P9-CCR-789

		DATE DUE	

DEADLINE IN ATHENS

WATERLOO PUBLIC LIBRARY
33420010198373

Petros Markaris

DEADLINE IN ATHENS

Translated from the Greek by
David Connolly

GROVE PRESS
NEW YORK

Copyright © 2004 by Petros Markaris
Translation copyright © 2004 by David Connolly

All rights reserved. No part of this book may be reproduced in any form or by any electronic or mechanical means, including information storage and retrieval systems, without permission in writing from the publisher, except by a reviewer, who may quote brief passages in a review. Any members of educational institutions wishing to photocopy part or all of the work for classroom use, or publishers who would like to obtain permission to include the work in an anthology, should send their inquiries to Grove/Atlantic, Inc., 841 Broadway, New York, NY 10003.

Originally published in Greek under the title *Nychterino Deltio.*

Published simultaneously in Canada
Printed in the United States of America

FIRST EDITION

Library of Congress Cataloging-in-Publication Data
Markaris, Petros, 1937–
[Nychterino deltio. English]
Deadline in Athens : an inspector Costas Haritos mystery / Petros Markaris ; translated from the Greek by David Connolly.
p. cm.
ISBN 0-8021-1778-3
I. Connolly, David, professor.   II. Title.

PA5624.A27N93 2004
889'.334—dc22   2004049136

Grove Press
841 Broadway
New York, NY 10003

04   05   06   07   08   10   9   8   7   6   5   4   3   2   1

To
Sophia
Rania
Philippos

albeit with some delay

DRAMATIS PERSONÍ

Antonakaki, Anna	– daughter of Mina
Antonakaki, Mina	– sister of Yanna Karayoryi
Antonakakis, Vassos	– husband of Mina
Delopoulos, Kyriakos	– studio director, Hellas Channel
Delopoulou, Nena	– daughter
Dimitris	– technician, records department
Dourou, Eleni	– schoolteacher
Ghikas, Nikolaos	– superintendent, chief of police, headquarters
Hacek, Alois	– Czech politician
Haritos, Costas	– chief inspector, CID
Haritou, Adriani	– wife of Costas
Haritou, Katerina	– daughter
Hourdakis, Lefteris	– customs officer
Karayoryi, Yanna	– TV news reporter, Hellas Channel
Kolakoglou, Petros	– former tax consultant
Kostarakou, Martha	– TV news reporter, Hellas Channel
Kostaras	– former police inspector
Koula	– police officer and secretary to Chief Superintendent Ghikas
Krenek, Gustav	– businessman
Manisalis	– news director, Hellas Channel
Markidis, Petros	– coroner
Mehmet	– husband of Pakize, Albanian
Milionis, Evangelos	– truck driver
Pakize	– wife of Mehmet, Albanian
Panos	– boyfriend of Katerina Haritou
Papadopoulos, Christos	– truck driver
Petratos, Nestor	– news editor, Hellas Channel

Petridi	– public examiner
Politou, Aspasia	– judge, official investigator for the public prosecutor's office
Pylarinos, Christos	– businessman
Seki, Ramiz	– Albanian
Sotiriou	– solicitor of Nestor Petratos
Sotiris, Vlassopoulos	– lieutenant, CID
Sotiropoulos	– TV news reporter
Sovatzis, Demos	– businessman
Sperantzas, Pavlos	– newscaster, Hellas Channel
Starakis	– solicitor of Demos Sovatzis
Stellio	– records department
Vlastos, Thanassis	– sergeant, CID
Yannis	– archivist, records department
Zissis, Lambros	– former prisoner of the junta
Zoumadaki, Dimitra	– assistant, Hellas Channel

CHAPTER 1

Every morning at nine, we would stare at each other. He would stand in front of my desk with his gaze fixed on me, not exactly at eye level, but somewhere between my forehead and my eyebrows. "I'm a moron," he would say.

He didn't say it with words; he said it with his eyes. I sat behind my desk and looked him straight in the eye, no higher and no lower. Because I was his boss and could look him in the eye, whereas he couldn't do the same with me. "I know you're a moron," I'd tell him. No word escaped me either; my eyes did the speaking. We had this conversation five days a week, every week of the year, excluding the two months that we were both on leave. From Monday to Friday, without our saying as much as a word, just through our eyes. "I'm a moron"—"I know you're a moron."

Every division has its share of losers. They can't all be high-flyers; you're bound to get stuck with a few dimwits like Thanassis. He entered the police academy but quit halfway through. With a great deal of effort, he managed to get to the rank of sergeant, and there he stopped. He didn't aspire to achieve anything higher. From his first day in the division, he made it clear to me that he was a moron. And I showed due appreciation, because his honesty saved him from difficult assignments, night duties, roadblocks, and car chases. I kept him in the office. An easy interrogation, filing, liaison with the coroner's office and the ministry. But because we had a chronic shortage of men on the force and simply couldn't deal with all the work, he made sure he reminded me every day that he was a moron, so that I wouldn't forget and assign him by mistake to a patrol car.

I glanced at my desk and saw that the coffee and croissant were missing. His only regular assignment was to bring me these every morning. I looked up at him questioningly.

"So, where's my breakfast today, Thanassis? Have you forgotten it?" When I first entered the force, we used to eat biscuits. We'd wipe the crumbs off the desk while some murderer or robber or common pickpocket by the name of Demos or Lambros or Menios sat across from us.

Thanassis smiled. "The chief phoned to say that he wants to see you right away, so I thought I'd bring it to you when that was done with."

He wanted to talk to me about that Albanian who had been seen lurking near the home of the couple we'd found murdered on Tuesday afternoon. The front door of the house had been open all morning, but no one had been inside. Who'd go into a decrepit hovel with one window missing and the other boarded over? Even burglars would turn up their noses at the prospect. Eventually, around noon, a neighbor who'd noticed the door open all morning with apparently no one around went to take a look. It was an hour before she contacted us because she had fainted. When we arrived on the scene, two women were still trying to revive her spirits by sprinkling water over her face, as if they were trying to make a fish look fresh.

A bare mattress was laid on the concrete floor. The woman was sprawled on it on her back. She must have been around twenty-five. Her throat had been slashed wide open, as if someone had cut her a bloody second mouth. Her right hand was clutching at the mattress. I couldn't tell what color her nightdress had been, but now it seemed to be dark red all over. The man beside her must have been about five years older. He was sprawled facedown and lying over the edge of the mattress. His eyes seemed to be fixed on a passing cockroach. He had five stab wounds in the back; three in a horizontal line from the level of the heart to his right shoulder and the other two beneath the middle horizontal stab wound, one after the other, as if the murderer had been trying to carve a T on the man's back. The rest of the house looked like the house of anyone else who leaves one hell to go to the next: a folding table, two plastic chairs, a gas stove.

Two dead Albanians is of interest to no one but the TV channels, and then only if the murder is sensational enough to turn the stomachs of those watching the nine o'clock news before sitting down to dinner. In the old days it was biscuits and Greeks. Now it's croissants and Albanians.

It took us the better part of an hour to get through the initial stage of photographing the two corpses, looking for fingerprints, putting the few pieces of evidence in plastic bags, and sealing the door. The coroner didn't even bother to come. He preferred to have the corpses delivered to the mortuary. There was no need for any investigation. What was there to investigate? There wasn't so much as a cupboard in the house. The woman's few rags were hanging on a hook screwed into the wall. The man's were lying beside him on the concrete floor.

"Should we check if there's any money?" Sotiris asked. He was a lieutenant and always did things by the book.

"If you find any, it's yours, but you won't find a cent. Either they didn't have any, or the murderer took it. And that doesn't mean that he killed them for their money. He'd have taken the money even if it was revenge. His kind wouldn't find money and leave it." Nevertheless, he poked around and found a hole in the mattress. No money.

None of the neighbors had seen anything. Or so they said. They may well have been hiding something for the cameras in order to make a little money for themselves. All that was left for us to do was to get back to the station for the second and final stage: a report that would go straight to the files, because looking for whoever killed them would be a waste of effort.

She popped up just as we were sealing off the house. Chubby-faced, wearing a sparkling blouse that looked about to burst open and her breasts spring out of it, plus a tight skirt that was shorter at the back because her backside stopped it from hanging properly, and with mauve slippers. I was sitting in the patrol car when I saw her approaching the two men boarding up the door. After she said something to them and they pointed to where I was in the car, she turned and came over to me.

"Where can I talk to you?" she asked, as if expecting me to make her a private appointment.

"Here. What is it?"

"Over the past few days I've seen a man snooping around the house. Every time he knocked on the door the woman would slam it in his face. He was average height, fair-haired, and had a scar on his left cheek. He was wearing a blue anorak, jeans that were patched at the knees, and tennis shoes. The last time I saw him was the day before yesterday. It was in the evening, and he was knocking on the door."

"And why didn't you tell all this to the officer who took your statement?"

"I needed time to think. The last thing I need is to be bundled off to police stations and courtrooms."

How long did she sit and stare at the street, at the neighbors and passersby? Evidently, she made her bed in the morning, put the pan on the stove, and then took up her watch at the window.

"Okay. If we need you, we'll contact you."

When I got back to the office, my first thought was to have the case put on file. What with terrorism, robberies, and drugs, who has time to worry about Albanians? If they'd killed a Greek, one of ours, one of the fast-food- and crêpe-eating Greeks of today, that would be different. But they could do what they liked to each other. It was enough that we provided ambulances to take them away.

Who says we learn from our mistakes? I sure don't. At first, I always say I'm not going to do anything, and then something starts needling me. Either because the office gets to me and I feel bored, or because, despite the routine, I still have something of the policeman's instinct left in me, I'm overcome by an urge to take it a stage further. So I put out a call to all the other stations with the woman's description of the Albanian. To be honest, you don't need to carry out prolonged investigations. All you have to do is go around all the squares: Omonoia Square, Vathi Square, Kotzias Square, Koumoundouros Square, the Station Square in Kifissia, all the squares. . . . The place has become an ass-backward zoo. They've shut up the people in cages, and the animals stroll around the squares staring at us.

Even before I began, I knew that any efforts I made would come to nothing. Finding him was hopeless. And yet within three days, they'd sent him to me gift-wrapped from Loutsa.

The chubby woman came to see me wearing the same striking getup. Except that this time she was wearing shoes, old-fashioned ones with high heels that sagged under her weight so that the heels slid first inward, then outward, as if about to embrace each other, before changing their minds and going their separate ways. "That's him!" she cried as soon as she saw the Albanian. I believed her at once and thanked God that she wasn't my neighbor watching me from morning to night. He was just as she'd described him to me. She'd missed nothing that mattered.

This was why the chief wanted to see me. To ask how the case was going. And Thanassis hadn't brought me my breakfast, because he was certain that once I heard that the chief wanted to see me, I'd drop everything and rush upstairs.

"Your job is to bring me my coffee and croissant. I'll decide when I see the chief," I told him angrily and leaned back into my chair to show him that I had no intention of budging from my desk all morning.

The smile immediately vanished from his face. All his assuredness went out the window. "Yes, sir," he mumbled.

"Well—what are you waiting for?"

He turned on his heel and bolted. I waited a minute or two and then got up to go see the chief. I wouldn't have put it past Thanassis to let it be known that the chief wanted to see me and that I was playing the smart alec. And the chief knew every trick in the book; you had to watch your back with him. Not to mention that he was a bundle of neuroses.

CHAPTER 2

My office was on the third floor, number 321. The office of the chief of security was on the fifth. The elevator usually took five or ten minutes, depending on whether it had decided to get on your nerves. If you got irritated and started pressing the button continually, it could take up to fifteen minutes. You heard it on the second floor, thought it was coming up, and then, without warning, it changed direction and went back down. Or the other way around. It came down to the fourth floor and instead of coming on down, went back up again. Sometimes I'd decide "To hell with it" and take the stairs two at a time, more to blow off steam than because I was in a hurry. At other times, I dug in my heels and reflected that since no one else was in any hurry, I'd have to be insane to rush. They'd even calibrated the elevator doors to open slowly, enough to drive you crazy.

All the big brains are on the fifth floor, either so they can think collectively or so they'll be isolated before they ruin our brains too. It depends on how you look at it. The office of the chief of security is number 504, but he's had the number removed from the door. He considered it demeaning to have a number on his door like in hospitals or hotels. He had a plaque put up in its place: NIKOLAOS GHIKAS—CHIEF OF SECURITY. "In America, there are no numbers on the doors. Just names," he went on saying crossly for a good three months. He said it again and again till he finally had the number removed and his name put in its place. And all because he'd spent six months on a training program with the FBI.

"Go straight in, he's expecting you," said Koula, the policewoman who did the job of his secretary but looked more like a supermodel.

The office was large and bright with a carpeted floor and curtained windows. They intended to give us all curtains, but the money ran out, so they limited them to the fifth floor. Just inside the door was an oblong conference table with six chairs. The chief was sitting with his back to the window, and his desk must have been all of three yards long. One of those modern ones with metal corners. If you want to get a document lying at either edge of the desk, you need a pair of tongs to reach it.

He looked up at me. "What more on the Albanian?" he said.

"Nothing more, sir. We're still interrogating him."

"Incriminating evidence?" Short sharp questions, short sharp answers; just the basics to show that he's (a) busy as hell, (b) efficient, and (c) direct and to the point. American tricks, we told ourselves.

"No, but we have an eyewitness who recognized him, like I said."

"That's not necessarily going to get you a conviction. She saw him in the vicinity of the house. She didn't see him either entering or leaving. Fingerprints?"

"Lots. Most belonging to the couple. But none to the suspect. No trace of a murder weapon." The ass had me speaking in shorthand, like him.

"I see. Tell the reporters that there'll be no statement for the time being."

He didn't have to tell me that. If there was a statement to make, he would have made it himself. And not only that, but he would have got me to write it all down for him so he could learn it by heart. I'm not complaining; it doesn't bother me in the least. Reporters are always on my back. It's just like the biscuits and croissants. Once it was newspapermen and newspapers; now it's reporters and cameras.

Using the secretary's telephone, I sent word for the Albanian to be brought to me for questioning. Interrogations take place in an office with bare walls, a table, and three chairs. When I entered, the Albanian was sitting handcuffed in one of the chairs.

"Should I remove the handcuffs?" asked the officer who'd brought him.

"Leave him and let's see whether he's cooperative or wants to play tough."

I looked at the Albanian. His hands were resting on the table. Two calloused hands, with thick fingers and long nails, black around the edges; misery's mark of mourning. He was staring at them as if seeing them for the first time, as if surprised. Surprised at what? That he'd killed with them? Or that they were rough and dirty? Or that God created him with hands?

"Are you going to tell me why you killed them?" I said to him.

He slowly raised his eyes from his hands. "Got cigarette?"

"Give him one of yours," I said to the officer.

He looked at me in shock. He thought I was messing with him. That's how sharp he was. He smoked Marlboros, whereas I'd stayed with the old Greek Karelia. I was giving the Albanian a Marlboros, to win him over. The officer put it in the suspect's mouth and I lit it for him. He took a couple of drags, beaming with satisfaction. He held the smoke as if to imprison it, and then let it out as sparingly as possible, not wanting to waste any of it. He raised his hands and squeezed the cigarette between the thumb and forefinger of his right hand.

"I no kill," he said, and, at the same moment, his two hands moved like one lizard and wedged the cigarette between his lips, while his chest heaved to make space for the smoke. His instinct told him that I might take the cigarette away now that he hadn't told me what I'd wanted to hear, and he hastened to inhale what he could.

"Don't play with me, you lousy Albanian!" I yelled at him. "I'll have you for every unsolved murder of Albanian lowlife on our files for the last three years, and you'll go down for life times ten, damn your country and damn its leaders!"

"I not here three years. I come—" he stopped to search for a way to say "last year." "I come 'ninety-two," he said, pleased with himself for having solved his vocabulary problem. Now his hands were stowed under the table, presumably so that I would forget about the cigarette.

"And how do you intend to prove that, dickhead? From your passport?"

I lunged at him, grabbing him and dragging him to his feet. He wasn't expecting it; his hands banged hard on the underside of the table and the cigarette dropped to the floor. He cast a quick glance, full of concern, at the fallen cigarette and then looked at me anxiously. The officer stretched out his foot and stepped on the cigarette, while grinning at the Albanian. Smart kid, catches on very nicely.

"You entered Greece illegally. There's no record of you anywhere, no visa, no stamp, nothing. I could dispose of you and no one would ever ask what happened to you. I've never seen you or heard of you, because you don't exist. Are you listening? You don't exist!"

"I go for woman," he said in fear, as I shook him.

"Fancied her?" I let him sink back onto the chair.

"Yes."

"That's why you were creeping around the house all day. You wanted to go in and do her, and she wouldn't open the door for you."

"Yes," he said again and smiled this time, enjoying the psychoanalysis.

"And when she didn't open the door, you went crazy and broke in at night and murdered them!"

"No!" he shouted in alarm.

I sat in the chair facing him and stared into his eyes. I let some time pass. He grew anxious. Luckily he didn't realize that I'd come to a dead end. What else could I do to him? Let him go hungry? He wouldn't give a rat's ass. He was used to eating one day in three and then only if he was lucky. Get two strong-armed boys from upstairs to give him a going-over? He'd had so many goings-over in his life that he wouldn't think twice about it.

"Listen," I said to him in a calm and friendly voice, "I'll write down everything we say on a piece of paper, you'll sign it, and you'll have nothing more to worry about."

He said nothing. He just looked at me with indecision and doubt. It wasn't that he was afraid of going to prison; he'd simply learned to be suspicious. He did not have it in his experience to believe that suffering comes to an end somewhere and you find relief. He was afraid that if you accept one thing, you'll have to face a second and third, because that had always been his fate. The poor wretch needed some gentle persuasion.

"After all, it won't be so bad in prison," I said to him in a conversational way. "You'll have your own bed, three meals a day, all courtesy of the state. You won't have to do anything, and you'll be taken care of, just like it was in your own country back then. And if you have any brains, after a couple of months you'll join one of the gangs, and you'll make a bit on the side as well. Prison is the only place where there's no unemployment. If you have your wits about you, you'll come out with a nice little nest egg."

He went on staring at me, except that now his eyes were glinting, as if he liked the idea, but he continued to say nothing. I knew he wanted to think about it, and I got up. "You don't have to give me an answer now," I said. "Think about it, and we'll talk again tomorrow."

As I was going toward the door, I saw the officer taking out his pack of Marlboros and offering him one. I made a mental note to get the kid transferred and have him work with me.

I found them all milling around in front of my office. Some were holding microphones, others pocket recorders. All of them with that greedy and impatient look: a pack of wolves hungry for a statement, soldiers waiting for their rations. The cameramen saw me coming and hoisted the cameras to their shoulders.

"Step inside, all of you." I opened the door to my office, muttering under my breath, "Go to hell, you bastards, and leave me in peace." They burst through the door behind me and planted their microphones with the logo of their TV channels, their cables, and their pocket recorders all over my desk. In less than a minute, it had come to resemble the stall of an immigrant vendor in Athinas Street.

"Do you have anything more to tell us about the Albanian, Inspector?" It was Sotiropoulos, with his Armani checked shirt, his English raincoat, his Timberland moccasins, and his spectacles with their round metallic frames, the kind once worn by poor old Himmler and now worn by intellectuals. He'd stopped calling me by name some time before and now just addressed me as "Inspector." And he always began with "Do you have anything to tell us" or "What can you tell us," in order to make you feel that you were being examined and graded. He believed, you see, that he represented the conscience of the people, and the conscience of the people treated everyone equally: no name or sign of respect, courtesies that only lead to distinctions between citizens. And his eyes were always fixed on you, wary and ready to denounce you at any moment. A modern day Robespierre with a camera and a microphone.

I ignored him and addressed myself to them all as a body. If he wanted equality, he'd have it. "I have nothing to tell you," I said genially. "We're still interrogating the suspect."

They looked at me in disappointment. A tiny, freckled woman wearing red stockings tried to get something more out of me, refusing to go down without a fight.

"Do you have any evidence that he's the murderer?" she said.

"I told you, we're still interrogating him," I said again, and to let them know that the interview was over, I picked up the croissant that Thanassis had brought me, removed the cellophane, and bit into it.

They began packing away their paraphernalia, and my office recovered its normal appearance, like the patient who, once out of danger, is unhooked from the machines.

Yanna Karayoryi was the last to leave. She hung back deliberately and allowed the others to go out. I disliked her even more than all the rest of them. For no particular reason. She couldn't have been more than thirty-five and was always dressed elegantly without being showy. Wide trousers, cardigan, with an expensive chain and cross around her neck. I don't know why, but I had got it into my head that she was a lesbian. She was a good-looking woman, but her short hair and her style of dressing gave her something of a masculine appearance. Now she was standing beside the door. She glanced outside to see that the others had gone, and then closed it. I went on eating my croissant as if I hadn't noticed that she was still in my office.

"Do you know whether the murdered couple had any children?" she said.

I turned, surprised. Her arrogant gaze was where it always was, and she was smiling at me ironically. That's what irritated me: those meaningless questions that she suddenly came out with and that she underlined with an ironic smile to make you think that she knew something more but wasn't going to tell you, just to annoy you. In fact, she knew nothing, she just liked to fish.

"Do you think there were children there and we didn't notice them?"

"Maybe they weren't there when you got there."

"What do you want me to say? If they sent them to study in America, we haven't located them, not yet at any rate," I said.

"I'm not talking about grown-up children. I'm talking about babies," she answered. "Two years old at most."

She did know something, and it was amusing her to play with me. I decided to go easy, be friendly, try to win her over. I pointed to the chair in front of my desk.

"Why don't you sit down and let's talk," I said.

"Can't. I have to get back to the studio. Another time." She was all of a sudden in a hurry. The bitch wanted to leave me wondering.

As she was opening the door to leave, she bumped into Thanassis, who was coming in at that moment with a document. They exchanged a look, and Karayoryi smiled at him. Thanassis averted his gaze, but Karayoryi kept hers fixed provocatively on him. She seemed fond of him. Truth to tell, she had every right to because Thanassis was a good-looking fellow. Tall, dark, well built. It occurred to me to get him to establish a relationship with her. That way he'd be able to answer both of my questions: whether she did, in fact, know anything about the Albanians and was hiding it from me, and whether she was a lesbian.

She waved to me, ostensibly saying good-bye, but actually it was as if she were saying, "Sit there and stew, you dummy." She closed the door behind her. Thanassis came over and handed me the document.

"The coroner's report on the two Albanians," he said. Karayoryi's smile had embarrassed him, and his hand was trembling as he handed me the paper. He didn't know if I'd noticed or how I'd react.

"Fine," I said. "Leave it and go." I was in no mood to read it. In any case, what could it tell me? Whatever the bodies had to reveal was obvious enough to the naked eye—apart from the time of the murder, but that was of no importance. It wasn't as if the Albanian was going to come up with a convincing alibi that we'd have to disprove. And Karayoryi didn't know anything. Like all reporters she was bluffing. She wanted to arouse my curiosity so that she would be the first I'd open up to and she'd be able to get more out of me. There were no children. If there were and we hadn't found them, the neighbors would have told us.

CHAPTER 3

Adriani was watching TV. She still hadn't noticed me, though I'd been in the living room for a good five minutes. Her hand was clutching the remote control; her forefinger was on the button, ready to switch channels as soon as the ads came on. On the screen, a wavy-haired policeman was yelling his head off at a redhead. He was on every evening, and he was either interrogating someone or he was suffering pangs of remorse. And in both cases, he was always yelling. If all police officers were like him, every one of us would be dead from a heart attack before forty.

"Why is he forever yelling, the moron?" I said. I added "moron" because I knew how cross she became when I showed contempt for the heroes in her favorite shows. I wanted to annoy her into giving me some attention, but it didn't work.

"Shhh!" she said curtly, while her gaze remained fixed on the wavy-haired actor in uniform. "What are you staring at, you fathead? Say something!" my father would shout at me, and give me a clip around the ear. I'd like to know what he'd do now that everyone stares instead of talking. Luckily for him, the old man's no longer around; he'd have a fit.

Every evening, I sought refuge in the bedroom and took Dimitrakos's *Dictionary* down from the bookcase. Bookcase? That was what we called it to make it sound grander than it was. In fact, it was only four shelves. On the upper shelf were all the dictionaries: Liddell & Scott's *Greek Lexicon*, Dimitrakos's *Dictionary of Modern Greek*, Vostantzoglou's *Thesaurus*, N. P. Andriotis's *Dictionary of Koine Greek*, and Tegopoulos-Fytrakis's *Modern Greek Dictionary*. It was my only hobby: dictionaries. No soccer, no do-it-yourself, nothing. If anyone else were to glance at the bookcase, they'd be shocked. The upper shelf was full of dictionaries. It was impressive. Then you moved down to the lower shelves and it was all Viper, Nora, Bell, Harlequin, and Bianca. In other words, I'd kept the penthouse for myself and left the three floors below for Adriani. On top, a veneer of knowledge, and underneath, degradation. A portrait of Greece in four shelves.

I lay on the bed with Dimitrakos. I opened it at "see." *See = the power of sight.* The mind sees and the mind hears, that is what my father used to say. Every night, half an hour before he'd come home, I'd open the books on the kitchen table and get down to studying to show him that I was doing my best. He'd come in wearing his sergeant's uniform, stand in the doorway, and stare at me. I'd make no sound. I was so immersed in my study that I failed to perceive his presence, as Dimitrakos might put it. He'd suddenly come up to me, take hold of me by the ear, and pull me from the chair.

"Only four again in math, you fathead," he'd say to me.

I'd have no idea. I'd find out the following day from the math teacher. He'd always know the day before.

"How do you know?" I'd ask, amazed.

Till one day I happened to be in his office in the gendarmerie, and then I understood that it wasn't that he was telepathic, but that, quite simply, the telephone rang. My father had once done the math teacher a favor, helping him to get a hunting license or some such thing, and the teacher, as a way of repaying the debt, would phone him as soon as he'd seen my exam sheet to tell him the mark. The strange thing is that most of the time I was sure that I'd done well, but all I ever got were fours and fives.

"Have you got your shoes on the bed again?" I heard Adriani's shrill voice and jumped up. That was the end of my daydreaming. What does a dream correspond to in terms of time? To a television show. The show ends and the dream with it.

"The moment you come home, you stick your head in that stupid book instead of talking to me, when I've been on my own all day. And if that's not enough, you dirty the bed with your filthy shoes."

"What do you want me to say to you when you're glued to the TV and you don't even say hello to me?"

"It had just reached a crucial moment. It wouldn't have hurt you to wait five minutes, would it? But you found an excuse to run to your creepy-crawlies!" "Creepy-crawlies" is what she called the letters in the dictionary. "Aren't you tired of reading the same words over and over again for twenty years! I'd have learned them all by now!"

"And what do you expect me to do, woman? Sit and watch that brainless copper? If he were working under me, I'd have him sent to the storeroom to count bullets! Or should I wait for the second half with that old hen who plays the prosecutor and after six hundred episodes still can't decide whether she wants to do her husband?"

"Naturally," she replied scornfully. "You're just a slob, and you can't stand anything that's even faintly glamorous." She turned and stormed out. But she'd succeeded in rankling me because I had no idea what "glamorous" meant, or where she'd got it from to dangle before me like that.

I went over to the shelf and took down the Oxford English-Greek *Learner's Dictionary*, the only English dictionary I had. I'd bought it in '77 when I was in the drugs squad and we had to interrogate some foreigners who'd gone to India, supposedly in search of a guru, and had come back with saris, a load of trinkets, and half a kilo of heroin hidden up their arses like a suppository. It was then that I'd decided to learn half a dozen words in English for fear that some pasty-faced redhead might hit on me and come out with the odd "fuck you!" and I wouldn't know if she was cursing me or asking me for a cheese pie.

I searched for *glamurous* but found nothing. So I looked under *glamourus* and again nothing. The damned English write it using *o* and *ou* just to make life difficult. So: *glamorous = possessing glamour, alluring and fascinating; beautiful and smart.* Glamorous film stars. So that's what she'd meant—that I don't like what's alluring and fascinating or, by inference, film stars who are alluring and fascinating, because I'm a ragamuffin. It's taken you thirty years to graduate from biscuits to croissants and she calls you a ragamuffin because you can't stomach her stupid soap stars.

I put up the shutters and went to watch the television. It had already turned nine, and I wanted to listen to the news in case they said anything about the Albanians. Half the news was taken up with political issues, the situation in Bosnia, two junkies who'd overdosed and an eighty-year-old who'd raped and murdered his seventy-year-old sister-in-law. Just as I was feeling a sense of relief that we'd been left out, the newscaster put on a grievous expression. His face darkened, his hands rose slightly from the desk in a show of despair at the upset he was going to cause the viewers, and he gave forth a sigh that was barely perceptible. The words emerged disjointed, one by one, like the last customers out of a café just before it closes who scatter into the street. He always had that handkerchief in his jacket pocket. I kept expecting him to take it out and wipe away his tears, but he'd never done it. He should have kept it up his sleeve for when the ratings fell.

"And in other crime, ladies and gentlemen," he said, "in the brutal murder of the two Albanians, there have been no further developments."

Yanna Karayoryi appeared right on cue. She was holding the microphone and wearing the same attire that she'd been wearing that morning. It was hardly surprising, as she was speaking in the corridor with her back to my office.

"The police have no new evidence concerning the murders, other than the arrest of an Albanian, who is being held at Athens Security Headquarters. According to a statement made by the head of homicide, Inspector Costas Haritos, the interrogation of the Albanian is continuing. The police suspect that the couple had a child, who has not yet been found."

Furious, I lunged to grab hold of her on the screen. But she disappeared, and in her place appeared the chubby woman who'd identified him. She began spouting into the microphone about the Albanian and about how she had notified us. It was the third straight evening that they'd shown the same scene. With the woman saying exactly the same things, wearing the same eye-catching blouse and the same skirt hitched up at the back, not at all glamorous. And how would I explain to the chief the next day that this was a fabrication on Karayoryi's part and that everything was under control?

"Now, who's glued to the screen?" I heard Adriani's gloating voice from the kitchen.

"I have some news," she said, just as I'd put the fork with the moussaka to my mouth.

"What news?"

"Katerina phoned today," she said, smiling.

"Why didn't you tell me before?"

"I wanted to tell you over supper, to give you an appetite."

Rubbish. She kept it from me on purpose to get back at me for not watching TV with her. She knew what a soft spot I had for our daughter.

"She's coming for Christmas, after all," she said with a satisfied grin.

Katerina was studying law in Thessaloniki. She was breezing through her second year. Her aim when she finished was to become a public prosecutor. Deep down, I only hoped I wouldn't have retired, so I'd be able to send her plenty of defendants. And then I'd sit in the courtroom and feel a father's pride as she read the charge, questioned the witnesses, and addressed the court.

"I must send her some money for the airfare."

"Don't bother—she said that she'd take the coach, with Panos," Adriani said.

Of course, I'd forgotten about that hulk. Or rather, I was trying not to remember him. He wasn't a bad kid underneath; he was studying to be an agriculturist. It bothered me, though, that he was muscular, the athletic type, always in a sweatshirt, jeans, and sneakers. The ones we had like that on the force were all dimwits. But it wasn't his fault; he was one of that fifties generation. Not the first post-war generation, but the one of today. I call them the fifties generation because their vocabulary extends to no more than fifty words. And if you exclude "fuck," "creep," and "asshole," you're left with a net taxable income of forty-seven, as the revenue people would say. I remember the period between '71 and '73, the events at the Polytechnic, the student demonstrations, the sit-ins at the universities, the slogan "Food, Freedom, Education," and I recall how they'd send us to keep them under control or even to break them up. Confrontations, chases through the streets, broken limbs, with them swearing at us and with us cursing them. How could we have known then that all the fighting was just so that we would arrive today at those fifty words? We might as well have all gone home, because it simply wasn't worth the effort.

"Do you have the money for the airfare, or did you intend to borrow it?" It sounded like an innocent question, but I could see the cunning in her eyes.

"No, I have it," I replied. "I've put a bit aside from the back pay we got."

"As you're not going to need it for the fare, why don't you give it to me so I can buy those boots I was telling you about?" She tried for a seductive smile, but it only gave her away.

"We'll see." I'd give it to her, but I left it open on purpose to rankle her and get a bit of my own back. The first stage of family life is the joy of living together. The second is children. The third and longest stage is getting your own back at every opportunity. When you get to that stage, you know that you're secure and nothing is going to change. Your kids are off on their own, and you come home each evening knowing that waiting for you is your wife, your meal, and those little opportunities to get your own back.

"Oh, come on, Costas. I haven't got any boots for going out in!"

"We'll see!" I said sharply, putting an end to the conversation.

In bed, she cuddled up to me. She put her arm around my waist and began kissing me on my ear and neck. I lay there motionless. She brought her leg up to my knee and began rhythmically sliding it up and down from my shin to my penis.

"How much do you need for the boots?" I said.

"I saw a really lovely pair, but they're a bit expensive. Thirty-five thousand drachmas. But they'll last me for years."

"All right. I'll buy them for you."

Her leg slid down for the last time, like the elevator from the third floor to the ground floor, and it stopped there. She removed her arm from around my waist. She gave me a kiss on the cheek and immediately withdrew into her own territorial waters.

"'Night," she said, with relief in her voice.

"'Night," I said, also with relief, and I opened my Liddell & Scott, which I'd taken down from the shelf before getting into bed.

But it was impossible for me to concentrate. My mind was on Karayoryi and the matter of the child she kept going on about. She couldn't have simply invented it, out of thin air; she was keeping something from me. It suddenly came to me: Ask the Albanian. He might know something. I'd ask him first and then worry about Karayoryi. If nothing else, I could do what I'd thought of that morning. I'd tell Thanassis to get it on with her and see what he could discover.

In my dream, I was in the home of the two Albanians. Except that their corpses were no longer there and the mattress was covered with a blanket. On the folding table was a bassinet. I leaned over and saw a baby. It was no more than three months old and was crying its eyes out. Standing by the gas stove, I saw Karayoryi warming the baby's bottle.

"What are you doing here?" I said.

"Babysitting," she said.

CHAPTER 4

I'd swallowed my first mouthful of croissant and was taking my first gulp of coffee when the door opened and in walked Thanassis. He looked at me and smiled. It was one of the rare occasions on which he didn't tell me that he was a moron. This happened once a year, twice at most.

"This is for you," he said, handing me a piece of paper.

"Okay. Leave it there."

Over the years I've developed a standard practice: never to take papers handed to me. Usually, they're orders, restrictions, cutbacks, something, at any rate, to get your goat. So I let them lie on my desk and psychologically prepare myself to read them. Thanassis, however, stood there holding it out to me and said, triumphantly: "It's the Albanian's confession."

I froze. I reached out and took the statement. "How did you manage it?" I said, unable to conceal my incredulity.

"Vlassis told me," he said with a smile.

"Vlassis?"

"He's the officer on cell duty. We were having a coffee in the canteen, and he told me that you wanted to convince the Albanian that he'd be better off in prison. So I sat down, typed out a statement, and took it to him. He signed it straight away."

I looked at the third page. A couple of inches from the foot of the sheet was a scribble that looked like a child's drawing of Mount Hymettus. Apparently it was the Albanian's signature. I read swiftly through the statement, skimming the formal parts. Everything was there, exactly as he'd told it to me the previous day during the interrogation: how he'd met the girl in Albania and fallen for her, how he'd skulked around the house for days even though she'd sent him packing. He'd felt insulted and had decided to break into the house and rape her. He'd removed one of the boards from the window and squeezed inside. He'd thought that her husband was away and had been terrified when he'd seen him lying beside her. And when the man rushed at him, he'd taken out his knife and murdered first him and then the girl. Everything was plain and simple, all very neat, no gaps or loose ends.

"Well done, Thanassis," I said with admiration. "Perfect."

He looked at me, and his eyes shone with pleasure. At that moment the phone rang. I picked up the receiver.

"Haritos."

This too was part of the FBI-type reforms imposed on us by Ghikas. We no longer answered, "Hello" or "Yes," but "Haritos," "Sotiriou," "Papatriandafyllopoulos." And regardless of whether you got cut off halfway through "Papatriandafyllopoulos," you still went on with it.

"The child. What do you know about it?" As always, short, sharp, and to the point.

"There is no child, Chief. I've got the Albanian's confession in front of me. There's no mention of a child. That's nonsense thought up by Karayoryi. Her ambition will be the death of her."

I said this expressly to provoke him, because I knew that he had a high regard for her.

"Has he confessed?" he said, as if unwilling to believe it.

"Yes. Confessed. Crime of passion. No child involved."

"Right. Send me your report. And a summary too, so I can make a statement." He put down the phone without even a word of thanks. Now I was going to have to write him a report that a schoolboy could understand so that he could learn it by heart.

Normally, the case would have closed there. The Albanian had made his confession and would be sent for trial, the stuff about the child had proved to be a fabrication, the chief of security would stand before the reporters and come out with his spiel—we'd wrapped it up. But I had a broomstick up my backside. I couldn't let things rest, and I always ended up paying for it.

"Listen, Thanassis, did he say anything about a child?"

"Child?" he said and became all confused. Thanassis's kind are like that. When you're least expecting it, they come up with a bright idea and arrive at something that, by their standards, is nothing short of a miracle. But as soon as you burden them with something else, something unexpected, they overload, blow a fuse, and the lights go out on them.

I looked at my watch. It was only nine-thirty. I had two hours before the reporters showed up.

It was more than enough time for me to write the report for Ghikas.

"Have them bring the Albanian for questioning."

He looked at me, and all the satisfaction drained out of him. "But he's confessed," he muttered.

"I know, but that Karayoryi woman put a damper on it last night on the news, by saying that there was a child involved. Ghikas heard it, and now he's on to me about it. I know there's nothing in it, but I want to be 100 percent sure that everything's in order. Have him brought to me, and you come along too." I would take him with me to show my appreciation, and he liked it. He left the office smiling from ear to ear.

The Albanian was sitting in the same place, but he wasn't handcuffed as on the previous day. When we walked in, he looked at us apprehensively. I offered him a cigarette.

"I say you everything," he said to me as he drew on the cigarette. "He come and I say all." He pointed to Thanassis.

"I know. Don't be alarmed. Everything's okay. I just want to ask you one question out of curiosity. Do you know whether the couple you murdered had any kids?"

"Keeds?"

He looked at me as though it were the most unlikely thing in the world for an Albanian couple to have kids. He didn't answer, but his gaze turned slowly toward Thanassis. Thanassis suddenly reached for him, took him by the anorak, and dragged him to his feet, screaming: "Out with it, you bastard! Did the Albanians have a child? Out with it, or you're dead meat!"

It's the quiet ones you have to watch when they're riled, as my old mother used to say. He'd succeeded in getting a confession; now his blood was up and he was playing the tough guy. I freed the Albanian from his grip and sat him down again on the chair.

"Gently does it, Thanassis. If he knows anything, he'll tell us without any rough stuff. Isn't that so?"

This last phrase was addressed to the Albanian. He was shaking from head to toe; why, I had no idea. It was just a simple question. He had nothing to be afraid of. Thanassis had just butted in and scared him with his excessive zeal.

"No," he said. "Pakize have no keeds."

Pakize was the name of the woman he'd murdered. "Okay, that was all," I said, friendly at last. "I won't need you for anything else."

He gazed at me in relief, as if a burden had been taken from him.

I returned to my office and sat down to write the schoolboy report for Ghikas. He didn't want much. A single page in my own handwriting, with my big, round letters. Just the facts, in précis. He could add the garnishing himself. I soon finished it and turned to the analytical report. This took me a bit longer, but I had finished inside an hour. I had them both sent to Ghikas.

I decided to have the rest of my croissant and drink my coffee, which was now stone cold. A cat was sunning itself on the balcony opposite. It was sprawled out with its head on the tiles that were baking in the sun. It was one of the few creatures to delight in the oven-like heat. The old woman came onto the balcony with a saucer. She put it down in front of the cat. She waited for it to open its eyes and see the food, but the cat showed complete indifference. The old woman waited patiently, stroking its head, talking to it, sweet talk most probably, but the cat couldn't have cared less. In the end, she gave up, left the saucer, and went back into the room. I reflected on the cat's arrogance, how it had its food brought to its feet, and I remembered the two Albanians lying on the bare mattress, the folding table, the two plastic chairs, the gas stove. Not that I'm especially partial to Albanians, but it got to me. So did the lousy weather, which gave no prospect of rain.

The door suddenly opened and in waltzed Karayoryi. Without even knocking, as if it were her own office. I should have given her a key. She was different. She was wearing jeans and a T-shirt. She had her cardigan on top of her bag, which was hanging across her shoulder. She closed the door and smiled at me. I looked at her without saying a word. I wanted to give her a mouthful, but we were under orders from the fifth floor to give reporters the kid-glove treatment. It wasn't always this way.

"Congratulations. I hear that the Albanian confessed. You've closed the case." Her smile was ironic, her expression haughty.

I was in no mood for playing cat and mouse. "Why did you lie in your television report last night?" I said. "You knew very well that there was no child, nor do we suspect anything of the sort."

She smiled. "Never mind," she replied indifferently. "All you have to do is deny it."

"Why did you come out with all that yesterday?"

"All what?"

"About the child. What was on your mind? Or were you just fishing?"

"I told you because I like you," she said, unexpectably amiable. "I know you can't stand me, but I don't care, I like you anyway. I have my weaknesses, you see."

The way she said it, straight out, she perplexed me. "I neither like you nor dislike you," I said, hoping that a neutral approach would seem more convincing. "You get on my nerves, and I get on yours, it's part of the job. But I don't dislike you any more than the rest of your colleagues."

"I'm sure you do," she said, still smiling. "With the exception, perhaps, of Sotiropoulos."

The bitch was razor sharp; nothing escaped her. "And why do you like me?" I said, to get out of a difficult position.

"Because you're the only one with an ounce of brains around here. Though don't go puffing yourself up too much on that account. Just that one eye's better than none. But you're way off the mark this time."

She made for the door and was gone before I could continue the discussion.

Once again I had to wonder: Was she playing with me or was she keeping something from me? If she came out with something afterward, I'd be the one they'd all come down on. Prosecutor, judge, police chief, all of them. There'd be no end to it. And it wasn't as if I had a lot of time on my side—I didn't. Ghikas would be making his statement before long. The file would be sent to the prosecutor the next day, and it wouldn't take him more than a couple of days to arrange for the court hearing. From then on, the case would be completely out of my hands, and if anything were to explode, at that point there'd be no picking up the pieces.

I picked up the telephone and told Sotiris, the lieutenant, to come into my office.

"Listen, Sotiris, when we were searching the Albanians' place, did you notice anything that might indicate the presence of children?"

"Children?" he said, a good deal surprised.

"Anything at all. Rattles? Bibs? Baby clothes? Toys?"

He looked at me as if he were up against a lunatic. And he had every right. "No, we found nothing of the sort." He thought for a moment and then said, "Apart from a box that had diapers in it."

"Diapers?" I cried and leapt to my feet.

"Yes, they were using it as a makeshift cupboard. In it, there was sugar, coffee, and half a packet of dried beans."

The cat had woken up now and was eating, just like the glamorous stars who have their breakfast at eleven. The old woman was standing over it with pride. She was probably pleased that it had an appetite so she wouldn't have to give it iron tablets and vitamins. The leaves drooping from the potted plants looked down on the tiles like demure virgins. The old woman had watered them only the previous day, and they were withering already. Imagine being in a car in that heat, breathing the exhaust fumes, with the plastic seats so scorching you and your backside gradually become soaked.

"Have them bring a patrol car, and we'll be on our way. Just the two of us."

"Where are we going?"

"To the Albanians' place. To search it again."

He was about to say something, but he thought better of it and left. Five minutes later, they informed me that the patrol car was waiting.

CHAPTER 5

It took us almost an hour to get to Rendi, even though Sotiris had turned on the siren. Throughout the journey, sitting next to Sotiris, I toyed with the window. I'd open it and be suffocated by the smog. I'd close it and be suffocated by the heat. In the end, I gave up and left it half open. Perhaps it was the congestion that was to blame for my irritability. A sudden feeling of impatience took hold of me. I wanted to get to the Albanians' place, search it, and be done. I was pissed off at Karayoryi for getting me all fired up so damned easily and with myself for having gone along with her game, and with the Albanians for not having a brat beside them on the mattress whom we could send to social services and who would let us wash our hands of the matter. Sotiris was driving without saying a word, very much down in the dumps. The low spirits were no doubt on my account, for putting him to all this trouble without good cause, when he should have been sitting at his desk, flipping through some document and telling the others about the chassis on the Hyundai Excel he'd recently bought by selling a piece of land he had in his village. At least that's what he said.

When we got into the house, I became even more uptight. One bare room, with the few rags on view; you could take it all in at a glance. What had I come to look for? Secret drawers, hollow walls serving as cubbyholes? The diaper box was on the folding table, as Sotiris had recalled. I opened it and found what he'd described: a hundred-gram packet of coffee, a packet of sugar, and half a bag of dried beans. They'd picked up the box from the street, to put their food in, so the rats wouldn't get at it.

"What are we looking for?" asked Sotiris, who was watching me.

"Anything indicating children, do I have to say it again?" I said testily.

I took the woman's clothes from the hook, let them drop to the floor, and spread them out with my foot. Perhaps there was something tucked inside them that we'd missed. But all I found was a pair of slacks, a blouse, and some tights. I looked again at the man's clothes, still lying beside the mattress. He, too, had nothing but a shirt, a pair of trousers, and his socks. And their shoes. Hers flat slip-ons, his lace-ups. Didn't they have any underwear? Not even for a change? I know they come here with no more than what they stand up in, but when you came face-to-face with the literalness of that, something just didn't seem right. I wondered whether this might be significant.

"Lend a hand to lift up the mattress," I said.

We got hold of it at both ends and doubled it up. Three cock-roaches raced out, scampering in alarm over the bare concrete floor. One was a bit slower than the others, and I succeeded in stamping on it. The other two escaped. So this was all we had to show for our search: one dead cockroach, two at large.

"Let's be off," I said to Sotiris in relief and dropped my side of the mattress. If we hadn't found anything, there was nothing to find.

"Just a minute. I need to use the toilet."

"Careful not to touch anywhere with your willy. You'll be asking me for sick leave when you end up with an infection."

I opened the door and went out. The chubby woman was stand-ing there. "So you're still looking for something, huh?" she asked me in a familiar tone, ready to invite me in for a coffee to learn the rest.

"What business is it of yours, missus? Go back into your house," I said curtly, in part because I was irritated at the thought of having to drive back through the center of Athens. After the compliments and praise she'd received in my office for being so observant, this took her aback. She gave me a nasty look, turned, and began walking away with as much speed as an overloaded truck can muster.

Suddenly I had an idea. "One moment!" I called to her.

She pulled up, undecided, with her back still turned. Then she swung around and came back to me, still looking offended.

"Would you know whether the Albanians had any kids?"

"Kids?" she parroted, and the question seemed to make her forget the insult. "No . . . whenever they came here, I never saw them with any children."

"What's that supposed to mean?" I said. "Are you saying that they didn't live here all the time?"

"They'd be here for a couple of days, leave, and turn up again after a week or so. When I asked the girl, she told me once that she'd been to stay with her in-laws in Yannina, and another time she told me she'd gone back to Albania because her father was ill . . ."

That's why we hadn't found any other clothes, because sometimes they stayed here, sometimes elsewhere, exemplary vagrants. I was considering what might be behind all this when I heard Sotiris calling from inside the dwelling.

"Sir, can you come for a minute?"

I went back inside. Sotiris was standing in the middle of the room. As soon as he saw me, he went toward the toilet without saying a word. I found him standing in front of the lavatory. My nostrils suddenly started burning from the stench, and I began to sneeze. The bowl was bare, without any plastic seat. A pile of dried-up shit in the shape of a cone was stuck to it right in the middle. There were shoe prints all around the top of the bowl. Those who'd relieved themselves had climbed onto it and squatted there, Albanian style. The cistern was one of those cylindrical ones that look like a tiny boiler, with a button that you press upward.

"I went to flush it, but the button won't budge," Sotiris said.

"And what would you have me do, call a plumber?"

"Go on, you try," he insisted.

I was ready to give him hell, but something in his expression made me pause. I pressed the button, and it wouldn't budge. Something was stopping it. I tried again, using more force this time, but nothing happened.

"The mechanism has jammed."

Without answering, Sotiris removed the top of the cistern and put his hand inside. First he pulled out a big stone, then dipped his hand inside again. This time, his hand came out with a cellophane packet, in which were wrapped five-thousand-drachma notes. I stood there, staring at the notes with my mouth wide open.

"I told you we'd find money, but you didn't believe me." He was trying to put one over on me, and he made no effort to conceal his smugness.

"You didn't find anything because you didn't look properly. When I said you wouldn't find any money, I meant in the mattress, not in the whole house. If you'd been a bit more methodical, we'd have found it the first time."

The smile faded from his lips, and his exhilaration melted like a lollipop. Serves him right. He tried to make it seem like my fault, and now I'd shouldered him with the omission, whereas normally I'd have given him credit for finding it. He had to learn that mistakes are always the fault of subordinates. Superiors never make mistakes.

"Count it!"

He went on counting and counting. "Five hundred thousand."

Speechless, I gazed at the heap of notes and remembered the report I'd written. I tried to recall a point in it where I could fit this new evidence, albeit at the last minute, without Ghikas finding out and screaming that we hadn't done our job properly.

CHAPTER 6

The families on Karadimas Street were condemned to live both together and alone. Because the street itself was no more than three meters wide and the houses were arranged on either side of it. Whoever sat at the window saw into the opposite house, talked into the opposite house, lived in the opposite house, whether wanting to or not. The houses were arranged without rhyme or reason: Three houses were stuck close together, then there was an empty lot, then a house with a tiny garden beside two other houses stuck together like Siamese twins. On one side of the street was a haberdasher's and on the other a grocer's. Most of the houses were single story and only occasionally was there a two-story one. Some of the roofs had TV antennas, others had iron uprights sticking out of the concrete; some straight and others now bent, but anyway signs of hope that one day there would be a second floor added. For the time being, the hope had been abandoned, and many of the houses were so narrow that you didn't need a tape measure to calculate their width; you could do it with your arms. The poorest houses had nice wooden doors, painted blue, red, and green. The more imposing ones had wrought-iron doors with patterns recalling fossilized flowers or branches from a burnt forest.

The house where the Albanian couple lived was at the end of the street, next to an abandoned timber warehouse. Whereas almost all the houses looked into each other, no one could see into the Albanians' house. I stood outside with Sotiris, facing the empty lot across the way, and I cursed my bad luck. Back to the beginning with the questioning, the door-to-door inquiries, one person telling you one thing, another something different, and all you're left with is a headful of nothing, as my father used to say.

"You take one side, and I'll take the other," I said to Sotiris. He understood and headed toward the haberdasher's. I made for the grocer's.

The grocer had a slab of Gruyère on his counter, and he was slicing it down the middle. He trimmed the edges, nibbling the bits. He looked up and remembered me immediately.

"About the Albanians again?" he said, as he placed half the slab of cheese inside the fridge.

"Do you know whether they lived here all the time? I was told that they came here for a while and then left." My mind was more on what the chubby woman had told me than on the five hundred thousand.

"All I know is that the woman came here twice to shop. The first time she bought a packet of spaghetti and a tub of margarine, the second time a packet of beans."

"That's some memory," I told him, mainly to flatter him so that he'd come out with more.

"Not memory, slack business. People here buy so little that you remember it like the national anthem."

"Presumably, if they lived here all the time, they'd shop more often."

"Pardon me for saying so, but you know nothing. They can get by for ten days on a packet of beans."

"Did you happen to see anyone strange going in and out of the house?"

"Strange?"

"Anyone not from around here."

He'd begun to grow impatient, I could see it in his look. "Listen, Inspector," he said, "far be it from me to tell you your job, but why all this fuss about two Albanians? You've got the one who murdered them, what more do you want? After all, with two fewer Albanians and another one in prison, Greece is a better place."

"If I'm asking, it means that I have my reasons. Do you think I'm doing it for fun?" I turned and was heading for the door when behind me I heard him say, "One evening, must be a month ago now, I saw a truck parked outside their door."

I stopped dead. "What kind of truck?"

"One of those hard-top ones. You know, what are they called? Vans . . . but it was dark, and I can't tell you what make it was."

He said all this as he was arranging things in the fridge. Arranging not a lot, given that it was as empty as a bachelor pad. A whole salami, a cut of ham, half a slab of Gruyère, and some round boxes of Ayeladitsa cream cheese. And on the wall, where a bachelor would have stacked his books, he'd stacked dozens of jars of mixed pickles.

"Not that it's of any importance, it might just be a coincidence," he went on, "but I told you anyway because I don't like people leaving my shop with empty hands."

"Do you eat so many pickles around here?"

"No, I got them at cost price. But no one buys them."

"So why bother with them if no one wants them?"

"If I didn't make that kind of mistake, I wouldn't be a grocer in Rendi, I'd have my own supermarket," he said, leaving me with nothing to say.

The last house on the right side of the street, the one at an angle to the Albanians' house, had a green door and a square window, a small one, only just big enough for a head to poke through and gaze up and down the street. But on the inside, it was covered with white linen curtains, embroidered with tiny bonbons. They were parted in the middle to form two curves and tied back at the bottom.

"Can I offer you some of my orange preserves?" said the old woman. She was about eighty, short and bony. She dragged her feet as she walked, as if her skin were stuck to her bones and her feet to the floor. She was wearing a dressing gown with clovers embroidered on it, and her face was wizened, like crumpled paper that you open out again, because you've noted something on it.

"No, thank you. I won't be staying long," I said, to keep it short.

"Do try a spoonful. It's homemade," the old women insisted. I humored her, though I hate preserves, and I swilled it down with water so it wouldn't stick in my throat and also to wash the taste from my mouth.

"My daughter sends it to me from Kalamata. Bless her. And she sends me oil and olives, too, every year. Last New Year's, she bought me a television."

And she pointed to a seventeen-inch television on a small table. There was a cloth covering on the table, also white, but embroidered with little flowers. Whenever I see embroidery like that, I think of my mother, who never left any surface in the house uncovered and was always warning my father and me not to dirty them. He with his cigarette ash, me with my dirty hands.

"But she doesn't want me living with her," the old woman said, a note of grievance in her voice. "Not her, that is, but her husband. He won't hear of it; doesn't want his mother-in-law getting under his feet. When you're a *young* woman, it's your mother-in-law who doesn't want you; when you're old, it's your son-in-law. The best age is between forty and fifty. It's the age when they want you, but you don't want them."

"The Albanians, can you tell me anything about them, Dimitra?" I hastened to cut her off before she began on her second cousins.

"What can I say, Inspector? Quiet people, without a hope in the world. Though the way things are today, it's only the frightened ones we call quiet."

"And which were they, quiet or frightened?"

She looked at me and smiled. As her mouth twitched, all her wrinkles concentrated in her cheeks like pine needles. "What would you say about me?" she asked me. "Quiet or frightened?"

"Quiet."

"That's how I might seem, but I'm not." She sat in her chair and looked me in the eye. "You see the phone?" She pointed to the telephone beside the television. "They put it in for me last year. Till last year, I was all alone and without a phone. If I'd died, the neighbors would only have found out from the stench. By rights, what I should do is give my daughter a talking-to for living in the lap of luxury and leaving me in this hovel. I don't mean that she should have me live with her, since she can't, but they sent my granddaughter to university here in Athens and bought her a two-room flat in Pangrati. Would it have killed them to buy a bigger one so I could have moved in with her? I should tell my daughter all that to her face, but I cross myself and keep quiet. And do you know why? Because I'm afraid of angering her in case she stops sending the oil, the olives, and the eighty thousand she sends me—every month she says, but it's more like every two. You see me quiet because I'm afraid. But inside, I'm fuming."

"Are you saying that they seemed quiet, but that they might have been afraid?"

"I don't know. You saw them coming and going, and it made you wonder."

"Why did it make you wonder?"

"Because they'd leave as if someone was after them, and they'd come back like thieves in the night. It was always late at night. You'd wake up in the morning and they'd be here. One evening, I'd switched off the television, and I was sitting at the window. Me, I sit in front of the television from three in the afternoon, and I watch everything. It's only when they start with politics and love stories that I get bored and switch it off. When it's politics, because I don't understand a word they're saying. And when it's love stories, all the lies get on my nerves. I watch them pining, suffering, arguing, and when I grow tired of swearing at them, I switch it off. I lived forty years with my husband. We argued about food, about money, about our daughter, but never about love. You don't think that my daughter married this fellow in Kalamata out of love, do you? She wanted a good life for herself, and he wanted to get her into bed. But the little vixen wouldn't even let him hold her hand. He wouldn't give up, and so, to get her into bed in the end, he married her."

"And what's that got to do with the Albanians?"

"Don't be in so much of a hurry," she said. "Everything is connected, because if that love story hadn't been on that night, I wouldn't have been sitting at the window and I wouldn't have seen them coming in that limousine."

"What limo?" I said, remembering what the grocer had told me about the van parked outside.

"I call it a limousine because I don't know a thing about cars. Anyhow, it was a huge car with a hard top, must have held a good ten people. He got out with the girl. They hurried into the house, and the vehicle drove straight off. Before long, the light from the gas burner was on—they didn't have electricity. It all took less than a minute or so. They didn't have any bags with them or anything. The girl had a bundle with her, that was all." She looked at me, and her smile once again produced the pine needles on her cheeks.

I thought about the dried shit in the lavatory and the five hundred thousand in the cistern, the food in the diaper box, and the van that brought them there in the night. And if that wasn't enough, there was the Albanian murderer, about to be sent for the official hearing. How was anyone to find the thread that linked all this nonsense together?

I left the old woman's house and cursed those young policemen who make such a mess of things by trying to wrap it all up with a few quick questions. If, when we'd carried out our first investigations, someone had been patient enough to sit down with this old woman and listen to her grievances, we'd have known all this before we'd even taken the corpses to the mortuary. You could say about us, it seems, what homosexuals say about their own kind: It's one thing to be gay and another to be a pansy. Similarly, it's one thing to wear the uniform and another thing to be a policeman.

CHAPTER 7

"Out with it, you louse-ridden bum, or I'll make mincemeat of you and send you back to Korytsa so your own kind can have something to eat!" The Albanian was shaking because exactly what he had most feared had happened to him. He'd confessed to find a bit of peace, and now we were turning the screws.

"Where did those good-for-nothings get hold of the five hundred thousand? Out with it!"

"I not know . . . not know anything," he said, looking up fearfully at Thanassis, who was standing over him.

Thanassis grabbed him by the anorak and lifted him off his feet. The Albanian's legs dangled in the air. Thanassis swung around and pinned him against the wall. He held him there, a good foot off the floor.

"Be very careful what you say, because you'll blow it, you bastard!" he screamed, his face so close to the Albanian's that you didn't know whether he might kiss him or bite him. "You won't get out of here alive!"

One second he was holding him tight, and the next he let go of him. For an instant the Albanian remained in the air, but as soon as his feet touched the ground, he collapsed in a heap, quivering with fear.

"Get up!" Thanassis barked at him, just as he'd barely touched the floor. The Albanian flattened himself against the wall, of his own free will this time, and began crawling up it like a caterpillar. He managed to pull himself upright, and the climbing stopped. Thanassis immediately took hold of him again and sat him down in the chair.

"Out with it! Now!" he shouted. "Out with it!"

"I not know anything," the Albanian insisted. "I go for Pakize."

He kept a terrified watch on Thanassis, ignoring me. I'd done right to bring Thanassis with me. And I was wrong to have stopped him in the morning when he'd started getting rough with the Albanian. I should have let him get on with it. We might have learned the truth there and then, and I wouldn't have had to send a half-baked report to Ghikas.

"What dealings did you have with Pakize's husband?" Now I was the one to get rough. "Thefts? Drugs? You quarreled over sharing the loot and you murdered him! But you didn't find the money because he'd hidden it in too safe a place!"

He latched on to what I'd just said and looked at me meaningfully. "Mehmet, husband Pakize, maybe robbery, maybe drugs," he said, "I, no. I work building, work Rendi, vegetable market. I not know Mehmet. Know Pakize only."

"You mean to tell me you were creeping around outside their house all those days and you didn't ever see them coming home in a van?"

Thanassis looked at me in astonishment. I hadn't told him that detail. He was hearing it for the first time.

"A neighbor saw a van or a very big car dropping them off outside their front door. Late one evening, in secret," I explained and turned back to the Albanian. "Who was it who brought them in the van? What's his name? Where is he? Tell us!"

"When I go, Pakize home," he said shaking. "I no see van." Then he had an idea and rapidly said: "Pakize clean houses, take care kids. Maybe boss take her in van."

Thanassis grabbed him by his collar. "You're asking for it," he threatened. "You've given us nothing, and you're going to pay for this."

"No, no!" the Albanian cried out in alarm. "I kill Pakize and husband. But not know anything."

Thanassis let him fall back into the chair. If we went on like that all night, we'd still get nothing out of him, I thought to myself, starting to tire of it. He'd confessed that he'd killed them; that was clear-cut. That didn't necessarily mean that he knew about the five hundred thousand and the van. The most probable scenario was that we were dealing with a crime of passion, and that it was only by accident that we'd come up with something else, without the two things being linked. After all, we'd found the five hundred thousand, but we'd found no drugs or stolen goods or guns. They must have had some other hideaway. All that about trips to Yannina and Albania was bullshit. But how was anyone to discover what other dirty business was behind all this? Besides, it didn't concern us. Given that they were both dead, all proceedings would come to a halt.

"He's telling the truth. He knows nothing," I heard Thanassis say as he stood beside me in the lift, as if wanting to confirm my thoughts. So Thanassis, this self-confessed moron, agreed with me, and I took refuge behind that simple statement and felt relieved. The only thing still bothering me was that I had yet to alter my report.

I left Thanassis on the third floor, and I went up to the fifth. I stood and stared at the plaque: NIKOLAOS GHIKAS—CHIEF OF SECURITY. I read it maybe ten times while trying to think of some excuse for getting my report back without arousing suspicion. In the end, I put on a big smile and opened the door.

"Hello, Koula," I said cheerfully. The mannequin in uniform was sitting at her desk. She furtively bundled the mirror and tweezers she was using to pluck her eyebrows into a drawer.

"Hello, Inspector Haritos!" She had forgotten her usually cold look and was being nice because I'd caught her red-handed. "You can't go in, I'm afraid. He's busy," she said in an apologetic tone.

"Again? Ah, poor Koula, I'm amazed at how you manage with so much coming and going in here."

"You can't imagine, I don't have time to draw breath."

I was about to tell her that I could see that, that she didn't even have time to pluck her eyebrows, but instead I said: "I don't know what he'd do without you. And not only him, but us too. Everything goes through your hands."

"Do you know what time I left yesterday? Nine o'clock!"

"Shall I ask him to transfer you to my department? And pick ten of mine to put in here? Because you're worth ten."

"He wouldn't let me," she said and giggled, obviously flattered.

"He'd be mad to let you go. Where would he find anyone as sharp as you?" She was oozing with satisfaction. I leaned over her desk, lowered my voice, and said to her conspiratorially, "Koula, can I ask you a favor?"

"Of course," she said immediately, ecstatic still and willing to do anything for me.

"I have to get back the report I left this morning. I forgot to include something. But I don't want him to know."

"It's still on his desk. I'll go and get it with the things from the out-tray. He won't know anything."

"Let's hope that he won't ask for it while I've got it."

"I'll tell him that I've sent it to be photocopied, and I'll call you so you can bring it back to me." She gave me a crafty smile and went into his office.

That's great, the fox and the hen have hit it off and there's no one to touch them. A moment later, she came out holding a pile of papers. She went through them, found the report, and gave it to me.

"You're a treasure," I gushed.

I wasn't in any mood to put up with the elevator, so I took the stairs. "I'm up to the ears and I'm not here if anyone calls," I shouted to Thanassis and closed my office door.

I sat down and began going through the report. As luck would have it, he hadn't read it—there were none of his notes on it. He'd read the summary I'd sent him to get it down pat for the reporters, and he'd left the report for later, like always. Fortune was on my side that day: The final page had only five lines on it. I could easily add the new information to the end. If he asked me why I hadn't mentioned the five hundred thousand in the summary, I'd tell him that was why I'd sent the report along too, so that he could read the details there. I'd have him showing himself up for not having read the report promptly. I'd earn plus points without losing any. The points system was another one of the innovations that Ghikas had brought back with him from the FBI. When you solved a case, you got positive points; when you messed up, you got negative ones. All this is recorded in your file, and when the Official Council convenes to consider promotions, they study your file and count the positive and negative points. In the end, each new government appoints its own people, and you remain in the same position with your points in hand.

I began feverishly to write the last page so as not to waste time, but I hit a snag because something else was bugging me. The old woman had told me that the Albanian girl had been holding a bundle. If she was holding it in her hands, that meant it couldn't have been large. What could have been inside it, clothes? We didn't find any clothes. Jewelry, gold, antiques? This was the most likely. How else would these gypsy immigrants have come up with five hundred thousand? They were either thieves or go-betweens taking a cut. And the hovel in Karadimas Street was their hideaway. They stayed there till they'd handed over the goods and got the money. Afterward, they moved somewhere else. The good thing about this was that it left the Albanian out of it. Certainly if he'd killed them for the loot, he wasn't going to have left the money in the cistern. No, he was a jarring note in the case; he'd killed on account of Pakize. So, the business with the Albanian was settled; we could send him all wrapped up to the prosecutor's office. As for the rest, Ghikas could read the report and decide if he wanted to continue the investigation and who he'd assign it to. I'd collect the points and end up sitting pretty.

Then Karayoryi sprang to mind. Hadn't everything started with her? Wasn't she the one who'd got me all worked up about the child and sent me off to investigate? We hadn't found a child, of course, but the old women had seen something that looked like a bundle. What if it was a baby wrapped in a blanket? How could she have made that distinction in the dark?

I picked up the internal phone and told Thanassis to come into my office. While he was on his way, I added the last bit of information to the report and handed it to him.

"Give this to Koula and then come back, because I need you for something," I said to give myself a little time to make my decision.

Why did I want to get involved? Why didn't I let the case, if there was a case, take its official course? I'd had the department on its feet thousands of times, and in the end, nothing came of it and instead of points all I got was a tongue-lashing. This was why I'd never been sent for further training, not even to the Panteion School for seminars, let alone to the FBI.

Thanassis returned before long. He thought I had a job for him, and he stared at me with that look that said, "I'm a moron." "I know you're a moron," I replied, again with a look, "but I need your help."

"Be honest with me, Thanassis," I said to him, "is that Karayoryi woman hot for you, or am I wrong there?"

He wasn't expecting it, and he was flummoxed. He looked at me in both surprise and alarm. "What makes you think that, sir?" he mumbled. He didn't know what else to say.

"I'm asking because I happened to notice the way she looks at you, the smiles she gives you. . . . Come on, don't tell me you haven't noticed yourself?"

"It's just your imagination," he said quickly. "Why would she fancy me?"

"It depends. . . . She might be after you because you're a fine young thing. Or she may be coming on to you because she wants access to the department and wants a scoop . . . or maybe both . . ."

"Am I one to talk?" he said in an offended tone. Not that he'd be the first.

"That's exactly what I want, for you to talk to her. I want you to phone her, supposedly confidentially, and tell her that you have some information for her. And when you're with her, I want you to find out what she knows about the child."

He stared at me dumbly. I waited for it to sink in, because, after all, he was a moron, as we said. "Let me explain, so you know," I said, after giving him a moment to think. "Two days ago, Karayoryi asked me whether the Albanians had a child. And yesterday, on the news, she said that we were looking for a child. It was a lie, but she must have had some reason for saying it. Today an old woman neighbor told me that she'd seen the couple getting out of a van and that the girl was carrying a bundle. The bundle might have been a baby that she couldn't see clearly in the dark. So I want you to find out just what it is that she knows and why she keeps dropping hints."

"Don't make me do this, please, sir," he stammered in obvious distress.

"What am I making you do, dimwit?" I don't call him a moron because we say that silently, like conspirators. "For years, you've got by in here through skiving, and I've always turned a blind eye! And once in a blue moon, when I send you on a job and pay your expenses and find you a chick, you start being difficult!"

"I don't want to get into trouble, sir. If anyone sees me and the people upstairs get to hear of it, I'll be in deep shit."

"Why should you get into any trouble? At worst, I'm the one who'll be in trouble for sending you. Or are you afraid that if it gets out, I'll play the fool and blame it all on you?"

"No," he said quickly, but then he began hemming and hawing again. "And then there's my girlfriend. If she finds out I was with another woman, I'll have real problems, and how am I going to explain things to her?"

"Send her to me and I'll give it to her in writing that you went on official business. Now get out of here and don't come back without the information."

He stood there and stared at me like a frightened pup. "Be off with you!" I shouted, and he took to his heels.

I didn't give a shit about the points.

CHAPTER 8

Before going home, I stopped by the bank to get the thirty-five thousand that Adriani had asked me for. I wasn't proposing to give it to her that particular day, but everything had worked out well for me and I was in a good mood. First of all, I was sure about the Albanian. With him, at least, I was in no danger of slipping up. And second, I'd adjusted the report without Ghikas getting wind of it. Of course, the business with Karayoryi was far from foolproof because Thanassis wasn't the smartest guy on two wheels and if he let it slip that it was me who'd sent him to fish for information, Karayoryi would make it front-page news and I'd have a hurricane on my hands. But you can't have all the hatches secured; you have to take the occasional risk.

I had a bank card. It was Adriani's idea. For her own selfish ends, but, anyway, it was convenient for me. At first, she pestered me to open a joint account, but that I wouldn't hear of. I'd have been witless to make her a partner to my money and end up tearing my hair out when there was nothing left in the account. Not that she was a spendthrift, but I decided to leave her on a diet before she could work up an appetite. When she saw that she wasn't getting anywhere, she changed her tune and persuaded me to get a bank card. She thought that she'd be able to discover the code and sneak off with the card to withdraw whatever she wanted, but it never happened. I gave her thirty thousand each week for the housekeeping, and whenever she asked me for more, I let her wait a few days before forking it over. I always gave in, but not before making her life difficult so she wouldn't get carried away. The only thing she'd succeeded in doing was to send me off shopping now and again, supposedly because she hadn't time, so she could put the money she saved to one side.

I put the card into the slot. "Touch here for Greek," the message came on the screen, to show that it was cosmopolitan and I was a peasant. I decided to put one over on it though and touched the second key, which said: "Touch here for English." Not that I understood everything it said in English, but I knew the sequence of keys blindfolded and I didn't care. It was as though I was repeating the conversation with Thanassis here too, silently, through the eyes: "I'm a moron"—"I know you're a moron." Except that I was the moron now because the machine told me everything I had to do, spelling it out, just in case I didn't understand and flubbed.

I withdrew fifty thousand and went home. Adriani was sitting in her usual spot, in her armchair, with the remote control in her hand. Except that this time it wasn't the policeman she was watching, it was some other guy who'd married the mother and wanted to screw the daughter, but the daughter was having none of it. I stood over her, and, just as every other evening, she was either not aware of me or she simply ignored me. I took the thirty-five thousand, which I'd already counted, out of my pocket, and, without saying a word, I let it fall into her lap. It surprised her, totally absorbed as she was by the daughter and stepfather; the girl was swearing at him, and he, evidently a masochist, was sweet-talking her. Just for a moment Adriani moved her gaze from the screen and stared into her lap. Her left hand suddenly grabbed the five-thousand notes while her right let go of the remote control. She leapt up, and the control fell to the floor.

"Costas, dear!" she cried in delight, "Thank you, darling!" She held me to her and put her lips to my cheek.

On the screen, the daughter slapped her stepfather, and the scene was brusquely concluded. The policeman reappeared and at once began bellowing. But Adriani had forgotten all about this and was holding me tight in her arms as if she already had her hands on the boots. And when she let go of me, she stooped and picked up the control.

"To hell with it. I'm fed up with it. All the same stuff!" she said crossly and pressed the button while looking at me with a crafty smile, as if to say: "You see? If you bought me a pair of boots every day, I'd never watch TV again!"

For the rest of the evening, till it was time for the news bulletin, she hung on to me and her tongue never stopped wagging. She went on and on—about how life had become so much more expensive, and how five years before, a pair of shoes had cost only five or six thousand, whereas now you needed twenty thousand, about the expensive supermarket across the street and how she went to Sklavenitis's, which was three blocks away but was cheaper, and how glad she was that Katerina was coming because she missed her terribly. It was all bullshit, wool over my eyes, apart from the Katerina bit. Because she did miss her terribly, as I did. She'd literally wilted since the day Katerina left for Thessaloniki, and lived only for her coming home at Christmas, Easter, and during the summer holidays. The periods between were empty waiting periods that she filled with housework, television, and the little daily games of getting her own back on me.

At nine o'clock, I switched on the television to watch the news, and who should be on but Ghikas. He wasn't at all short, but sitting behind that enormous desk, he was barely visible, like a man drowning, struggling to stay above water. He seemed to be sinking under the microphones. He'd reeled off the summary by heart, without getting stuck anywhere. Kouvelos, our history teacher at high school, would have given him ten out of ten. He said nothing about the five hundred thousand or the van, a sign that he hadn't taken the trouble to read the full account. If the reporters discovered it later, he'd get around it by saying that the investigations were ongoing and he was unable to give any more details.

We lounged around for another two hours, first supper, then the ads with breaks for a film on TV, a bit of chat, and, by eleven, we'd had enough and went to bed. I was already tucked up and ready to prop Liddell & Scott on my stomach when Adriani came and lay down next to me. She was wearing a pale blue nightdress with embroidery on the chest. It was virtually transparent, because her white panties shone through underneath. She was ready to reach for her

Viper on the bedside table when I put down Liddell & Scott and reached for her. I pulled her on top of me with one hand while I thrust the other under her nightdress and began caressing her left leg. I took her by surprise, and, at first, she froze, then she stretched out her arm and began caressing my back, giving me a back massage. It wasn't that I was desperate to make love, but somehow she had to pay me back for the thirty-five thousand and for my making things easy for her. My generosity deserved some reward. My hand moved higher, got as far as the elastic in her panties and tugged at it. She bent her knees slightly to help me, then straightened them again and held them tight together because she knew how I liked to shove my hand between her legs and part them.

About halfway through, I was already regretting it and wanted to get up and go, as if from a boring play at the intermission. Adriani's moaning and groaning made things worse. Half the time, the bitch faked orgasm and thought I wasn't aware of it. If every time it happened, I nabbed her and took her in, she'd have received a life sentence for repeated fraud. I'd look at Katerina and wonder how I'd produced a girl like that from a faked orgasm.

Adriani's groans ceased the instant I came. She leapt up and left the bedroom. She didn't realize that that was how I knew she was faking. When we come and she stays in bed counting her breaths, it means that she had a real orgasm. When she rushes to the bathroom to wash herself, as if I had gonorrhea, then she's faking.

I was holding Liddell & Scott and about to open it when I heard the phone ring in the living room. That was another one of Adriani's little quirks. She wouldn't agree to having a line in the bedroom because she didn't want it to wake her on those occasional nights when they needed to contact me, with the result that I had to spring in a panic from the bedroom to the living room, not to mention that I slept every night with the fear of not hearing the damn thing.

It had rung a dozen times or so before I lifted the receiver.

"Hello," I said, out of breath.

"Get over to Hellas Channel immediately," Ghikas said sharply at the other end of the line. "I want you to go yourself. Don't send anyone else."

"Is it something serious?" I asked like a moron, as it had to be serious or he wouldn't be sending me.

"Yanna Karayoryi's been murdered." I was thunderstruck, unable to utter a word. "I want you in my office at nine in the morning with all the details. Before you have your croissant." He stressed this last to demonstrate that he had his eyes everywhere and that nothing escaped him.

I heard him hang up, but I remained rooted to the spot, the receiver stuck to my hand.

CHAPTER 9

I found her sitting in front of the wall of mirrors. She wasn't looking into the mirror. She was leaning back in the chair, her head thrown back, and she was looking up at the ceiling. It was as if she'd been murdered while stretching. Her arms hung lifeless at her sides. She was wearing an olive green dress with gold buttons, and she had a scarf around her neck. It was the first time I'd seen her in a dress, and I stood there taking it all in. It made me wonder what suited her best, a dress or trousers—as if it mattered now. She was all made up: eyeliner, rouge, and a faded red lipstick, like the blood left by barbecued meat. There were no signs of violence on her face and the makeup was untouched. She'd been getting ready, it seemed, to appear on the late-night news. That was strange, because they usually have the live reports on the nine o'clock news and put the rehashed stuff on late at night.

The metal rod had gone through her left side, below the lung, and had come out slanting upward, pinning her to the chair. It reminded one somewhat of the jousting of medieval knights, who ran each other through: Ivanhoe or Richard the Lionhearted. Not that I'd ever read about them as such; I only read dictionaries, but my father once tried to educate me and bought me all the "Illustrated Classics." That's how I know them, from the printed form of TV, literature as cartoons.

"What sort of rod is that?" I asked Stellio from the records department, who was photographing the corpse so that they could remove the murder weapon and Markidis, the coroner, could get to work.

"A light stand," he said, and his camera flashed four times in quick succession. He altered the angle and there were four more flashes.

When I'd gone in, I'd had a quick look around, but I'd focused my attention on Karayoryi. Now I looked around again. It was a big room. Along the length of the wall beside the door they'd fixed a bench, just like those you find in government offices or doctors' waiting rooms, except that the officials' desks were missing. In their place was a long, rectangular mirror covering the whole wall. Three chairs had been placed in a row in front of the bench. Still sitting in the first one was Karayoryi, awaiting the coroner. The other two were empty. Karayoryi's was facing the mirror. The second, however, was turned toward Karayoryi. If it hadn't been moved by whoever discovered the body, then that might be a clue. Someone had been sitting beside Karayoryi, perhaps talking to her. If it was her murderer, this meant that she knew him and had had dealings with him.

Piled in the opposite corner of the room were projectors and spotlights and various lights still attached to their stands. Some spare stands were propped against the wall. He hadn't come to kill her, I thought; he'd come to talk to her. Something must have upset him; he'd picked up one of the stands and run her through with it. But what was it that had upset him? Passion? Professional jealousy? Revenge by someone she'd exposed? I reminded myself not to be in too much of a hurry, it was still early days. But at least I had something to go on. If it indeed turned out that the chair had been in that position.

"Are you done, here?" I asked Dimitris, the other technician from records.

"We're done, all right. We're packing up."

There was a closed cupboard on the adjoining wall. I opened it. Men's suits and women's dresses; the kind that fashion companies supply the newscasters with in order to get their names in the credits and so get some free advertising. I'd worn a tie for the first time when I'd entered the academy. It came with the uniform. And I'd acquired a suit when I graduated. From Kappa-Maroussis's "almost-ready-to-wear department." They brought me a brown suit, covered in stitching, that was big enough for a second Haritos. "Don't worry," the assistant had said. "That's why you choose it 'almost-ready.' Once we tailor it precisely to your size it'll fit you like a glove." Two days later, the ready-to-wear was as baggy on me as the almost-ready-to-wear. "It's just your imagination," the assistant had snapped at me. "You've still not worn it in, that's why." Meanwhile, Kappa-Maroussis burned down, whereas I moved up in the world and started going to Vardas, which also makes its money on tailored suits.

I looked swiftly through the clothes, but found nothing. The women's dresses had no pockets, the men's suits had empty pockets.

I went back to the bench, beside Yanna Karayoryi, who'd had the rod removed from her. Markidis was bent over her, poking around. I picked up her handbag and emptied it out onto the bench. Lipstick, powder, eyeliner, exactly what she had on. No one was going to take it off now; she'd go to the grave with her makeup. A packet of Ro-1 cigarettes and a silver Dynon lighter, very expensive. A key ring with car keys and what must have been the keys to her house. And her purse. It contained three five-thousand notes, four one-thousand notes, a bank card, and a Diner's Club card. In the photograph on her identity card, she couldn't have been much more than fifteen, with long hair and a stern expression. I looked at the year of birth, 1953. So she was forty, and she hadn't looked it at all. I kept the keys and put everything else back in the bag for forensics.

Markidis was done and came up to me. He was short, bald, with thick-rimmed glasses, and had been wearing the same suit for two decades. Either it never got dirty or he'd found a way of sending it to the dry cleaners on Sundays. He invariably had the expression of a whipped dog, whether as a result of the force or of his wife, I can't say. Anyway, it always got on my nerves.

"I'm fed up with seeing corpses," he said. "There are days when I see as many as three and four. I knew I should have become a microbiologist."

"It's not my fault that you chose corpses instead of urine," I said. "Come on, let's have it quick. I might still get an hour's sleep."

"The rod entered beneath the left thorax at an angle of approximately fifteeen degrees. It pierced the heart and came out through her shoulder. The murderer was standing behind her."

"Why behind her?"

"From the front he wouldn't have been able to run her through with such force without knocking over the chair." He went and got one of the metal stands. "He must have killed her something like this." He held it in both hands just above the middle, raised it, and brought it down with force. "He must have been quite tall and muscular."

"How do you figure?"

"If he was short, either the wound would have been higher, or he wouldn't have been able to run her through at all because he would have lost some of his strength when leaning over."

He may have seemed grumpy and dispirited, but he knew his job. "What can you tell me about the time?"

"Two or three hours. No more than three, but no less than two. I might be able to be more exact after the autopsy."

He left without saying good-bye. "Sir," said Sotiris, whom I'd notified and who had meanwhile arrived. "There are a lot of reporters outside asking to see you. And Mr. Sperantzas, the newscaster, is annoyed that you're making him wait."

"I don't give a shit! First, I want to see whoever it was who found the body. Have him brought here."

"It wasn't a he, it was a she. A girl from the production team."

"Just get her here!"

How on earth could the murderer have come up to Karayoryi from behind, with the stand in his hands, without her having seen him in the mirror? She must have seen him, but not thought anything bad because she'd known him. So we were looking for a tall, well-built acquaintance of Yanna Karayoryi's who at the time of the murder, obviously, was at the studios.

The girl who came in couldn't have been more than twenty-two and was pretty nondescript. At most she was five one, or maybe five two. She was wearing jeans, a shirt, and boots. She was still shaking from the shock, and her eyes were swollen from crying. Sotiris stood her before me, holding her by the arm, so she couldn't get away from him, like the thoroughbred police officer that he was, instead of sitting her down on a chair so she might feel relaxed and we could get to the bottom of things.

"Have a seat," I said to her gently, and I had her sit in the third chair, which was the only one available. She sat with her legs drawn in, her hands clamped on her knees, and she stared at me silently.

"What's your name?"

"Dimitra . . . Dimitra Zoumadaki . . ."

"Listen, Dimitra, there's nothing to be afraid of. Just tell me what you know, in your own time. If you forget anything, don't worry, you can add it later."

She remained silent for a while to collect her thoughts. It wasn't easy for her. She unclamped her hands and began rubbing them on her jeans. "We were about to move on to the news bulletin when we suddenly saw that a spotlight had burnt out, and so Mr. Manisalis sent me to get another one—"

"Who is Mr. Manisalis?"

"The director . . . I'm his assistant . . ."

"Okay . . . go on . . ."

"I came running in here, and I didn't notice her. I was in a hurry to replace the spotlight. But when I turned around to leave, I suddenly saw—" she covered her face with her hands as if wanting to block out the memory.

"You saw the metal rod sticking out of her back," I said coaxingly, to help her. She nodded emphatically and began sobbing.

"Open your eyes," I told her, but she kept them shut. "Open your eyes. There's nothing to be afraid of." She opened them and looked, first at me, then, hesitantly, all around her. The room had been emptied. The corpse was in an ambulance on its way to the mortuary, and the forensics boys had left. There was only Sotiris, who was standing discreetly outside her line of vision.

"Try to remember, Dimitra. Was this chair here, as it is now, or was it turned toward the mirror?"

She stared at the chair and thought for a moment.

"It must have been like that because I didn't touch anything, I'm sure of that. I screamed and ran outside. And Mr. Manisalis, who came back with me afterward, didn't enter the room at all. He looked in from the door and went at once to the phone."

"When you were coming to get the spotlight, did you see anyone outside in the corridor? Anyone coming out of the room or leaving?"

"I didn't see anyone, but I heard something."

"What did you hear?"

"Footsteps. Someone was running. But I didn't pay any attention, because there's always someone running in here. We're all run off our feet."

"That's my girl, you reeled it off like an expert. I'll let you know when to come to make an official statement, but there's no urgency. Tomorrow, the day after, when you've got over the shock. Go on home now and have some rest. But find someone to take you, don't go on your own."

She smiled at me, relieved. As soon as she opened the door to go out, they all poured in, pushing her back inside. I'd put an officer on guard outside, but he got caught up in the bedlam too and ended up inside the room. At their head was Sotiropoulos, leader in the Taking of the Bastille.

"What happened is tragic," he announced to me sorrowfully. That's to say, only the tone of his voice was sorrowful, because his expression revealed nothing, unshaven as he was, and as for his eyes, these looked, behind his round glasses, like two tiny beads that reacted only to intense light.

"Yanna Karayoryi was the personification of the honest and conscientious journalist, who went fearlessly and determinedly in search of the truth. She will be sorely missed."

I listened to this worthless spiel in silence. He raised the tone of his voice—not because I said nothing. He would have done it anyway, he'd rehearsed it. "And while the journalistic world is in turmoil, the police provocatively keep silent and have made no statement. We demand, Inspector, that you tell us what you know about the heinous murder of our colleague Yanna Karayoryi."

"I have no intention whatsoever of telling you anything, Mr. Sotiropoulos." He was at a loss as to how to react to the officiousness of my manner.

"That's unacceptable, Inspector," he said, in an equally officious tone. "You cannot treat us in this way when we give our lives for the truth."

"I can't make any statement, or reveal any aspect of the investigation, before questioning every one of you."

"Question us?" A brouhaha consisting of three ingredients rose up from them: bewilderment, alarm, and protest. Two cups of water, four cups of flour, and half a cup of sugar, as Adriani says when she gives the recipe for her famous cake, which—just between us—is inedible.

"There is evidence that the victim knew the murderer. And you were all colleagues or friends of Karayoryi. It's perfectly obvious that we would want to question you."

"Are we regarded as suspects?"

"I can reveal no part of the investigation to you before questioning you. That's all. Tomorrow morning, I want every one of you in my office, and that's not because I intend to make a statement. Sotiris, take all their names before you show them out."

"Everyone is innocent until proven guilty. That's a fundamental rule of law, or perhaps they didn't teach you that in the academy."

"That's what the lawyers say. In the eyes of the police, everyone is guilty until proven innocent." I pushed through the crowd and went out into the corridor.

Behind me swirls of protest and indignation rose and fell, but I was content. Of course, the next day Ghikas would give me a chewing out for ruining his good relations with the media, but I'd been through far worse.

CHAPTER 10

Sperantzas was sitting where he sits when he reads the news, behind the oval table. He was alone because on the late-night news, he appears without any entourage. He wasn't the one with the handkerchief in the breast pocket of his jacket to wipe away the tears; he was the other one, the one who shouted the news as if he were selling watermelons in the market. He looked at me as I came in and couldn't decide whether he should lead with displeasure at being kept waiting or distress at the murder of his colleague. In the end, he settled for a deep sigh that covered both. I went and sat next to him in the seat of the girl who presents the sports news.

"How did they all find out?" I asked, referring to the reporters in the corridor, who were making so much noise that they could be heard even from where we were.

"They must have heard about it on the news."

I couldn't believe my ears. "You mean you reported Karayoryi's murder on the news, before you'd even informed us?"

"The whole of Greece was shocked," he replied passionately. "That kind of breaking news report has never happened before. The phone lines just about caught fire. I'd just begun to present the news about the new economic measures when they took me off the air and went into a commercial break. Before I'd had time to ask what was happening, Manisalis, the director, came charging in and told me that Yanna had been murdered. I shouted to them to keep on with the commercials and I sent a camera to the makeup room. When I went on the air again, I was grief-stricken. 'Ladies and gentlemen,' I said, 'at this moment in our own studios a tragedy has taken place. Our crime reporter, Yanna Karayoryi—the sleuth, as she was known to her colleagues—is lying dead in the next room, murdered. We don't know who the perpetrator of this heinous crime is. Sadly, the truth has many enemies. Nevertheless, Hellas Channel, the channel renowned for its exclusive reports, the leading channel for up-to-the-minute news, has an obligation to inform you, its viewers, before anyone else. Ladies and gentlemen, you are hearing about the tragic end of Yanna Karayoryi at almost the same time that the fatal incident occurred, even before the police have been informed.' And right on cue I showed the scene in the makeup room, with Yanna exactly as you found her. I mean, we're talking documentary art here. We have the video. You can see it if you want."

Why didn't I chew him out? Why didn't I smack him in the face? Why didn't I set up two chairs and tie him between them, remove his socks and shoes, and subject him to an hour of bastinado? The police officer who abandons the rough stuff is like a smoker who's quit cigarettes. Even though, logically, you know you were right to give it up, inside you're dying to let fly, just like an ex-smoker who deep down longs for a drag.

"Do you know what I should do to you?" I said to him. "I should frog-march you down to the station, lock you up in a cell with murderers, thugs, and pushers, and let them pin you down and shoot craps on your ass!" Words, shouting, empty threats. I'd given up cigarettes, and I was deceiving myself with chewing gum.

"How dare you talk to me like that? Who gave you the right? We will protest in the strongest possible terms to your superiors, and publicly too. You're living in the past, it seems." His voice was trembling as if he were shivering.

"First of all, it's against the law to publicize a murder before informing the police. We're the ones who decide when to make it known to the public and what evidence to reveal. Secondly, when you make known at what time the body was found, you may be helping the murderer to escape and so, albeit unwittingly, become his accomplice. If you protest, all that will happen is that I will be severely criticized for not arresting you."

"I'm a journalist and I did my duty. If Yanna were alive, she'd salute me."

She'd not only have saluted him, she'd have rubbed her hands in glee because he'd put one over on us. That much I knew to be true, so I said nothing.

"Why was Karayoryi due to appear on the late-night news? So far as I know, there was nothing new on the crime report."

"She was about to make a startling revelation."

"What kind of revelation?"

"I don't know. She didn't tell me."

I became irate again. "You'd better not be hiding anything from me, Sperantzas, just so you can reveal whatever it is and get all the credit. Because if you are, I'll have you hopping like a Muslim in Bosnia."

"I'm not hiding anything. I'm telling you the truth."

"And just what is the truth? That she came and announced to you she was about to make a startling revelation, without telling you what it was she was about to reveal and without asking permission from anyone? Are you saying that anyone can appear on your channel and say what they like, is that it?"

"Not anyone. Yanna Karayoryi," he replied under his breath, at the same time looking over to where the cameras were, as though afraid he might be being filmed.

"What's that supposed to mean?"

He hesitated before answering. He found it hard to get the words out. "Yanna made her own decisions. She answered to no one." He bent forward and lowered his voice. "Listen. Don't expect to get it all from me. I can't tell you any more."

Hiding beneath the tailored suit was a frightened and insecure little man. I was surprised to feel a sudden liking for him, and lost all desire to push him any further.

"When did she tell you about this revelation?"

"I was in the newsroom, having a final look at the bulletin. About half an hour before I was due to go on the air."

"What time did you go on the air? Twelve?"

"Three minutes past twelve. The program on before the news was running three minutes late, and we decided not to interrupt it. We let it go on."

"Was she alone?"

"Of course," he said. "Who would she be with?"

"That's what I'd like to know." I got to my feet.

"Where's the newsroom?"

"Next to makeup."

"Inspector." I was almost at the door, and I turned around. "There aren't too many in here who'll shed any tears for Karayoryi. Talk to Martha Kostarakou. She does the medical reports. She knows plenty."

That said, he began rapidly to gather the papers on the desk, avoiding my gaze.

"Come with me to the newsroom."

"I've told you what I know. If you need me for anything else, I'm always here at the studio. But right now I'm going home because I'm beat."

"Come with me." From his expression, it was obvious that he wanted to tear me off a strip, but he controlled himself. He picked up his papers and went with me.

The reporters had all left, and the corridor was empty; we bumped into the director, so I didn't have to go looking for him. In any case, as it turned out, Manisalis knew nothing of any importance. After the news bulletin had begun, his girl assistant had come running in and told him that she'd found Karayoryi dead. He had taken a quick look from the makeup room doorway and realized that there was no point in going into the room. He'd gone on running the ads, but he hadn't rushed to the phone as Zoumadaki had told me. First, he had informed Sperantzas. He had telephoned the police only after first sending a camera to makeup at around ten past twelve.

I still had no idea why she had been killed, but at least I was clear as to how and when the murder had occurred. Sometime between eleven-thirty and twelve, Karayoryi had gone to see Sperantzas and told him that she wanted a slot on the late-night news. At three minutes past twelve, Zoumadaki had found her dead. So the murder had taken place in the course of that half hour. She had known the murderer. He'd been sitting beside her in makeup, talking to her. He'd got up, probably still talking, and had started playing with the light stand. He'd gone up to her, still chatting away. She'd seen him in the mirror while she was putting on her makeup, but her thoughts hadn't turned to anything bad. And once he'd got behind her, he'd raised the rod and run her through with it. If there were fingerprints on the rod, his might be among them. If there weren't any, that meant he'd wiped it before opening the door and disappearing. If the murderer was someone from outside the Hellas Channel, then I had to keep my fingers crossed and hope that he had been seen entering or leaving. If he was someone who worked there, then we were sailing in the southern Aegean against a gale-force wind.

The newsroom was a large open area with ten desks arranged in three rows of three, three, and four. The walls were bare. No one had thought to hang a picture, even a calendar—a sign that those who used it were merely passing through. They stayed there as long as they needed to do their work and then left, either for the studio or the street. At one end was a space separated by a glass partition. It was small, like a cubicle, just big enough for a desk and two chairs with a coffee table between them.

"The news editor's office," Sperantzas said.

"Which was Karayoryi's desk?" He pointed it out, the second one in the second row. I took out her keys, found the one that fitted the drawer, and opened it. "I won't be needing you any further," I said to Sperantzas, as I began looking through its contents. He appeared to hesitate. He was curious and wanted to stay. "I thought you said you were beat? Go on then." He'd said it and he couldn't take it back, so he turned and left.

Her desk was one of the smaller ones and it had only two drawers on the right-hand side. In the first drawer I found two notepads, a reporter's pad and a larger one for correspondence, and some cheap Biros, the kind that companies issue to their staff. I opened the second drawer. At the front was a small packet of colorfully wrapped toffees. It seemed that she liked chewing, perhaps to help her come up with ideas when she got stuck with her writing. There was a desk set, consisting of a letter opener and some scissors, in an expensive leather case still in the cellophane wrapping. Obviously a gift that she hadn't opened. And at the back there was a desk diary bearing the logo of some insurance company. I flicked through the diary. It was empty; she'd made no notes.

Puzzled, I stood over the drawers. There was something missing. Didn't she have a Filofax, damn it? It was unheard of for a reporter not to have a Filofax. That was where they noted everything: telephone numbers, information, loans and debts, professional and personal contacts, loves and hates, friendships and enmities. Filofax, the gospel of the modern Christian. Didn't Karayoryi have a gospel? Impossible. So where had it disappeared to? Usually, they carried it with them, so it should have been in her bag, but it wasn't. She might have locked it in her desk, but it wasn't there either. Could she have left it at home? Perhaps, but I thought it unlikely. Most probably the murderer had taken it, either because he was looking for something, or because it contained some incriminating information about him.

"Delopoulos, the studio director, would like to see you in his office," said Sotiris from the doorway.

"Right. Tell him I'll be along shortly."

"Do you want me for anything else, or can I go home?" he said, significantly.

"You can stay here," I told him severely. "You can go and find the security guard who was on duty around eleven at the entrance and tell him to wait for me, because I want to talk to him."

"Yes, sir," he said and went off sulking. I could have taken care of it over the phone from Delopoulos's office, but it didn't seem right to me for a subordinate to be at home snoring in his bed while his superior was slaving away into the small hours. These new officers were all milksops. They wanted to do nothing but lounge about all day at their desks wittering on about their Hyundai Excel or their Toyota Starlet. If there was a way to do it, they'd issue a memo demanding that crimes take place only between nine and five, not including Sundays and federal holidays.

CHAPTER 11

Delopoulos's office was a three-roomed penthouse suite, seventy meters square, with a lounge, dining area, bedroom, hall, and bathroom, all open plan, except for the bathroom. He was sitting behind a desk that was a basketball court compared to Ghikas's Ping-Pong table. On the south-facing side of the suite, there was a huge oblong table with ten high-backed chairs around it. The chair at the head of the table had a higher back and arms, whereas the others were armless. Across from Delopoulos's desk was a TV screen, five times bigger than the normal ones. It was off and the screen reflected his face and mine.

I wondered whether I should play the TV soap policeman who yelled all the time, given that I was in a TV studio, but that dickhead only shouted at women and small fries, whereas I had to deal with Delopoulos.

He was a tall, lanky man, balding, and with a sour expression. Right now his expression was a picture of grief, but given his face, this too appeared sour.

"I am completely shocked, Inspector Haritos," and he repeated it so as to leave me in no doubt. "Completely shocked. Yanna Karayoryi was an exceptional woman and a talented reporter. Her colleagues called her the sleuth. I regarded that as a mark of honor, one she had most justly earned." He paused, looked at me, and added, stressing each word, "And apart from being a colleague here at the channel, she was also a personal friend."

I had to stop myself from wondering aloud if she was also his bit on the side, because the way that Karayoryi did as she pleased meant that she had someone high up watching over her.

"Do you have any clues? Any information to give me? Is there anyone you suspect?"

"It's too early to say, Mr. Delopoulos. We do know, at least, the time of the murder and that the murderer was someone she knew because, before he killed her, they were chatting together in makeup."

"Then it must be someone she'd exposed, someone who had been damaged by her revelations and was looking for revenge. That's where you should begin your investigations."

Now he was telling me where I should start looking. I'd got another Ghikas on my hands. "Mr. Sperantzas told me that Karayoryi had asked to appear on the late-night news because she had a bombshell to deliver."

"That's what Sperantzas told me too, but I knew nothing. And I didn't need to know what it was; I had total confidence in her."

"Do you know what she was investigating in particular of late?"

"No, but even if there was something in particular, I wouldn't have known. Karayoryi never disclosed what she was working on, or the information she had unearthed. She never got it wrong, and I'd given instructions that she be left alone to get on with her work." He stopped, leaned toward me, and said, "Come what may, you will have as much help as you need from us. Tomorrow morning, I will put two of my reporters on the case. They will be in constant contact with you."

"Let them search, of course. Any help is welcome," I said with an excessive willingness, which seemed to please him. "But let's not make any bets as to who finds something first, and let's make sure we don't get under each other's feet."

That took the wind out of his sails, because he suddenly turned cold toward me. "What do you mean exactly? Speak openly. You realize, of course, that Yanna Karayoryi was one of our star reporters and her murder is of direct concern to us."

"I do realize that, Mr. Delopoulos. But this evening, Mr. Sperantzas gave the news of Karayoryi's murder on the late-night bulletin before informing the police. I'm not saying that this will cause us serious problems, but it could. So it would be wise if your people consulted you before taking any similar initiatives."

"A reporter's work is to inform the public, Inspector Haritos," he said in the same icy tone. "Swiftly and accurately. When he steals a march on a rival, even on the police, that is a bonus for the channel. I should congratulate Mr. Sperantzas and not threaten him, as you did."

I should have expected it. Sperantzas had shot off his mouth about Kostarakou, his colleague; why wouldn't he have done the same about me?

"We wish to cooperate with the police. But for us, Karayoryi's murder is in the nature of a family matter. I require, therefore, that *you* keep *us* informed as to the course of your investigations, and exclusively us, not the other channels. Objectivity and impartiality do not apply in this case." He paused, looked at me, and went on deliberately: "Otherwise, I shall have no choice but to convey the information we gather to the minister responsible, who as it happens is a friend of mine, and you'll get it relayed to you from him."

In case the point needed underlining, he also gave me a meaningful look—apparently he regarded all police officers as backward third worlders, so speaking to them rudely wasn't enough; you also had to browbeat them with looks and hints to be sure the message had sunk in.

"I'm sure that our cooperation will be of the best possible kind," he said, cordial once more and holding out his hand.

As I was shaking his hand, it occurred to me that I was at that moment inaugurating an agreement between the FBI and CNN and that we wouldn't catch the murderer in a month of Sundays, unless, that is, we bumped into a good fortune teller.

I left with my tail between my legs.

Sotiris was waiting for me in the entrance. Standing beside him was a young kid dressed like a security guard. Blue-eyed with close-cropped hair, he held his arms and legs apart to make himself seem stockier. A chubby backstreet marine. And a lucky kid. If he'd been in a gang selling protection, we might very well have run him in.

Whereas now he was working for a company, drawing a salary every month and eyeing me like a colleague.

"Did you know Karayoryi?" I asked him.

"Of course I knew her. I know them all, every one of them. My memory is like a computer."

"Forget the computers and tell me about Karayoryi. What time did she arrive tonight?"

"Eleven-fifteen. I always check."

He was playing with fire, this one. He'd no idea how close I was to the end of my tether. "Was she alone?"

"All alone."

"Perhaps she came with someone who left her at the gate."

"If someone dropped her outside on the road, that I wouldn't know, because you can't see it from here. She was alone when she got to the studio."

"Did you see anyone unfamiliar leaving the studio? Or someone you've never seen before?"

"No. No one."

"Did you leave your post at any time?"

He didn't answer this last question immediately. He appeared to be giving it some thought. Finally, he mumbled, "For two minutes only. Vangelis, my colleague, who was on duty in the boss's office, came and told me that Karayoryi had been found dead. I ran back upstairs with him, because I thought that most people are inexperienced in such matters—they might have made a mess of it."

"And you, with all your years of experience, what were you going to do? Bring her back to life?" I screamed, furiously. It seemed that this computer had crashed, because he didn't know how to answer and remained silent.

"Take his details and arrange for him to come to make a statement," I said to Sotiris.

As I went out to the street to retrieve my car, which I had left parked up on the curb, it began drizzling. That, at least, was something.

CHAPTER 12

Karayoryi lived in Lycabettus, not far from the Doxiadis building. She woke up every morning, saw the wood from her window, and lived with the illusion of being in the countryside. Now, too, it was morning, nine o'clock, except that it was raining cats and dogs. The windshield wipers on my Mirafiori were working only at slow. By the time they'd swept one wave of water off and were ready to get to work in reverse, the windshield was awash again. I had to strain my eyes to maintain a steady distance from the car crawling in front of me. I missed the house. I'd almost gone past it when I saw the patrol car parked outside and I braked sharply. "Where did you learn to drive, moron?" shouted the driver of the car behind me. "Is that how you brake on a wet road? You'd have been better off sticking to a donkey!" And all this to the accompaniment of his horn. In the end, he held up the flat of his hand to me, end quotes. I pretended not to notice any of it. There was a space behind the patrol car. I backed into it.

The house was an old two-story building, yellow with orange shutters and a wrought-iron door with leaf patterns. It recalled the elegant houses on Akritas Street in the good days. I switched off the engine but stayed in the car. I'd slept for no more than two hours and had woken up with a fearful headache. The aspirin I'd taken before leaving home did nothing for me. My head was bursting and my temples felt as if they were clamped in a vise. I looked at the door to the house, which was half open. From the car to the front door was three strides, but in the rain it seemed enormous and I didn't dare move.

I must have looked suspicious to the two police officers in the patrol car because one of them got out and came over to me. I opened the door and sprang out. "Inspector Haritos," I barked as I hurried

past him. By the time I got into the house I was soaking and my
socks were squelching inside my shoes. God-awful weather.

The hall was small, marble-floored, and had two doors, one to the
right and one to the left. At the far end was a narrow wooden stair-
case, with a polished handrail, leading to the second floor. I opened
the door on the right and found myself in Karayoryi's study. Dimitris, from records, was standing in front of a small fitted bookcase,
looking through some folders.

"Do we have anything?"

He looked at me and shrugged his shoulders. "Computers," he
said.

I looked at the computer screen facing the desk chair and I realized what he meant. They'd have to take the computer and all the
disks to the lab to begin looking: to see what was stored, to do a first
check, to print out whatever was there, and then send it all to us for
evaluation. At the rate they worked in the lab, it would be three to
four days at best. Long gone were the good old days when we had to
deal with handwritten scripts, typed pages, notes on scraps of paper,
on cigarette boxes, on the backs of old bills. We'd take them down to
the station and find clues from the style of the handwriting or from
a typewriter's *a* missing its tail. Nowadays, you don't know whether
you're watching *Ben Hur* or reading a purchase agreement. You don't
know where to start.

"Leave that to me and go and do something else," I said to Dimitris. He didn't need telling twice. He was off before I could change
my mind.

The room was square, as in all the old houses. The desk was a
wooden one, with carved legs. A solicitor's desk. She must have in-
herited it from her father or an uncle. When you sat at the desk, you
could see the Lycabettus bypass through the window. The rain was
coming down in torrents still, and the traffic poured on, nose to tail,
horns honking like the devil. The window was small, and the room
must have been dark even when the sun was out. Now, with the rain,
if you didn't put the light on, you'd be feeling your way in the dark.

On either side of the window were two old leather armchairs, which matched the desk.

The wall on the right was floor-to-ceiling shelves. In places the books were tightly packed, and in others they were sparse. They were arranged according to subject. I was more interested in the fitted bookcase on the left-hand wall because there were files on the top shelf, while on the rest were heaps of envelopes and papers, either loose or in plastic folders.

I'd be a real moron to waste my whole day going through that pile of paper. It was the job of the boys in records, after all, to sort it and bring me the findings. But, as if wanting to prove that I was a moron, I reached up and took down the first file. I flicked through it and put it down immediately. It was full of bills: electricity, telephone, and water bills. I took the second file down: her tax declarations. For the previous year, she'd declared twelve million drachmas net. The largest amount, 8,400,000, was her salary at the channel. I did a quick calculation. She earned six hundred thousand a month. Six hundred thousand for getting information from me and coming out with it on the screen. Whereas I, who handed it to her on a plate, had worked for twenty-five years to get to the point of earning half what she earned. Given the chasm that separated us, it was only natural that she should look down on me and that I should think she was a lesbian.

The rest of her income was from renting a two-room apartment she owned in Ambelokipi and from a book she'd published, entitled *A Quiet Man.* Attached to the declaration was a copy of the statement from the publishing company. I went over to the large bookcase, took it down from the third shelf, and saw that the book was based on her big success investigating the Kolakoglou affair.

Petros Kolakoglou was a tax consultant who had been convicted three years ago of the rape of two young girls. One was his goddaughter, who was only nine at the time. Kolakoglou had taken her out one afternoon to buy her clothes. The little girl had later told her mother that her godfather had taken her to his home. There, he'd undressed her, on the pretext that she try on the clothes, and had started caressing her. Straightaway the parents had gone to the local police station. It seems, however, that they came to some arrangement with Kolakoglou during the course of the initial investigations, because the girl suddenly retracted her statement, the parents withdrew their accusation, and the case was put on file. At precisely that point, Karayoryi came on the scene with one of her amazing revelations: There had been a second child, the daughter of Kolakoglou's assistant in his tax adviser business. The woman took her daughter to work with her during the school breaks, as she had nowhere to leave her. Kolakoglou showed a great fondness for the girl, bought her sweets and gifts, and she called him uncle. But, once again, there were some dark aspects, so it seems, that Karayoryi discovered, and she persuaded the mother to go to the police. The second case reignited the first. The goddaughter's parents gave way and brought the charge again. Kolakoglou got eight years, reduced to six in the appeals court. That series of startling revelations made Karayoryi famous. Her last had been the death of her.

I put the book down as it came to me why I had gone there so early in the morning: to look for Karayoryi's Filofax. There were cupboard doors on each side of the desk, as on most old desks. You opened the cupboards and the drawers shot out, three on each side. In the first drawer on the right I found a Nikon camera, a very expensive one, with all the accessories, including a telescopic lens. I looked at how many exposures had been used: none. There probably wasn't any film inside, but, just to be sure, I left it on top of the desk for the records people. In the bottom drawer on the left, I found four color photographs of a couple sitting arm in arm on a sofa. The woman was Karayoryi, just as I'd known her. The man was unrecognizable because someone had marked up his face with a black felt-tip pen. They'd added a mustache and beard and had lengthened his nose to look like an eggplant. In one of the photographs, they'd even given him a hat.

In the top drawer on the right, I saw a folder. There was nothing else in the drawer, and the folder was lying there, seemingly forgotten. Opening it, I discovered six letters, all addressed to Karayoryi.

All written in the same handwriting, a scribble of the kind for which, had we done it at school, the teacher would have rapped our knuckles with the sharp edge of her ruler. The most recent one was dated two weeks before; the oldest was from 1992, eighteen months earlier. All began with the same plain form of address: "Yanna." In the first one, the writer described his surprise at meeting her by accident after so many years and asked her to "meet up for a chat." It seemed, however, that Karayoryi didn't do as he asked, because a month later he was back with another letter and asked her again. After the third one, the letters became more interesting. It was clear that the writer wanted something from Karayoryi, something that she had and wouldn't give him. He never said what it was exactly; he was always vague, as if it were something very familiar that they had discussed on innumerable occasions. At first, he implored and entreated. It sounded as though Karayoryi had simply played with him, because he became more and more demanding, until in the last letter, he threatened her straight out:

> For so long now I have been doing what you asked, believing that you would keep your word, but all you do is play with me. I now know that you have no intention of doing what I ask. You only want to keep me on a string so you can blackmail me and get what you want. But no more. This time I won't give way. Don't force my hand because you'll be sorry and you'll only have yourself to blame.

There was no signature as such on the letters, just "N." I sat there staring at it. What name was hidden behind that *N*? Nikos, Nondas, Notis, Nikitas, Nikiforos? Whoever it was, this N was known to her and had threatened her. And Karayoryi had been talking to her murderer before he killed her.

The other two drawers were empty. No sign of her Filofax. To be honest, I hadn't expected to find it. As it wasn't in her bag or in her desk, it was probably taken by the murderer. There was nothing else either; nothing about kids, other than the book about Kolakoglou.

No file, no paper, nothing. So why, then, had she dropped me the bait in connection with the Albanians? Unless, of course, we were going to find something in her computer files.

I took the folder with the letters, gathered up the photographs, and went out of the room. In that rain, I would need at least an hour, crawling along, to get to the office. I had all the time in the world to do my thinking.

CHAPTER 13

I found my croissant and my coffee on my desk and three urgent messages from Ghikas saying that he wanted to see me. The journey from Karayoryi's place to security headquarters had only made my headache worse. I opened my drawer, took out two aspirins, and swallowed them with the cold coffee, which turned my stomach. I leaned back in my chair and closed my eyes, hoping that the pounding would go away. Hopeless. It was as if I were in dry dock and they were beating my keel with giant hammers. I gave up. I grabbed the file and the photographs and set off for Ghikas's office.

As soon as I opened my door, I saw them. Sotiropoulos at their head. Now that Karayoryi was gone, no one was going to dispute his role as leader.

"So what's going to happen, Inspector?" he asked, in a tone implying that he'd taken all he could from me and was about to set up the guillotine.

"Don't go away. I want to see you."

The way I said it, vaguely and unspecifically, I might have meant that I wanted to question them, or that I was going to make a statement. Because they didn't want to miss the chance of the latter, they were willing to risk the former. I left them wondering and made for the elevator. It must have intuited the state I was in and taken pity on me, because it came immediately.

Koula had been waiting for me in the chief's outer office and launched straight in. "What a thing to happen to Karayoryi. I heard about it this morning."

That gave me a boost without her knowing it. I reflected that Sperantzas's supposed bombshell had turned out in the end to be a damp squid, because most people at that time of night are getting ready for bed and are in no mood for hearing about murders, rapes, famines, earthquakes, and deluges.

"A crime of passion, you mark my words," Koula rattled on confidently.

"What makes you think that?"

"Listen to me, I had her figured out. She knew how to drive men crazy. She didn't give a damn about them, and she had them all running after her like little puppies. In the end, one of them must have flipped and killed her. But doesn't it seem strange to you that they ran her through with a metal rod?"

"No, why?"

"It symbolizes the penis," she said triumphantly.

"Is he in?" I asked quickly, before she began analyzing me too.

"Yes, and he's expecting you."

As I closed the door, Ghikas raised his head, leaned back into his chair, and folded his arms. His expression beckoned me to approach his desk, the better that he could give me a roasting. Before I'd got halfway there, he launched his attack.

"I said I wanted you in my office at nine o'clock. I've been calling you all morning."

I said nothing. I stood there with the file under my arm and stared at him.

"We have a star reporter, the leading name in crime reporting, murdered. Newspapers, radio stations, TV channels are all going to descend on us. In cases like this, the FBI works on a twenty-four–hour basis."

"I work on a twenty-hour basis. I need four hours to get myself back on form," I said calmly. "I left the channel at five in the morning, slept for less than three hours, and at nine o'clock I was at Karayoryi's house."

"What were you doing at Karayoryi's. That's records' job. I want you here."

Without a word, I put the file in front of him and opened it. I'd put the photographs on top.

"Who's that?" he said, gesturing at the defaced photograph.

"I don't know yet."

"Why have you brought it to me. It's not carnival time, is it?"

I left him wondering. It was dawning on him that the case was not one to be solved telegrammatically, in five lines, so he decided to read the letters. "Right," he mumbled when he'd finished. "Someone called N was threatening Karayoryi. It's a clue, agreed. But where are you going to find him? It means sifting half the male population of Greece."

"Unless N is the man scrawled over in the photographs."

"It's a possibility. Look into it!" he said, certain that he'd opened my eyes to something I myself would never have thought of. "Any other evidence? And don't tell me about the murder because I know how it happened. Sotiris told me."

"Her Filofax is missing. It was most likely taken by the murderer."

"Any connection with the Albanians?"

I'd been waiting for him to ask that. It would have suited him if she'd been bumped off by an Albanian. The newspapers would have made it front-page news with huge headlines as black as a mourning veil; the TV channels would have organized roundtable discussions on imported crime and would have been wallowing in commercials. Three days later the mourning would have been over, and Karayoryi's time would have lapsed.

"So far we've found nothing, but there is still her computer. Something might turn up there."

"I want you to keep me informed on a daily basis. And when I say informed, I mean that you tell me everything. Not write half in your summary and bury the other half in your report like you did with the Albanians."

"I write in the summary what I consider can be announced to the public. The rest goes in the report. That's why I send them to you together." I picked up the file and the photographs, and left feeling satisfied that I'd come out on top.

They were still waiting for me outside my office. As soon as they saw me, they blocked my way. I stood confronting Sotiropoulos.

"Let's start with you. You've been around longer than most and you knew her as well as anyone among you." Their question was answered. They realized that I'd kept them waiting there to be questioned and not to make a statement. Sotiropoulos glared at me. If I forced him to give in, the rest of the herd would follow.

"Are you coming?" I asked coldly. "Or should I have a writ issued so you'll have to present yourself within twenty-four hours?"

I opened the door and waited. He hesitated for a moment, then followed me into my office.

"Sit down." I pointed to the chair opposite mine.

"Shouldn't I remain standing, given that I'm a suspect?"

"So you take Karayoryi's murder for a laughing matter, do you, Sotiropoulos? She was your colleague, damn it. You should be the first to come forward so that we might get somewhere. Instead of which, you make an issue of the fact that we want to ask you a few questions."

My shot hit him right between the eyes. He may have hated Karayoryi, but he didn't want to show his delight that her job would go to some greenhorn who he'd have under his thumb. He sat down in the chair.

"So then . . . fire away," he said, serious now.

"I'm not going to ask anything. You're the one who's going to do the talking. You're an experienced reporter. You know what might be of use to me."

I'd learned this approach from Inspector Kostaras, during the dictatorship, when I'd been assigned for a time to security headquarters on Bouboulinas Street. Whenever he was sent someone new, he'd put him for a couple of days with the prisoners being tortured, to scare the living daylights out of him. On the third day, he'd sit him down and say to him: "I'm not going to ask you anything; you know what you have to say to me. If I like what I hear, I might just take pity on you." And the poor wretch coughed up everything, just to be sure. My job was to escort the prisoners for interrogation. I stood in one corner, observing Kostaras and admiring his technique. Now I knew that it was all bullshit; he had absolutely nothing to go on and was simply fishing blindly to see what he'd catch. Good luck to him.

Sotiropoulos was staring at me thoughtfully. He was trying to decide what he should say to me. "There's nothing I can tell you," he said eventually.

I saw red. "What do you think you're playing at? Don't invoke that journalistic crap about not being able to reveal your sources. We'll end up very seriously at loggerheads, you and I."

"I don't intend to invoke anything," he said calmly. "I'm only telling you the truth. I can't tell you anything." He fell silent and was obviously thinking. It was as if he were trying to find an excuse, more for himself than anything. "Karayoryi kept to herself," he went on, slowly. "She never showed her cards to anyone, neither on a professional level nor on a personal one. Besides, none of us shows our cards in our professional lives. She lived on the Lycabettus bypass. Alone. And I emphasize the "alone," because I never saw her with anyone. Whenever a group of us went out for a drink, she was always on her own."

What he said put the idea into my head again. "Was she a lesbian, do you know?"

He burst out laughing, but his eyes, behind those little round Himmler-type glasses, fixed on me as if he wanted to send me to a concentration camp. "You police officers are all perverse, like all the petits bourgeois. As soon as you hear that a woman goes around alone, you call her a lesbian." Evidently, he was making a distinction between the police and himself, who wasn't a petit bourgeois. That much I understood. What I didn't know was where he placed himself, among the leftists or among the bourgeois proper, with their Armani shirts and Timberland footwear. Most probably, he was both. We used to get by with a little soup; now we feed ourselves on salads.

"If I'm to judge from what various people said," Sotiropoulos said, "she was most likely the very opposite."

"Meaning what, exactly?"

"A nympho. A slut." Then he saw that his spite had escaped its leash and he hastened to get it back under control. "But I may be doing her an injustice, because I know nothing definite. It was all just rumors."

"And what did the rumors say?"

"That she never had any steady relationships. That she went from one to the other. But she always chose men with clout. Businessmen . . . politicians . . . mixed business with pleasure, as we used to say. But let's be clear, I've heard all this from others."

"Do you know if she was working on anything?"

"I can tell you, generally speaking, that she was never not investigating something. She was a ruthless little ferret. She poked around everywhere and stopped at nothing. She had a thing about bursting out with a story, so she never confided in anyone. Not even Delopoulos, who worshipped her."

"Was she a good reporter? I want your professional opinion, with no trimmings."

"Everyone disliked her, so she must have been good," he said. "A reporter's job is to be disliked. The more disliked he is, the better he is."

His definition applied as much to him as it did to Karayoryi. He succeeded in making me like him through what he'd said, which confirmed my opinion that he wasn't a good reporter. I kept staring at him in silence. He realized that I had nothing more to ask him and got to his feet.

"So what's going to happen? Will you make a statement so that we'll have something to tell the public?"

"What statement can I make when I don't have any evidence? All I know is what we found out last night. Be patient for a couple of days. Something will turn up."

As he was going out, the telephone rang. "Haritos," I said, faithful as ever to FBI protocol.

"This is Mina Antonakaki, Yanna Karayoryi's sister," said a broken voice. "When can I collect my sister's body for burial and from where?"

"In a couple of days, Mrs. Antonakaki, from the mortuary. But we have to meet first."

"Not now. I'm in no state to meet anyone."

"Mrs. Antonakaki, yesterday someone murdered your sister. We're trying to find the murderer, and we need information. I understand the state you must be in, but we do have to see you. If you'd prefer, I can come to you. But we mustn't delay."

She seemed to weigh this for a moment. "You'd better come around here. I'll be in," she said in a faint voice, and she gave me her address.

I still hadn't received any information from records, or the coroner's report, and I decided to run through the rest of the reporters so no one would depart feeling left out. No one could tell me anything more useful than Sotiropoulos had told me already. They knew nothing. Karayoryi confided in no one; she never revealed her cards.

When the last reporter had left, I tried to make sense of what I now knew. Outside, the rain was still torrential. The old woman opposite was standing at the balcony door saying something to the cat in her arms. I couldn't tell whether she was chatting with it or singing "Raindrops Keep Falling on My Head" to it, but the cat appeared to be enjoying it. I was so carried away by the cat's contentment that I didn't hear the door open. A discreet cough brought me back to my senses.

Standing at the door was a thirty-year-old woman, neither tall nor short, neither pretty nor plain. She was wearing boots and a beige raincoat belted tightly around the waist, perhaps in an attempt to look more sexy, but the result was lukewarm.

"Good morning, I'm Martha Kostarakou," she said with a smile.

I suddenly saw her in a different light. Kostarakou was my one hope of learning something specific—that is, if Sperantzas had been telling me the truth.

"As of today, I'm taking over Yanna Karayoryi's job." She said it with some difficulty, still smiling embarrassedly. "Mr. Delopoulos told me to come and see you. He also told me that you would keep me personally informed concerning the investigation into Yanna's murder, and exclusively so." Unconsciously, she let out a sigh, as if a burden had been lifted from her. She was the polar opposite of Karayoryi. Neither aggressive nor arrogant, but rather a demure young thing, the kind you feel sorry for and toss a bone to. Like a third world country that you give aid to and that can't thank you

enough—until, that is, it discovers oil and tells you into which ori-
fice you can insert yourself.

"Why did you dislike Karayoryi? What had she ever done to you?"

Her smile faded, her hands clutched at her bag, squeezing it
tightly, and she stared at me, speechless. Just when she'd thought
everything was going smoothly, I'd suddenly turned the tables on
her, and now she was the one who was going to have to talk, not me.

"Who told you that?" she asked in a trembling voice. "Yanna and I
were colleagues. We weren't exactly friends, but I didn't dislike her,
and I certainly didn't wish her any harm."

"Do you mean to tell me that what she did to you was of no importance and you forgot it straightaway?" Like Kostaras, I was fishing blindly to see what I might come up with.

"Did what? That she got me taken off crime reporting so she
could take my place and had me put on the medical reports? To be
honest, I was better off there. There was less work and I didn't have
to run around all day. Not to mention that I was dealing with scien-
tists and not muggers and murderers."

"Who was behind her? From what I've heard, you're good at your
job. So she must have had to pull a few strings to get you out of the
way."

She understood that I was playing up to her vanity and smiled,
ironically this time.

"Listen to me," I said, adopting a tougher tone. "You were responsible for the crime reporting. Karayoryi came along, took your place,
and landed you with the medical reports. Don't tell me that it didn't
bother you. You might not have said anything, but deep down you
were furious with her. And suddenly, one evening, somebody murders Karayoryi. And the very next morning, you're back in your old
job. You're the first to have something to gain from her death. Do
you know what that means?"

She got the message because she jumped up and shouted: "What
are you trying to say? That I'm the one who killed her?"

"No, I'm not saying that. At least not at the moment. Of course, I
don't know what I'm going to come up with tomorrow if I start

looking. But tongues will start wagging from today. And the longer it goes on, the more wagging there'll be. So the sooner we get to the bottom of it the better for you if you want to keep people's mouths shut tight. Tell me who was behind her. Was it Delopoulos?"

She laughed, as though what I'd said seemed genuinely funny to her. "Is that what they told you? That she did as she pleased because she was sleeping with the boss?" Her laughter stopped abruptly. "You're quite wrong. Yanna was smart and methodical. When she came to the channel, she undertook the medical reporting, but she wasn't particularly interested in it because there was nothing sensational, no hard-hitting news. Just the occasional mention at the end of the news bulletin. Inside a month, she'd got herself involved with Petratos, the news editor. It took her another two weeks to get her hands on my job. But I have to be honest with you. She wasn't only ambitious, she was talented too, much more talented than me. She came up with exclusive reports, delved into cases, unmasked people. She latched on to the Kolakoglou case and forced Delopoulos to give her the freedom to explore as she wished. Once that happened, she gave Petratos the boot. Of course, he took it badly. He would have been happy to have been shut of her, but it was too late, he couldn't say anything to her anymore." She fell silent and once again let out a sigh, as if relieved to have got that much off her chest. "No, Yanna didn't need to sleep with Delopoulos in order to have clout. She managed it with her talent. She used Petratos to get her chance, but everything else she did on her own."

I hadn't liked Karayoryi at all and I'd branded her a lesbian. Sotiropoulos, who also disliked her, and who in his Robespierre role defended all the people on society's fringes, preferred to call her a nympho and a slut. And now this half-baked girl had come along to put things in their proper place. I began to feel a certain respect for Kostarakou, but my instinct told me not to get carried away. What if her honesty was simply a front?

"Where were you last night between ten and twelve?"

"Alone at home, like every other night," she said calmly, almost sorrowfully. "First with a salad, then with a whiskey, and always with the TV on." She stopped, looked me in the eye, and added with barely perceptible emphasis: "Till eleven, when Yanna called me."

"Karayoryi phoned you at eleven?"

"Yes. To tell me that she had a report ready for the late-night news that would cause a sensation."

Who else had she told apart from Kostarakou and Sperantzas? If I found that out, I'd be getting closer to finding her murderer.

"She told me something else, too."

"What was that?"

"She told me to watch the bulletin, because if anything happened to her, I was to continue the investigation. To be honest, I didn't take what she said at face value. On the contrary, I thought it was spite, that she was saying it to provoke me, and I hung up on her. Perhaps because of the loneliness, perhaps because of my fury at what Yanna had said, I felt suffocated in the house. I got into the car and drove around aimlessly. It was about one o'clock when I got back home."

"Didn't she tell you what the report was going to be about?"

"No. All she told me was to watch the news."

"All right." I called Thanassis and sent her with him to fill out a statement. "Wait, don't go." I said as she reached the door. I took out the photograph of Karayoryi and the man she'd scrawled over. "This man here, do you know him?"

She looked at the photograph and laughed out loud.

"Why are you laughing? Do you know him?"

"Of course I know him!"

"Who is it?"

"It's Petratos, the news editor at Hellas Channel. My boss."

CHAPTER 14

Mina Antonakaki lived on Chryssippou Street in Zografou. I found myself stopping every ten meters on Olof Palme Street, with time enough for a coffee before moving forward again. Throughout the journey I kept seeing Karayoryi's sister before me, sitting on a sofa, with red eyes and a handkerchief in her hand, and I grew steadily more despondent. The headache that had eased a little with the two aspirins started to get worse again. The traffic was as bad on Papandreou Avenue. By the time I turned off on Gaiou Street, my luck changed. I found an empty parking space.

The woman who opened the door was around forty-five and was wearing black. "Inspector Haritos? Come in. I'm Mina Antonakaki."

It wasn't often I'd come across sisters so different. If she hadn't told me who she was, I'd have taken her for a friend who'd come to lend a hand. Yanna was tall, thin, and imposing. Mina was a short, plump, nondescript little woman. Yanna was a brunette. Her sister had dark hair but was going gray at the roots. Yanna always looked at you haughtily. This woman had the look of a calf on its way to slaughter, which made you think less of her, and instead of feeling pity, you wanted to shout at her.

She led me into a small living room, had me sit on the sofa, and then sat opposite me. I hadn't been wrong. Her eyes were deep red and she was clutching her handkerchief, but was probably too lazy to use it, finding it less trouble to keep sniffing. Her living room was like mine, like my sister-in-law's, and like all the other living rooms I've seen in twenty-two years on the force: a sofa, two armchairs, a coffee table, two chairs, and a stand for the television.

It seems she sensed my surprise because she said with a bitter smile: "Yanna and I are not at all alike, are we?" She corrected herself in a subdued voice: "Weren't alike, I mean." She paused as if trying to find strength and then continued. "Yanna took after my mother. I'm more like my father. Though we were very close. We saw each other almost every day. You see, I live pretty much alone with my daughter. My husband is a sailor and is always at sea."

I could see her lips trembling, and I knew I'd have to be quick before she fell apart or I'd end up picking up the pieces. "We need some information about your sister, Mrs. Antonakaki. We have to complete the picture so that we'll know where to start looking for her murderer."

There are some questions that you ask because you want to find out something, or to trap someone or to clarify a matter. And there are others of no particular importance that you ask just to keep someone's mind busy and help them to find their feet. Mina Antonakaki fell into the last category. She attached great importance to what I was about to ask her and braced herself.

"Ask me," she said. Her voice was steady now.

"When was the last time you saw your sister?"

"The day before yesterday, in the evening. She was going to stop by last night, but she phoned to say something had come up and she couldn't make it."

"What time did she plan to stop by?"

"She usually came around nine and stayed for a couple of hours."

"And what time did she phone you?"

"It must have been around six."

So it was at about six o'clock that she decided to drop her bombshell on the late-night news. But if she'd already made the decision at six, why didn't she appear on the nine o'clock news, which is watched by many more people, instead of waiting for the late-night news?

"Mrs. Antonakaki, what do you know about your sister's relationship with a Mr. Petratos?"

"Petratos?" She seemed alarmed and repeated the name mechanically. "What *should* I know about it?"

"Your sister had an affair with Petratos and left him. It's no secret. Everyone knows about it. Did Yanna ever talk to you about him?"

She hesitated and said reluctantly, "All I know is that it wasn't an affair as you or I would understand it."

"What exactly was it?" I said.

"That's something only she could tell you." She said quickly. Then she applied the brakes and began searching for the right words. "She didn't have a very high opinion of him. She thought him ridiculous and made fun of him. He's an asshole, she'd say, if you'll pardon the expression. But those were her exact words. He didn't know if he was coming or going. And when I asked her how a big-time news editor for a TV channel could be an asshole, she simply laughed. He goes on because he's a panderer and a yes-man, she'd tell me. He runs after Delopoulos like a little puppy and agrees with everything he says." She stopped to take a breath; her words were now coming out with more difficulty. "And when she made love to him, she felt sick and was repelled by him. A forty-year-old lump, and he still doesn't know how to make love, she'd say. I have to take him by the hand and lead him along, like a kiddy in the park."

"If she didn't want him, why did she stay with him?" I asked, though I knew the answer.

"Because she was using him. There you have it, straight, just as she told me herself. She got involved with him and got into Hellas Channel on a good salary. She gritted her teeth and slept with him so he'd give her the position she wanted and so she'd have direct access to Delopoulos. And as soon as she had that, she dumped him. I remember it as if it were today. It was just after her success with Kolakoglou that Delopoulos said to her, 'From today, Yanna, you have my permission to run whatever story you want on the news bulletin.' She jumped with joy, and she told me that the very next day she was going to give Petratos his marching orders."

My mind went to the scrawled-over face on the photograph. She'd take him out of her drawer, look at him, and feel pleased with herself, and she'd made him exactly as she'd seen him.

"What is Mr. Petratos's first name? Do you know?"

"Nestor, I think. Nestor Petratos."

So, not Nikos, or Notis, or Nikitas, but Nestor. The unknown *N* on the letters. Lady Luck was smiling on me, but too readily. I restrained myself so as not to fall into her trap.

"I've kept nothing from you," Antonakaki went on, "because Yanna kept nothing hidden either. She told me everything, bit by bit." She let out a sigh. "But it wasn't only Petratos. My sister was repelled by men in general, Inspector."

"Why was that?"

"What can I say? She said that we women have to put up with the worst things in the world because of men, and they always do what they want to us even though they're worthless cowards. And that you should only keep them as long as they're of use to you, then you should get rid of them. 'Do you know why I'm sad?' she'd say to me. 'Because being a lesbian isn't my style.' My hair would stand on end."

Yanna Karayoryi appeared before me with her arrogant smile, her haughty air, ready to show her scorn for me. You see, I was in the same category as Petratos and Delopoulos and all the others. Okay, she may not have been a lesbian, I may not have got it entirely right, but I'd been close.

"For a time, she tried to get me away from my Vassos," Antonakaki went on. "She said he was worthless too, and she made my life a misery trying to get me to leave him. But my Vassos is nothing like her Petratos. He's a good husband, a good father, and works like a dog at sea to keep us, me and Anna. Don't worry, I'd tell her, one day you'll find a man who's right for you and then you'll see that things aren't as you think."

At this last memory, she broke down and the weeping started again. This time, however, she remembered her handkerchief and wiped her nose instead of sniffing. I didn't even try to comfort her because my mind was fixed on Karayoryi's affair with Petratos. On Yanna and her defaced Nestor.

"All right, that's enough. You've been crying all morning. You've even got the police coming to you, when you should be running about trying to find out what's gone on. As if crying's going to change anything."

I turned and saw a girl in the doorway. She must have been about the same age as Katerina, possibly a little younger. I stared at her open-mouthed.

"My daughter, Anna," I heard Antonakaki say.

It was as if Yanna Karayoryi were there, twenty years younger, roughly the age in the photograph on her identity card. She was a tall, slender girl, with the same austere beauty and the same arrogant look that Yanna had. As if nature had taken all the features of the sister and given them to the niece. The girl wasn't wearing black. She was dressed simply in a T-shirt, jeans, and tennis shoes. She stood there, cold and haughty, and turned her gaze toward me. I was overwhelmed by a desire to ignore her, just as I'd ignored her aunt. Not out of arrogance or antagonism, but because deep down I was afraid of getting into an argument with her. I preferred the mother, who wanted to talk in order to unburden herself.

"Had your sister spoken to you about some big story that she was about to break last night?"

"No. Yanna never spoke to me about her work."

"Do you know if she was being threatened? If she was afraid for her life?"

The girl got in first. "She *was* afraid," she said. "She was constantly afraid. She said that one day she'd come to a bad end. She laughed about it, but deep down she believed it. My aunt was a difficult person. When she got something into her head, she wouldn't rest, even if all hell broke loose around her."

"Anna, what are you saying?" her mother cried, terrified.

"The truth." She calmly turned back to me. "My aunt liked getting people's backs up. It amused her, but it also frightened her. Once, after I told her I wanted to become a reporter, she spent months browbeating me, trying to get me to change my mind. She listed all the disadvantages: how the profession had become degraded, how you now had to crawl or be cunning, and how everyone else was just waiting for you to slip up. And how she made so many compromises that what she ought to have done every morning was to spit at herself in the mirror. In the end, she convinced me, and I went to medical school."

"Anna, please! I won't allow you to insult Yanna's memory like that!"

The girl gave her mother a cold, angry look. I felt, however, that the look was simply a mask and that the person behind it was ready to burst into tears.

My headache had returned. I could barely hold my head up. A terrible feeling of tiredness came over me, and I stood up. I couldn't think of anything else to ask.

"Thank you. If we require any further information, we will call you."

The mother nodded good-bye to me, as she'd begun to weep again. The daughter got up with a blank expression to show me out. I was reaching for the front door latch when she stopped me.

"Inspector—"

"Yes."

"Nothing—," she said quickly, as if thinking better of it.

"You were going to say something."

"No. If I had wanted to say something, I would have said it."

She clammed up and became aggressive in order to cut me short. I realized that I'd better not pursue it. Perhaps she'd been in too much of a hurry and needed time to think.

"Anyway, if you want to reach me, your mother has my number," I said, giving her a friendly smile. She gave me an indifferent look and closed the door.

From Chryssippou Street, I emerged once again onto Papandreou Avenue and turned down Olof Palme Street. My mind was on the relationship between Karayoryi and Petratos. Antonakaki had told me that they'd broken up right after the Kolakoglou affair. But the letters from N began a year after the Kolakoglou case. If Petratos was the letter writer, then the relationship must have continued in some other form and ended in threats. I made a mental note to get hold of a sample of Petratos's handwriting to compare it with that of the unknown N. The other matter tormenting me was why Karayoryi had chosen to appear on the late-night news.

From Hymettou Street, I turned onto Iphicratous Street and looked for a place to park somewhere between Protesilaou, Aroni, and Aristokleous Streets. Naturally, I didn't find one and I began the same old business, just like every other evening: going around and around the block till I came across someone leaving their space.

Light rain was falling, fine like mist. My head was splitting and I was cursing when, all of a sudden, I spotted Thanassis at the corner of Tzavela and Aristokleous Streets pacing back and forth and glancing first down one street then down the other. I pulled up beside him and rolled down the window.

"What's up? Has anything happened?" I asked him, alarmed. For him to have come all the way out there meant that something truly serious was going on. He opened the door and got into the car. He sat beside me in silence.

"Why didn't you go to my house instead of standing outside and getting wet?"

"I wanted to see you alone."

He took a deep breath. Somebody else who was taking deep breaths. Everyone I'd come into contact with that day was either crying or sighing. I couldn't stay put on the corner. I drove away and once more began going around and around the block.

"I was with her last night. That's why I wanted to see you alone. I didn't want to tell you in front of others."

I froze. I stepped on the brake without thinking. The Mirafiori shook and came to a halt, while the driver behind me started sounding his horn, enraged. But I could hear nothing. My eyes were fixed on Thanassis. He avoided them and looked out through the windshield.

"Why did you send me?" he said. "I didn't want to go. You were the one who forced me to go."

I knew where he was leading. If the next day it got around that he was with Karayoryi just before she was murdered, he'd say that I'd sent him, that he was carrying out my orders. Of course, I'd made it clear to him from the very first that I'd take full responsibility, but he was reminding me just in case, so that he wouldn't have to worry his head. He might tell me every morning at nine that he was a moron, but as soon as things got rough, he used that to duck all responsibility. I didn't hold it against him. In his position I would have done the same. If Thanassis were found to be mixed up in Karayoryi's murder, there'd be such a scandal that Ghikas would undoubtedly have me suspended. The thought made me shudder. "Where did you go with her?" I asked, to get some idea of who might have seen them together.

"To a small bar-restaurant in Psyrri, near Agion Anargyron Square."

So that's why she'd phoned her sister to say that she wouldn't be able to make it. Not because of any revelation, but because she'd arranged to go out with Thanassis.

"Did anyone see you?"

"Just a couple, friends of hers, but she didn't introduce me. Nobody I knew saw us, I'm sure, because it was one of those places for those poseurs who pretend to be lowlife and hang about between Psyrri, Gazi, and Metaxourgeio."

"Where did you meet?"

"In Agion Anargyron Square. We went in separate cars." He thought a moment and said: "The only place we might have been seen together was when I waited for her in front of the church while she went to the kiosk for cigarettes. Then again, I doubt it."

"What time was that?"

"Just after nine. . . . We were going to meet at nine, but she was about fifteen minutes late." He quickly added, "Don't worry, I didn't get out. I waited for her in the car. In any case, I was careful."

"And did you leave separately?"

"Yes. Ya—" He was going to say her name, but it stuck in his throat and he stopped. "She left at around eleven. I paid and left a couple of minutes later."

He took the receipt out of his pocket and handed it to me. The bill was for 11,800 drachmas. Six thousand apiece to eat in a dive in Psyrri. Everywhere else, the smart ones sharpen their minds in the schools and universities. In Greece, they sharpen them on the suckers. The more suckers there are around, the more smart ones there are.

"I'll hang on to the receipt. And as for Karayoryi, you won't say a word to anyone. You haven't seen her or spoken to her. Otherwise, we'll both be up the creek."

"Okay."

I put the receipt in my pocket, took out my wallet, and counted out 12,000 drachmas. As I was handing him the money, I felt as if I were staking my all in an illegal gambling joint. At least there were two things in that hideous mess that gave me relief. One was that Thanassis had in all probability not been seen with Karayoryi. The other was that I now knew for certain what Karayoryi had been doing from about nine that evening till the time she was killed.

Thanassis was about to get out, but I stopped him. "Did Karayoryi make any phone calls while you were together?"

"Yes, just before she left. To be exact, she called and left." He looked at me puzzled. "Why?" he asked.

"She called Kostarakou, a colleague of hers. She told her to make sure she watched the late-night news because she was going to drop a bombshell. She also told her that if anything happened to her, she wanted Kostarakou to carry on the investigation."

"What was the bombshell?"

"Kostarakou says she doesn't know. But she might be hiding it to get it on the air herself and feather her own nest. Did she say anything to you about being in danger or being afraid?"

"No," he answered straightaway. "If she'd said anything like that to me, I'd have told you immediately. Just the opposite. She was in high spirits and kept teasing me about the force."

Then I remembered why I'd sent him to get in with Karayoryi. "What about that business with the Albanians and the kids, did you find out anything?" Not that I was particularly interested any longer, but at least I'd have something to show for my twelve thousand.

He smiled. "Over dinner, I kept bringing the conversation around to that, but she was as slippery as an eel. In the end she told me that she wanted to sleep with me first and that if I was good in bed, she might tell me something more."

A little earlier, the niece had told me that her aunt made compromises and then took it out on herself. A nymphomaniac and a seductress, but one who felt remorse. So Robespierre was right. Revolutionaries are like that. They make a mess of the revolution, but they are on the right wavelength with the girls at the barricades.

CHAPTER 15

I closed the door and expected to hear the soap cop yelling or the prosecutor whining, but I heard nothing. The living room was dark and the TV was off. In the kitchen I found a saucepan full of spinach and rice. Adriani had disappeared. I wondered where on earth she might have gone, because she hardly ever went out in the evenings. Then I realized that I had the house to myself and that put me in a good mood.

I took down Dimitrakos and jumped onto the bed in my clothes. I did remove my shoes. I didn't want to give Adriani any excuse, because, given the state I was in, I was simply waiting for someone to let fly at and she would be the one to bear the brunt of it. I opened the dictionary and fell randomly on the letter *D. Deface = to spoil or mar the surface, legibility or appearance of; disfigure. Defaceable (adj.); defacement (n.); defacer (n.).* Karayoryi had defaced him, all right. She'd got him out of her face in double-quick time. But what was the game she had been playing with Petratos? She had got what she wanted from him. But what about him? What did he want from her that made him threaten her? And what did it mean in that first letter when he said he'd been surprised to see her? He saw her at the studio every day. Had he seen her somewhere else? Sure, his asking to see her to talk to her was easily explained. He couldn't talk to her at the studio, fair enough, and he wanted them to meet away from the office.

"Are you here?" Over the top of the dictionary I saw Adriani standing in the doorway and smiling at me. "Good boy, you took your shoes off," she said.

"Where have you been?"

"You'll see. I've a surprise for you."

She dashed out. Outside I could hear the sound of plastic bags, boxes being opened, paper being torn. In a few minutes she came back into the room, but her hands were empty.

"What do you think? Do they suit me?"

She stretched out a leg, like a veteran ballerina, and only then did I notice the boots. They reached almost to her knee and were dark brown and shiny.

"Well?" Adriani said, impatiently.

She was expecting me to express my admiration, and, I have to say, the boots were impressive. But I was overcome by an unexpected vexation, born no doubt of stinginess. I'd paid thirty-five thousand for them, and, as if that weren't enough, I'd forked out another twelve thousand for Thanassis's restaurant bill, so that in two days I'd spent fifty thousand, money down the drain. I was annoyed with myself: If I'd adopted my usual tactics, I'd only have been twelve thousand poorer and she would still be sweet-talking me.

"They're okay," I said half-heartedly and went back to Dimitrakos.

"Okay? Is that all you have to say about them?"

"What else do you want me to say? When all's said and done, they're boots just like all the others."

"No, not like all the others. These are from Petrides."

"Okay. So Petrides's boots are different. That's why you paid thirty-five thousand for them, when anywhere else they'd only be twenty."

"What do you mean? That I squander money just for the label?"

"No, I'm not saying that. Anyway, they suit you fine."

The compliment didn't satisfy her at all. "You're always putting a damper on other people's pleasure," she said bitterly. "You're really good at that."

"Don't be ungrateful!" I shouted, and Dimitrakos flew to the foot of the bed. "I paid thirty-five thousand for your pleasure! Isn't that enough?"

"It most certainly is and thank you very much. But you know what my mother used to say? 'Don't give with one hand what you take back with the other!'" She stormed out of the room before I had time to answer.

I needed to relax but all I'd succeeded in doing was getting myself worked up. I reached for Dimitrakos again. I took hold of it clumsily and some pages got crumpled. As I tried to straighten them, my eye fell on the word *sucker*. I thought that it summed me up perfectly, and I began to read, to discover my roots. *Sucker = fool, idiot, (sl.) moron.* Definitely. A fool for giving Adriani the thirty-five thousand and for letting myself be taken to task by her into the bargain. An idiot for wanting at all costs to find out why Karayoryi was dropping hints about kids when she had it all worked out already. And a moron for getting Thanassis involved so that I could find out what I wanted. Being a sucker would be the least of my problems if Ghikas were to find out about Thanassis. I'd be in the doghouse, no question. My father used to call me a whelp, though I didn't know what it meant then and I didn't dare ask, because whenever he used it, he was always furious with me. He'd have thought I was trying to be clever and he'd have hit me upside my head. It was the first word I looked up when I got hold of a dictionary. *Whelp (n). = 1. a young offspring of certain animals, esp. of a wolf or dog. 2. disparaging; a young man or youth. 3. jocular; a young child.* So, the young dog was heading for the doghouse. I wasn't complaining. It was the way of the world.

The voices on the TV brought me back to reality and I remembered that I'd wanted to watch the news. I looked at my watch. I had two minutes. I was certain that Karayoryi would be the main story. I left Dimitrakos on the bed and rushed into the living room. Adriani was in the armchair, in her usual position. Her eyes were glued to the screen and she made a show of ignoring me to emphasize her wounded pride.

I'd just managed to get comfortable on the sofa when the first of the main stories was announced: "An investigation by Hellas Channel reveals unknown aspects of Yanna Karayoryi's brutal murder." It was as well that I had been expecting something, and I accepted it calmly. Grief was oozing from the features of the newscaster, like snot from a runny nose. If he didn't get out his handkerchief to wipe his tears now, he never would. But he didn't. I guess he sensed that even hypocrisy has its limits.

"Mystery continues to surround the killing of Yanna Karayoryi. The determination of the police not to reveal any information has caused an unprecedented uproar. The channel's telephone lines have been busy all day. Viewers have been desperately seeking information and expressing their indignation at the police's indifference to public opinion. Over and above anything else, one vital question remains to be answered: What was the story that Yanna Karayoryi had intended to break on our late-night news bulletin? Let's hear what Martha Kostarakou has to say."

Martha Kostarakou appeared and spoke about the telephone call Karayoryi had made to her. She gave the bare bones, without any trimmings. Perhaps that's why she seemed so bland alongside the newscaster.

"Why did Yanna Karayoryi phone Martha Kostarakou? And why did she ask her to carry on the investigation should anything happen to her? Who was Yanna Karayoryi afraid of?" The newscaster looked penetratingly into the camera, as though waiting for the viewers to solve the mystery. "Our own reporters have been working to find an answer to this question and have come up with a sensational discovery." He paused for a moment, then fixed his gaze, as though looking at each of us individually, and asked: "Ladies and gentlemen, do you remember this man?"

The scene changed and we were in the grounds of the law courts in Evelpidon Street. The camera came to rest on a short, thin man. He was wearing a dark suit, white shirt, and tie, and looked like a bank official or some bureaucrat. But this first impression was immediately undermined because the man was in handcuffs and was being escorted by two plainclothes policemen, who were pushing him through a crowd of reporters. I recognized him immediately. It was Petros Kolakoglou.

The scene changed again. A girl was speaking with her back to the camera so she couldn't be identified. The voice asking the questions belonged to Karayoryi.

"And then what did he do to you?"

"He fondled me," said the girl with her face hidden.

"Where did he fondle you?"

There was a pause. Then the girl broke into tears.

"What we've shown you today, ladies and gentlemen, requires no comment. It speaks for itself." The newscaster was there again. His expression had changed, and he was all smiles. Self-satisfaction had replaced the mask of mourning. We'd wept for our aunt, now it was time for the inheritance and we were rubbing our hands with glee.

Back to Evelpidon Street. Kolakoglou, the two policemen at his sides, was walking toward the police van. His head was bowed, and he kept his gaze focused on the ground. As he was approaching the van, a crowd of reporters swarmed around him, their microphones held out like bayonets. Karayoryi was in the vanguard.

"What do you have to say about the court's decision, Mr. Kolakoglou?" she asked him.

Kolakoglou suddenly raised his head and fixed his gaze on her. "You're the one who got me sent down, you bitch!" he screamed in fury. "But you'll pay for it! You'll pay big-time!" The policemen broke through the ring of reporters and bundled him into the back of the van. The camera remained on Karayoryi, who followed Kolakoglou with her eyes, smiling her satisfaction.

The newscaster appeared once more. "Ladies and gentlemen, Petros Kolakoglou was released on parole just one month ago for good conduct. The Kolakoglou case was one that Yanna Karayoryi took intensely seriously. She regarded Kolakoglou as a dangerous individual. She had already published a book on the subject, but we have reason to believe that she was continuing her investigations and that's why she had reason to fear for her life." He stared into the camera with a grave expression, leaving open every possibility. "We have searched for Kolakoglou, but we have not yet been able to locate him. No one knows where he is, or, at least, no one is willing to talk."

I stopped following what was happening on the screen. The scenes flashed before me, but I didn't see them. Now all of Greece would believe that Karayoryi's murderer was Petros Kolakoglou. Tomorrow, reporters from every channel would rush out to find him. And whoever found him first would be the channel's *plat du jour*.

Not a minute had passed before my thoughts were confirmed, at least as to the first part. "It's a good thing that there are reporters to bring certain things to light. Because if we waited for the police . . ."

I heard Adriani's disdainful commentary, and I felt doubly infuriated. The police force fed us, clothed us, paid for our child's education, and yet she was having a go at it. You don't bite the hand that feeds you. And second, because she was doing it expressly because I hadn't gone overboard in my enthusiasm for her new boots.

"What do you know about police investigations to even have an opinion, you stupid shit?" I yelled at her.

"Don't you talk to me like that!" She jumped up in anger.

"What do you think the police are like? Like that arsehole that you watch every evening yelling his head off? They make them like that to delude credulous cows like you!"

"I won't allow you to talk to me like that!"

"As if I need your permission. Go on, get your boots on and get me something to eat!"

"Get it yourself, you pig! You bastard!" She went out, shaking from head to foot, just at the moment that I picked up the coffee table and threw it back down. It was like the coffee table that Antonakaki had in her living room, except that ours had a vase of flowers on it that fell over and soaked the carpet.

All I'd needed was one small provocation. I'd had it bottled up inside me all day and I'd taken it out on her. But I'd done it on this occasion because I'd wanted to take her down a peg or two. I knew what would be waiting for me otherwise. She'd make my life unbearable. She'd want to verify every little piece of nonsense that she heard on TV about Karayoryi's murder and ask me for details about the investigation. And I wasn't going to make two reports a day. One to Ghikas in the morning and one to Adriani in the evening. She'd stop talking to me for at least two weeks now. I'd lie on the bed with my dictionary, and I'd get some peace.

I switched off the TV and tried to put my thoughts into some order. So Kolakoglou had been released from prison after serving three-fifths of his sentence. And he had openly threatened Karayoryi, there was no denying that. He'd spent three and a half years in prison with the thought of revenge. That's all that had kept him going. During this time, Karayoryi had published her book, which was only fat on the fire. Within a month of getting out, he'd done her in. The fact that he'd disappeared from the face of the earth was the more incriminating, together with the fact that Karayoryi was afraid for her life. She had heard that Kolakoglou had been released, and that's why she'd been frightened. The whole scenario suited me to a T, as it left out Petratos. You grab a pederast, who's already done three and a half years inside, you lock him up again, this time for life, and everybody's happy, above all Ghikas, who credits me with another twenty-five points.

Fine so far, but there was one snag in the whole imbroglio. Why would Kolakoglou risk going to the studio to kill Karayoryi? He certainly ran the risk of being recognized at any moment. Wouldn't it have been easier and safer if he'd waited for her on some street corner at night? Let's suppose, however, that he'd decided to take the risk and that he'd gone there. Wouldn't he have had a knife or something with him to cut her throat, or a rope to strangle her? Would he have left it to chance, hoping that he'd find a light stand there to do the job? I had no liking at all for Kolakoglou—I'd have been only too happy to put him away again. That was one thing, but it was another matter entirely to arrest the first villain who came to mind. Besides, there was the threatening letter among Karayoryi's papers. Kolakoglou's first name was Petros. There was no persuasive connection with the N who had signed the letters. And since there *was* no connection, there must have been someone else, someone other than Kolakoglou, who was threatening Karayoryi.

All this got my goat because the tidy solution I'd come up with, that left out Petratos, didn't seem so tidy in the end. I picked up the telephone and called the studio. I asked the operator, who answered in a couldn't-care-less tone, to put me through to Petratos.

"Yes," said a sharp voice.

"This is Inspector Haritos, Mr. Petratos. I saw your report about

Karayoryi's murder on the news and I'd like to talk to you. Please remain there and I'll be right over."

"I can appreciate your urgency," he said with heavy irony. "Come on over. I'll be waiting for you."

It was an opportunity for me to get out of the dilemma of having to get my own meal and of losing face before Adriani. I thought that on the way back I'd stop and get a couple of souvlaki with all the spicy garnishing rather than have the spinach and rice that I hated. Not to mention that I'd reek of garlic from fifty paces and Adriani wouldn't get a wink of sleep because of the smell.

CHAPTER 16

At last, I saw the man from the defaced photograph in the flesh. He was a porky forty-something with chubby cheeks, hair cropped short at the sides and bushy on top—a real doughboy. In appearance, he played on two fronts: that of the serious news editor, with his dark gray suit; and that of the casual reporter, with turtleneck sweater, without ties or formalities.

We were inside Petratos's cubicle and I was facing him, but at an angle. Facing me was the newscaster, with his tailored suit and the handkerchief in his breast pocket. They smiled at me. Smiles full of condescension for the poor police officer who'd come to pay his respects. I played the fool because it suited me that way.

"Kolakoglou is an interesting case," I said in a friendly tone. "Of course, it's a little too early to say for sure that he's our murderer. We will need to continue investigating."

They swapped more smiles and Petratos shrugged. "We're done with our investigation," he said. "But you go ahead. When all's said and done, it's your job to investigate."

"That's why I'm here to see you. Do you have any other evidence, that you haven't yet revealed to your audience and that might help our investigation?"

"We don't keep cards up our sleeves, Inspector," the newscaster broke in. "What evidence we have, we come out with it, so that the public may be informed."

Petratos rested his elbows on the desk and put his hands together. "Let's speak openly, Inspector Haritos. Yesterday, Mr. Delopoulos suggested that we work together. You'd give us precedence in informing us about the course of your investigation and we'd give you whatever evidence we have. This morning I sent Kostarakou to see you. Not only did you not tell her anything, but you even interrogated her. And now you're asking us to give you evidence. That's not the way it works."

"I didn't give any information to Miss Kostarakou because I had nothing to tell her. We're still in the dark. You're already one step ahead of us." If it seemed as if I was sucking up to them, I wasn't; it was a tactical maneuver. Not one learned from the FBI, but one learned in the Greek village. "That's why I came to ask for your help. From tomorrow morning, we'll be inundated with phone calls. Every two minutes someone tells us that they've seen Kolakoglou. We don't know where this mass hysteria will take Kolakoglou. So we have to find him, and quickly."

"We disagree on that too, Inspector Haritos." He looked at me as if I were a person with special needs, who had to be taught basic literacy. "Would that the public were so concerned about Yanna Karayoryi's murder as to take to the streets tomorrow and look for her murderer. That would not only be a huge journalistic coup, but also a mark of recognition for everything Yanna achieved."

"And what if the murderer was someone else? Okay, there's incriminating evidence with regard to Kolakoglou, but we cannot yet be certain that he killed her. He may be innocent."

"What are you afraid of?" the newscaster said. "That you might tarnish the reputation of a pederast who was sentenced to six years in prison?"

"No. I'm afraid that we may waste time looking for the wrong person."

"First of all, it's not our job to prove Kolakoglou's guilt," Petratos broke in. "We're simply handing him over. Everything else is up to you."

In other words, they were lumbering us with Kolakoglou. It was for us to run around and prove his guilt. Meanwhile, they'd fill their news bulletins with the story and up their ratings.

"Anyway, you're worrying for nothing," Petratos went on. "It's ninety percent certain that he's the murderer. If it hadn't been for Yanna, he'd have got away with his squalid little crimes. He's the only one with a motive."

"You're wrong," I said quietly. "There are others who had motives too. Even you."

He stared at me open-mouthed and the image of the doughboy was complete. He couldn't decide whether I'd said it seriously or in jest. In the end, he evidently plumped for the latter, because he let out a howl of merriment.

"Me? You are pulling my leg, of course."

I didn't reply, but turned to the newscaster, who was trying to recover his poise. "Would you leave us, please?"

The newscaster was taken aback and didn't know what to do. He responded, however, to Petratos's nod and got up.

"I don't like your tone at all, Inspector," he said to me icily.

"Nor I yours, especially when you're presenting the news." It left him speechless. He would happily have slammed the door behind him, but it was made of aluminum and he was probably afraid of bringing the whole cubicle down behind him.

"So, Inspector? What motive did I have for killing Yanna Karayoryi?"

"You had an affair with her. She used you to scramble up the ladder, and when she'd got where she wanted, she dumped you."

He made an effort to maintain his ironic smile but failed, because he hadn't liked what he'd heard.

"Who told you that?"

"We asked and we found out. That's our job."

"Just because we had an affair and split up—I stress that she didn't dump me, we split up—that doesn't mean that I had a reason to kill her."

"I heard it differently, Mr. Petratos. You didn't split up, she dumped you as soon as she had direct access to Mr. Delopoulos and could do as she liked without having to go through you. She offended not only your male but also your professional pride. You would have given anything to teach her a lesson, but she had Mr. Delopoulos behind her. You could neither control her nor fire her. And from what I know of Karayoryi, she would have made sure she reminded you of that every working day, which of course made you furious." If I'd had the photographs with me, I'd have stuck them in his undefaced face, but I'd left them in my office.

He was fuming inside but was trying hard to appear calm. "That's all speculation on your part, there's no evidence whatsoever for it."

"It's not speculation. It's the conclusion from statements made by witnesses. Karayoryi's murder has all the elements of a crime of passion. That fits Kolakoglou's case, but it also fits yours, given that you'd written her threatening letters."

His surprise seemed genuine, at least as genuine as a journalist could get. "Me?" he said after some time. "I wrote Yanna threatening letters?"

"We found them in the drawer of her desk. In the last one you openly threaten her."

"And is my signature on those letters?"

Now it was me who was in a tight spot. "You signed them N. Your name is Nestor, if I'm not mistaken."

"And because you found some threatening letters signed by someone with the initial N, you automatically concluded that I wrote them? What can I say? The police force should be proud of you."

I ignored the insult and said, very calmly: "It's easy for us to prove who's right. The letters are written by hand. Give me a sample of your handwriting and I'll compare it with that on the letters."

"No!" he answered in a rage. "If you want a sample of my handwriting, you can take me down to the station for interrogation and ask for it officially, in the presence of my lawyer! And if you're wrong, I'll drag your name through the gutters!"

And the whole of the police force with it. From the minister down. I'd be lucky to get away with a transfer to the VIP guard.

"First, you have to prove that I had the opportunity to kill her. Yanna came to the studio at around eleven-thirty. I'd left by ten. At least four people saw me leaving."

"They saw you entering the elevator. That doesn't necessarily mean that you left."

"So where did I hide? In a cupboard or maybe inside a wardrobe?"

"In the parking lot," I said. "You took the elevator down to the parking garage, hid there, and came back up just before the late-night news."

So far I'd been doing quite well, but then he lost his temper, jumped to his feet, and started shouting: "You won't get away with this. You can't go around making unfounded accusations."

"What accusations?" I said in all innocence. "Weren't you the one to suggest we exchange information? I'm giving you what I have. You can hardly complain."

By the time he realized that he'd walked into the trap, I was outside his office.

As I crossed the newsroom, some young reporters who were still at their desks turned and looked at me inquisitively. I walked out without paying any attention to them. I'd pressed the button for the elevator when, coming down the corridor, I saw Kostarakou.

"Hello," she said rather formally and walked on past me. I let the elevator go and went after her.

"Are you sure that Karayoryi didn't say anything else to you on the phone?"

"I told you all I know this morning," she said coldly. "There's nothing more. Because of you, I got into hot water with Petratos."

"Did you say anything to Petratos about the photograph I showed you?"

"Of course not. If I'd told him about the photograph as well, he'd have canned me on the spot, given the vile mood he was in."

"If Karayoryi spoke to you on the phone about the story she was preparing, it would be better for you to tell me now, before it's too late."

She didn't even trouble to reply. She shot me a poisonous look and walked off.

When I stepped out of the elevator, I ran into the backstreet marine. He puffed up his body, his arms and legs apart.

"Here again? Any developments?"

"Why do you always stand like that with your legs apart? Are you chapped?" I asked, and went off to find some souvlaki.

CHAPTER 17

"The profile fits at any rate."

It was the first time he'd used the English word *profile*. I made a note to look it up later in the *OED*. It was nine-thirty in the morning and I was giving my report to Ghikas concerning Kolakoglou. He guessed that I hadn't understood "profile" and was waiting to see how I'd react. But I was wise to what he meant—that Kolakoglou would do quite nicely for the murderer—and I began listing everything that didn't ring true. It didn't ring true that Kolakoglou had gone to the studio and risked being recognized. It didn't ring true that he'd have gone without a murder weapon if he'd gone to kill her. And I reminded him that Kolakoglou was not the only suspect.

"I know," he said. "We have the unknown N and his letters."

"Did you know that Petratos's name is Nestor . . . ?"

He studied me in silence. He was trying to connect the man in the photograph with the Nestor of the letters, and the two seemed to him to fit, just as they seemed to me to fit. "Stay away from Petratos," he said. "You won't go near him unless you have enough incriminating evidence to convince me. I don't want to find myself at daggers drawn with the minister."

His look stopped me in my tracks and I didn't dare to tell him about the conversation I'd had with Petratos the previous evening. If he found out that I'd asked him for a sample of his handwriting, he'd have my ass.

"Find Kolakoglou quickly and get him behind bars."

This was a classic way for a superior to say to his subordinate: "All right, I've listened to your bullshit, now do what you have to." He wanted the tidy solution, just like Delopoulos, Petratos, the newscaster, and everybody else. No complications and no ministerial interventions because of the involvement of upstanding citizens, etc. The reprobate was the easy solution. Always.

"The only incriminating evidence we have on Kolakoglou is that he threatened Karayoryi after the trial. What if he can prove that he was elsewhere at the time of the murder?"

"The alibi of a pederast with a criminal record doesn't hold water," he said. "When all's said and done, he should have spent six years in prison and he got away with three. It won't hurt him to spend another couple of weeks in jail. He's used to it."

There was no point in arguing. I collected my papers and turned to leave.

"You still don't get it, do you?" I looked at him surprised, and without hiding the fact that he was amused by my foolishnes. "Get Kolakoglou behind bars. Maybe he's the murderer, maybe not. We'll say that we're holding him for interrogation. Meanwhile, they'll publicize all the dirt on him. They'll rake up everything from the trial again and go knocking on the doors of the girls he raped to get interviews from them. If in the end Kolakoglou proves to be the murderer, then we come out and say that we owe our success to our valuable collaboration with the media and everybody will be happy. If it's not Kolakoglou, and we produce the real murderer, then they won't know where to turn first. Either way, we come out smelling of roses."

You had to hand it to Ghikas! Now I know why he became chief and I remained a humble inspector. He rarely got a smile of admiration from me, but this time he deserved one. He saw it and laughed, obviously pleased with himself.

"As for Petratos, check him out, but at a distance. Discreetly," he said generously because I'd made his day. "And make sure you find out what *profile* means. In a few years' time, we'll all be using it."

The herd of reporters was massing in the corridor, outside Koula's office, waiting. They'd got nothing out of me the previous day, and so they were now knocking on my boss's door hoping to get something out of him. Among them was Kostarakou, but she didn't add her gaze to the collective, provocative look that the others gave me. She avoided my eyes.

I told Thanassis to come in. We hadn't spoken since the previous evening and he looked at me as though frightened. He thought I was going to start on about his meeting with Karayoryi. As soon as I told him that I wanted a large-scale hunt to find Kolakoglou, that I wanted his photograph circulated and a call put out to all patrol cars and so on, he looked relieved, as if he'd just emptied his bowels after ten days of constipation. He was good at organizing. I also told him to find out where Kolakoglou's mother lived and to get me a car and backup ready.

"Will you require a search warrant, too?"

"As if I needed a search warrant to get into a pederast's house. That would take the cake!"

The croissant was on my desk, in its cellophane. I opened it and took a bite. Souvlaki at night, croissant in the morning. I wondered when they'd serve souvlaki wrapped in croissant with tzatziki, tomato, and onion. I recalled some paintings depicting war chiefs in the court of King Otto, dressed in fustanellas with their dress coats over the top. The profile fitted, as Ghikas might say.

I bit into the croissant and addressed the pile of documents on my desk. I began with Markidis's report. Nothing new there, other than that Karayoryi had eaten approximately two hours before her death, which confirmed what Thanassis had said. The murder had taken place between eleven and twelve. I knew that too. I put the coroner's report aside and looked over the files from Karayoryi's computer. I didn't find anything of interest there either. Articles, interviews, and ideas for topics. There was nothing in them about Kolakoglou. Nothing among her papers either. How the hell could she be investigating something and not keep any notes? I reached the bottom of the pile as the telephone rang.

"Haritos."

"Haritou," I heard a girl's voice say, laughing. It was Katerina. Katerina didn't have a phone in the house where she lived and so we weren't able to call her. When she called us, it was usually at night. It was very rare for her to call me at the office. Every time she did call me, I was immediately filled with worry that something had happened to her.

"How's things, Daddy?" She sounded happy, carefree.

"As always, love. Too much work. How come you're calling me in the morning? Is anything wrong?" I thought it better to make sure. "Nothing's wrong, I'm fine. I phoned Mum at home first and she told me you had had a scrap again."

If I'd had Adriani in front of me, I'd have given her what for. What did she mean by upsetting the girl? When you're a long way away, everything seems bigger than it is.

"Come on, Daddy. You know how she is. She's alone, I'm away, and she's always on edge. She flares up at the slightest thing."

"You don't have to tell me. But sometimes she gets my back up with her ingratitude."

"She's a bit touchy, but don't pay any attention to her. Make it up. I can't bear knowing that you've had a fight and you're not speaking."

"All right. I'll make an effort." I said it halfheartedly, because I'd made a whole strategic plan to find a little peace and now I was going to have to retreat in disarray. But I couldn't say no to Katerina.

"You're such a sweetie," she cried, overjoyed that she'd succeeded, and I simply melted. "And because you're the sweetest daddy in the world, I'll tell you something else. Sismanis, my criminal law tutor, suggested that I do a doctorate with him. He even told me that he'd manage to dig up some funds from somewhere so I could work in the department and get paid."

"Well done, my princess!" I wanted to shout, but my voice cracked with pride and emotion.

"I kept that for last to put you in a good mood. Anyway, I'm going to hang up now, otherwise I'll spend my whole lunch break on the phone. You have best wishes from Panos."

We'd never talked about it, but she knew I couldn't stomach that hulk that she dragged around with her. But she always gives me his best wishes. It's her way of telling me that she's still with him.

"Give him mine too," I said, politely but halfheartedly.

I heard her hang up and I put down the receiver. They'd all gone out of my mind, Karayoryi, Kolakoglou, Petratos, all of them, leaving only Katerina. Who was she after all? The daughter of a police inspector, who'd begun as a cop, who'd taken twenty-five years to get to be head of homicide and who'd never been able to learn the trick to make that big stride forward. It wasn't as if she had any background or had gone to the best schools; she'd attended the local high school and had had a few lessons on the side, and that only in the last year before the university entrance exams. Now look at her. They were telling her to go on to do a doctorate even before she'd taken her first degree. And look at me, I thought to myself. I'm running myself down, humbling myself in order to increase my happiness, to make myself feel even more proud of her.

I made an effort to come back down to earth, because I was ready to let the sleuth reporter, the defaced news editor, and the pederast tax consultant go to hell. I called Sotiris on the internal line. I told him to find out everything he could about Petratos. Who he mixed with at the studio, who he was at odds with, who his friends were, the places he frequented. And above all, what time he'd left the studio on the night of the murder, if anyone had seen him leaving, and where he'd gone after he left. And all that discreetly, without him getting wind of the inquiries.

When Sotiris had gone, I realized that I had to do everything in my life discreetly, and I began cursing my fate. I had to be discreet with Petratos so that Delopoulos wouldn't find out and make my life difficult. I had to be discreet with Adriani so as not to upset Katerina. I had to be discreet with Ghikas so as not to lose points. Fortunately, at that moment, Thanassis came in to say that the patrol car was ready and stopped me sinking any further into the pit.

CHAPTER 18

It wasn't raining now, but the sky and I had that popular song in common. Gray clouds and gray moods. Kolakoglou's mother lived in Kallithea, on Argonafton Street, which ran parallel to Davaki Street. I told the driver to switch the siren on; otherwise we'd have taken an hour to get from Vassileos Konstantinou Avenue to Amalias Avenue and then to Thiseos Street. Fortunately, the traffic wasn't too heavy on Thiseos Street and we switched off the siren because it gets on my nerves. We soon got to Davaki Street. It took us less than five minutes to get from there to Argonafton Street.

Mrs. Kolakoglou lived on the second floor of a four-story building. It was a cheap construction that had already begun decaying. The balconies had iron railings and geraniums. The builder skimped on the railings and the tenants on the geraniums. I told the sergeant who had come with me to ring one of the other bells. Not that Kolakoglou would have been there, but you never know. We didn't want to warn him and let him get away.

There were four flats on the second floor. Mrs. Kolakoglou's was next to the elevator. She opened the door as though she'd been expecting us. She was a shriveled, gray-haired old woman dressed in black. She may have been in mourning for her husband and for the calamity that had befallen her four years previously. She didn't know me, but as soon as she set eyes on the others in uniform, she froze. I pushed her aside and entered the flat.

"Search it!" I said to the others in a tough voice. "Turn everything upside down!" But what was there to turn upside down? A living room and two bedrooms, kitchen and bathroom, seventy square meters at most. The first bedroom was the mother's; the second was the

son's. I went into the second one. The bed had a cover and embroidered pillows. On the bedside table was an alarm clock, a
battery-operated radio, and a box of sleeping pills. I opened the fitted cupboards. Three suits, not tailored ones but ready-to-wear, and
five shirts that Sotiropoulos would never have worn, because they
weren't Armani, but had the air of a factory. They were all hanging
in a row and with space between them so that they wouldn't get
creased. The meticulousness of the housewife.

"He's not here, I swear it." I heard her whimpering voice behind me.
I spun around. "Where is he?" I snapped.

"I don't know."

"You do know and you're hiding him."

"No, I swear. I don't know and I'm worried."

"If you want what's best for him, tell him to come out of hiding
because it'll end badly for him. He's looking at a life sentence."

"Why a life sentence? What has he done?"

I didn't answer because I didn't know the answer. "When did you
see him last?"

"On the day they killed—" She couldn't get Karayoryi's name out.
"On the day they killed her. He went out early that evening. I waited
for him at night, but he didn't come back. He called me to say he was
all right and told me not to worry."

"What time did he call?"

"About one in the morning. I'd gone to bed and he woke me."

He disappeared because he'd murdered Karayoryi or because he
was scared when he saw it on the TV and so went into hiding?

"Where might he be hiding? Does he have any friends or relatives?"

"We don't have anyone. They all turned their backs on Petros and
me. There's just the two of us now." Her shriveled body collapsed on
the bed and she began weeping. "He wasn't even a month in his own
home. I left the old neighborhood and came here, where no one
knows him, to change surroundings and help him to forget. And in
less than a month, he's on the run again like a wild animal."

"Where did you live before?"

"In Keratsini. But people kept pointing me out, and I couldn't live there anymore."

The sergeant came in and indicated to me that they had found nothing. I didn't expect them to find anything. It was simply a ruse. If any reporter asked her, she'd say that we'd been around looking for him. I was shutting mouths, as Ghikas would say.

"Tell your son to come out of hiding. Sooner or later we'll find him. He's only making it worse for himself."

"If he calls me, I'll tell him," she said, between sobs. Even if she did tell him, he'd follow the first rule of prison, which teaches you to hide and stay there, whether you're guilty or not.

When I got back to the station, I found Sotiropoulos standing in front of my office door, waiting for me.

"What are you doing here at this time? Have you run out of stories?" Usually by one o'clock they'd all gone back to their studios to get their reports ready.

He smiled and followed me into the room. "It's my turn to make a little coup."

He sat down and stretched out his legs to his great pleasure. I pretended not to hear what he'd said and thumbed through the papers that I'd read that morning as though I was revising my lesson.

"Be quick about it, because I'm up to my neck."

"Just between us, honestly now, do you think it was Kolakoglou who killed her?"

"I don't know. We're trying to find him. When we do, we'll question him. I'll let you know."

He laughed again. "You're wasting your time. All that's bullshit thought up by Petratos. Only an idiot like Petratos would go on air with a red herring like that."

"It's no red herring. He threatened Karayoryi in public, or have you forgotten?"

"Pity, I thought you were smarter than that. Kolakoglou is small fry. A pervert, but small fry. He did his thing by using candy and chocolate. Can you imagine him killing anyone, and in such a savage way? Not to mention that he might have also ended up a victim."

"Victim? How come?"

He had succeeded in getting my attention. Behind his round glasses, he had a wily glint in his eyes, just like Himmler when he flushed out Jews hidden in attics.

"Have you been around to Kolakoglou's old office recently?"

"No. Neither recently nor in the past. I've never been there."

"You'll find yourself in an enormous office for what it is, accounting and tax matters. They're lousy with money. And do you know who owns it?"

"Who?"

"The parents of the two girls. They banded together and kept the business going." He fell silent and stared at me. I waited for him to go on. "Who's to say they didn't get him denounced as a pederast to get their hands on his business? Kolakoglou was fond of the two little girls, he never tried to hide it. It wasn't difficult for the parents to claim that there was some grubbier motive behind the sweets and cakes. And it's easy to tell two little girls what to say. I'm not saying that that's what happened, but it's worth looking into. The girls must be in high school now. If I can talk to them, they might have a very different story to tell today."

He came out with it all in one go. He took a deep breath and stared at me, pleased as punch with himself. Before we came up with Karayoryi's murderer, we'd end up with a dozen indictments, a couple of suicides, and who knows what else.

"If I turn out to be right, that'll be the coup de grâce for Petratos. He's already on the way out."

"Petratos?"

"Didn't you know? Delopoulos has him lined up for dismissal. But what with Karayoryi's murder and everything, he's safe for the time being. That's why he stirred up all the business with Kolakoglou. He's desperate for a big story so as to keep his job. But he's made a pig's ear of that too." He adopted his wily look again. "Word has it that Delopoulos had Karayoryi earmarked for his job."

"Why didn't you tell me all this yesterday?" I said curtly.

"What was there to tell? There was no Kolakoglou on the scene yesterday. He came into the equation last night." He thought he'd left me speechless. "I didn't say anything to you yesterday, because I didn't know anything. Now that I do know, I've come to tell you. It shows my good intentions." He got to his feet, but he didn't leave. He stood there, looking at me. "You owe me one," he said.

Of course, I was under no delusion that everything he'd told me was purely out of kindness. "Okay, but all I can give you is a post-dated check. When I learn something, I'll let you know."

"Come on, Inspector. What did you get out of Kolakoglou's mother?" he asked in a tone that showed there was nothing he didn't know.

"Nothing. He disappeared on the day of the murder and hasn't been home since. All he did was call to say he was all right. At least, that's what his mother says."

He didn't believe me, but that didn't bother him, especially as he'd come with another purpose. He'd wanted to make Petratos seem unreliable and he'd succeeded. Why did Petratos keep cropping up? Without knowing it, Sotiropoulos had provided me with another piece of information. Karayorgi had wanted his job, and so he'd had another reason to hate her. What man wouldn't hate the bitch who first used him, then dumped him, and finally stole his job?

When Sotiropoulos had gone, I shouted Thanassis in and told him to put out a call to the police stations in Keratsini, Perama, and Nikaia to be on the lookout for Kolakoglou. Logically, he wouldn't go where everyone knew him, but in this line of work, you often find a lead where you're least expecting it.

CHAPTER 19

I found her just like every evening, in front of the TV, the remote control in her hand. I thought of going straight into the bedroom and getting comfortable with my dictionary, but I recalled the promise I'd made to Katerina and I went into the living room.

"Good evening."

She didn't reply, or even turn around to look at me. She simply straightened her head slightly, at the same time sticking out her lower jaw—as Markidis might put it—while her hand squeezed the remote control, a sign that she'd heard me but was determined to ignore me. I understood. It wasn't enough that I'd made the first step with my good evening greeting. She wanted me to sit down beside her and begin the mollycoddling, while she pulled away and told me that she wasn't going to put up with my vile manners anymore and while I told her that she was in the right, that it was the pressures and stress of work that were to blame, and after wasting the best part of three-quarters of an hour like that, she'd finally come around, warning me that it was the last time she was going to give in, while in real life it would always be the time before the last time, because the last time would never come. She didn't get a chance though, because by talking to her I'd fulfilled my obligation to Katerina, and I had no intention of going any further. To my great delight, I was able to stick to my original plan. If Katerina phoned me, I'd say that I'd made an effort, but that it was Adriani who was still sulking and I'd let her get on to her mother.

Produce . . . profess . . . I was lying on the bed, looking up Ghikas's "profile" in the *Oxford English-Greek Learner's Dictionary*. I'd kept my shoes on deliberately to annoy Adriani, so she'd start shouting and be forced to talk to me or go on sulking, in which case I'd lie on the bed every evening with my shoes on for as long as we weren't talking. There it was: *Profile = 1. a side view, outline, or representation of a human object, esp. of a human face or head. 2. a short biographical sketch of a subject.* So that's what he'd meant. We used to call it a description, now it had become a profile. The description of Kolakoglou fits the description of Karayoryi's murderer. Plain language, so we knew what we were talking about. But did it fit? Apart from the threat, which had nothing to do with his description, nothing else fitted. Sotiropoulos had been right. We were trying to turn Kolakoglou, who'd seduced two little girls with candy and chocolate, into a cold-blooded murderer. Apart from the likelihood of his coming up with an alibi and making us look foolish, there was one other consideration. According to the coroner's report, the murderer had to have been tall and strongly built. That's what Markidis had told me on the night of the murder, and he'd repeated it in his report. Kolakoglou was five foot nothing in height and all shriveled up like his mother. Where would he have found the strength to strike a blow like that at Karayoryi? Then again, if in the end it turned out that Kolakoglou had indeed been the killer, it wouldn't have been the first time that the coroner had made a mistake.

The profile—I decided to use the word so as to get used to it, given that sooner or later I'd be getting it thrown at me all the time—fitted Petratos much better. First of all, he had the necessary build. He was around six foot and stocky. He gave the impression of being a milksop, but he would definitely have had the strength to stick the lamp stand into Karayoryi's breast. Which would also explain why a knife or pistol or some other murder weapon wasn't used. Petratos hadn't gone with the intention of killing her. He'd made up his mind on the spot; the rod was in hand and he'd run her through with it. He'd had a motive: Karayoryi was digging his grave. But then so did Kolakoglou: She'd dug his three years earlier. Karayoryi had known them both; she wouldn't have been surprised to see either of them there. She would have been more cautious in Kolakoglou's case, since he had threatened her, but she was so self-assured and so arrogant she may not have given much thought to it.

A knock at the door woke me from my thoughts. I was surprised, as Adriani hadn't accustomed me to such niceties. When the door opened, it was Thanassis I saw, looking at me with an embarrassed smile.

"Excuse me, but your wife told me that you weren't sleeping."

I jumped up from the bed. "What's going on?"

"Nothing," he said reassuringly. "I was just passing, and I thought I'd update you on Kolakoglou."

He did that occasionally. He showed overwhelming zeal in order to get himself into my good graces, but only when he was sure that it wouldn't result in his having to run about or sacrifice his comforts.

I led him into the living room. Adriani had realized that we would be coming in there and had switched off the TV. She was excessively sweet and polite to Thanassis. She asked him how he was, how his family was, gave him coffee and cookies. She didn't even give me a glance, let alone a coffee.

"We had our work cut out with Kolakoglou," Thanassis said, after having had his fill of Adriani's attentions. "By six o'clock, we'd had thirty calls. Twenty-five local ones, two from Thessaloniki, one from Larissa, one from Kastoria, and one from Rhodes."

"What did you expect? They've put him up for auction. Are there any developments?"

He fell silent, but evidently he had a card up his sleeve that he thought was an ace and he was getting ready to produce it. "He was recognized by a clerk while buying a ticket at the bus station, in Kifisos."

"When?"

"Yesterday. From what he remembers, he bought a ticket for Thessaloniki." That was it. Not an ace—at a pinch, a seven of spades. But he wasn't aware of it and he went on undeterred. "So the calls from Thessaloniki must have been genuine."

"And the one from Rhodes?" I said peaceably. "From Thessaloniki he took the plane to Rhodes for a holiday?"

It was only then that it dawned on him that something wasn't right with his logic and he reassumed the profile of the moron.

"Did you find the ticket inspector from the bus?"

"None of the inspectors remembers seeing him, but that doesn't mean much. The inspectors don't look at the passengers, they only look at the tickets. If he hid his face behind a newspaper, the inspector wouldn't have seen him at all."

"Did it occur to you that he might never have boarded the bus, that he might have bought the ticket to throw us off? Or that he might have got off at some other stop?"

"Do you think he's that smart?"

"Every lowlife that's ever been to prison learns half a dozen things in order to be able to survive. That's as smart as he needs to be. Does he have relatives or friends in Thessaloniki?"

My question put him in a difficult position. "I don't know. We haven't looked into that yet."

"You should have looked into that first. Because if he doesn't have people there he can trust, where's he going to hide? Wherever he goes, we'll find him. You want my opinion? He's still here, in Athens. He can lie low here better than anywhere else. And if those shitty reporters find him before we do, Ghikas will have something to say about it."

I remembered that it was time for the news and I pressed the remote control. Nervous and anxious, Thanassis watched me. I really did hope that Sotiropoulos and his crew hadn't flushed him out. He could say whatever he liked, but I was sure that he was looking for him, too, if for no other reason than to put one over on Petratos. He was the only one who might find him. Kostarakou didn't inspire much confidence.

That was why I tuned first to Horizon, Sotiropoulos's channel. He was in an office, holding a microphone and talking to a woman with dark hair and well past her best. I didn't know who she was because I'd not been involved in the Kolakoglou case. From his questions, I gathered that she was the mother of one of the girls, one of the ones who had got their hands on the consultancy business. Sotiropoulos was trying to get her to explain how she and the father of the other girl had come to be co-owners of Kolakoglou's business. The woman was furious, refused to answer, told him to leave, but he stood there undeterred. In the end, the woman threatened to call the police. The poor woman didn't realize that this was precisely what Sotiropoulos was after: to show her angry, scared, and hostile.

The scene changed and Sotiropoulos next appeared in the corridor of an apartment block in front of a closed door. He was pointing to the door and talking to the camera.

"This is the house of the second family whose child was molested by Kolakoglou. Sadly, they refused to talk to us. It is, of course, understandable, ladies and gentlemen, that these people want to erase the past, to forget the tragic events that they and their children went through. On the other hand, there are some burning questions that remain to be answered. How, for example, did the victims find the emotional strength to buy the business owned by the culprit, the man who had molested their children? And how, if they want to forget the past, do they manage to live and work in a place that reminds them of that past every day? Questions that demand answers."

Sotiropoulos was a crafty devil. He said nothing about his suspicions that Kolakoglou might have been innocent and that the parents of the two girls might have set him up in order to get their hands on his business. He simply engaged in a bit of mudslinging at the parents. But not too much. He'd started the poison dripping and was letting it do its work. When, the next day or the day after, he came out and said, as he was sure to, that Kolakoglou may have been the victim of a conspiracy, one section of the public would be ready to accept it, at least as a possibility.

As soon as I switched over to Hellas Channel, I knew I'd been right. Martha Kostarakou was badgering Mrs. Kolakoglou, who was standing in the doorway to her flat. She was asking the same questions I had and was getting the same answers. I thought of suggesting to her that we exchange jobs, given that we do the same work. Let her have my position and I'd go to Hellas Channel and make six hundred thousand a month.

"Do you know that your son is wanted by the police?"

"I do know. They came here this morning and turned everything

upside down." I congratulated myself. Things had turned out as I'd
foreseen. "What has he done?" Mrs. Kolakoglou wailed. "Haven't we
been through enough? Leave us in peace, can't you." Her anger at us
caught up Kostarakou too.

"The police believe that your son murdered Yanna Karayoryi.
What do you have to say about that?"

I leapt to my feet as if I'd just sat on a pin. When had we ever said
that Kolakoglou had murdered Karayoryi? They were the ones who
wanted to make him into a murderer and they were using us as a
front. I suddenly saw a very different Kostarakou. She was trying to
imitate Karayoryi but lacked her intelligence and innate audacity. All
she succeeded in doing was to appear even more cruel and callous
than her predecessor. The old woman began to cry. A mute kind of
crying, like a ritual lament.

"My son never killed anyone. My Petros is no murderer. Isn't it
enough that he rotted in prison for so many years, an innocent man?
Are you trying to pin something else on him now?"

Kostarakou looked amazed. The birdbrain thought that she was
on to something. "Are you implying, Mrs. Kolakoglou, that your son
was wrongfully sent to prison?"

"Ask those who sent him there and who got their hands on his
business. As for that woman who got him put away, I won't say I'm
glad she was killed, but there's such a thing as divine retribution," she
said, crossing herself, as the tears rolled down her cheeks.

Would Delopoulos and Petratos realize, I wondered, that they
were playing Sotiropoulos's game? It was as if he'd foreseen the report by Kostarakou and had taken pains to emphasize the parents'
unwillingness to talk so that they would appear guilty. I was wrong
to think of him as a Robespierre. He was an out-and-out Rasputin.

"Is that how they think they'll find Kolakoglou?" quipped Thanassis, who was sitting beside me on the sofa.

"Don't you get it?" I said. "They don't want to find Kolakoglou. It
suits them for him to remain at large so they can throw more fat on
the fire."

He gazed at me as if I'd come out with a pearl of wisdom.

"Why are you still here?" I suddenly said. "Back to the office and on with the search. Check out the cafés, the bars, all the joints frequented by the lowlife. He may well be lying low during the day and only going out at night." He leapt up immediately, said good-bye, and rushed out. Sotiropoulos might have been right, but Ghikas was right too. Let's get him behind bars first, and then we'd see what was what.

The kitchen table had been laid for one. A saucepan was simmering on the stove. I took the lid off and found the spinach and rice from the previous day. I wasn't going to get away with it, it seemed. I put some on my plate and sat down to eat alone. As I was eating, I reflected that it was Petratos who had started the hunt for Kolakoglou. If he was the one who had killed Karayoryi, then he'd done it deliberately to turn our attention away from him so that he'd have nothing to worry about. This thought led me to leave my meal unfinished. What the hell, spinach and rice always made me want to gag.

CHAPTER 20

Thanassis swore on everything he held holy that he'd been coordinating the search till two in the morning. He'd put a further call out to the patrol cars to comb the cafés, the bars, and all the joints that the people Kolakoglou had knocked around with in prison now might frequent. He came up with nothing. No one recognized Kolakoglou from his photograph. A few who remembered him from the trial had never actually seen him. Or so they said. It was only to be expected. Prison is a kind of mutual aid society. Once you've been there, you'll always find someone to help you out. Just the fact that the police were after him was enough to enable him to find a place to lie low and friends to help him. I told Thanassis to carry on with his investigations and to send me Sotiris.

Sotiris immediately began reeling off his findings. The reporters had indeed seen Petratos leaving at ten. But no one had actually seen him leaving the newsroom. Of course, he may have taken his car from the parking lot and left. Because I'd told him to act discreetly, Sotiris didn't want to ask without my approval whether anyone had seen Petratos's car in the parking lot after ten. Half an hour after midnight, Petratos had made an appearance at a bar behind the Panathinaikos Stadium where reporters hang out. The barman clearly recalled when he'd come and when he'd left, just after two. Yet from ten o'clock until the time he'd gone to the bar, his whereabouts were unknown. No one had seen him either going into or out of his house. The most important thing he kept for last: Karayoryi had phoned the studio after the nine o'clock news and had told them to keep a slot for her on the late-night news.

"Who did she talk to? To Petratos?"

"No. To Kontaxi, a girl who works in the newsroom. She told her to notify Sperantzas that she wanted a minute on the late-night news."

"Sperantzas hadn't known anything about it. First, he heard it was from Karayoryi."

"Yes, because he still hadn't arrived at the studio. Kontaxi told Petratos so she wouldn't have to worry about it, and then went home."

"So Petratos knew that Karayoryi wanted to break some story on the late-night news, but he didn't know what the story was," I said to Sotiris. And he said nothing about it to Sperantzas. He didn't even leave him a note. He just left. Why? Out of indifference, or did he have some ulterior motive? I'd begun to get excited over this new evidence that Sotiris had turned up when the phone rang and cut me short.

"Haritos."

"Come up to my office! Now!"

"Ghikas wants me. We'll carry on later." From Ghikas's tone, I realized that a storm was brewing and I was going to get the brunt of it.

His expression was gale force and it hit me head-on. "Who told you to send Vlassopoulos to investigate Petratos?"

Vlassopoulos was Sotiris. I should have known that some busybody would spill the beans to Petratos, no matter how discreetly he'd gone about it. I did my best to pass it off as routine.

"It wasn't an investigation. It was just a formality. We were checking the movements of all those connected with Karayoryi."

"You're not telling me the truth. The evening before last when you went to see Petratos about Kolakoglou, you told him that he was a suspect! You even asked him for a sample of his handwriting to see whether he was the one who'd sent the letters to Karayoryi!"

I began calculating how many points this was going to cost me, and I felt as if I were going through a whole month's salary at the Mount Parnes Casino. "I told you that Petratos's first name was Nestor, like the N who signed the letters."

"Yes, you did! But you didn't mention anything about a handwriting sample!"

"I thought I'd told you about that too, but perhaps it slipped my memory." More lost points. "However, I have it on good authority that Delopoulos intended to get rid of Petratos and put Karayoryi in his place."

"And so you automatically assume that Petratos killed her to keep his job, is that it?" he demanded sarcastically.

"I don't assume anything. But as soon as there's a motive, and a triple one at that, an emotional one, a professional one, and the letters, then I'm obliged to investigate."

"So it wasn't the formality you were trying to pass it off as," he said, and I shut up, while he carried on even more caustically: "A short while ago, Delopoulos himself called and gave me the benefit of his displeasure, for a good half hour. He had plenty to say: how disgraceful it is that we should suspect a distinguished employee of Hellas Channel; that he intends to protest in person to the minister and condemn our outrageous methods; that from the evening of the murder when he first met you, he'd seen that you had a hostile attitude toward the channel and that you weren't at all cooperative; that in addition to Petratos, you also put Kostarakou in the dock, and that the aim of all this is to make criminals of the unfortunate victims. He demanded that I take you off the case and assign it to someone else."

He said it all in one breath and was panting, like when he went jogging with the FBI. As for me, I felt my blood rising.

"All right, we'll take it easy, no problem, but there's a strong indication that he may be the killer."

"We agreed that you'd look for Kolakoglou. Have you found him?"

"Not yet, he's vanished."

"That's what Delopoulos told me. He said that because you're unable to catch the real culprit, you're simply stirring things up to show that you're doing something."

"We've only been looking for him for twenty-four hours. How are we supposed to find him in a day? He'd have to be sitting drinking coffee in Kolonaki Square!"

He did not hurry to reply. He looked at me and said very slowly so that it would sink in: "You will go now and find Delopoulos. He's expecting you. He wants you to explain everything to him in person. Otherwise, he says, he'll speak to the minister. You understand what that means. I can only cover for you up to a point. Watch how you tread with him. And see that you get Kolakoglou behind bars. Then we might get some peace."

As soon as he'd finished, he picked up a document from his desk and pretended to study it. In other words: Get things sorted out and see that I am left in peace, because I've got more serious matters to deal with.

Throughout the journey to the Hellas Channel studios, I tried to calm down and decide how I would confront Delopoulos. The difference between Ghikas and me was that I knew him, I'd come face-to-face with him, whereas Ghikas had only spoken to him on the phone and had no idea who he was dealing with. Delopoulos was play-acting in order to blackmail me. At first he'd pretended to be friendly to win me over, but then he'd seen that I was investigating his own people, Kostarakou and Petratos, and he'd got cross. Besides, he was no fool. He knew that if Kolakoglou turned out not to be the murderer, then he'd be up the creek, because that would vindicate Sotiropoulos and Horizon, who were trying to make him out to be the victim in the piece. So he'd decided to lean on me, the last spoke in the wheel, the most vulnerable of all. If he did have clout with the minister, then Ghikas would make sure he saved his own ass and he'd leave me up the creek. Without doubt I had to swallow my pride. But I've never known how much to swallow—I might end up choking.

As soon as I gave my name to his secretary, she sprang up, opened the door, and bustled me into Delopoulos's spacious office. Petratos was with him. He was sitting in one of the two armchairs stuck in front of Delopoulos's desk and looked at me as might a spider at a fly caught in its web.

"Sit down," said Delopoulos coldly, and he pointed to the other armchair. Before my ass had even touched the leather, he launched into me.

"I'm delighted that you've seen fit to do us the honor of coming in

person instead of sending your subordinate again." From behind his
desk, he looked imposing, but his expression did not bother to be severe. It reminded me of Kostaras's ironic, scournful expression before the questioning began.

"I'm afraid that what was nothing more than a routine verifica-
tion has been blown up into something bigger than it was, Mr. Delopoulos. Perhaps Sergeant Sotiris is to blame for that. Plainly we are
obliged to check on the movements of anyone connected with the
victim. You will understand, I'm sure, that I too have people over my
head to whom I have to report. I don't want them telling me tomorrow that I haven't done my job properly."

"Superintendent Ghikas assured me that he had not instructed
you to investigate Mr. Petratos. You did it on your own initiative."

"Superintendent Ghikas is chief of security and has hundreds of
important matters to deal with every day. Heaven help him if we
were to inform him of every routine investigation. He'd never be
done. But if, tomorrow, there's some oversight in the process, you
can be sure that he'll require me to answer for it."

I was cowering and playing the luckless cop, instrument of the
law, doing everything according to the book, living in fear of his superiors. Apparently I didn't convince them because Petratos launched
into me next.

"I don't believe a word you're saying, Inspector Haritos. You're the
one who told me on the evening that you came to my office that you
considered me a suspect. You even asked me for a sample of my
handwriting."

"I never said that I saw you as a suspect. It's just that because you
insisted that the only suspect is Kolakoglou, I wanted to show you
that, theoretically, there are other suspects too, yourself included.
You had an affair with Karayoryi and she dumped you as soon as she
had secured a free hand for herself from Mr. Delopoulos. I only offered this as an example of a possible motive. You obviously took it
to heart."

He was pretty much bowled over and didn't know how to re-
spond. Delopoulos shot him an angry look, before turning to me.

"Who told you all that nonsense?" he said in a pompous tone. "Mr. Petratos had no problem at all with Karayoryi's free hand. In fact, he was the one who suggested to me that we give her all the freedom she wanted since she got better results that way."

He didn't appreciate that what he was saying put Petratos in an even worse position. Because if that were the case, it meant that Petratos had secured complete independence for her and she, as a token of her gratitude, had left him.

"Please understand, Mr. Delopoulos, Superintendent Ghikas advised me to tell you everything, to keep nothing back." This seemed to please him. He leaned back in his chair, knitted his fingers, and waited for my full capitulation. "Our work obliges us to investigate every piece of information, every piece of hearsay, no matter how implausible it may seem. Well, there are certain rumors circulating among the reporters that you intended to get rid of Mr. Petratos and to give his job to Karayoryi."

Petratos jumped to his feet. He was shaking from head to toe with anger and indignation. And Delopoulos looked furious too. He forgot his easygoing attitude, banged his hand on his desk, and shouted: "I categorically deny it. I have total confidence in Mr. Petratos and I can assure you that his position was never in any jeopardy on Karayoryi's account."

"All this is a cheap diversion," Petratos fumed, still shaking. "You're unable to find Kolakoglou, who's the murderer, and you're trying to throw dust in our eyes."

"What have you done about Kolakoglou?" Delopoulos wanted to know, looking as if he would gladly throw me out with the trash.

"Nothing yet."

"Ha!" cried Petratos, triumphantly.

"All we have up to now is some information from a clerk in the ticket office at the bus station in Kifisos. He remembers him buying a ticket to Thessaloniki."

"And why didn't you tell us that before? From our first meeting I told you that I want you to give us priority with regard to any information you might obtain. Mr. Petratos told you the same thing. Yet you continue to keep us in the dark, in a matter that is of intimate concern to our channel."

"I didn't want the information to leak out and for Kolakoglou to hear of it. When you're hunting for someone, you don't say where you've seen him, or you'll help him get away. At any rate, that, I can assure you, is the only information we have."

"I tend to believe that Mr. Petratos was right," Delopoulos said. "You are incompetent, and I'm seriously thinking of asking the minister to have you replaced. It will depend on whether you—"

Before I had time to learn what would depend on me, the telephone rang. He lifted the receiver, answered with a sharp "Yes," and handed the receiver to me.

"It's for you."

"Hello." I only use "Haritos" at the station. At the other end of the line, I heard Sotiris's worried voice.

"Martha Kostarakou has been found dead in her home, Inspector."

It took a few moments for the news to work its way around my circuit and for me to reassemble my thoughts. "When did you learn this?"

"A very short while ago. An anonymous telephone call. I've sent a patrol car. I'm on my way there now, but I thought that perhaps you'd want to come too. The address is Twenty-one Ieronos Street, Pangrati."

"Okay. I'm on my way."

Delopoulos, who was waiting for me to hang up, went on regardless. "I was saying, then, that it will depend on whether you—"

But he paused, like Rommel in the desert, and he lost the advantage. "I have some exclusive information to give you, Mr. Delopoulos. A short while ago, Martha Kostarakou was found dead in her home."

I saw them freeze on the spot, speechless, and suddenly Mrs. Kolakoglou's words came to mind: "I won't say I'm glad she was killed, but there's such a thing as divine retribution."

CHAPTER 21

"Can you tell me what time it happened?"

Markidis slowly got up from the corpse. He didn't reply straight-away. He looked at his watch and did his calculations.

"It's twelve now. I'd say about seventeen hours have passed, so that means she was killed between six and eight yesterday evening."

Great. While I was listening to Thanassis giving me the report on Kolakoglou, someone was murdering Martha Kostarakou ten blocks up from my house.

She was lying facedown in front of me, next to the sofa. One arm was under her body, while the other, the left one, was stretched out at her side. As though she'd tripped after getting blind drunk and had fallen flat on the floor. She was wearing jeans, a pullover, and those Dutch clogs.

"She was strangled, right?"

"Yes. With wire or wire cord."

He bent down and pulled her hair back. Her head was resting to one side and was facing her arm. A scar, rather like a gash, ran along the left side of her neck. The trickle of blood to either side of it had dried.

"That wound was made by wire," Markidis said. "Rope and cord don't leave scars like that. He strangled her while she was on her feet and let her fall to the floor when she was dead."

"Was he strong?"

"Yes, just like with the other woman. We're probably talking about the same person."

I knew what this meant and I didn't like it at all. If he'd strangled her with her own scarf or with a cord, then it would have been the same as in the case of Karayoryi. It would mean that he hadn't come with the intention of killing her but had decided on the spot, taking hold of whatever he could find to do the job. But in this case, the murderer had come prepared. And if he was the same person, as Markidis supposed, then he'd progressed from a murder committed on impulse to a premeditated one. In other words, from bad to worse.

Besides, the flat spoke for itself. Someone had ransacked it. Drawers hung open, papers were strewn all over the floor. The books from the fitted bookcase were scattered to the four corners of the room. He'd been frantically looking for something that Kostarakou had— that's why he'd killed her, I thought to myself. The officers who'd arrived in the patrol car had found the front door to the flat half open, but the lock hadn't been broken. Kostarakou must have let him in. Just as Karayoryi had been sitting with him before he killed her. Markidis's theory seemed to be right. It was the same murderer and he was known to both of them. So, it must have been someone from their circle. Petratos again came to mind. Maybe his affair with Karayoryi had been even more complicated. Maybe Karayoryi had found out something about him, from when they were together, and was blackmailing him. But why would Petratos suppose that Karayoryi had told his secret to Kostarakou? He knew that they couldn't stand each other. One thing for sure was that Kostarakou had known far more than she'd told me. I'd told her the night I was coming out of Petratos's office that she'd land herself in trouble, but she hadn't listened.

The letter I'd found in Karayoryi's desk now acquired even greater importance. If the one who had threatened her in writing was Nestor Petratos, then it was all as clear as daylight. He'd learned from Kostarakou about the telephone call she'd received from Karayoryi, but he hadn't believed her. He was sure that he'd find in Kostarakou's place what he was looking for and killed her in order to get it. That was why the door hadn't been forced. Kostarakou wouldn't have thought twice about opening the door to Petratos. But if N was not Petratos, we were in a real mess, because it meant that there had to be a third suspect.

Sotiris came out of the bedroom and interrupted my thoughts. "It's just as bad in there," he said.

"Have you found anything?"

"Like what? It's not like we know what we're looking for."

"The anonymous telephone call. Was it from a man or a woman?"

"From a woman, but she didn't call us. She called the Emergency Unit."

"He must have been in a hurry. Otherwise he'd have seen that he hadn't closed the front door properly."

"Can we exclude the possibility that the woman who found her had a key? She entered the flat, saw the body in front of her, and in her confusion ran out and left the door open."

"We can't exclude it, no, but it's unlikely. If it was someone who had a key, a cleaner for example, she'd have started screaming and alerted the neighbors. The woman who found her couldn't have known Kostarakou. The door was open, she came in, saw her dead, and left quietly. Then she called to inform us, or the Emergency Unit, without giving her name so as to avoid getting involved."

Sotiris looked at me pensively. "Who could that have been?" he said, at a loss because no one came to mind.

"It was probably one of those women who carry out research or advertising campaigns. She'd have taken to her heels, afraid she might lose a day's work. Have you found any wire or wire cord?"

"No."

"That's what he used to strangle her with. Have you talked to the neighbors?"

"Yes. The ones above and below were at home yesterday evening, but they heard nothing."

For them not to have heard any disturbance meant that Kostarakou didn't put up a struggle. He'd killed her just like Karayoryi, suddenly, when she wasn't expecting it. Both of them had known him and hadn't suspected him. That's how he'd been able to take them unawares. He did what he'd come to do, put the wire back in his pocket, and left as quietly as he'd come.

"Did they see any stranger coming or going between six and eight, when the murder took place?"

"I asked, but they saw no one. There's no super in the building. The woman in the shop opposite says that it's a big block and there are always lots of people coming and going. She didn't see anyone who looked odd to her."

"Why should the murderer look odd to her, Sotiris? He wouldn't have a sign on his forehead, would he?"

I was in a vile temper and I took it out on him, though he was in no way to blame. He understood and remained calm.

"I'm gonna go see Ghikas," I said and patted him on the back. "He'll be waiting for a report. If you find out anything new, call me at the station."

Koula had been waiting for me. As soon as she saw me come in, she jumped to her feet.

"God, what's happened now?" she said, trying to pass her curiosity off as concern. "Are all your people suffering from a death epidemic?"

"My people? Since when do I work for the TV channels?"

"That's not what I meant," she replied, giving me one of those playful smiles that she used to bring Ghikas to his knees. "It's just that with all the dealings you have with them, you've become rather hand in glove. They're downstairs now, waiting for you." She nodded in the direction of Ghikas's office. "He didn't want to see them and sent them to you."

The good guy and the bad guy. He was the good guy who gave them the good news and feathered his own nest. I was the bad guy who was left to sort out the mess.

"Can I go in?" I asked Koula.

"Do you have to ask? He's like a cat on hot bricks."

Apparently Koula meant what she said because I found Ghikas standing behind his desk. He indicated that I should sit down in a chair while he sat on the edge of his own.

"Well?" he said impatiently.

I gave him all the information, piece by piece, along with Markidis's view that we were dealing with the same murderer. He looked at me thoughtfully.

"Do you think it's the same person?" He said eventually.

"All the evidence points to that."

He let out a huge sigh as if he'd missed winning the lottery by just one number. "Then the likelihood of Kolakoglou being the culprit becomes more remote. Even if he made good on his threat and killed Karayoryi, he had no motive whatsoever for killing Kostarakou."

With difficulty I refrained from saying, "I told you so," but he took the sting out of my tail.

"And for the same reason, Petratos couldn't have killed them either," he added, without concealing his satisfaction at having proven me wrong. "You got me into hot water with Delopoulos for no reason. Let's suppose that he killed Karayoryi because she left him and was a threat to his job. It's a bit far-fetched, but let's suppose it's true. Why, then, did he kill Kostarakou?"

"He'd have a reason if she was blackmailing him."

"Blackmailing him? Kostarakou?" It seemed incredible to him.

"Let's say she had some evidence to prove that Petratos had murdered Karayoryi. She said nothing about it to me when I questioned her, but she went to Petratos and blackmailed him. She saw it as an opportunity to get something out of it for herself. Let's not forget that he'd brushed her aside to promote Karayoryi. Petratos told her that he'd come to her flat so they could discuss it. He went armed with the wire and strangled her. Then he turned her home inside out, searching for the incriminating evidence. Karayoryi sat down and talked to the killer. Wouldn't she have talked to Petratos? Kostarakou opened the door to him. She wouldn't have opened it to Kolakoglou, most likely, but to Petratos, why not? And both victims were killed instantly, unsuspecting. Would it have crossed their minds that they were in danger from Petratos? The profile fits perfectly."

I'd kept the "profile" for the end. It was the icing on the cake. He listened pensively and silently.

"All that might work as a hypothesis," he said cautiously, "on condition that Petratos is without an alibi. If, for example, he was in the studio at the time of the second murder, then your entire theory falls to pieces."

"He goes to the studio at seven-thirty, an hour and a half before the main news bulletin. I verified it before coming to see you. Markidis says that the murder happened between six and eight. If he killed her around six, he'd have an hour and a half to get from Ieronos Street to Spata. In his haste, he left the front door open. My mistake was that I didn't investigate him more thoroughly from the beginning."

It was as if I were saying to him: "My mistake was that I let myself be talked out of it by you, you and Delopoulos, and that I didn't do what I knew was right." He swallowed the bitter pill just as I used to swallow the cod-liver oil my mother used to give me to make me strong.

"In other words, we've found the murderer? So we can give up on Kolakoglou?"

He was fishing for any other little morsel. Keep hold of yourself, Haritos, don't let this one run away with itself, I thought to myself. Blow hot and cold.

"No, it's still a hypothesis. We're still looking for Kolakoglou."

"If we had a sample of Petratos's handwriting, that would shed some useful light," he said with some reluctance.

I'd willingly have got my own back, but the more I thought of it, the more my satisfaction abated. "To some extent."

"Why only to some extent?"

"Let's suppose that it was Petratos who wrote the letters. That doesn't prove that he killed her. And vice versa. Karayoryi had her finger in a number of pies. Maybe someone else had threatened her, and that doesn't leave Petratos in the clear. There's a pile of other incriminating evidence. Let me first find out where Petratos was yesterday evening between six and eight. We can take it from there."

"If we suppose that Kostarakou was killed by the other person, the one she was blackmailing, how did he know that what he was look-ing for was at Kostarakou's?"

"From the news. They made Karayoryi's phone call to Kostarakou public knowledge."

All he could find to say to me before I left was to keep him in-formed. For no other reason than to cling to a little honor.

As soon as they saw me coming along the hall, they ran up to me, as if I were returning from some long journey. I looked around, trying to pick out some unknown face among them, the new reporter for Hel-las Channel, but all the faces were familiar and I was left wondering.

"I appreciate your concern and I know what you're feeling at this moment," I said in a mournful tone. "This makes two of your col-leagues murdered in the space of a few days. But for the time being, all I can tell you about is the actual murder."

And I began to let them have it, holding nothing back. They pushed their microphones at me and listened in silence. I finished, and they still kept silent. The shock prevented them from pressuring me to give them something more as they normally did. Only that tiny woman, the one with the red stockings, asked me eventually: "Do you believe the murderer to be the same person, Inspector?"

"The first indications suggest to us that we are dealing with the same person."

Another one plucked up courage and asked: "Do you still believe the murderer to be Kolakoglou?"

"At this moment in time, we are investigating every possibility. We cannot exclude anything."

So saying, I took a step forward to break through the wall they'd formed around me. They silently stepped back and let me pass. Thanassis, who'd been listening to my statement from the door of the office, followed behind me.

"What are we going to do about Kolakoglou?" he said. "Shall we continue the search?"

Logic dictated that I call off the hunt and leave him in peace. Even Ghikas would have no objections now. On the other hand, though, the hunt for Kolakoglou did, as they said, throw dust in the eyes of Delopoulos and Petratos, and it left me with a free hand.

"Continue with it until I give the word to stop," I said to Thanassis.

"But do you seriously believe that Kolakoglou killed both Karayoryi and Kostarakou?"

I heard Sotiropoulos's voice behind me and turned. He'd entered unheard. He leaned against the wall, next to the door, and gave me an ironic look.

"Carry on, I'll see you later," I said to Thanassis.

Sotiropoulos watched Thanassis leave, then sat, uninvited, in the chair facing me.

"Petratos died along with Kostarakou," he said, not disguising his pleasure.

"How so?"

"Don't you see. He built Kolakoglou up to be the murderer, and now he'll have to admit that he was wrong. He's embarrassed the channel, and Delopoulos won't forgive him for it." He gazed at me. Behind the round glasses, his two beady eyes were full of glee. "Did you see my report yesterday?" he said.

"Yes."

"Tonight, I'm going to take it a bit further. Who benefited from Kolakoglou's conviction. And who are the ones still using him as a scapegoat? As of tomorrow, Petratos will be yesterday's news."

"Why do you dislike him so much?"

He was surprised by my question. Then he grew serious and seemed to hesitate.

"I have my reasons, but they're personal," he said eventually. "But one thing I will tell you. Petratos got to where he is by treading on others. I'll be only too pleased if he comes toppling down."

"You'd be even more pleased if he was the murderer."

He stared at me, trying to guess where I was going. "Why?" he said. "Do you suspect him?"

"Hate always gives rise to suspicions. In every direction."

He burst out laughing. "Do you suspect me too?"

I didn't reply. I left it in the air, to make him come out with more. "I admit that I'd enjoy seeing him in handcuffs, and I'd enjoy sticking the microphone in his face so he could tell me why he killed them. But that's just a pipe dream. Petratos didn't kill them. You have to look elsewhere."

"You're keeping something from me."

"No, on my word. But instinct tells me that something else is behind the two murders, something that we can't imagine." He got up and went toward the door. "You'll see that I'm right. My instinct never fails me," he said as he went out.

I turned my gaze to the window and tried to guess what he meant. Was he keeping something from me? Very probably.

On the old woman's balcony, the cat had squeezed between two plant pots and was looking at the passersby on the street, with its face pressed against the railings. It was already December, and if you excluded two days of bitter cold, outside it was like an oven. The weather was all over the place.

CHAPTER 22

Petratos lived on Assimakopoulou Street, next to the Aghia Paraskevi Youth Center. It was one of those new apartment buildings built
for PR people, business executives, and academics living off EU-
funded programs. There was no place to park in front of the entrance, as was usually the case, but instead a garden with a lawn and
flowers. There was a separate underground garage. The doorbells
were connected to a closed-circuit TV, so that they could refuse to let
you in if they didn't like the look of you.

I picked a name at random and was about to ring when I saw a
woman coming out of the elevator. As she opened the door, I darted
inside. Petratos lived on the second floor. Each floor had three flats:
two side by side and the other one on its own, across from the other
two. I began with the one nearest to the elevator.

"Yes?" said the Filipino girl who opened the door.

The times were long past when well-to-do families brought girls
from the villages to do all the chores and, in addition, give their darling son his first lessons in screwing. Today, you ring the bell, some
Filipino girl opens the door, her English is broken, yours is irrepara-
ble, and you're supposed to communicate.

As soon as I said the word "police," she began trembling. Presumably, she was working illegally. "No problem, no here for you," I said
to her, and my fluent English immediately put her at ease. I asked her
whether she knew Petratos, whether she'd seen him the previous
evening either coming or going and at what time. The answer to my
first question was yes, to the other two no, and after the second no,
she shut the door in my face.

I rang the bell of the flat that was next to Petratos's and this time fortune smiled on me. A sixty-year-old woman, and one of our people, opened the door. I explained who I was, showed her my badge, and she ushered me in. When I asked her about Petratos, she went into raptures.

"But of course I know Mr. Petratos! A wonderful man!"

"Do you happen to know what time he usually leaves his house in the evenings?"

"Why?" she said, suddenly suspicious.

I leaned over toward her as if about to divulge a Masonic secret. "You'll have heard of the murder of the two reporters at Hellas Channel, where Mr. Petratos works."

"I heard it on the news. Young women. Tragic!"

"We're trying to make sure there won't be any more victims, so we're watching the homes of all the reporters who work at Hellas Channel. That's why we want to know when they're at home, especially in the evening and at night. Yesterday evening, for example, did you happen to see him coming or leaving?"

"Why don't you ask him?"

"Reporters are strange people. They don't want the police under their feet. In any case, we're trying to be discreet, not to alarm anyone."

My reply apparently convinced her because she gave it some thought. "What can I tell you?" she said eventually. "In the morning he leaves around eleven. I know because I'm often coming back from doing my shopping at that time and we bump into each other on the landing. I rarely see him in the evening."

"When you do see him, what time is it?"

"Between six-thirty and seven. But yesterday I didn't see him at all."

I was about to go when she suddenly remembered something that I would rather she had forgotten. "The day before yesterday, there was another one of your men here asking questions," she said.

Sotiris's inquiries that had made Delopoulos and Petratos furious. "Yes, it was following the first murder. We'd suggested even then to Mr. Petratos and to the others to let us have their houses watched, but they'd refused. The result was that we had the second murder. That's why we decided to watch them discreetly, without them knowing, till we've found the murderer. You realize, I'm sure, that if there's a third victim, we'll have everyone down on our heads."

"Ah, what a line of work to be in!" she said with understanding.

I took my leave of her, but went away with empty hands. The same was true of the other flats. Most people didn't even ask me in but kept me standing at the door. And their answers were all alike: "I don't know," "I rarely see him," "Ask him yourself."

The higher I went in the building, the more my hopes fell, but I'd started to get the bit between my teeth. On the one hand, there was Kostarakou's murder and, on the other, my set-to with the gang of three—Ghikas, Delopoulos, and Petratos—not to mention Sotiropoulos, who kept sticking his nose in. All this had dented my pride. I wanted to get some evidence so I could bring Petratos in for questioning and begin to put the screws to him.

I had reached the fourth floor and was talking to a tall, lanky woman with strikingly thin lips. She told me that she minded her own business and wasn't in the slightest bit interested in what her neighbors did. This sermon was interrupted by a tall, gangly kid with shaved head and earring, who pushed past her to get out.

He'd obviously heard us talking, because he turned and said to me: "For what it's worth, his car wasn't in its parking place yesterday around six when I was putting mine in the parking lot."

"What business is that of yours?" said the woman crossly.

"What does it matter, Mum? The man asked a question, I knew the answer, and I told him. When I don't know the answers at school, you go crazy. Now, when I do know them, you still go crazy."

The woman went inside, slamming the door behind her. Her rudeness didn't bother me at all. In fact, she was doing me a favor, as I wanted to get her son on his own.

"Are you sure his car was gone?" I said.

"Look, he's the only one in the building with a black Renegade. It's a really cool set of wheels and whenever I see it, I can't take my eyes off it. I've tried to persuade the old man to get me one, but he won't hear of it. 'What's wrong with the Starlet? It's a great little car,' he always says. Anyway, yesterday when I parked the Starlet, the Renegade wasn't there."

"Let's go down to the garage so you can show me where he parks it." I wanted to take a look myself.

"Sure, come on," he said.

It was a spacious garage, easily big enough for twenty cars. Most of the parking spots were empty. Only five of them were occupied, one by the black Renegade. The car to the right of it was covered over; the space on the left side was empty.

"There it is!" the kid shouted in admiration. "Cool, eh?"

I looked at my watch. It was already four. It seems he came back late in the afternoon, took a rest, and returned to the studio around seven-thirty. It wasn't at all improbable that the woman in the flat next to Petratos's had rung his bell and told him absolutely everything I'd said. I couldn't care less. Let him phone Delopoulos and tell him that I was still harassing him. I walked around the Renegade, but saw nothing from the outside that looked unusual. I went closer and looked through the window. There were some videocassettes on the passenger seat. The backseat was strewn with newspapers and magazines. That was all. The kid walked over to the Starlet.

"Are you staying here?" he called.

"No, I'm coming."

"As I turned to walk to the exit, something under the covered car caught my eye. I bent down and saw a length of wire, carelessly wound up.

"Just come here a second!" I called to the young man.

He turned and looked askance at me. "My mum was right, I should have kept my mouth shut," he said, irritated.

"Come here, I said!" My tone brooked no objection, and he came over.

"What's that there, under the car?"

Curious, he bent down and took hold of the wire. "A piece of wire," he said, not giving a damn. He had no idea that this wire might possibly lead him to court as a prosecution witness to testify that he had found it next to Petratos's car.

"How long has it been there?"

"How should I know?" That's Kalafatis's car. He died three months ago. It's just been standing there ever since. Why, is it important?"

"Important. Of course it's important. Don't you know that wire can puncture the tires? And you want a Renegade." I took the wire from him. He shot me a venomous look and went to his Starlet. He started it up, opened the garage door using a magnetic card, and sped off. I followed him out, while the door slowly closed behind me.

I sat in my Mirafiori and looked at the wire, which I'd put on the seat beside me. It seems I'd underestimated Petratos. The second murder may have been premeditated, but the murder weapon had again been something at hand, something chosen at random, as was the case with Karayoryi's murder. He'd seen the wire as he was getting into his car; he'd cut off a piece and later used it to strangle Kostarakou before pocketing it and leaving. If it had been a knife or a gun, we would have been able to prove that it was his or find out where he'd got it from. But the wire? You could find it in any hardware store, in homes, all over the place. How could anyone prove that the murder had been committed with that particular piece of wire, tossed down next to his car? Any two-bit lawyer would be able to get the evidence thrown out immediately. Perhaps that was why he hadn't bothered to get rid of the rest of the wire. It had been lying there for three months under the dead man's car. "If I'd killed her, would I have left the wire lying there? Wouldn't I have gotten rid of it?" Most certainly, the judge would agree, you don't find murderers as stupid as that, not even made to order.

It took me around a quarter of an hour to get from Aghia Paraskevi to Hellas Channel in Spata. There was only Sperantzas in the newsroom. He was preparing the six o'clock news bulletin. He'd lost his resentful expression and stared at me with a nervous, frightened look.

"Who's going to be next?" he said. "Are we all going to get caught up in this?"

I made no effort to reassure him. Having him frightened suited me. "Did no one wonder where Kostarakou was when she didn't turn up at the studio yesterday evening?"

"Why should she turn up here? She came, handed over her report, already edited, and left at around five. She'd have come back only if something special had come up for the nine o'clock news. We don't clock in here."

"So not even Petratos is here all the time?"

"Not even him. He leaves around four and comes back between seven and seven-thirty."

"What time did he get back yesterday?" He looked at me inquisitively. "Don't go getting any ideas," I told him. "I'm just trying to form a clear picture."

"I have no idea. But he wasn't back at seven, which is when I left."

I left him to get on with his work in peace. On my way back from Spata, I dropped in at the lab and gave the wire to Dimitris. He took a look at it, and when I saw him shrug his shoulders, my fears were confirmed.

"We can examine it," he said, "but as soon as the prosecutor gets hold of it, he'll chuck it straight out. It's easy for us to prove that he strangled her with a wire *like* this one, but practically impossible for us to prove that the murder was committed with this one that you found in the garage."

"I know," I replied, disappointed all the same. "But examine it anyway."

A wind had kicked up and the air smelled like an autumn downpour. As I drove back to the office, I reflected that everything pointed to Petratos, but I had no evidence. If it had been anyone else, I would have hauled them down to the station and put the screws on until they confessed. But for Petratos, I needed Ghikas's okay. And I didn't think he'd give it to me.

CHAPTER 23

I hurried to be in time for the nine o'clock news. Kostarakou's murder was sure to be the main story, and I didn't want to miss it. I got my breath back as I walked into the living room.

Adriani was in her usual place, clutching the remote control. I walked in front of her to sit in the other armchair. She pretended not to see me. Her eyes remained fixed on the screen. I shot a quick glance at her and found it all very amusing. I knew how much it rankled her not to be able to hear the news about Kostarakou firsthand and to have to make do with the news on TV like a common mortal. She'd lost her privileged position, but she accepted it with dignity, I had to give her that. She maintained her self-respect and wasn't going to allow her curiosity to get the better of her pride.

Kostarakou's place. The living room where she'd been found murdered. All around were papers on the floor and scattered books, just as we'd found it. Only the body had been taken away. In its place was a chalk outline. The newscaster wore his classic, sorrowful expression, but for the very first time he convinced me that his regret was genuine. The words came slower and fainter out of his mouth. He held his hands out in the usual sign of despair. Even his tailored jacket seemed to be sagging at the shoulders.

"Unfortunately, at this moment in time, we have no further information, ladies and gentlemen," he said. "The police believe the two murders are connected and are continuing their investigations with all possible urgency under the direct supervision of the chief of Athens security, Superintendent Ghikas."

Because I'd come out on top in the matter of Petratos, Ghikas was elbowing me aside, to get back his own. Now he was taking charge, and I would get pushed into the wings. Not that it hurt my pride, it simply bothered me that as of the very next day, I'd have to report to him and get his permission for my every move.

I'd become absorbed in my thoughts and was no longer concentrating on the news. I came around when I suddenly saw Petratos on the screen, beside the newscaster.

"Good evening, Nestor," the newcaster said. "For the second time in just a few days, the Hellas Channel has suffered a shattering blow. First Yanna Karayoryi, and now Martha Kostarakou, too, has come to a sad end at the hands of a ruthless killer who remains at large."

"As you say, Pavlos," Petratos said, "in the space of just a few days, our channel has suffered two devastating losses."

In the past, when two people patted each other's back like that, we called it mutual adulation and asked them what club they belonged to. Now we call it journalism.

"I'd like your assessment of the way the investigation is going, Nestor," the newscaster said. "How soon can we hope for some results? I ask because, as you know, our channel is receiving thousands of telephone calls every day from viewers anxious to find out what's happening, and we owe them an answer."

"I'll tell you what I think, Pavlos." Petratos paused a theatrical moment to show that he was thinking. "There's an upside and a downside. The upside is that the chief of Athens security, Superintendent Ghikas, has decided to take charge of the investigations personally. I regret to have to say that the investigations until now had taken a completely wrong turn and valuable time has been lost. I don't know whether the ministry intends to apportion blame for this negligence, but at least we can now be hopeful that the investigations will at last move in the right direction."

Suddenly, Adriani threw down the remote control and stormed out of the room. She continued to sulk, but this was her way of showing how angry she was at what she'd just heard. I stayed where I was. I reckoned that I would be lucky if I avoided suspension.

"And what is the downside?" the newscaster said.

Petratos sighed, as if the answer he was about to give was tormenting him. "If Kolakoglou is the murderer, and this possibility is seriously being looked into by the police, then we're dealing with a psychopathic killer. It seems he didn't only hate Yanna Karayoryi. He hates all reporters because he believes they wronged him, and he is killing out of revenge. If you look at it like that, it is only natural that he should be striking back first against our channel, because it was our channel that brought him to justice. Don't forget that the resolution of the Kolakoglou case was one of Hellas Channel's outstanding journalistic success stories."

"So what you're saying is that we're all in danger?" He said it as if Kolakoglou were standing behind him, ready to cut his throat.

"That's what I said before that the police lost valuable time. They allowed Kolakoglou to circulate freely even though they knew, from the first time they arrested him, that he was a psychopath. We have to hope that from now on they will be more methodical in their work."

The newscaster thanked him and Petratos departed from the screen. You underestimated him, Sotiropoulos, I thought to myself. Both you and Karayoryi underestimated him. Not only did he not try to justify himself for getting it wrong about Kolakoglou, he even upgraded him, presenting him now as a psychopathic killer. How could you explain to the public that a psychopathic killer always kills in the same way; it's his trademark. He doesn't use first a lamp stand, then a piece of wire, and then a chainsaw. That said, Ghikas was right about one thing. We should have caught Kolakoglou and put him behind bars. We'd have found some peace. Just as I was thinking that the next day Thanassis was going to get a rough time of it, the phone rang.

"Did you hear?" Ghikas didn't even bother saying his name.

"Yes, I heard," I said, sharply.

"In half an hour, I want you in the minister's office and you'll hear the rest," he said, and hung up.

I began to understand that things were more serious than I had imagined. It seemed that, after all, Delopoulos would succeed in getting me dismissed. They'd send me to take charge of some suburban station, investigating claims of theft, dealing with calls reporting disturbances of the peace, or settling disputes in car crashes. I heard Adriani setting the table in the kitchen, and I was filled with a desire to talk to her, to tell her where I was going and what was awaiting me. But something held me back at the last moment. Perhaps it was my lousy pride. I didn't want her to think I was talking to her out of weakness, just because I was in need of a kind word and a little encouragement. But that's exactly what I wanted. I slammed the door behind me so she'd know that I'd left.

From Hymettou Avenue to Eratosthenous Street, I didn't meet with any traffic, but I got stuck on Vassileos Konstantinou Avenue. Then, on Mesogheion Avenue, the cars were bumper-to-bumper and the drivers blew off steam by making frequent use of their horns. I arrived at the Ministry of Public Order on Katechaki Avenue a quarter of an hour late.

"Inspector Haritos. To see the minister," I told the young guard on duty.

He consulted the list in front of him and with a "Go straight in, Inspector," he let me drive in.

I came out of the elevator and almost ran down the hall, as if one minute's less delay was of any importance. But I was in a hurry to get it over with.

When she heard my name, the secretary said: "Go straight in. They're waiting for you."

Compared to Delopoulos's three-room suite, the minister's office was a closet with a hall. As soon as I entered, I found the Holy Trinity there waiting for me. Minister, Ghikas, Delopoulos—Father, Son, and Holy Ghost. The minister and Delopoulos were side by side on the sofa, as if to make it clear to me that they were close friends. Ghikas was sitting in the armchair next to the minister, and all three had their eyes fixed on me.

"I'm sorry I'm late, but there was a lot of traffic."

"Sit down, Inspector." The minister pointed to the empty armchair, but his expression told me that he'd have preferred to keep me standing.

The scene spoke for itself. Delopoulos wanted my head on a plate;

the minister wanted to humor him in order to keep in with him. As
for Ghikas, he had his own ambitions and didn't want to go against
them. I didn't know how it would end, but I did know that I wasn't
going to get out of there in one piece.

"What's happening with the investigation into the murders of the
two Hellas Channel reporters, Inspector Haritos?" the minister said.
"Of late, I've heard nothing but complaints about you."

Ghikas was trying as best he could to avoid my eyes, but because
he was facing me, he didn't know where to look. In the end, he directed his gaze above and behind me, to where the wall met the ceiling. He was visibly uncomfortable. On the other hand, Delopoulos
had his gaze fixed on me and didn't hide his satisfaction. Perhaps
this collective assault was their mistake. Because when things are in
the balance, you take things gently, you make tactical withdrawals,
even bow and scrape. But when you're up against it with your back
to the wall, you jump straight in and throw caution to the wind. I
decided to come out with everything and let them suspend me if
they wanted. At least I would have the satisfaction of a heroic last
stand.

"The investigation is proceeding slowly, as usually happens in
such cases, Minister. But at least it's proceeding."

"From what I've heard, it's on the wrong track. Superintendent
Ghikas gave you a clear order to arrest Kolakoglou, which you ignored in order to concentrate on other things."

"I didn't ignore it at all. At this very moment, the entire police
force is engaged in the search for Kolakoglou. It's not easy to find
someone with prison connections who can thereby easily find a
place to hide."

"So you allow a psychopathic murderer to run loose and kill at
will," Delopoulos quipped ironically. Either he'd seen the news bulletin together with the minister, or he'd agreed with Petratos to turn
Kolakoglou into a psychopath, which was more likely.

Delopoulos turned to the minister. "You can pass as many crime-
fighting laws as you like, but if you don't have competent people in
the security force, the laws won't have any effect whatsoever."

"Not many laws are required for fighting crime, Mr. Delopoulos," I said calmly. "One would be enough."

"And what one would that be?" said the minister.

"Young people at the end of their military service should be required to spend six months in a prison for further training. Have you ever seen a soldier who's got his discharge papers wanting to return to the army? Much less would he want to return to a prison."

Ghikas turned around and looked at the conference table, which was against the facing wall. He wanted to laugh, but he restrained himself.

"I didn't ask you here to hear your views on crime," I heard the minister's icy voice say. "I want you to tell me about Kolakoglou."

"I would be astonished if Kolakoglou turned out to be a psychopathic killer, Minister." And I gave him the whole spiel about psychopaths, how they always use the same weapon, how all their killings are identical, and all the rest. "I'm sure Superintendent Ghikas must have told you all this," I added.

Ghikas knew all that, but I was certain he hadn't said anything to them, because it was in his interests to follow their tack. He realized, however, that he couldn't go on keeping to himself. "What Inspector Haritos says is fundamentally true. There are, of course, exceptions," he said, to cover himself. I wanted to tell him that the FBI saw it differently, but I let it go.

Delopoulos saw that he was losing ground and went on the attack. "Do I have your blessing to go public with all this, Minister? I'm curious to know what public opinion will make of all these theories."

It was exactly what I'd been afraid of. He'd stirred up the public against Kolakoglou, turned Kolakoglou into public enemy number one, and if he were to come out now and say that the police ruled out the possibility of his being the murderer, they'd all turn on us. The minister must have thought the same thing, because he more or less implored him: "Let's not be in too much of a hurry, Mr. Delopoulos. Leave it a few days more. I feel confident we'll find Kolakoglou and it will all be cleared up."

"So be it. I respect your wishes," Delopoulos acquiesced. "Besides,

I have every confidence in Superintendent Ghikas. And in order to show just how cooperative we are, here you are."

From his pocket he took a folded piece of paper and gave it to the minister, who took it and examined it. "What's this?" he said surprised.

"The sample of Mr. Petratos's handwriting that your subordinate had been seeking. You can compare it with the handwriting on the letters that you found in Karayoryi's house. But on one condition. That you remove your subordinate from the case, or at least stop him from harassing us. He unjustly made accusations against a distinguished newsman simply because the man once had a brief affair with Karayoryi, and he shouldn't be allowed to get away with it."

So that was the price for my head: a sample of Petratos's handwriting. Delopoulos was so sure of himself that he thought it unnecessary to even mention my name and referred to me as the "subordinate."

"That was the case this morning, Mr. Delopoulos," I said, still very calmly. "In the meantime, new evidence has come to light."

"What new evidence?" It was Ghikas who asked.

"First of all, I verified that Mr. Petratos was absent both from his house and from the studio at the time that Kostarakou was killed."

"Along with another five million Greeks, most likely," Delopoulos said sarcastically. "Can't you put a stop, for heaven's sake, to your obstinacy and your prejudices?"

"Mr. Petratos had in his possession something that the other five million didn't have. The wire that was used to strangle Martha Kostarakou."

"What was that?" The minister almost jumped out of his seat. Delopoulos stared at me blankly. He didn't know how to react.

"In the garage of his apartment building, next to the space where Mr. Petratos parks his car, I found a length of wire identical to that which was used to strangle Kostarakou. I have a witness to the finding."

"Are you positive that this is what was used to strangle Kostarakou?" Ghikas said.

"I handed it over this evening to the lab people. We'll know more as soon as we have the results of the tests. You'll have my written report on your desk tomorrow morning."

All three of them remained silent. They realized only too well the implications of what I had said. If they took me off the case and I turned out to be right, someone would come across my report and would haul them over the coals.

"Very well. You can go, Inspector," the minister said.

I said good-bye, but no one was taking any notice of me. They were all lost in thought. Ghikas had a barely perceptible smile on his face, and there was a wily glint in his eyes. He seemed to be enjoying it, though I'd got nothing out of it. He was playing his own game.

I left with the satisfaction, at least, that I'd gone against the tide. Not as a lamb to the slaughter, but as a slaughterer of lambs.

CHAPTER 24

I was holding the croissant in my left hand and writing furiously with my right. I wanted to get my report to Ghikas before being suspended or transferred. I had made up my mind not to deal with anything else, but I'd reckoned without Thanassis, who I found waiting for me, just like every morning.

"Go away, I have work to do," I told him curtly, needing to get rid of him. But he didn't budge. And not only that, he didn't have his usual moron look.

"We have a lead on Kolakoglou."

That was just great. If he'd told me this the previous day, I'd have been pleased and had a good word to say to him. But right now, having woken up resolved to get off the case, I'd convinced myself that it was no longer my concern. Let Ghikas tear his hair out since he'd taken charge of it. On the other hand, I didn't want to provoke comment and so I asked, purely as a formality: "What lead?"

"He was seen yesterday, around midnight, in a bar on Michael Voda Street, with another man. The owner recognized him and called 100, but by the time the patrol car got there, they'd gone."

"You see what I said about him still being in Athens?" When you're getting a pasting on all fronts, even the least bit of vindication is a comfort.

"The owner recognized the other man. His name is Sourpis and he's known in the street as a fence, a loan shark. The owner doesn't know where he lives, but he goes to the bar now and again to pick up a girl. As of today, I'll have one of our men waiting there. As soon as either of them shows up, he'll nab him."

"Fine. Put it all in your report."

"Report?"

He was expecting a pat on the back, but I was more concerned about my own situation. I'd send his report to Ghikas along with my own, so he'd see that I hadn't confined myself to Petratos, but that I had pressed on with the search for Kolakoglou. I wanted him to see that he'd treated me unfairly. From then on, he could do as he thought fit. Thanassis went on staring at me in surprise. He was about to say something, but thought better of it and left the office.

I bit into my croissant without much appetite, more out of habit than anything, and I kept writing. I wondered if I'd find croissants in the place they were going to send me or if I'd have to make do with a run-of-the-mill cheese pie. Most probably Adriani would have to pack me sandwiches, wrapped in tinfoil.

When I got home the previous evening, she'd pretended to be asleep. But I'd found the table set and the food simmering on the stove. It was another of her ways of showing that, even though we weren't talking, she still worried about me. I hadn't slept a wink. She'd felt me tossing and turning beside her but had said not a word. When I got up in the morning, she was asleep, perhaps because it had been late when she finally dozed off. Before I left, I had put the housekeeping money on the table together with five thousand more. An ambiguous gesture. Had I done it deliberately or because I'd miscounted the money? She could decide.

I had filled two sides of A4 paper and I was getting to the conclusions when Sotiris came in.

"Not now," I said, without lifting my head, like a student taking an exam.

"There's a girl outside who wants to see you."

"When I'm finished."

"She says she's Yanna Karayoryi's niece."

I stopped in midsentence. Anna Antonakaki was the last person I'd expected to see that morning. "Show her in," I said to Sotiris.

She was wearing black trousers tucked into cowboy boots, a gray pullover, and a black leather jacket on top. She was carrying a plastic bag. Once again, I was taken aback by her likeness to Yanna. That same haughty air. Except that she was still young and didn't have the irony in her look yet. She was simply cold and kept the world at arm's length. She stood next to the door, staring at me. I wondered if she shared her aunt's loathing for men.

"Come in, sit down."

She sat on the edge of the chair and continued to stare at me. "I don't know if what I'm doing is right," she said after a while.

She remained silent after that, as if she expected something from me. Maybe she was waiting for me to make it easy for her. But what could I say? I didn't know why she'd come, or what her intentions were, so I let her work it out for herself.

"I was thinking about it all night and didn't get any sleep."

"Since you have come here, it means that you have already decided to talk to me. So tell me why you've come and we'll see."

She reached into the plastic bag and pulled out a thick, bound file, like those we'd found in Karayoryi's apartment. She was about to hand it to me, but then she changed her mind and held on to it tightly.

"My aunt gave me this file to keep hidden from my mother. She told me that if anything happened to her, I should give it to Martha Kostarakou."

So that was the explanation for Karayoryi's mysterious telephone call to Kostarakou. She'd wanted Kostarakou to see the report with the revelation, though she died before she could broadcast it, so the other woman would know what it was all about if the file came into her hands. We'd been searching in Karayoryi's computer files, and all the while the stuff had been in the hands of her niece.

"Yesterday, when I heard that Kostarakou had—died—" The words "been murdered" had stuck in her throat. "—I didn't know what to do. I was afraid to tell my mother, because she gets terrified at the slightest thing. That's why I lay awake all night. In the end, I resolved to hand it over it to you."

This time, her mind made up, she held out the file, and I took it. I was in no hurry to open it. I wanted to go through it in my own good time. The girl considered her mission completed, and she got up to leave.

"Why didn't you give the file to Kostarakou while she was still alive?"

She was taken aback by my question. She tried to come up with an excuse. "I would have taken it to her, but various things cropped up. Also I had my classes at the university. Besides, how was I to know that they would murder her too?"

"You went to give it to her yesterday morning, but you found her dead and ran off. When you'd recovered, you went to a phone booth, called 100, and informed us without giving your name."

Some ideas come to you on the spur of the moment. You haven't given them a second's thought, they're not the result of some association, and yet you know you're right. I knew for certain that I was right when I saw the expression on Anna Antonakaki's face. She turned pale, her face lost its cold expression, and her face filled with fear. She began shouting, but her shouts had something hysterical about them, as they always do when people shout to try to come out on top.

"Are you crazy? I spent all day at the university yesterday. I heard about Kostarakou last night on the news."

"Listen, Anna," I said very gently. "It would be easy for me to verify whether or not you went to Kostarakou's house yesterday. All I have to do is comb the neighborhood, door to door, with a photograph of you in my hand, till I find someone who recognizes you."

"Do what you want," she said stubbornly. "It's my own fault for bringing you the file."

"You were right to bring it to me. Something tells me that it was because of this file that Kostarakou and your aunt were killed. You had no reason whatsoever to kill them, so you're not under suspicion. All I want to know is what time you found Kostarakou dead. It's important for our investigations."

She sat down again and stayed still. She was looking at me, but her mind was elsewhere. "I don't want to get mixed up with it. If the reporters find out, they'll start pestering my mother . . . me. . . . We won't get any peace."

"No one will find out anything. I'm not going to ask you for a statement for the time being, and it will remain between us. If—tomorrow or the day after—we need a statement from you, then you can come and make one."

She continued to look at me suspiciously, but the fact that she wouldn't have to make a statement now reassured her somewhat. When she began to talk, her voice came out like a whisper. "I'd called her the day before to arrange to go and see her."

"What time was it when you called her?"

"At nine-thirty in the morning, but she had to leave. Then it was difficult for us to find a time convenient for both of us, so we agreed that I'd stop by the next day, before I went to my classes."

"Do you remember what time it was that you got there?"

"It must have been around ten-thirty because I had a class at eleven at the General Hospital in Goudi. If I'd rung the doorbell downstairs, she wouldn't have answered and I'd have left. But I found the door to the building open and I went straight in. I went up to the third floor and rang her bell a couple of times. No one answered. I was about to leave when I noticed that although the two door flaps were touching, the door was not locked. I pushed it open and went in. I began calling her name but got no reply. I thought about leaving the file and going, because I was in a hurry to get to my lesson. But then I thought that she must be around somewhere to have left the door open, so I went into the living room to wait for her."

She stopped and began to tremble. The tears were about to come, but she managed to restrain herself. She spoke with difficulty, faltering at every word.

"Suddenly I saw her in front of me, on the floor. Her eyes were wide open, fixed on the doorway where I was standing. It was as if she were looking at me—"

She couldn't contain herself any longer. She put her hands to her face and broke into sobs. I let her cry to relieve her feelings.

"How was the room?" I asked after a while.

"A total shambles, as if there'd been an earthquake."

"Did you touch anything?"

"I couldn't have been there for more than a minute. After I'd got over the initial shock, I took off. When I got out on to the street, I remembered I had left the door open, but I didn't dare go back. In any case, it was open when I found it."

"Where did you call us from?"

"From the hospital. At first, it didn't occur to me to call you. But before I went into my class, I realized that I had to do something, so I called 100."

"All right, Anna. We're done. And don't worry, nobody's going to find out anything. You have my word."

"Thank you." She wiped away her tears and stood up. She still had the empty plastic bag in her hands and didn't know what to do with it.

"Give it to me." I took it from her and put the file back in it. Better that no one see it until I had had time to go through it.

Anna had reached the door when it opened and in walked Thanassis.

"I've brought you the report," he said.

His gaze fell upon Anna and he froze. He kept staring at her and couldn't take his eyes off her. She gave him a casual glance, said "Bye" to me, and went out.

"Karayoryi's niece," I said, once he'd closed the door, to help him recover from his shock.

"Her *niece*?"

"Yes. Her name's Anna Antonakaki and she's the daughter of Karayoryi's sister. Did you see the resemblance?"

It was as if he hadn't heard me. His eyes were still on the door. Eventually, he came over and handed me the report.

"Incredible," he mumbled.

He was still saying "incredible" as he went out of the office. The same thing had happened to me when I'd first set eyes on her.

CHAPTER 25

The file was tied with a double knot on three sides. Logic dictated that I put it to one side and get on with my report. If I sent it to Ghikas, together with Thanassis's report on Kolakoglou and Karayoryi's file, I'd show him that I hadn't been concentrating on Petratos in particular but had been carrying out three simultaneous investigations. The minister and Ghikas would have to eat their words. That's what logic dictated, but my instinct told me to let logic go to hell and to open the file.

I pulled it to me and began to unfasten the knots. On top was a Kodak envelope containing negatives. I held them to the light. They were images of people and various vehicles: buses and cabs, but I couldn't make out any details. Beneath it was a newspaper cutting with a photograph of Pylarinos. I suddenly felt proud of my instinct, which had guided me correctly once again. Christos Pylarinos was one of those businessmen who had sprung up from nowhere in the last decade. An old leftist, he had fought with Markos in the resistance and, following the defeat, had ended up in an Eastern European country. In '76, he had sent his application from Prague to be repatriated. He had turned up in Athens one fine morning and had bought a tourist agency that was on the brink of going bust. Within ten years, he'd opened branches of Prespes Travel throughout Europe, with coaches on regular routes abroad. And he hadn't stopped there. He'd set up Transpilar, an overseas freight company, with a whole fleet of refrigeration trucks. Now he'd become the leading name in tourism and in overland transport.

There were other clippings from the daily press and from financial magazines. The majority of them related to the successes of the "Pylarinos Group," as if it were a soccer team that had won the championship.

Beneath the clippings was a map of the world, taken from a school atlas. Someone, using a red felt-tip pen, had marked almost all the main cities of the Balkans and Central Europe, as well as those of America and Canada. These had been connected using different colors. For example, seven green arrows began from Amsterdam, Frankfurt, London, New York, Los Angeles, Montreal, and Toronto and ended in Athens. Three yellow arrows linked Tiranë with Prague, Sofia with Warsaw, and Bucharest with Budapest. A blue arrow linked Tiranë with Athens.

I racked my brain trying to understand why Karayoryi had marked the map. Okay, the different colors referred to different activities; that was easy. The question was why she'd been gathering all that information about Pylarinos. What was she doing? Investigating him? Or was there something else involved? I remembered what Sperantzas had told me: that Karayoryi had friends in high places. She might have been having an affair with Pylarinos, or been in business with him, or maybe she'd had something on him and was blackmailing him. If I'd had her Filofax, I might have found some clue. First of all from her telephone numbers. She must have had the telephone numbers of Pylarinos's businesses, surely. But which number? The main switchboard? Or the number of one of the executives? Or Pylarinos's personal number? From that I would have been able to draw some conclusions.

My hopes that I'd find some paper or some notes of Karayoryi's that would enlighten me had begun to fade when I found a report sheet, like those I used, folded in two. I opened it and found a handwritten list:

Arrival date	From	Type	Arrival date	From	Type
6/20/91	Tiranë	Refrigerator	6/22/91	London	Charter
8/25/91	Tiranë	Refrigerator	8/30/91	Amsterdam	Charter
10/30/91	Tiranë	Refrigerator	11/5/91	New York	Excursion
4/22/92	Tiranë	Refrigerator	4/25/92	Amsterdam	Excursion

7/18/92	Tiranë	Refrigerator	7/22/92	Los Angeles	Charter
9/25/92	Tiranë	Refrigerator	9/29/92	Montreal	Charter
11/5/92	Tiranë	Refrigerator	11/10/92	Frankfurt	Excursion
2/6/93	Tiranë	Refrigerator	2/10/93	Toronto	Excursion

It made no sense to me. The only things that matched somewhat were the dates: 6/20–6/22, 8/25–8/30/.... The longest gap between two dates in the same line was five days. But for the rest, what connection was there between Tiranë and London, Amsterdam, New York, and so on? What was going on? Surely tourists weren't coming from Tiranë by refrigerator truck and continuing on an excursion or charter to Frankfurt or London? Or perhaps we were talking about goods and not tourists? Bullshit! As if the Albanians would have that kind of network for exporting goods! And even in the unlikely case that it were true, then the list should have recorded arrivals and departures and not two arrivals at the same time. Whatever it was that the refrigerators were carrying, it was intended for those arriving from Frankfurt, London, and the other cities—at least, that's what the dates indicated. That much was clear, except that the list didn't mention what was being carried.

I turned the report sheet over and found two more lists, which confused things even more.

Departure date	From	Destination	Type
6/25/91	Tiranë	Prague	Coach
8/16/91	Sofia	Warsaw	Coach
10/30/91	Bucharest	Budapest	Coach
1/5/92	Tiranë	Prague	Coach
3/6/92	Bucharest	Budapest	Coach
6/12/92	Sofia	Warsaw	Coach
9/3/92	Tiranë	Prague	Coach
12/5/92	Tiranë	Prague	Coach

Name	Date	Destination	Means
Yannis Emiroglou	6/30/91	Prague	Coach
?????	?????	Warsaw??	?????
Alexandros Fotiou	11/5/91	Budapest	Air

Eleni Scaltsa	1/12/92	Prague	Air
Spyros Gonatas	3/15/92	Budapest	Coach
?????	?????	Warsaw??	?????
Vassiliki Petassi	9/12/92	Prague	Coach
?????	?????	Prague??	?????

The lists were undoubtedly connected, at least with regard to the dates. On 6/25/91 a coach left Tiranë for Prague and on 6/30/91 someone by the name of Yannis Emiroglou also left for Prague. On 10/30 another train left from Bucharest for Budapest and on 11/5 Alexandros Fotiou also left for Budapest by air. More enlightening, however, were the trains that left from Sofia for Warsaw on 8/16/91 and on 6/12/92, together with the one that left from Tiranë for Prague on 12/5/92. It seemed that Karayoryi hadn't been able to link these and had put question marks by them. But even so, I couldn't understand who the Greeks traveling to Prague, Warsaw, and Budapest were going to meet. And why didn't those who left Tiranë, Sofia, or Bucharest come to Athens instead of making our people travel thousands of kilometers to meet them?

It was going to take a lot of digging before I'd be able to make any sense of it. Whatever the secret behind it all was, Karayoryi had taken it with her to the grave. What *was* clear to me was that if the murders were connected with the contents of the file, then the murderer had killed Karayoryi to stop her digging and had killed Kostarakou to get the file from her. But if he'd wanted the file so badly, then why hadn't he searched Karayoryi's house too? One possibility was that he didn't have enough time. Another was that it was only later that he'd found out that the file contained incriminating evidence and decided that he had to get hold of it.

I was itching to give orders to Sotiris to begin investigating, but I restrained myself. The best thing would be if I handed the file over to Ghikas. Let him make the decision. Anyway, I ought to be pleased that things had now taken a different turn and it seemed as if I would come out of it unscathed.

I had almost got to the end when I stumbled across another file; a thin one this time and blue, like the ones lawyers use. As soon as I opened it, my hand remained in midair holding the edge of it, while, thunderstruck, I stared at its contents. In it were photocopies of police reports, some of them ours and some from other stations that had come to us. The first concerned the disappearance of two babies from a maternity clinic in 1990. A nurse had been accused at the time, but nothing had been proved against her and the case had been put on file. The second referred to the case of illegal Bulgarian immigrants, who had attempted to cross the borders in a truck going to Thessaloniki in 1991, but they'd been caught and sent back. Among them were four mothers with their babies. This point had been underlined in red, obviously by Karayoryi. There were six more reports on file, all referring to the disappearance or selling of children. The most recent of them was my own report about the Albanian couple and the five hundred thousand that had been found in their cistern. This too was underlined in red.

Now I realized why Karayoryi had persisted in asking me whether the Albanians had any children. She believed that their murder had been connected with either the selling or the abduction of children and had wanted to point me in that direction. I leaned back, closed my eyes, and tried to bring the image of her into my mind. Strange woman. She'd had Petratos as her lover and at the same time had despised him. And yet she'd trusted me, though she knew I disliked her, and Kostarakou, who had every reason to hate her.

Petratos wasn't N. I was virtually certain that his handwriting wouldn't match. The unknown N was the one who had asked her for the file and who was threatening her. And it was certain that this was Karayoryi's bombshell. But who had given her the information from our own files? Whose palm had she been greasing? I knew only too well what the consequences of that discovery would be, and I didn't want be burdened with any more responsibilities. My points total was already like my bank account, in the red. I picked up the phone and asked Koula to put me through to Ghikas.

He answered with a sharp yes.

"I need to see you right away."

"I'm busy. If it's about your report, send it to me."

"It's not about the report. It's something much more serious."

"In connection with the case?"

"Yes, but it also has a connection with us. Someone was feeding Karayoryi information from our files."

Silence for a moment, then "Come up," and the line went dead.

I collected Karayoryi's file, put it back into Antonakaki's plastic bag, and made for the elevator.

CHAPTER 26

The files lay open before him. To his right was the large file with the photographs and Karayoryi's lists; to his left was the blue file with the photocopies of our reports. Ghikas's attention was focused on the first. I was standing watching him. I'd put the Kodak envelope underneath so he'd look at the newspaper clippings first.

"Pylarinos!" he shouted, and pulled his hand away as if he'd burnt it.

"There's more."

He glared at me, not having decided yet whether he should be surprised or afraid. He took in the thickness of the file and decided to be afraid. He took a deep breath and began thumbing through it. He saw the rest of the clippings, the map, and Karayoryi's lists. He looked desperate.

"What do you intend to do with all this?" he asked me. "As if Petratos wasn't enough, now we've got Pylarinos to deal with. It appears his hands are dirty, but that doesn't necessarily mean that he killed the two women or that he had someone do it for him. The two things may be quite unconnected. So what do you intend to do?"

I knew what I was going to do, but I was keeping it to myself. "Whatever you tell me. You're in charge of the investigation."

He looked at me. "Sit down," he said.

He'd only just spotted that I was being cold and formal with him. He leaned forward and put on a friendly expression, even intimate, as if we were old childhood buddies.

"Listen, Costas, you're a good officer. You've got brains and you're eager. But you have one fault. You're unbending. You don't know how to be flexible. You jump in headfirst, come up against a wall, and bang your head on it. When you're dealing with people like Delopoulos or Pylarinos, you have to be as slippery as an eel, or they'll wrap you up in a sheet of paper and throw you in the wastepaper basket."

I kept quiet because I knew he was right. I *was* unbending, and whenever I got something into my head, I was unable to let it go, no matter where it led me.

"I said that I was personally taking charge of the investigation to take the pressure off you and to protect you. Last night, after Delopoulos left, I told the minister that you were the only one who could solve the case. You just have to be a bit more discreet and keep me posted so that I can watch your back."

Was he telling me all this because he believed it or because he wanted to demonstrate to me how to be as slippery as an eel? After having me up for suspension, now he was playing my guardian angel. As soon as he realized he was going to get involved with Pylarinos, he'd turned tail and was trying to get himself out of it.

"So, tell me then, what do you intend to do?"

"I'll send a written request to customs to find out what the refrigerator trucks that Karayoryi refers to were carrying. I'll ask at the airport to find out if there are passenger lists for the groups and the charter flights."

"And if there aren't?"

"I won't do anything for the time being. I don't want to have to ask for them from Pylarinos's company because it'll create suspicion, and we don't want that. I'll send the film to be developed so that we can see what's on it. And I'll question the Greeks who went to Prague, Warsaw, and Budapest. I want to know why they went."

"But how are we going to get close to Pylarinos without stirring up a hornets' nest?"

"I know someone who can give us information. He's not one of us. He's a personal friend of mine and I can't reveal who he is. But he's a reliable source."

He looked at me and smiled. "Okay. What's going to happen with Petratos?"

"I will wait for the report on the handwriting and the lab report on the wire. But, just between us, I'm not too optimistic. The wire's the common variety—you can find it at any hardware shop. As for the letters, I no longer believe that they were written by Petratos. No, they were written by whoever wanted the file from Karayoryi. It's not out of the question that the two cases are unconnected, as you said, and that Petratos is the murderer. But it requires further investigation." I remained silent and looked at him. "There's something else. Good news."

I told him about Kolakoglou. He listened to me and his face lit up. "Why didn't you tell me before?" he said enthusiastically.

He grabbed the telephone and told Koula to get Delopoulos on the line. I gazed at him, amazed. He noticed and smiled.

"You're wondering what I'm doing, right?" he said. "Now you'll see what it means to be flexible."

When Delopoulos came on the line, he told him everything, apart from the name and address of the bar. He put the phone down, obviously pleased with himself. "Delopoulos is over the moon. From now on, he'll call me. He'll leave you alone to get on with your work. And something else. I want those two reports, yours and the other one on Kolakoglou, to send to the minister. You have to know how to keep mouths shut."

His gaze turned to the other file, the blue one. He opened it and skimmed through it quickly. Slowly he raised his head. "You understand that I'm obliged to order an immediate internal inquiry," he said.

"I understand, but I would prefer you to delay it."

"Why?"

"First of all, Karayoryi's dead and she's not going to steal any more reports from us. But whoever was providing her with them may have some deeper involvement. Now he's not worried, because he thinks that no one's on to him. If you order an internal inquiry, you'll alert him. Let's proceed with the investigation and see what other evidence comes up."

"All right," he said after reflecting for a moment. "I'll inform the minister orally and tell him that I'll delay it." He collected the file and handed it to me. "Lock it in your drawer. It would be better if no one else knew of its existence."

I was so eager to get going that I didn't have the patience to wait for the elevator. I went down the stairs two at a time. When I turned into the hall, I saw the familiar throng at my door.

"To Superintendent Ghikas for any statements. As you know, he's taken charge of the case."

They knew and didn't press me. They began moving toward the elevator. Sotiropoulos pretended to follow them but stayed behind.

"Can we have a word?"

"They have me gagged. Don't put me in a difficult position."

He smiled, he quite understood, and he gave me a friendly pat on the back. "A passing storm," he said in a soothing tone.

I took a sheet of paper and copied first the arrivals of the refrigerator trucks and then the arrivals of the groups and the charters. On another sheet, I copied the five names from Karayoryi's second list. I summoned Sotiris in.

"Ask customs what these refrigerator trucks were carrying. They most likely belong to Transpilar, Pylarinos's company. And ask at the airport if they have the passenger lists for these groups and charters. They were probably met by some tourist agency also owned by Pylarinos. And I want you to question these five in person. I want to know why they were traveling."

He took the two pieces of paper, but he didn't leave. Pylarinos's name had aroused his curiosity and he wanted to know more.

"Stop dawdling. I'll tell you eventually. And send Thanassis in."

While waiting for Thanassis, I started to put the finishing touches to my report, but I didn't have time. In less than a minute, he was in my office.

"They called from the lab," he said. "The wire is the same as that used to kill Kostarakou, but they can't say whether or not it's the wire actually used in the murder. If we'd found the wire used by the murderer, they might have been able to tell whether it had been cut from the same piece. At any rate, they're certain that the wire wasn't cut using scissors or pliers, but broken by hand."

That was something. If Petratos had seen the wire by chance and the idea had suddenly come to him to use it, he would have cut it by hand in his rush. Of course, anyone wanting a piece of wire who couldn't be bothered to go and get a pair of pliers would have done the same.

"Petratos drives a black Renegade. I want you to comb the area where Kostarakou lived and find out if anyone saw it around the time of the murder. It's unlikely that they'll have remembered the license number, but make a note of it anyway. It's XRA 4318. And give this film to the lab to be developed."

I got rid of Thanassis and settled down to the report. In less than a quarter of an hour, it was done. Before handing it in, I phoned Politou, the examiner who'd undertaken the Albanian's case, and informed her of the new evidence that had come to light.

"How strong is the likelihood that we're dealing with a trade in babies?" she asked me.

"Too early to say. But it's not unlikely that the Albanian murdered the couple for the reasons that Karayoryi suspected and not for those he claims in his confession."

"I see. I'll let you know as soon as I call him for the inquest," she said and hung up.

I submitted the two reports to Koula and then went down to the basement, where the records are kept.

The officer in charge was surprised to see me. "It's not often we see you, Inspector Haritos."

He was around forty and always had a smile on his face. He'd had the misfortune, a couple of years back, to have a run-in with a minister's son, who'd had a row in a bar and had seriously injured one of the customers. The minister had exerted pressure to get his son off on a plea of self-defense, but Yannis was irritated by the boy's arrogance and wouldn't give way. In the end, the boy got a six-month suspended sentence and Yannis ended up in records.

"Yannis, I need a personal favor from you."

"If I can be of help, of course."

"I need to know what files from our division have been asked for in the last year and a half and who took them."

"Last year and a half?" he said, and it was plain that his spirits had well and truly sunk.

"Yes, and I want it to remain between us. I don't want anyone at all to learn of it."

I knew this would be a real chore. He'd have to search all the lists one by one. But I didn't know the numbers of the files and I didn't want to ask for them from my own boys, because that could alert Karayoryi's accomplice.

"What am I going to do? Say no?" Yannis said. "But it's going to take some time."

"Be as quick as you can be." I shook his hand warmly to show him my appreciation.

It had started to drizzle. I got into my Mirafiori and went to find Zissis. This was my friend, the one I'd kept hidden from Ghikas.

CHAPTER 27

Lambros Zissis lived on Ekavis Street in Nea Philadelphia. If you set off around one o'clock, as I did, you need at least an hour and a half to get down from Galatsiou Avenue to Patission Street, to come out onto Acharnon Street, and, from Treis Yephyres, to get onto Dekelias Avenue. Ekavis Street lies in a fork, between Dekelias Avenue and Pindou Street, and runs parallel to Iokastis Street. Hecuba and Jocasta, two fallen queens. It was as if they'd put them together to tell of their sufferings and console one another.

I'd met Zissis at security headquarters on Bouboulinas Street in '71 when I was a cell guard. Kostaras had always insisted that we be present at the interrogations, supposedly so that—greenhorns that we were—we might learn something, or so he said. Deep down, he didn't give a damn about our "training." It was simply that he prided himself that there was no one he couldn't break, and to prove it he set up a whole show at which we greenhorns were the audience.

But in Zissis, he found his master. Zissis had begun his career in the dungeons of the SS on Merlin Street, had gone on to the Haidari prison, had taken his diploma in the detention camp on the island of Makronissos, and was as tough as they came. He sat staring Kostaras straight in the eye, and never opened his mouth. Kostaras was fuming. He tried all his advanced technology on Zissis: beatings, bastinado, fake executions. He'd let him soak for hours in his clothes in a barrel of freezing water, take him up to the roof above Bouboulinas Street and threaten to throw him off; he even tried electroshock, but all he managed to get out of Zissis were his screams of pain. He never uttered so much as a word. Whenever I took him back to his cell, I'd have to hold him under the arms and drag him because it was impossible for him to stand on his own feet.

At first, I'd taken him for a plucky but misguided lunatic who would break sooner or later. But while it lasted, I began making bets with myself to pass the time, given that I was obliged to sit in silence and witness the whole spectacle. It was as if I had placed a bet that Zissis wouldn't break. Perhaps that bet was how we came to know each other. They had him in strict isolation and wouldn't even let him go to pee. During the night shift, when I was alone in the cells, I'd let him out of his cell to get a bit of air and stretch his legs. I'd give him a cigarette, and if Kostaras had had him in the barrel, I'd let him lean against the radiator to let it soak up a little of the dampness. Whenever I heard footsteps, I'd lock him back into his cell. I told myself I was doing it so that he'd keep up his strength and I'd win my bet. When I took him to empty the slop pail and he spilled it because he didn't have the strength to lift it, or when I dragged him back to his cell after an interrogation, I'd give him the odd backhander in front of the others so they wouldn't think I was being soft on a commie. That way I'd get in trouble. I never explained to him why I did it, nor did he ever thank me. Afterward, they took him on a stretcher to the Averof prison and I lost touch with him.

I met him again, completely by chance, in the corridors of the security headquarters in '82. His hair had turned white, his face was covered in wrinkles, and he was walking with a stoop. But the look in his eyes still inspired you to bet on him. We stood there staring at each other in silence. We both felt embarrassed. Neither of us dared make the first step. Suddenly, Zissis held out his hand to me and, shaking mine, said: "You're okay, man. Too bad when you became a policeman."

I don't know what I was thinking. I said: "Would you let a policeman buy you a coffee?" I was sure he'd say no, but he laughed. "Let's have one, now that we commies are legal and you fascists are all democrats," he said. "Who knows what'll happen tomorrow." Over coffee, he told me he'd come to the security headquarters because he needed a certificate to enable him to draw the pension given to members of the resistance, but he was being messed around. I undertook to take care of it for him. It was then that he told me he lived in his family house on Ekavis Street in Nea Philadelphia.

At that time I was on the drugs squad and had begun to learn my broken English. One day, we got a call from the police station in Nea Philadelphia. They had information that a house on Medeas Street was a hideaway for illicit drug dealing, and they asked us to investigate. The chief sent me so that they could fill me in. Zissis's certificate had been issued in the meantime, and, as I'd be in the area, I thought of letting him know he could come and pick it up. It wasn't just to do him a favor. I hoped he could give me some information about the area.

He lived in one of those houses built without planning permission that were added to the town plan just before the general elections. The small front yard was filled with cutoff oil cans, painted in various colors, containing geraniums, carnations, lemon plants, and begonias. He welcomed me without much enthusiasm, though he offered to make me a coffee.

"You didn't have to go to so much trouble over the certificate," he told me. "I would have called you."

When I explained to him why I'd come, he shot me a scornful glance and shook his head fatalistically. "Ah, you people will never change. You're always chasing after the last spoke in the wheel. Harmanis is the man you want."

The Harmanis in question had a motorbike business that he used as a front for pushing drugs. Everyone knew it, even the police at the local station, but he was a former army officer and had friends in high places. I was surprised that Zissis knew all this.

"As long as I can remember, you've been keeping tabs on me," he laughed. "Now, I've decided to keep tabs on a few of your people. Just to get some of my own back. Who knows, in the future I might write a book on all these sharks and need the information on them." And he smiled wryly.

But when I asked him to show me his files, he grew serious. "I'm not even going to even tell you where they are. I wouldn't put it past you to confiscate them."

As for Harmanis, what he told me proved to be true. We nabbed him, and it was one of our biggest successes in all the time I was in the drugs squad. Later, after we grew closer, Zissis came to trust me and showed me his files. I was flabbergasted. Compared to him, we were in complete darkness. This guy had files on around five hundred people, some of them well known, some I'd never heard of. It seemed that for years he'd been collecting information, bit by bit, like an ant. From then on, whenever I was stuck in any investigation that was connected with dirty money, I'd go to him. It was a relationship that no one but the two of us knew about. Of course, that didn't stop him from complaining or being difficult every time I asked him for information.

That's how it was in this case. We sat facing each other across the table with our coffee. His house was strangely decorated, as if he'd brought the balcony into the living room. Four folding canvas chairs and a small, folding metal table, like the ones in the old-style cafés. The only other piece of furniture in the room was an enormous bookcase all across the wall behind him, with bricks for its base and planks for the shelves. It was filled with books, stacked upright or flat, right up to the ceiling.

"They've hounded you your whole life, and now you're living on a measly resistance pension. Where did you find the money to buy all those books?" I asked him. The question had been nagging me for a long time.

He chuckled. "Wake up, you silly copper. The bookshops are there so that we can steal from them," he said proudly.

"So you steal? You?"

"In a capitalist society, you either have to pay for knowledge or steal it. There's no other way."

I was about to inform him that education in Greece was free, but then I suddenly remembered how much Katerina's studies in Thessaloniki were costing me and I kept my mouth shut.

Zissis said: "You haven't come to talk about my books, you're here for some other reason. You want something from me again."

As he'd brought it up, I'd no reason to hide it. "Pylarinos," I said. "Christos Pylarinos. Does that name mean anything to you?"

"Why do you come to me?" he said, annoyed. "Why the hell did I have to go and tell you about the files I keep for personal use. You have your own files, you have the Security Service—"

"Information Agency," I interrupted. "That's what it's called now. The Information Agency."

"All right, Information Agency. Same difference . . . What business is it of mine? I'm not one of your agents and I'm not a squealer that you can blackmail into giving you information."

"He's a former leftist," I said undeterred, because each time we dug up the same skeletons and rattled the same bones. "Like you."

"I know who he is," he replied in a disdainful tone, though I couldn't tell if the disdain was directed at me or at Pylarinos. "Except that I'm not a former leftist, I'm just retired."

"But he *is* a former leftist. Because now he's gone over to the other side. In the last fifteen years, he's made barrels of money. And money that comes so easily is usually dirty money."

I saw him break into that wry smile of his, the one he produced when he knew he was going to come out on top. "When was it you graduated from the academy?"

"Sixty-eight."

He shook his head. "They taught you to hate all leftists, to hunt them down like bandits. They told you that they'd make commies of you all. . . . But what they didn't teach you is how leftists think, what methods they use, what tricks they devise. You know nothing about all that."

He remained silent, thinking. I knew him now, and I knew he was deciding what to tell me and what to keep from me.

"Pylarinos is a swine who's brought a lot of people down. But dirty money is like fire to him and he's too clever to touch it. He's involved in other rackets."

We stared at each other. That had stayed with us since Bouboulinas Street. When I gave him a few backhanders in front of the others, we'd exchange a conspiratorial look because we knew that that was the way it had to be if we were going to have our heads free of worry. The same thing was happening now. In the past I wouldn't explain anything. Now he was the one who wouldn't explain; he waited for me to understand.

"Have you heard of Yanna Karayoryi?"

"That she was murdered? I read it in the papers."

"It's quite possible that Pylarinos was somehow involved in her murder."

"And why have you come to me?" he said, annoyed at my persistence. "You have a whole intelligence agency. Start looking if you want to get to the bottom of it."

"If I had something concrete, I could take out a warrant for his arrest. But I don't and I can't start investigating him because I'll have all the bigwigs on my back, from the chief of security to the minister, and my hands will be tied."

"You can be sure of that," he said with a sudden outburst of sincerity. He let out a deep sigh and shook his head. "I never believed that we'd get into power. But if you'd told me when we first met that I was rotting in the cells so that Pylarinos's kind could get rich, I'd have spit in your face."

"Karayoryi had a huge file on him. That's what put a flea in my ear. She was evidently investigating him for some shady business, but she didn't find any incriminating evidence. The only explanation is that he's involved in illegal dealings. That's why I came to you."

He looked at me for a while, but now there was a glint in his eye. Illegal dealings had become second nature to him, and as soon as he heard the magic words, he was ready to go to work.

"Look what you're doing to me," he said. "I was about to paint the house because the damp is killing me. Now I'm going to have to leave it and start rushing around."

I got up. "When shall I call for an update?"

"I'll call *you*."

"You still don't have a phone? I can understand you not wanting a TV, but a phone?"

"Don't get me started. I've been waiting two years for one. And I need one. The way that your buddies have screwed me, if anything were to happen to me, the neighbors would find me from the stench."

I looked at him in silence. What could I say? But he read my look and was annoyed because he didn't like to be pitied. He made a joke of it.

"Look at me," he said. "Investigating former leftists. If I were a businessman, at least I could say that I was expanding my activities."

Outside, a raging wind blew and the drizzle had turned into sleet. The wind had blown over the lemon plant. I stooped to pick it up. Only ten days before we'd been under a sweltering heat, and now we were shivering with the cold. God-awful weather.

CHAPTER 28

Flexible = 1. *able to be bent easily without breaking, pliable.* 2. *adaptable or variable.* 3. *able to be persuaded easily, tractable.* Interesting word. Now, which sense best suited Ghikas, and which one best suited me? Ghikas was fairly easy. He bent easily when it came to the minister and Delopoulos, or when he was dealing with the media. And in the end, he'd have us all bending to their wishes. Me, I was more in the adaptable and variable category.

It was almost seven-thirty by the time I got home. The TV was on full blast, but Adriani wasn't in the living room; she was preparing something in the kitchen. She'd often do that. When she had something to do in the kitchen, she'd turn up the sound so that she could at least hear her soap and not miss what was happening. I lay on the bed and breathed a sigh of relief. The pressures of the day together with three hours behind the wheel had left me exhausted. I lay down to relax a bit, using my chest as a lectern for Liddell & Scott.

Soon it was five to nine, but I wasn't in the mood to listen to the news. What they had to say about Kolakoglou I already knew, and what I knew about Pylarinos they didn't know, so I could have a night off. The only thing I'd eaten all day was half a croissant, and I was absolutely famished. I got up to see what Adriani was preparing in the kitchen. As I went through the living room, I saw her in her armchair, watching the news.

The kitchen table was adorned with a dish of stuffed tomatoes. I immediately got the message. It was Adriani's way of telling me it was time to make up. This had stayed with us since our very first quarrel. We were newlyweds then and not speaking to each other was something we'd taken to heart. But we kept it up to test each other's limits. Until, one day, Adriani made me stuffed tomatoes. She knew that I had a particular weakness for them, but she'd never made them for me before. As soon as I'd seen them, I'd melted. "They're great, better even than my mother's!" I told her. It was a lie. My mother's were much tastier, but on the one hand I was looking for an opportunity to speak to her, and, on the other, we'd only been married for six months and I hadn't had my hands around her for a whole three days. It had been the same ever since. Whenever she wanted us to make up, she made me stuffed tomatoes. I told her how tasty they were, and it broke the ice. Except that now I didn't have to lie about it. She really did make them better than my mother.

"This time, you've outdone yourself. They're great," I told her.

She turned from the TV and smiled at me. "Did you eat?" I asked.

"I just took a mouthful to try them, but I was waiting for you to come and eat."

She switched off the TV and followed me into the kitchen. She served me, put one tomato on her own plate, and sat down facing me. In the light, I could see that her eyes were all red and swollen.

"What's wrong?" I asked her, concerned.

"Nothing."

"What do you mean, nothing! You've been crying!"

"I got upset last night. I heard those two idiots on the news, then I saw you leaving all agitated, and I realized it was something serious. And this morning I woke up racked with worry."

"There's no need to worry. They did put me on the spot, that's all, but then they were forced to backpedal."

She didn't seem reassured by what I said. She kept on looking at me distraught till she finally blurted out the secret. "Katerina's not coming home for Christmas. She called today to tell me."

"Why?"

"She wants to study over the break."

"And she made up her mind, just like that? The last time I spoke to her on the phone, she was certainly coming."

"She made out a work program, she said, and saw that she won't have time to finish everything before June if she takes a holiday now."

I lost my appetite on the spot. I pushed my plate away. If I'd eaten the stuffed tomato, it would have sat on my stomach. Adriani made an effort to smile.

"I'll tell you something," she said with difficulty, "but I want you to promise me that you won't breathe a word to her. She's staying there on account of Panos."

"Panos?"

"Yes. He has to hand in an assignment after the break, and she's staying with him to keep him company. She promised me that she would definitely come for Easter."

As soon as I was over the initial shock, I thought of that hulk with his T-shirts and gym shoes, and I began to fume.

"What kind of assignment can a student greengrocer be doing? Investigating how apples fall from apple trees or the best way to prune nettles?"

"He's not a greengrocer. The boy's studying to be an agriculturalist."

"And is he such a blockhead that he needs someone beside him to hold his hand?" If I'd been able to get my hands on him at that moment, I'd have given it to him, though he'd probably have made mincemeat of me with all those muscles of his.

"I know it's hard for us to swallow, but when you love someone, you want to be with them. There comes a time when parents have to take a back seat."

Usually, whenever she trots out that kind of armchair philosophy that she's picked up from one of her soaps, I hit the roof. But now I couldn't bear to start shouting at her, because I knew how much she was suffering.

"Do you want to go and spend Christmas up there with her?"

I don't know how it came to me, maybe because I saw the tears in her eyes again. She wasn't expecting it, and for a moment I saw her eyes shine through the tears. But then she immediately resumed her severe expression, more to restrain herself than me.

"And leave you on your own at Christmas? Out of the question!"

"Forget about me. This Karayoryi business has become so complicated that it's touch and go whether we'll even be able to eat together on Christmas Day. And I'll be up to the ears in it. And you'll be sitting alone at home with a heavy heart."

"It'll cost a pile of money and there's no reason for it."

"How much will it cost? The train ticket, Katerina's present that we were going to get anyway, and something for your expenses each day. Eighty thousand would be more than enough."

What I had left in the bank, together with my Christmas bonus, would just about enable me to cover her expenses and Katerina's allowance for January. Of course, I'd be left without a penny, but what the hell, I'd get by somehow. Now that I was making it easy for her, Adriani began to waver.

"Do you think I should go?" she asked me hesitantly, as though afraid that if she showed how happy she was, I'd change my mind.

"Just think how thrilled Katerina will be. She may want to please that bulldog of hers, but she won't like it at all that she's leaving us on our own."

Of course, I was doing it for Adriani and for Katerina. At least they would have a good time over Christmas. But there was something else that made me feel good about it: that I was turning the tables on that shirker. He'd succeeded in keeping Katerina in Thessaloniki, but now that Adriani was going to go up there, he wouldn't just have her as his personal handmaid. Not to mention that he wouldn't be able to get her on her own, because he'd have to drag his prospective mother-in-law along too. Adriani threw her arms around my neck and her lips stuck to my cheek like a lollipop.

"You're a real treasure," she whispered, when she'd finished kissing me. "I know you fly off the handle sometimes and you don't know what you're saying, but deep down you're a little lamb."

Was that a compliment or not? I didn't know. But at any rate she pushed the plate of stuffed tomatoes back in front of me. "C'mon, eat now," she said, becoming bossy. "I'll take it personally if you leave it. I made it specially."

And she made me eat it. She'd outdone herself, and my appetite came back. She just nibbled and watched me, pleased with herself.

"Is that why they put you on the spot last night?" she said suddenly. "Because it's a difficult case?"

"Never mind, they've only got themselves to blame."

"If they had any sense, they'd let you get on with your work and get them out of the mess, instead of playing the big shots."

She'd changed her tune. Now I was right about everything. Not that it bothers me when I'm on the receiving end of compliments, even if I'd paid for it in part. It's not at all unpleasant to be fawned upon. But, actually, I wasn't pleased because of this but because I'd managed to lift her spirits.

CHAPTER 29

The stuffed tomatoes did give me indigestion and I had nightmares all night long. At first, they were about Ghikas, who'd suspended me because I'd put Kolakoglou behind bars. I'd done it, he said, to throw the investigations off course because I was on the take from Pylarinos. He was the one who'd raped the girls and not Kolakoglou. I tried to convince him that I had evidence and proposed to interrogate Kolakoglou in his presence. But when they brought him, it wasn't Kolakoglou; it was Petratos. They sat him down in a chair in front of me and I began shouting at him: "Tell me who gave you the duplicator so you could print the leaflets, otherwise I'll rip your heart out, you commie bastard! You'll go out of here in a coffin!" And Ghikas had taken the place of Kostaras. "That's it. You're doing fine, you're learning," he said with satisfaction. But Petratos kept his mouth shut. Then I began hitting him furiously and at that moment I woke up in a sweat.

Still sleepy, I was sitting at the wheel of the Mirafiori. The indigestion hadn't gone and I kept belching. I was trying to put the information I'd gathered up to now in some kind of order. I still didn't know if I was dealing with one case or two. If the murders of Karayoryi and Kostarakou had any connection with the file Anna Antonakaki had given me, then the murderer was Pylarinos, or someone paid by him. If they weren't connected, then Petratos was still the prime suspect. But one thing kept bugging me: Why did the murderer ransack Kostarakou's apartment when he hadn't touched Karayoryi's? If he was looking for something, shouldn't he have looked there first? Unless he didn't know about this thing when he killed her. Maybe when he heard on the news that Karayoryi had phoned Kostarakou, he'd got a flea in his ear and had gone to see her. The other question was the letter from the unknown N. That pointed to Petratos; it didn't point at all to Pylarinos, whose given name was Christos. If Petratos's handwriting didn't match that of the letter writer, then we had a third candidate on our hands. And we didn't have a shred of evidence to point to any third person. A real mess.

From a distance I caught sight of Thanassis waiting for me in the entrance. As soon as he saw me, he came charging up.

"I called you at home but you'd already left."

"What's going on?"

"We've found Kolakoglou."

From his expression, I guessed that something wasn't right. Normally, he would have swelled up like a peacock. But he seemed worried and scared.

"Where did you find him?"

"He's been staying under another name at the City, a hotel on Nirvana Street, between Acharnon Street and Ionias Avenue." His words came out like blood out of a stone. "He's on the roof of the hotel, holding a gun to his head, and he's threatening to blow his brains out."

"Get a patrol car," I said abruptly.

"I've got one ready. It's waiting for you."

The car's siren moved all the other vehicles aside. We raced down Alexandras Avenue without stopping at any red lights and turned onto Ioulianou Street. That's where it got difficult, because the road was narrow and we kept getting stuck in the traffic.

"Who let us know?" I asked Thanassis, who was sitting next to the driver.

"The crew from Hellas Channel."

"What was Hellas Channel doing there?"

"They were the ones who found him," he replied, and then I understood why he had his head down.

Once again we had our wordless dialogue, like every other morning, but now it was a little later than usual and through the rearview mirror.

He tried to change subjects. "I have something new on Petratos's car."

"Tell me later, because now we've got our work cut out."

Two motorcycle policemen had stopped the traffic at the level of Vourdoupa Street, where Treis Yephyres is. The block between Ionias Avenue, Acharnon Street, and Nirvana and Stephanou Vyzantiou Streets was sealed off by patrol cars, police, and TV crews.

The hotel looked onto the left-hand side of Ionias Avenue. We got out of the car and crossed the bridge over the train tracks on foot. As we passed through the cordon, I glimpsed the Horizon Channel van in front of the hotel entrance, but I couldn't see the crew anywhere. Then, when I got to the hotel, I saw Ionias Avenue and Nirvana Street teeming with uniformed policemen, reporters, and cameramen. They were all looking up, as though watching a kite on Shrove Tuesday. I, too, looked up so as not to appear odd.

The balconies on the surrounding apartment blocks were empty and the shutters were down. Evidently, our boys had ordered the neighbors to keep back, and they were watching through the cracks.

"C'mon, get on with it. Some of us have to get to work!" How conscientious of this professional to be on his way to work at ten o'clock.

Kolakoglou was on the roof ledge. He was standing still, with the gun to his head. Dressed in a jacket and tie, he looked like a small-time businessman who was about to kill himself because he was unable to pay his debts. Below, there was a huge commotion with police officers and reporters all shouting together as if all the noise would convince Kolakoglou to come down.

"Inspector Haritos. Who's in charge here?" I asked an officer standing beside me. He pointed to an older man in uniform, who was holding a bullhorn. I went over to him.

"Inspector Haritos, Homicide Division."

"Since television was invented, it's meant only trouble for us," the man said wearily.

"How did he get up there?"

"I'll tell you what the hotel owner told me." And he did. Kolakoglou had been in the hotel for three days. He'd given his name as

Spyrou. No one knew how he'd managed to hole up in there without being seen again.

They thought that someone must have booked the room for him and he'd sneaked in when the receptionist wasn't at her desk, because the owner swore he'd never set eyes on him before. Maybe it was booked for him by the man he was with in the bar. He'd kept himself locked up in his room all day. The reporters from Hellas Channel had shown up first thing in the morning. They'd played it both hot and cold. On the one hand, they'd terrified the owner saying that Kolakoglou was a dangerous criminal, and, on the other, they must have greased his palm so he'd take them up to Kolakoglou's room. They'd begun hammering on the door. He wouldn't open it to them. In the end, they'd threatened to turn him over to the police. And he'd jumped out in front of them, holding the gun to his head. He'd begun shouting that he'd blow his brains out. The other residents in the hotel had been alarmed, the owner had dialed 100. When Kolakoglou had seen our boys arriving, he'd found his way out onto the roof, still holding the gun to his head. That was an hour ago and he was still up there, motionless on the edge of the roof.

While the officer in charge was telling me all this, I saw Petratos and the newscaster coming out of the hotel.

"Excuse me a moment," I said to the officer, and I went over to them. They'd taken off their suits and were wearing combat gear: anoraks and pullovers.

"Beaten to it again, Inspector," Petratos said, with an ironic little grin.

I began to bristle, while inside I was cursing Thanassis, who'd screwed everything up again. "What is it with you people? You keep going after a scoop and all you do is make a bloody mess of things!" I shouted.

"What you can't stand, Inspector," the newscaster interrupted, "is that we do our job properly. And instead of thanking us for helping you, all you do is scream at us."

"If Kolakoglou suffers so much as a scratch, I'm taking you both in, you can be sure of that."

"On what charge?" Petratos said, as ironically as ever.

"Don't worry about that. I'll have you for needlessly pushing Kolakoglou to suicide and I'll have you both sent down. If you'd informed us promptly, we'd have waited for him outside the hotel and we'd have nabbed him as soon as he showed himself, without even a nosebleed." I would have gone on, but I was cut short by a heart-rending cry.

"Petros, my dearest! Put the gun down! Don't do anything stupid! I won't be able to bear it!"

It was Mrs. Kolakoglou, in her habitual black. Every eye was turned to her. She was being supported by Sotiropoulos. Robespierre's counter-move, I thought to myself. Sotiropoulos had brought her to compete with Petratos.

"Please, put the gun down and come down from there! Think of me!"

For the first time, her son showed some sign of movement. He was about to put the gun down, then remembered why he was up there and put it back up to his head. "Go away, Mother. There's no reason for you to be here!" he shouted at the same time.

Sotiropoulos, still holding her, leaned over and said something in her ear. I couldn't hear what he said, but she began screaming again: "Please, my dearest! Please, my darling boy. I know what you've been through, but don't do this. Don't break my heart!"

"Why did you bring her? Get her away from here!" Kolakoglou shouted from above. Evidently he thought that the police had brought her.

The officer in charge took advantage of the opportunity and spoke to him through the bullhorn. "Petros, think of your poor mother! Come down and put an end to this! No one's going to harm you! You have my word!"

"Do you hear, Petros? The officer's given his word that they won't harm you!" his mother shouted with renewed hope.

"I believed them once before and I paid a high price for it!" Kolakoglou held the gun firmly to his head.

"All right, if you don't believe me, tell me what it will take for you to come down from there!" said the officer through the bullhorn.

Kolakoglou didn't answer immediately. He reflected. Meanwhile, I was back next to the officer.

"I want my mother to go away. I want the police to leave the hotel. I want everyone to go. Clear the street of those reporter creeps and the patrol cars. Then I'll come down."

The officer lowered the bullhorn and turned to me. "Tell me what I should do," he said. "I have no reason to arrest him. At most, I could hold him for illegal possession of a firearm. You're the one who's after him—you decide."

I cursed the moment that I'd got mixed up with Kolakoglou. I'd reached the point of feeling sorry for him, the bastard. I was virtually certain that he had no involvement in the case, and yet we were pursuing him as if he were a kingpin.

"Have you cleared the hotel?" I asked the officer.

"Only our own men are still inside."

"Do what he asks." The officer looked at me undecided. He didn't like having to give in, and his expression showed it. "Listen," I said. "Kolakoglou is like a trapped animal. And his mother coming has made it worse. You have no way of knowing if he's going to put a bullet in his head or if he will start shooting anyone in his sight, out of desperation."

The officer didn't reply. He simply handed me the bullhorn. I put it to my mouth. "All right, Kolakoglou. We're going to do what you ask so that you'll come down."

Kolakoglou listened, perfectly still. All other eyes fell on me. That's it, I thought to myself. From now on, I'll be known as the chicken-shit inspector who can't take the heat.

"Come on, Mrs. Kolakoglou. Everything's going to be all right," Sotiropoulos said to the mother. Now that everything had been taken care of, he'd lost interest in Mrs. Kolakoglou. He handed her over to a policeman so that he wouldn't miss the rest of the show.

The officer in charge sent a sergeant to get our men out of the hotel. The other policemen began dispersing the reporters, together with the vans and patrol cars.

"You did the right thing," I heard a voice beside me say. I turned around and saw Sotiropoulos. "You know that I don't particularly like you, nor do I particularly trust you. But this time, I have to take my hat off to you. The poor schmuck has already paid in prison, and unjustly; he shouldn't have to pay with his life, too."

I again felt the deprivation of an ex-smoker dying for a drag. "I don't have time for your games, Sotiropoulos," I said, furiously. "And as for liking and trust, the feeling's mutual."

Before I'd finished with Sotiropoulos, I saw Petratos coming toward me. "Are you going to let him get away?" He was huffing and puffing.

"What other choice do I have after you've made such a mess of it?"

"Just as well I thought of bringing his mother, and everything got sorted out," said Sotiropoulos, looking provocatively at Petratos.

I nodded to one of the officers. "Get these two gentlemen out of here!" They exchanged a look and walked off in opposite directions.

One by one, the policemen came out of the hotel. The sergeant was the last out. "No one's left inside," he said to the officer.

I put the bullhorn to my mouth again. "Kolakoglou! They're all gone! You can come down now!"

Kolakoglou leaned over and looked, to make sure I was telling the truth. He began moving backward, still with the gun to his head.

The officer and I stood and waited without speaking. Before long, Kolakoglou appeared at the entrance to the hotel. He was still holding the gun to his head.

"Don't go near him! Let him go!" I shouted to our men through the bullhorn.

Kolakoglou had his back to the wall of the hotel and was looking all around him. He began moving along the wall, turned onto Nirvana Street, and vanished. The policemen were all looking at me. They were evidently waiting for me to make the first move. I did nothing. I remained where I was.

CHAPTER 30

On the way back, the driver of the patrol car changed his route. He turned off of Iakovaton Street and drove down Patission Street.

"You tell them that the person you're after frequents a certain bar, and it doesn't occur to them to make inquiries at the nearby hotels," Thanassis said. "The lousiest reporter is better at his job." He was looking at me through the rearview mirror.

"That's what you get when you organize the investigation by phone from your office instead of supervising it personally," I said, and he shut up. I held back on "You're a moron," because I didn't want to embarrass him in front of the driver, his subordinate.

I wondered if I'd done the right thing with Kolakoglou, or if I'd let my belief that he was innocent run away with me. But what else could I have done? After all, there was one positive thing to come out of all that business. It proved that Kolakoglou either didn't have a circle of friends to hide him or that he'd exhausted his limits and had been forced to stay in a hotel under a false name. So now we knew where to look and we'd be able to find him more easily. The only problem was Ghikas. Once again, I'd failed to inform him. I'd done what I'd thought best and I didn't know how he would take it.

The whole way to the traffic light on Alexandras Avenue Thanassis said not a word. "Do you want me to tell you now about Petratos?" he said as we were passing the Pedio to Areos Park.

"Go on." I preferred him to tell me then, because it was almost noon and I'd be up to my neck in the office. Not to mention that I had to report to Ghikas.

"I found someone who saw a black Renegade parked two streets down from Kostarakou's place."

"What time?"

"At six-thirty. He's a lawyer and he was going back to his office. He parked in front of the Renegade."

"Did he notice the license number?"

"No."

"Ask in the building where Petratos lives if anyone noticed the Renegade missing from the garage after around five."

"I already did. One of the tenants was in the garage just before six and is certain that Petratos's car wasn't there." He was congratulating himself for making up for his blunder with Kolakoglou.

"You see how far you get when you ride hard?" I said patronizingly. He took it as a sign of reconciliation and smiled in relief.

I went straight to see Ghikas. If I delayed, it would only make things worse. He listened to me without interrupting even once.

"Are you sure they went to the hotel without notifying us first?" he said at the end.

"Yes. They didn't inform us or the local police station."

"Are there any witnesses to confirm that?"

"The hotel owner, who called the station. And the police officers who found them there."

"You did right to let him go," he said, obviously pleased. "Now they won't dare say another word about Kolakoglou. We lost him because of them." He looked at me and smiled. "Yesterday, you were surprised that I contacted Delopoulos right away. He used the information, wanted to move behind our backs, and made a mess of it. That's what it means to be flexible. You throw him the cheese, he goes to bite it, and he falls into the trap."

I smiled at him. If I was lucky and Ghikas was to remain another couple of years in that position, then with all the tricks I was picking up from him, I'd be certain to get a promotion.

"So that's the good news. Now for the bad news," he said. "I received the handwriting report. We drew a blank. It's not Petratos's."

On the one hand, it rankled me. On the other, though, I was thankful that my intuition always led me to keep something up my sleeve. "I told you yesterday that would probably be the result. It doesn't mean a great deal, in any case." And I gave him the latest on Petratos's Renegade.

Things had taken a downturn with the negative report on the handwriting, and he was weighing how he was going to deal with it. "Leave it to me," he said eventually. "I'll sort it out and I'll let you know. Meanwhile, find out all you can about Pylarinos."

"I'm like a cat on hot bricks, that's why I'm moving slowly," I said, to show him that I was following his advice. "In a couple of days, I'll have something."

I wasn't at all surprised that the usual throng wasn't in the hall. They were all at their studios, editing their videocassettes and sound recordings for the day's big story. The same story all around and each of them with an exclusive report.

On my desk I found the photographs from Karayoryi's film.

In the first one, Pylarinos was holding up his drink, smiling, as if wanting to toast me. It was only natural that he was in good spirits, as he was partying in a nightclub with three others. Two of them were obviously foreigners, Germans, Belgians, Dutch, I'd no way of knowing—at any rate, they looked like northern Europeans. The other one was lank and surly. He was wearing gold-rimmed glasses, a dark suit, his hair was brushed back and stuck down. He didn't look to me like a businessman. More like the director of a ministerial department or of some public organization. While Pylarinos and the man next to him were plainly enjoying themselves, this one had a constipated smile, as if he were smiling out of obligation. There was something about his face that was familiar to me, but I couldn't remember where I'd seen it before. Sitting beside him was the last member of the group, a hefty, round-faced man with swollen cheeks. His hair was combed over his forehead. It seemed as if they'd put him beside the other one because he had the same reluctant smile. I'd bet money that those two weren't having any fun at all. Below right, the camera had recorded the date: 11/14/1990. Fine, so on November 14, 1990, four men were partying at the Diogenes Club. One of them was Pylarinos, the second one reminded me of someone, and the other two were foreign and unknown to me. What was special about it? Was it the photograph, or the date, or a combination of the two? I couldn't come up with an answer and I continued.

In the next photograph, the two with the sour smiles were in a cafeteria at a table beside the window. The photograph was taken from outside in the street and I couldn't make out their expressions because the glass was reflecting the light. The date at the bottom right was 11/17/1990. Three days after the Diogenes picture, the odd couple from the group had met to talk without the others. Why were these two meetings so important that Karayoryi had gone to the trouble of getting them on film?

It seemed that at some stage she'd grown tired of photographing people and had decided to focus on vehicles. Because the next four pictures were refrigerator trucks and coaches belonging to Pylarinos's company. The trucks bore the company name Transpilar, with the address and the telephone and fax numbers. On the left side of the coaches were the words "Prespes Travel," again with the company address, telephone, and fax numbers. Photographing people was one thing. Obviously, she had her reasons. But why was she photographing Pylarinos's fleet of vehicles? I couldn't understand it.

I heard the door open and looked up. Sotiris came cantering in.

"What is it?"

"I sent the written requests to the airport and customs. I'm waiting for a reply. They promised to phone me from customs as soon as they come up with anything, but as it's been two years all the documents have been filed away."

"What about the names I gave you?"

"I located all of them. Two of them came back dead. Fotiou died six months after returning. Petassi lived a bit longer. For a year. Died of AIDS. The only one still alive is Spyros Gonatas. I've got him outside waiting for you."

Of the five on Karayoryi's list, four were dead. We were off to a good start. "Bring him in," I said impatiently.

I opened the drawer and took out Karayoryi's file. I found the list. Gonatas was the one who'd traveled by bus to Budapest on March 3, 1992.

The door opened and Sotiris ushered in a couple. "Mr. and Mrs. Gonatas," he said, as he showed them where to sit.

Gonatas looked to be in his sixties, nearly bald, with just a few tufts of hair left around his temples. His jacket was a different color from his trousers. It wasn't a sports jacket and flannels, just the halves of two different suits. He was wearing a crewneck pullover, which left just enough room for the knot of his tie to stick out. His appearance suggested a small-time shop owner—haberdasher, stationer, milliner, something like that. The woman with him was a bit younger. She was wearing a loose, gray overcoat. Her hair was jet black, flecked with a few white hairs. Two ordinary people, who were now sitting opposite me, nervous and worried.

I put on my kindest expression to make them feel at ease. "Don't worry, it's not about anything serious," I said. "I just need to ask you a few questions." I saw them relax, but at that moment the phone rang.

"Haritos."

"Haritou." It was the voice of Katerina, who always laughed at her little joke.

"Hello. How's things?"

She immediately understood my tone, because usually I'm full of sweet talk. "Is someone with you?" she asked.

"Yes."

"Okay. I won't keep you. I just phoned to say that you're the best daddy in the world."

"Why?" I asked like a moron, as I felt a smile spread from one ear to the other.

"You know why. Because you're sending Mom up to me for the holidays."

"Are you pleased?"

"Yes, but only half pleased."

"Why only half?"

"Because the other half would be if you came. And you'll be all alone in Athens."

"You want everything," I said, teasing her to hide my emotion.

"No. You've always taught me to make do with a little." I knew why she said that. Because I was stingy with her allowance so that she wouldn't take everything for granted.

"I love you."

"And I love you, dear." I'd forgotten the couple and it slipped out. I heard her hang up and I put the phone down.

"My daughter," I said to the couple. "She's studying in Thessaloniki and called to say hello." So that they wouldn't think I was talking to my mistress, and also to break the ice. Evidently I succeeded in the latter because they smiled sympathetically.

"Mr. Gonatas. On March 15, 1992, you went on a journey to Budapest."

"That's right."

"Can you tell me the purpose of your journey? Was it for pleasure, business, or what?"

"I went for treatment, Inspector. I had a kidney transplant."

So that was it. They'd all gone abroad for organ transplants. That might explain Petassi's AIDS. Perhaps he'd got it from a blood transfusion.

"You can get a transplant in Greece. Why did you go to Budapest?"

"Because we'd been on the waiting list for seven years and we were desperate, Inspector," his wife said, intervening. "Seven years of hell. Going twice a week for dialysis and with no light at the end of the tunnel. God bless that woman—she saved us."

"What woman?"

"One afternoon, as I was coming out of dialysis, a woman came up to us," said Gonatas. "It was November 'ninety-one."

"No, it was October. I remember it well," his wife said, correcting him.

"Anyway. She asked me if I was interested in a transplant abroad. In Budapest, Warsaw, or Prague. Three million drachmas. Opera-

tion, hospital, hotel, tickets, all included, and paid for in Greece.
Yitsa and I sat down and thought about it. We might have been waiting for another seven years here. We didn't have the money for Paris
or London. So we took a chance, agreed to the deal, and I was saved."

"What was the name of this woman?"

Gonatas glanced briefly at his wife. Then they both looked at me,
once again nervous and perplexed.

"Do you think there was anything illegal in what you did?" I asked
innocently.

"Heavens, no!" the woman cried. "My Spyros got his health back,
that's all!" She didn't know that the other four had died and that only
a miracle had saved her husband.

"Then why won't you tell me her name? You've nothing to fear,
and neither does she."

"Her name was Dourou," Gonatas said with resolve. "Eleni
Dourou."

Where had I seen that name? I couldn't recall. "Do you have an
address for her? Phone number?"

"We don't have anything," his wife answered. "She had our number and she was always the one who communicated with us. She
brought us the tickets, together with the voucher for the hotel and a
paper for the hospital saying we'd been accepted, and the date that
we had to be in Budapest. We arranged everything else through the
travel agency."

"Which agency was it?" I asked, although I knew the answer already.

"Prespes. We went there by coach and came back by plane. It was
cheaper that way."

I remained silent and looked at the couple across from me. They'd
gone to Budapest, the man had regained his health, and they'd found
peace. Now I'd come along, opening up old wounds, and had
planted in them the worm of disquiet.

"All right. That's all. You can go home now. I don't have any reason to question you again."

This reassured them and they got up to leave. As soon as they'd gone, I called Sotiris in.

"Note down the name Eleni Dourou. Find her for me."

I picked up the two lists and looked at them. On June 25, 1991, a coach left Tiranë for Prague. On June 30, 1991, Yannis Emiroglou left Athens for Prague. On October 20, 1991, a bus left Bucharest for Budapest. On November 5, 1991, Alexandros Fotiou left for Budapest. Spyros Gonatas, who left Athens on March 15, 1992, was linked with a bus that left Bucharest on March 6, 1992. It didn't take much to realize what was going on. They found various poor wretches, Albanians, Romanians, or Bulgarians, and bought one of their kidneys. They took the Albanians to Prague, the Romanians to Budapest, and the Bulgarians to Warsaw. Then they notified the patient in Greece, telling him where to go. There, they took the kidney from the donor and transplanted it in the patient. The Greeks returned home cured, and the Albanians and Romanians were left with one less kidney and a few banknotes in their pockets. Okay, four of the five had died, but we were talking about transplants and they were no joke. And, after all, anyone who had an objection could go and file a lawsuit in Prague, Budapest, or Warsaw. He could do absolutely nothing in Greece. There wasn't even an illegal export of currency involved.

This was all very well, but why would they murder Karayoryi and Kostarakou, supposing it was they who'd killed them? And why hadn't Dourou given out her address or number? Possibly so that she wouldn't get into any mess with the relatives if the patients died. But why had Karayoryi paid someone to supply her with the case records of the trade in children from the files of security headquarters? What connection was there between the transplants and the children? I was missing a piece of the puzzle.

Then I suddenly remembered where I'd seen Dourou's name. I again took out Karayoryi's file from the drawer and began searching through the photocopies. In one of these, Karayoryi had noted in the margin the name Eleni Dourou.

I called Mrs. Antonakaki and told her I wanted to see her.

"All right, but don't come before seven because I'll be out."

Outside, a north wind was howling. It had knocked two plant pots over on the balcony opposite. The old woman came out to pick them up. The cat was inside the house watching her through the open door. She must be mad to go out into the freezing cold for the sake of two wretched potted plants!

CHAPTER 31

She opened the door to me dressed in black.

"I'd gone to see about Yanna's headstone," she said, as if feeling the need to justify her going out while she was in mourning.

I sat on the sofa, in the same spot where I'd sat the first time. I was tired and was in no mood for chitchat.

"Mrs. Antonakaki, did you ever hear your sister mention anyone by the name of Pylarinos? Christos Pylarinos?"

"Isn't he the one who has the travel agencies? We went on a trip organized by his agency."

"When was that?"

"End of August, beginning of September, 1990."

"Was your sister with you?"

"Yes. There was Yanna, me, and Anna. Yanna had promised Anna that if she got into medical school, she'd take her on a trip as a present. We went to Vienna, Budapest, and Prague. For ten days." The memory upset her. She sniffed and her lip began to tremble. "I'll never forget that trip. It wasn't enough that we had guided tours all day long; Yanna wanted us to go out in the evenings too. I tried to restrain her, partly because I was tired and partly because I saw her spending money right and left. But my sister always did whatever she wanted."

"Apart from that trip, did you ever hear your sister mention Pylarinos?"

"No, never. Though I know she went twice more, after the trip we took together."

"When would those journeys have been?"

"The first time was in the winter. February, I think. And the second one was in May. But I couldn't tell you whether she went through Pylarinos's agency."

"On the trip that you went on together, did anything out of the ordinary occur? Anything that might have attracted your attention."

"Nothing. We were together all the time and had a lot of fun." She stopped, as if remembering something. "Apart from two mornings in Prague, when she went off to do her own work."

"What work was that?"

"I don't know. She didn't tell me."

"And she never said anything to you about Pylarinos?"

"No, never."

"Okay, Mrs. Antonakaki. That's all I needed to know."

As I was starting up the Mirafiori, it occurred to me that I should have another look through the folder with Karayoryi's receipts. To see if there were any clues about those trips. It wasn't unlikely that she'd discovered something on her first trip, quite by chance, and had started investigating. In 1990, she'd stumbled on the relationship between Pylarinos and the two foreigners in the photograph and then had made two other trips to get more information. Dourou was the key. If I could only find her, I might start getting somewhere with Pylarinos.

The TV was on in the living room and the picture showed the back of someone's head. The voice coming out was that of a young girl. Her words were confused, faltering, and came out sharply, as though someone was forcing them out, one by one:

"He used to buy me clothes . . ."

"What sort of clothes?"

"Blouses . . . skirts . . ."

"And then?"

"He'd take me to his home . . ."

"What did you do there?"

"He'd dress me in the new clothes . . ."

"Did he do anything else to you?"

"He would look at me."

"Only that?"

"He told me that I was a pretty little girl . . . and he touched me . . ."

"Where did he touch you?"

"On my hair . . . my arms . . . my legs, sometimes, not always . . ."

"Just that?"

"Yes."

The back of the girl's head vanished from the screen and in its place appeared Sotiropoulos's face, grave, expressionless. His eyes, however, had a glint in them. Two fireflies, behind round glasses.

"Ladies and gentlemen, a man was sentenced to six years in prison on the basis of only a journalist's report and the allegations made by two sets of parents," he said with the look of someone unraveling a massive travesty of justice. "I'm not saying that he was convicted unjustly, but without doubt the charge of indecent assault of a juvenile is open to question. The fact that Kolakoglou's tax consultancy firm passed into the hands of the parents of the two alleged victims also leaves questions to be asked. I couldn't say whether that is of any significance in the case. Maybe yes, maybe no. At any rate, today Kolakoglou is a wanted man. If he weren't living under the burden of his conviction, it is almost certain that no one would be seeking to arrest him." He allowed a moment to pass, then added in a meaningful tone: "We reporters are sometimes prey to excessive zeal and are sometimes blind to its consequences."

Catalytic, that's what Robespierre was. Adriani could bear it no more and pressed the remote control. "What's he up to? Is he trying to pretend Kolakoglou is an innocent lamb?" She was furious.

"No. He's simply trying to discredit Petratos and the rival Hellas Channel."

"And is that the right way to do it?"

I wanted to change the subject. I was in no mood to discuss Kolakoglou, Petratos, or Sotiropoulos in my own home. "I spoke to Katerina," I told her.

"Well, you should have heard her on the phone when I told her that I was going up to Thessaloniki. Just like a baby girl." She looked at me furtively. "Couldn't you come too for Christmas? It falls on a weekend this year."

I bit my lip to stop myself from saying yes. "It's impossible. I can't leave while this case is still open. Something might come up and I'd have to run back." It wasn't only the case. It was the cost of the trip and the hotel because we couldn't all stay at Katerina's place. Then I'd have to borrow money to send her in January.

Fortunately, my tone was categorical and Adriani didn't persist. Before we sat down to eat, the phone rang. Adriani answered. "Someone called Zissis," she whispered, and handed me the receiver.

"Greetings, Lambros."

"I have to see you. You know Hara's, the confectioner's that sells homemade ice cream at the end of Patission Street?"

"Yes."

"I'll be waiting for you there in half an hour and you can buy me an ice cream," he said and hung up.

I told Adriani I wouldn't have anything to eat as I had to go out again. In any case, my stomach still hadn't settled.

"Who is Zissis?"

"A colleague," I said, as vaguely as possible.

CHAPTER 32

We sat at a table by the window that looked onto Patission Street. Zissis was eating his parfait ice cream, while I made do with soda water. He was scraping the glass so clean with his spoon that it wouldn't need washing.

"Christos Pylarinos," he said eventually, sounding like a civil servant. "Son of political refugees. Born in Prague. Grew up there and studied economics there. Kept well away from party politics. As soon as he'd finished his studies, he entered a state-owned company. I think it was Czechoslovakian Airlines, but I was unable to verify that. He was competent and soon rose from the middle to the higher echelons of the company. He was unable to get to the top because only party members were appointed to the higher positions. At the beginning of the eighties, he suddenly appeared in Greece and opened a tourist business. The question is: Where did a company employee working in a socialist country get the money to open his own business in Greece?"

He looked at me with a crafty smile. I didn't have to rack my brain. I knew where he was leading. "The Czechs gave it to him."

"Just so. All the socialist states opened businesses of that kind in capitalist countries, because they needed the foreign currency. Some opened them through sister parties in the capitalist country, but more often than not they used individuals as fronts. Pylarinos belongs in the second category."

"And why would the Czechs trust the son of a Greek political refugee? How were they so sure that he wouldn't run off with their money?"

Zissis's smile was all condescension, as if he were talking to a mental retard. "They had a powerful control mechanism. First of all, they put one of their own people beside the individual acting as a front, to watch him on a daily basis. In addition, the sister party in the host country undertook a high level of supervision and regularly reported back to their comrades in the source country. And on top of all that, they also had a guarantee."

"What kind of guarantee?"

"Pylarinos's father died years ago, but his mother is still alive. She came back from Czechoslovakia in 1990."

"They used Pylarinos's mother as their guarantee?"

Zissis shrugged. "It wouldn't be the first time, but again I can't be sure. The party's finances were monitored by a very small circle of members. Even party leaders in high posts didn't know everything that was going on. But doesn't it seem strange to you that the son should have a huge fortune in Greece while the mother was living on her state pension in Prague?"

It wasn't only strange, it stuck out like a sore thumb. Zissis shook his head fatalistically.

"Controls, covering for each other, mechanisms—they thought of everything. There was only one thing they hadn't reckoned on. That all this would collapse like a house of cards in 'eighty-nine. And suddenly Pylarinos found himself with a vast fortune, all his own. The Communist Party of Czechoslovakia had disintegrated, its echelons had scattered, and those who came to power had no means to lay claim to all these fortunes. It's quite possible that the new people didn't even know of their existence."

"And suddenly, from being a marionette, Pylarinos became a businessman in his own right."

"I don't know about 'right'!" Zissis leaned toward me and lowered his voice. "Pylarinos is like a red flag. He appropriated money belonging to others, lots of money. I'm not the only one who despises him. He is despised by all the party members. They'd be happy to see him rot behind bars, but if they expose him, they'd have to bring a lot more to light. I'm telling you all this, so you'll understand that no one likes him." He shifted his position. He sat back in his chair, looked at me, and said with absolute certainty: "But there is no way he's involved in any dirty business."

"Why is that?"

"Think about it. As long as the socialist regime existed in Czechoslovakia, he didn't dare put a foot wrong. They'd have got rid of him. Now he has a fortune. Why would he get involved with dirty money?"

"Listen, Lambros. Karayoryi may have been ambitious, but she was no fool. She had a fat file on him with information that it would have taken us a year to amass. For her to be investigating him to that extent means that she'd discovered something."

"Are you sure she was investigating Pylarinos and not someone else in his company?"

The photographs that Karayoryi had taken came into my mind. The one with the group of men in the nightclub and the other with the two men talking in the cafeteria.

"Let's go for a drive," I said to Zissis.

"Where to?"

"To my office. There's something I want to show you."

"Don't even think about it," he said, as if he'd been bitten by a snake. "I'm not setting foot in security headquarters. I almost lost my pension because for three whole months I was thinking that I had to get a certificate from your people and I kept putting it off. I said I'd help you, but let's not overdo it."

"Let's split the difference," I said, laughing. "We'll go as far as the entrance. You'll wait in the car and I'll nip in to get something that I want you to see."

"If I can stay in the car, okay," he said and immediately got up.

It was after eleven and the traffic on the roads had cleared. From Amerikis Square at the point where Patission Street widens, we weren't held up by any traffic lights, and in twenty minutes we were at the security headquarters. On the way we talked about other things. He asked me about Katerina, how she was doing with her studies. He'd never met her, but he knew she was studying in Thessaloniki. I began to tell him how upset I was that she wouldn't be home for Christmas, and, without wanting to, I came out with all my bitterness about her hunk. Zissis listened to me without interrupting. He realized that I needed to talk and he let me.

He remained in the Mirafiori, while I got the two photographs taken by Karayoryi. I showed him the one from the nightclub first.

"That's Sovatzis," he said as soon as he looked at it, and he pointed to the man with the plastered hair and the constipated smile.

"Who's Sovatzis?"

"The party member that they put in place beside Pylarinos to watch him."

"And the other two?"

"Foreigners, for sure. I don't know this one at all. The other one sitting next to Pylarinos looks kind of familiar, but I can't remember where from." His finger rested not on the pudding-faced one with the fringe, but on the one sitting next to Pylarinos. Suddenly he cried out. "Of course, it's Alois Hacek! One of the top men of the party in Czechoslovakia! You don't have to be Sherlock Holmes. He was the party official responsible for finances and he came to Greece to check up on Pylarinos." I showed him the date, to the bottom right. He seemed surprised. "November 14, 1990," he muttered. "The party was already dissolved and he's taking a trip to Greece?"

I took out the other photograph, the one with the two of them talking in the cafeteria. He looked at the date: 11/17/90. He put the photographs side by side. I said nothing. I let him think in his own good time. He shook his head and sighed.

"Do you want to know what happened in Athens on those two dates?" he said. "I'll tell you, and I don't think I'll be far off." He stopped to collect his thoughts and then said: "Toward the end of 'eighty-nine, when the socialist regimes collapsed, the party leaders lost everything. The people were wringing their hands. The high positions were gone, the dachas were gone, the limousines were gone. Everyone was out of work. Except that it wasn't exactly like that. Because these people had had a monopoly on power for more than forty years. They were the only ones who knew anything about administration, the only ones to have any contacts and connections with the rest of the world. And they made use of them. From being party members, they became businessmen. Once they had talked politics; now they talked business. Alois Hacek belongs to that category. Obviously he had the evidence that Pylarinos had been financed by the party in Czechoslovakia. So in November 1990, he came to Athens to find him. 'Which would you prefer?' he probably told him. 'I give the information I have to the new government to lay claim to your business, or do we become partners?' What would you have done in Pylarinos's shoes? You would have made him a partner rather than risk losing everything."

I turned to the two photographs that were propped against the windscreen. Pylarinos was looking at me with his glass raised. He wasn't drinking to my health, of course, but to the success of his collaboration with Hacek.

"But there's a catch." Zissis's voice brought me back to earth.

"What's that?"

"The other two. I told you that the party mechanism operated on the basis that everyone covered each other. Sovatzis watched Pylarinos, and the other man, the one sitting beside him, watched Hacek. It was these middle members who took the brunt of the state's collapse. No one needed them, and they ended up on the garbage heap. Except that with Sovatzis and the other, things weren't so simple because they knew. What could Pylarinos and Hacek do? They gave them a few crumbs to keep their mouths shut. But the other two weren't content. Their smiles say it all. Their whole working lives they'd done the legwork, and now other people were getting the tasty bits and leaving them with the bones. So they decided to set up their own operation. They met three days later to discuss it. That's what the second photograph is about.

"What kind of operation?"

"How should I know? That's your job to find out."

I looked at the two seated side by side. The one with the plastered-down hair, the other with the fringe, both with the same sour smile. "Two operations. The one operating inside the other," I said to Zissis.

"The first one legal, the second illegal but making use of all the mechanisms of the first, along with the security it affords, because who would think of investigating Pylarinos's business for any dirty work?"

"That reporter woman did," Zissis reminded me.

"Karayoryi . . ."

"Karayoryi wasn't investigating Pylarinos—she was investigating Sovatzis."

I remembered where I'd seen Sovatzis's face. In the newspaper clippings, behind Pylarinos. All the pieces were falling into place. The photographs, in all of which Sovatzis appears, the map, the lists, everything. From the beginning, something just didn't fit with regard to Pylarinos. I thought it highly improbable that a businessman of his stamp would be dealing in dirty money. But what didn't fit in the case of Pylarinos did fit in the case of Sovatzis. I felt a burden removed from me, because Pylarinos was outside it all and everything had thereby become easier.

"Do you happen to know Sovatzis's first name?"

"Demos."

That was the only thing that didn't fit the puzzle: the letters from the unknown N. They couldn't have been from Sovatzis. But who was to say that the letters had to do with Karayoryi's investigation and not some other matter altogether?

"Does the name Eleni Dourou mean anything to you?"

"Dourou . . . no." He opened the door. "Anyway, I've clued you in and now I'm going to get some sleep," he said, pleased with himself.

"I'll take you."

"No need for you to go out of your way. I'll get a taxi."

"Why pay for a taxi? Come on, I'll drop you off."

"Do you know how many times I've done it on foot because I was broke?" he said. "At least I have the money to pay now."

As he was about to get out, I reached over and took hold of his arm. "Why do you help me, Lambros?" I asked him.

What was I expecting him to say? That he did it out of friendship? Out of love? Out of gratitude?

"When you don't have anything left to believe in, you believe in the police," he said with a smile filled with bitterness. "You're as low as it gets. I got that low and we found ourselves together. That's all."

He started to get out, then he changed his mind. "I also do it because you're all right," he said.

"What have I done to be all right?" My mind immediately went to Bouboulinas Street.

"I heard on the radio about that Kolakoglou. You did more than all right."

Through the windshield I watched him quickly walking away. A little farther on, he hailed a taxi and got in.

I shook my head. All the old-style leftists were the same. They think that the police are monsters who kill innocent folk and then live it up. And whenever they come upon someone who's different, they're surprised and happy, as if they'd discovered a new party member.

CHAPTER 33

"Eleni Dourou is nowhere to be found," Sotiris said to me the next morning. "The address on her identity card is Fourteen Skopelou Street in Kypseli, but she moved five or six years ago when her husband died. No one knows where she went. The phone in Kypseli was in her husband's name, and there's no phone now in her own name. I can't find a lead anywhere."

"Keep looking. We *have* to find her."

"I do have some answers from the customs people concerning the refrigeration trucks belonging to Transpilar."

"Go on."

"They were carrying goods to Albania for companies belonging to Greeks and people from northern Epirus. They came back empty."

"Empty?"

"Yes. But there's something about it that bugs me."

"For God's sake, Sotiris. Out with it. *What* is bugging you?"

"All the entry documents from Albania into Greece were signed by the same customs officer. Name of Lefteris Hourdakis. Strange that all the trucks belonging to Transpilar should happen upon the same customs official."

It wasn't just strange. It stank at one hundred kilometers. "Get hold of the customs people at the border. I want to talk to this Hourdakis."

"He's no longer there. He took early retirement."

"Hand the airport over to Thanassis and start looking for Hourdakis. I want that man without fail."

There was no question it was a con. Someone notified the drivers in Albania and they made sure they crossed the border when Hourdakis was on duty. I would bet good money that the drivers were the same ones each time too. I could have got their names from Transpilar, but Pylarinos would have heard of it and would have started asking questions of his own. I preferred to wait, until I had questioned Hourdakis.

The telephone sprang me from my thoughts. It was Ghikas. "Come up to my office." The usual sharp tone.

The elevator started acting up again. It kept going up and down between the third and fourth floors just to get on my nerves. In the end, I got out on the fourth and took the stairs. It arrived at the fifth at the same time I did.

Koula wasn't there and the outer office was empty. I walked straight into Ghikas's office without knocking. He had summoned me himself, so there was no need to stand on ceremony.

Ghikas was at his desk. Facing him was Petratos with another man, all spruced up. Koula was sitting at the edge of the desk with a pad on her knees, poised to take notes.

"Get a chair and sit down," Ghikas said to me. I took a chair from the conference table and put it at the other corner of the desk, opposite Koula. That way I'd have Petratos facing me.

"This is Mr. Sotiriou, Mr. Petratos's lawyer." Ghikas gestured at the other man. "Mr. Petratos has agreed to answer any questions we may have."

Petratos shot a venomous glance at me.

"Before we go any further," the lawyer said, "I'd like you to tell us the results of the test carried out on the handwriting sample provided by my client."

Ghikas turned and looked at me. Aha . . . he was assuming the role of the good guy for himself, making me the bad guy and leaving me to take the initiative. Okay, if the shoe fits, wear it.

"The results were negative," I said, as calmly as I could. Petratos's triumphant smile was worse than a slap across the face. "But that, by itself, means nothing."

"It means a great deal; otherwise you wouldn't have been so eager to get hold of it," the lawyer retorted.

"This conversation is unpleasant for all of us," Ghikas interrupted. "Let's get to the point."

I turned to Petratos. "At the time that Martha Kostarakou was murdered, your car was seen parked in Monis Sekou Street, two streets away from Ieronos Street, where Kostarakou lived. Can you tell me what you were doing there at the time of the murder?"

"Are you certain that it was my car?"

"It was a black Renegade, license number XRA 4318. That is your car, isn't it?" The witness hadn't made a note of the plate number, but I was fishing in the dark to see what I'd catch.

Flummoxed, Petratos looked to his lawyer, who didn't look at all alarmed. On the contrary, he smiled encouragingly at his client, full of self-confidence, it seemed.

"Tell the truth, Nestor, you've nothing to be afraid of."

"I don't know when exactly Martha Kostarakou was murdered, but I was in the area between five-thirty and seven-thirty that evening, yes. I'd gone to see a friend of mine."

"Who is this friend of yours? Name? Address?" At last, I could put pressure on him.

"Why do you want that information?"

"Come now, Mr. Petratos," said Ghikas, with a silky smile. "You know that we are obliged to verify what you say. We're not disputing the truth of your answers, it's simply standard procedure."

Petratos was even more discomfited. He hesitated and then said, "I'm sorry, but I can't give you the girl's details."

"Why?"

"There are certain reasons that bind me not to disclose her identity."

"We have no reason to embarrass the woman concerned unless it's absolutely necessary."

The lawyer interrupted once more. "Mr. Petratos is under no obligation to answer you."

"I'm well aware of that, but if he does answer, he'll be helping both himself and us. Otherwise, he'll be forcing us to look more deeply into the matter."

"Then look more deeply," the lawyer snapped. "You looked into the handwriting sample and found nothing. And you won't find anything now either, because there's no murder without a motive. And my client had no motive for murdering either Karayoryi or Kostarakou."

"Mr. Petratos had a romantic liaison with Karayoryi. He helped her move up professionally and she ditched him. We know that Karayoryi was looking to get Mr. Petratos's job. So he certainly had grounds for disliking her a great deal."

Petratos suddenly laughed. "Perhaps Karayoryi was after my job, but she didn't have the slightest chance of getting it. Not the slightest, Inspector. I can assure you of that." He said it with such conviction that I was astonished.

Sotiriou got to his feet. "I think our conversation has come to an end," he said. "If you're so sure that Mr. Petratos is the murderer, you have no option but to detain him. But I warn you that I'll inform the public prosecutor that you are holding him without any evidence. And I'll have the whole journalistic world drag your name through the mud."

I made one last move, knowing that it would come to nothing. "A piece of the wire used to murder Kostarakou was found under Mr. Petratos's car."

"If you try to prove that the murder was committed with that particular piece of wire, I'll prove to you that it could have been committed with wire from my own garden." He turned to Petratos. "Let's go, Nestor. We have nothing more to say." He turned to Ghikas. "My respects, Superintendent." It was a negligible thing to me, unnecessary to say anything.

"What have we got out of all this business?" Ghikas asked me once Koula had shown them out.

I was clutching at straws. "First, we didn't know whether the Renegade did actually belong to Petratos because our witness hadn't noticed the plate number. Now we know for certain that it was his. Second, we now have this business with Petratos's woman friend. Either he's bluffing, or he's covering for someone well known. Probably the latter."

"And what do we do now?"

"We'll try to find the woman so as not to leave any stone unturned."

From his look, I could tell that I hadn't convinced him. I changed
the subject, told him about Sovatzis, the transplants, and the refrigerator trucks belonging to Transpilar. After the smack in the eye with
Petratos, he seemed somewhat relieved that I wasn't going to light
any more fires by going straight after Pylarinos.

I saved the matter of the customs officer for the end. "I want to
find him, and as quickly as possible. You see, the worst thing about
this case is that we don't know what the motive for the murder was
and so have to look into every possibility. Petratos and Sovatzis, the
transplants and the refrigerator trucks, all the avenues."

"If we ever figure it out, I'll light a candle to the Virgin," he said
despairingly.

I found Sotiropoulos in front of my door. "Did you see my report
on the news yesterday?"

"Yes," I said drily.

"Just you wait. With a little more investigation, I'll show how the
whole Kolakoglou business was a setup."

"I'd like to be there when the girl's father files a suit against you."

"Do you think he'd risk it? He'd have to put her on the stand, and
the lawyers would tear her to pieces."

I turned the handle on my door in order to disappear into my office before I threw up, but he took hold of my arm.

"I have something else for you."

"What is it?"

He leaned toward my ear and whispered confidentially: "Delopoulos sacked Petratos last night."

"I've heard that before."

"This time it's certain. Tomorrow or the day after, the bomb will
go off. You're the first to learn about it."

"And why are you so pleased this time?"

"Because he'll come knocking on the door of our channel, and I'll
make sure he doesn't get in."

I was about to shut the door in his face when I saw Sotiris coming. "Sorry, but I have work to do," I said curtly.

"I've found Hourdakis," Sotiris said when we were alone. "He has a farm in Milessi."

"Where's Milessi?"

"Just beyond Malakassa. On the road you turn down to go to Oropos."

"Well done. Get ready and we'll be off."

He looked at me surprised. "Don't you want me to have him brought here?"

"No, I would rather that we go and find him." A little country air would do me good.

After we'd passed Filothei, the traffic on Kifissias Avenue thinned out and we were in Kifissia in less than half an hour. But just as we turned down from Nea Erythraia to get onto the motorway, the heavens opened and the rain came down cats and dogs. Fortunately, there was no traffic on the motorway and even though I didn't go over 60 kph, we soon arrived at Malakassa. The village was deserted, not a soul on the streets. I stopped in front of the police station and sent Sotiris in to ask if they knew the farm where Hourdakis lived. While I was waiting for him, I rolled down the window to inhale the smell of the wet pine, but the rain drenched my sleeve. I rolled up the window, cursing.

Sotiris came back on the double and jumped into the car. They didn't know where Hourdakis lived and advised us to ask at the kiosk when we got to Milessi. Why hadn't I thought of that? In Greece, whatever the police don't know you can find out by asking the kiosk vendors.

The road to Milessi was deserted. The plain stretched out to the right. On the left was the abandoned army camp of Malakassa, gradually going to ruin. Two kilometers farther on, the plain ended and we entered a pine forest. The rain had lost its force and was now falling slowly, tiredly. The road began to wind downward. As we rounded a corner, we found the kiosk in front of us, next to the bus stop. The vendor pointed out a narrow dirt track. The Mirafiori kept getting stuck in the mud. I would have to come back in reverse.

At the end of the track, to our left, an enormous farm came into view, reaching up the hillside and most likely stretching as far back as the Oropos road. The house stood out in the distance. It was a big three-story building. It was as if they'd uprooted a tower from the Mani and planted it in Milessi.

"Are we going in?" Sotoris said, when he'd recovered from his surprise.

"Why? To ask why he was always on duty when the Transpilar refrigerator trucks arrived at the border? His house says it all. Now you see why I wanted us to come here, to see what kind of house he lives in."

Sotiris looked at me without saying anything. I released the brake and began going back in reverse. A little farther and we got stuck in the mud. Sotiris got out to push. As I was stepping on the gas and Sotiris was pushing from the hood, one of the windows in Hourdakis's house opened and a woman leaned out. She remained there at the window, looking at the pickle we were in.

"Tomorrow, you're going to go through the whole of Hourdakis's family tree," I said to Sotiris, when, after much ado, we were back to the kiosk. "Himself, his wife, his children if he has any, his parents if they're still living. You'll ask for approval from the public prosecutor to look into the bank accounts of the whole family. I want to know what amounts went into the accounts, when, and who deposited them. We'll talk to him as soon as we're ready to stand him up against the wall." I had learned my lesson with Petratos. I didn't want to come anywhere near Hourdakis before I had first collected enough evidence.

The rain had stopped. When we were again passing through the pine forest, I opened the window and breathed in the scented air in order to clear my lungs.

CHAPTER 34

The next morning, I arrived half an hour earlier at the office, at eight-thirty, and went straight down to the records department in the basement.

"Your ears must have been burning," Yannis told me as soon as he saw me. "I was just getting ready to call you."

"Any luck?"

"I went through the lists one by one. No one has asked for those files from the day they came down to the records department. I can vouch for that."

"Thanks, Yannis."

So whoever had photocopied the reports and given them to Karayoryi had done it while they were still in the office, before they went down to records. That meant that someone in the division was making a bit on the side by selling departmental documents. I felt a tightening in my stomach. The files stayed in the office for up to six months. During that time, anyone could take a file from the cupboard, photocopy what they wanted, and put it back in its place. There was no way to find out who was doing the dirty on us.

As I came out into the hall, I saw a girl waiting for me outside the door of my office. She had blond hair tied in a ponytail. She was wearing flat shoes, and she must have been as tall as me, around five ten. She was wearing a black leather jacket, expensive, and a miniskirt, sparingly cut, as it barely covered her behind. From below the skirt streamed a pair of legs like the stems of tall crystal glasses. As I got closer to her, I saw that she couldn't have been more than twenty-five.

"Are you Inspector Haritos?" she asked me.

"Yes."

She was without any makeup, had blue eyes and a cold expression, which made me feel uncomfortable.

"I'm Nena Delopoulou, Kyriakos Delopoulos's daughter. I need to talk to you."

I'd heard that Delopoulos had a daughter, but I never imagined she would be such a dazzling bit of skirt. "Come in," I told her and opened my door, wondering why she'd cut short her beauty sleep.

She sat in the chair and crossed her legs. Her miniskirt slid upward, offering me a view of her thighs right up to her panties, which were white and shone through her black tights. I crossed my legs too, not in imitation, but to prevent an erection. I leaned back in my chair to appear relaxed, though I wasn't at all.

"So what's it about?"

"Nestor Petratos told me that you saw his car close to Martha Kostarakou's house and that you suspect him of two murders."

"We simply asked him for an explanation," I said cautiously. "If we suspected him, we'd be holding him in custody."

"Nestor was with me on the evening that Martha Kostarakou was murdered. Between about five-thirty and seven-thirty." She looked at me and added with a touch of irony: "He was with me the whole time. I'm telling you this so that you'll leave him alone."

So this was the woman friend that Petratos had been protecting, and why he wouldn't tell us her name.

"Where do you live?"

"I own the Erodios Art Gallery on the corner of Iphikratous and Aristarchou Streets. It's an old two-story house. The gallery is on the ground floor. I live upstairs. Ieronos Street is two blocks away. Nestor didn't want to tell you that he was with me, as our relationship is somewhat unconventional." She fell silent and then added with the same touch of irony: "At least, it was until yesterday."

It was unconventional because they had kept it hidden from Delopoulos. She hadn't wanted any trouble with her father, and Petratos hadn't wanted any with his boss. I gazed at her and Katerina came into my mind. Whether she eventually became a magistrate or a lawyer, it would be ten years before she had any career. Whereas this pretentious girl, who was only twenty-five and already had her own gallery, bought by her father, was carrying on behind his back.

Ms. Delopoulou considered our interview over and got up.

"Are you willing to sign a statement of what you've just told me?"

She held the door half open and turned around. "My father and I see each other every three months, Inspector Haritos. Last night, when I learned of his intention to fire Nestor, I told him that if he did it, he wouldn't see me for three years. That changed his mind. So I'll sign whatever you want."

She went out and closed the door behind her. Another one who didn't bother to say good-bye to me. What was that word? Boorish. Quite so.

Strangely enough, my first thought was of Sotiropoulos. He's turned the tables on you, Robespierre, I thought. You wrote him off, but he is sitting pretty.

Then I realized that it wasn't only Sotiropoulos who had come out of it badly, but me too. I could now forget about Petratos for good. Given that he was with Delopoulou, he couldn't have killed Kosta-rakou. And if he didn't kill Kostarakou, then he couldn't have killed Karayoryi either. The two murders went together, a pair. His solici-tor had turned out to be right. In the end, Petratos had no motive. Why would he waste time hating Karayoryi when he was screwing the boss's daughter? And why would he be afraid of losing his job? The proof being that he hadn't lost it. I didn't know whether I was sorry or relieved that Petratos had come out of it clean. At least I was now free to turn my attention exclusively to Sovatzis. I had to keep Ghikas abreast, but there was no rush. First, I had to come up with a way to get close to Sovatzis. The surest way was through Hourdakis. As soon as Sotiris got the evidence I needed, I'd put him through the mill.

Then I had an idea. I dug out the photocopies of the letters from the unknown N:

For so long now I have been doing what you asked, believing that you would keep your word, but all you do is play with me. I now know that you have no intention of doing what I ask. You only want to keep me on a string so you can blackmail me and get what you want. But no more. This time I won't give way. Don't force my hand because you'll come unstuck and you'll only have yourself to blame.

What if N was Nena Delopoulou? But what had she done for Karayoryi and why would Karayoryi be playing with her? Had she put in a good word with her father on her behalf? In exchange for Petratos? But then Karayoryi wouldn't let him go and Delopoulou threatened her, evidently, with dismissal. Until Karayoryi, who didn't want to sacrifice her career, surrendered him to Delopoulou. This version suited me because it tied up everything without burdening us with any other suspect.

The ringing of the telephone interrupted this train of my thoughts. It was Petridi, the public examiner.

"Do you remember Seki, that Albanian you asked us to question in connection with the trade in children?"

"Of course. I was going to call you; you beat me to it."

"I'd planned to interrogate him the day after tomorrow, but he was killed last night."

The news was an appalling blow. "Who killed him? Do they know?" I said, after a pause.

"One of his own kind. Stabbed him, in a lavatory."

"Does he give a reason?"

"The man claims that Seki had stolen from him. He asked for his money back, Seki denied that he owed him any money and was stabbed five times in the stomach. They took him to the General Hospital in Nikaia straightaway, but he died from loss of blood on the way. So Seki's case has been put on file."

"Thank you for telling me," I said politely and hung up.

I racked my brain trying to understand what the murder of the Albanian might mean. At first sight, nothing. Two Albanians had had a quarrel and one of them had knifed the other. It happened every day, inside and outside of prison. But was it a coincidence that he'd been killed just when Petridi was about to question him? Karayoryi again came into my mind, her obsession with the Albanian couple's kids. She'd gone so far as to pay to get her hands on my report. Was she so certain that the Albanian hadn't killed the couple because he fancied the woman, but because they were all involved in a circle of trade in children? Of course, this was one explanation for the five hundred thousand found in the cistern. In this case, Seki had suffered the same fate as Karayoryi and Kostarakou. As soon as they'd found out that he'd been called for further questioning, he'd been killed to keep his mouth shut. But how had they found out and from whom? Had the information been sold by the same person that Karayoryi had been bribing to get her hands on the reports? But who would he have given it to? Hourdakis? That was the only name going around the station.

The only solution was for me to go to Korydallos Prison to learn what happened firsthand. I thought of the journey, and my spirits sank, but there was no alternative.

From Alexandras Avenue to Larissa Railway Station I moved at a snail's pace, but at least I was moving. When I turned onto Konstantinoupoleos Avenue, however, I found a mile-long line of cars before me that kept stopping every ten meters. Cars kept getting stuck in the middle of the junctions, blocking the way; those drivers wanting to turn out of the side streets were furiously honking their horns: It was absolute bedlam. By the time I reached Petrou Ralli Street, my mind had begun to crumble like a rotten cauliflower. I'd forgotten Sovatzis, the Albanian, even Nena Delopoulou's legs. The Mirafiori couldn't take all that strain and I was afraid it would break down on me in the middle of the road.

On Petrou Ralli Street, the situation improved somewhat and the Mirafiori began to roll along. On Grigori Lambraki Street, there was even less traffic, and within another quarter of an hour I was at the gates of the prison.

When I explained to the warden what had brought me to Korydallos, he shrugged in a gesture of perplexity. "What can I tell you? Everything points to the fact that it was a common quarrel that ended in a stabbing."

"Are you sure that there was nothing behind it?"

"How can I be sure? They always talk in their own language. Our lot don't want anything to do with them. The murderer was on the outside—the leader of a gang—that killed and robbed their own kind. He does the same on the inside. He apparently wanted something from the victim, and because he was being difficult, he killed him. Afterward, he put it around, as an excuse, that the victim had stolen from him."

"Where did he get the knife?"

"He said he took it from the kitchen." His grim laugh made plain his disbelief. "We've got him in solitary confinement. Do you want to talk to him?"

What would he tell me? Even if he'd been put up to it, he would stick to his story. Just like Seki. "No. But I would like to take a look at the victim's personal effects."

"Come this way."

He took me to the storeroom, where they'd put the Albanian's belongings. When I saw them, my mouth fell open. New underwear, new socks, two new shirts, a pair of shoes, evidently unworn, and a brand new anorak. I asked the warden: "Where did he get all this from? When he left us, he was wearing an old anorak and a patched pair of jeans."

"I'll ask. Maybe a visitor brought them for him."

"You didn't find a wallet? Any money?"

"No, but if he had any on him, it would be at the General Hospital in Nikaia, together with the clothes that he was wearing."

From what the warden found out, the Albanian didn't have a single visitor all the time that he was in the prison.

I went back the same way along Grigori Lambraki Street, more worried than I had been on the outward journey. The new clothes lent even more credence to the idea that the Albanian had been killed to keep his mouth shut. For that good-for-nothing to have had enough money to buy an entire wardrobe meant that someone had been paying him for his trouble. And the only trouble he'd gone to was to kill the couple. How he had got hold of the money, yet had no visitors, was simple. They'd sent it to him by means of a guard. After the first interrogation, they hadn't been worried because he'd convinced me that he'd killed them on account of the girl. They'd paid him and their minds were at rest. But when the public examiner had called him for a second interrogation, they'd been scared and had bumped him off so as to leave no loose ends.

Preoccupied as I was, I missed the turn for Chrysostomou Smyrnis. I had to go back onto Petrou Ralli Street and return via Thivon Street.

The doctor who had dealt with the Albanian had gone, but I found a supervisor who was willing to help. She took me herself to the storeroom. The Albanian's clothes had been put into a large bag. I took everything out and went through them piece by piece. He had been wearing the same anorak he'd had when he left us, but his jeans were new. But again, I found no money.

"Didn't he have any cash on him?" I asked the supervisor, who had stayed to help me.

"If he did, it would be in the accounts department."

The head of the accounts department was getting ready to leave and made no attempt to conceal his displeasure at being delayed. He opened the safe and handed me a wallet. It was a cheap plastic one with a gold outline of the Acropolis on it, the kind you find at any of the kiosks in Omonia Square. It was stuffed and difficult to fold. I opened it and took out a fistful of 5,000-drachma notes and three 1,000-drachma notes. I counted the 5,000s. There were twenty-five. The scoundrel had been carrying 128,000 on him. Add to that what he'd spent on his wardrobe. He must have had around 200,000. The rest of what was in his wallet were papers written in Albanian, so I couldn't read what they said, but they resembled official documents. Last of all, I unfastened the pocket for loose change. I didn't find any coins, but I did find a crumpled piece of paper and I opened it up. Someone had written in Albanian characters and in capital letters: 34 KOUMANOUDI STREET, GIZI. I studied the paper, then shoved it into my pocket, thanked the supervisor, and left.

CHAPTER 35

My stomach had settled, but the coffee and croissant made me feel sick. I had spent the entire previous evening in the kitchen. No dictionaries, no nine o'clock news, nothing. Adriani had been cooking so that I would have plenty to eat while she was away, and I'd been keeping her company. We were going through one of our sloppy phases. Roast pork, fresh beans, fried meatballs, all meals you could eat cold so that I wouldn't have to warm them up. I looked at it all and felt sorry for all the expense because as soon as her back was turned I'd be into the souvlaki. Adriani doesn't let me eat them because, she says, they make them from old meat and fat and it's bad for my cholesterol. I didn't give a shit. I loved them. It wasn't likely that I'd eat more than two meals worth of the food she was preparing. A day or so before she came back from Thessaloniki, I'd throw it in the rubbish so she wouldn't find it in the fridge and whine about it.

"What did you do with the names of the passengers that Sotiris gave you?" I asked Thanassis, who was looking at me, like every morning.

He raised his hands in the air. "It was impossible for me to get anywhere with the airport. They asked me if they were scheduled flights or charters, and I didn't know. They asked me for the airline companies and the flight numbers. I didn't know that either. All I know is that they were arranged through Prespes Travel, but that's not enough. They referred me to the airline companies that fly those routes, but they can't help me either unless I give them more information. The only way is to get it direct from Prespes Travel."

I knew that myself, but that wasn't possible for the time being. Once I was alone, I called Koula. "I have to see the superintendent. It's urgent."

"One moment." She put me on hold while she conferred with him. Then she told me that he was free and I could come up.

This time, the elevator did me the favor of arriving right away. Ghikas listened to the story of the Albanian without interrupting me. I showed him the paper with the address in Gizi.

"When can I have a team from the Special Armed Force to go to Thirty-four Koumanoudi Street?"

"What do you want the SAF for?"

"I don't know what I'll find and I want to be ready for anything."

He telephoned the head of the SAF to discuss it with him. "They'll let you know as soon as they're ready. Count on about fifteen minutes."

I went back to my office to see what Sotiris was up to.

"Hourdakis has a wife, a son, and a mother-in-law. They all have bank accounts. His is with the National Bank, his wife's with the Commercial Bank, his mother-in-law's with the Credit Bank, and his son's with Citibank. I've already submitted a request to the public prosecutors'. Once we have the okay from the Magistrates' Council, we'll open them up."

"Get on with it, because I'm in a hurry."

I didn't take the Mirafiori. I went in the SAF van. We parked it one street away, on Soutsou Street, so as not to attract attention. While the SAF boys surrounded the block, I went to number 34 and looked at the doorbells. There were about fifteen flats. Most of them family homes. The exceptions were a dentist's, a commercial firm, and one bell rather vaguely labeled THE FOXES.

"Let's start with this one," I said to the two SAF men who had come with me.

I rang the bell of the commercial firm and they opened the front door. We went through the floors one by one. The Foxes' flat was on the third floor. The SAF men took up positions on either side of the door and I rang the bell.

"Who's there?" asked a woman's voice. From those two words alone, I knew she was foreign.

"Open up! Police!"

I got no answer and the door didn't open. All I heard was footsteps scampering away.

"Should we break down the door?" one of the SAF men asked me. "One kick and we're in."

"Wait. They might still open it."

"It's wrong for us to wait," said the other one, giving me a lesson. "If they're armed, they'll have time to organize themselves."

With all the noise, the doors of the other flats opened. In one doorway an obviously retired couple appeared and in the other a woman holding a little boy.

"Get back inside and lock your doors!" the SAF man shouted at them.

The woman pulled the boy inside and slammed the door, while the old woman cried out in real fear: "Don't! There are children inside!"

We've startled a hare, I thought to myself, while from inside the flat another voice, not foreign this time, said: "Who is it?"

"Come on, woman, get a move on. Police, open up!" I said.

"Who is it you want?"

"Will you open the door or do you want us to break it down?" said one of the SAF men, who was just looking for an excuse to play the tough TV detective.

The door opened and a tall, thin woman of around forty-five was standing there. Her hair was graying at the temples, and she wasn't wearing any makeup. She didn't seem to be startled by the SAF men and their automatic weapons.

"Who is it you want?"

I pushed her aside, without answering. The two SAF men followed behind me and closed the door. We found ourselves in a small, square hallway, facing a closed sliding glass door.

"Who gave you permission to barge into my home? I demand an explanation!" The tone of her voice had become severe, but her manner was still calm and composed.

Again, I didn't answer her. I opened the sliding door and found myself in the space of two adjoining rooms. One half was living room, the other half playroom. Opposite me in the two corners were two armchairs with a coffee table between them. The floor was covered by a grenadine carpet. Four young children, a boy and three girls, were playing on it. They seemed to be roughly the same age, two or three, and they were all poorly dressed but clean. Lying around them were dolls, toy cars, building bricks.

I squatted down next to a little girl who was playing with a doll and asked: "What's your name?" She didn't reply but pointed to her doll. "Do you like your doll?" Again, the girl didn't answer, but nodded yes. The little boy grabbed the doll from her. The girl burst into tears. They began quarreling in a language I didn't understand but that resembled Albanian.

"Will you kindly tell me what's going on?"

My silence and indifference had rankled her and she was shouting. I went on as before, ignoring her.

In the middle of the other room was a large playpen. Two toddlers were crawling around inside it, while a third was standing up, hanging on to the netting. I looked around and went back into the hall. The woman, who followed me out, realized she wasn't going to get anything out of me and turned to the SAF men.

"Who is this man? Would you mind telling me?" The SAF men pretended not to hear.

"You leave me no choice but to call the police to find out who you are and who gave you orders to barge into my home!" she said threateningly, but without carrying out her threat.

The hall opened into a corridor on the right. The kitchen was on the right of the corridor and, beside it, a closed door, presumably the bathroom. I glanced around the kitchen. A young woman was sitting with her arms resting on the table. She looked at me and was shaking all over from fear. Facing me was another room in the flat. I looked in through the open door and saw two bassinets. I went inside and saw three more, all five together in a row, all with babies in them. Infants of all ages and for every taste.

The woman had grown tired of following me around and had

stayed in the hall waiting for me. I turned and went up to her. "What's your name?" I asked her abruptly, Officer Bulldog now.

"Eleni Dourou."

"So, in addition to acting as an intermediary in kidney transplants, you also take care of children, Mrs. Dourou."

She was startled, but admirably maintained her composure. "I am a qualified child care provider and my nursery is operating legally, with a license from the Ministry of Social Services."

"And what kind of children do you take care of?"

"Any child whose parents can pay my fees. I do not discriminate."

"I want the list with the children's parents. All the details. Names, addresses, and phone numbers."

"What for?"

"Don't ask questions. Asking questions is my job. Just give me the list."

For the first time she lost her presence of mind and faltered. "I'll give it to you, but their parents are all abroad."

"All of them?"

"All."

"Where abroad?"

"I don't know where exactly. They go away for a length of time . . . weeks . . . months . . . and because they don't have anywhere to leave their children, I take care of them till they get back."

There was a telephone on the coffee table in the living room. I called Thanassis. "Send a female officer immediately to Thirty-four Koumanoudi Street in Gizi. Third floor. Name is 'The Foxes.' And phone the Ministry of Social Services. Get them to send a child carer to the same address. Do it right away, it's urgent."

"What's all that for?" Dourou said, when I hung up.

"You and the girl are coming with me to the station."

"Are you arresting me? On what charge?" Every time she felt threatened, her composure and audacity returned.

"For the present, all I want is to ask you a few questions. I'll decide on the rest later."

I wanted to jump for joy, but Dourou was smart and I held back so as not to give myself away. Leaving her in the dark would increase her anxiety and insecurity.

"Sit down," I said to Dourou. "We'll be off as soon as the female officer and child carer arrive."

She hesitated for a moment. Then she decided to put on a show of being unconcerned. We sat silent in the two armchairs, with the kiddies playing at our feet. Every so often, one of the kids would come up to her and show her a toy. She caressed them and talked to them. And when two of them started fighting, she'd take one into her arms to comfort them. I was surprised at how tenderly she behaved toward the kids. Standing opposite me were the two SAF men. They'd lowered their automatic weapons and were holding them discreetly at their sides. As soon as they got back to their base, they'd make me a laughing stock at the station for having got the SAF involved in an all-out assault on a nursery.

Half an hour later, the female officer arrived with the child carer. While I was giving instructions to the former, Dourou was telling the latter what to do. When to feed the children, when to change the babies' diapers, showing her the ropes.

"Let's go," I said, when we'd both finished. I shouted to the SAF men for one of them to bring the girl, who he'd been guarding in the kitchen.

The girl looked like a frightened animal.

"Don't be afraid, it's nothing," Dourou said to her in Greek, but the girl didn't appear convinced.

While we were waiting for the elevator, the girl suddenly broke free of the SAF man and bolted toward the stairs. The SAF man caught her on only the third step and brought her back.

The balconies and windows of the surrounding buildings were full of people taking in the spectacle. A band of reporters and cameramen had blocked the street in front of the buildings. They made straight for me, holding out their microphones. They were all speaking together and I couldn't hear what anyone was saying.

"No comment," I said, in answer to all of them, and I walked toward the van that the SAF men had brought right up to the door. The reporters ran after me and continued with their questions, but I pretended to neither see nor hear.

I watched Dourou and the girl get into the back of the van, and we set off for the station.

CHAPTER 36

"Come on, woman! I have all night, but let's get to the truth of the matter: How did you come by those children?"

"Where do the nurseries find the kids? Is it the parents who bring them?"

"And where are the parents?"

"This is the third time I've told you. They're abroad."

"Names, addresses, and phone numbers, please, so we can contact them."

"I've just told you they're abroad. You won't find any of them."

We were in the interrogation room. Eleni Dourou was sitting up straight on a chair at the end of the table. Her arms were crossed, resting on the wooden top, and she was staring at us calmly, almost provocatively. I was sitting on her right and Ghikas was opposite me. It was one of the rare occasions when he left his office to be present at an interrogation, no doubt to underline the importance of it.

"Do you take us for fools, Mrs. Dourou?" Ghikas said, in a moderate tone of voice. "Let's say that the parents left their children with you and went on their respective journeys. Who would you get in touch with if any of the children needed something? Who would you inform if one of them got sick?"

"I would have a pediatrician come to examine them. And if it was anything more serious, I'd take them to the hospital. I take care of everything and the parents have nothing to worry about."

"And how is it that they are all Albanian children, not even one Greek child among them? Stop trying to take us for a ride, Dourou! Those kids were brought into Greece illegally!" As usual, I was playing Officer Bad.

She shrugged as if it was no concern of hers. "I have no idea how every Albanian or Bulgarian enters Greece, and I'm not the slightest bit interested. What I know is that they are brought to me by their parents."

"All right, Mrs. Dourou," Ghikas said, intervening once again in a soft voice. "Give us those parents' addresses so that we can verify what you've told us and you will be free to go."

Inside, I had to give credit to Ghikas. He was telling her indirectly that if she didn't provide us with the information, she wouldn't be free to go anywhere. Dourou seemed to get the message.

"I don't have the addresses, but I can give you a phone number."

"Only one phone number?" I said, with some sarcasm. "Why is that? Do all the kids belong to the same parents, or perhaps to a society?"

She was beginning to feel the pressure and was taking pains not to make a false step. "Listen . . . the number I'll give you is in Tiranë. The parents are Albanians who can't raise their children properly in Albania. There are no doctors, medicines, proper food, nothing. So they bring them to Greece and give them to me to be looked after. The parents come every few months, see them, and then go back to Albania."

I got angry again. "Ah, another lie. One more and you're going to find yourself in really deep trouble. I'll tell you what you're up to. You buy the kids from their parents, bring them illegally into Greece, and sell them for adoption. You've set up a business in the selling of children."

"What are you talking about?" she cried indignantly. "I'm a qualified child carer. My nursery operates legally, with a license from the Ministry of Social Services. And you come and tell me that I'm engaged in selling children? What is your sick mind going to come up with next?"

"If you are a qualified child carer, what business do you have being mixed up in kidney transplants?" Ghikas said.

She had to have been expecting the question. She shrugged impressively and answered without hesitation: "I have acquaintances who are doctors, and they proposed that I send them patients from Greece for transplants."

"Who are these doctors?"

"Foreigners . . . Czechs . . . Polish . . . Hungarians. . . . I know people in those countries. Is there any law preventing patients from going abroad for treatment?" She knew there wasn't. Nor were we going to be able to prove that the organs had been bought from some down-at-heels in the Balkans.

I took up from where Ghikas had left off. "What connection do you have with Ramiz Seki?"

This was the only reliable piece of information that I'd been able to get out of the girl assistant. The murdered Albanian couple were not known to her. But I'd shown her a picture of Seki and she recognized him immediately. He had never come to the nursery while she had been there, but one afternoon, when she had been given time off, she had forgotten her keys. She had gone back for them and had found him talking to Dourou. She had also told me that someone called Ramiz had called on a number of occasions, asking for Dourou.

"Who's he?" she said, but without the usual assuredness.

"He is an Albanian who killed two of his countrymen. The day before yesterday he himself was killed by another Albanian who was imprisoned with him in Korydallos."

I showed her the photograph from forensics. She glanced at it and pushed it away.

"I've never set eyes on him."

"You have set eyes on him. Your assistant saw him in your flat and recognized him."

"How did she recognize him if he's dead?"

"From the photograph. Shall I show you her statement?"

"There's no need. I have never set eyes on him."

"It's not only the photograph. We found your address among his possessions. Can you explain how Ramiz Seki came to have your address?"

"How should I know? One of the parents might have given it to him so he could tell me something or give me something, and he never got around to it."

"And they trusted a murderer?"

"All Albanians turn into murderers eventually," she answered with scorn.

We went on like that for another half an hour, getting nowhere. When we went outside, Ghikas looked at me perplexed.

"What shall we do now?" I asked him. I was trying to kill two birds with one stone. On the one hand, I was asking for his opinion in order to get him to commit himself. If, the next day, something went wrong with Pylarinos, I didn't want to get it in the neck again, as had happened with Delopoulos. I couldn't count on my luck every day of the week. And on the other hand, he was more adept than me at handling situations and I wanted to let him take the initiative.

"How did they get the kids to the nursery?" he asked me.

"The girl had a day off once a week. Not always the same day. It was Dourou who arranged it. When the girl came back, she always found new kids there. Every so often, Dourou would take one of the kids to hand it over to his parents, so she told her."

Ghikas laughed. "She wasn't lying. She was handing them over to their adoptive parents." He became serious. "See what you can get out of Hourdakis. In the meantime, we'll let it be known that we've arrested Dourou, but we won't say anything about Sovatzis, or about Pylarinos's businesses. Let's wait and see what Sovatzis does. Then we'll decide whether to bring him in or talk first to Pylarinos."

From my office, I phoned the Ministry of Social Services and asked for the department responsible for overseeing nurseries. The director assured me that "The Foxes" had been issued a license two years previously and was operating legally. The file was clean. I asked whether the inspector had noted anything strange about the nursery.

"In what way strange?"

"That all the children were Albanian. That there wasn't a single Greek child."

"If there's anything strange, Inspector, it's that half of Greece is inhabited by Albanians."

There was no answer to that and I hung up. It seems that the news of Dourou's arrest had already got around, because Sotiris came bounding into the office.

"At last, we're getting somewhere, eh?"

"I don't know. We'll see."

"If not, we're up the creek, because Hourdakis seems to be another dead end."

"What do you mean?"

"I got a copy of the family's accounts from the banks."

"So soon?" I said, surprised.

"I convinced the public prosecutor that it was urgent. He gave me permission and the legal council will take care of it afterwards. But there are no big amounts anywhere. The largest is 300,000 drachmas."

And he laid the photocopies of the bank statements on my desk. I picked them up and looked at the deposits. It was true that there were no large amounts. The most activity occurred in the accounts belonging to Hourdakis and his son. I saw regular deposits of 250,000 and 300,000, but no more than that.

"How old is his son?"

"I don't know precisely, but he's grown up. He works in computers. A programmer, I think."

No doubt the son earned more than his father. But if Hourdakis had a second income from somewhere, that would explain the amounts. The accounts belonging to his wife and to his mother-in-law also showed deposits of 200,000 and 300,000, though less frequently.

"You're right. At first sight, there's nothing untoward here."

Sotiris shook his head in despair. "That's what I meant. Dourou is our last hope."

I looked again at the Hourdakis accounts, one after the other. I felt sure that I was missing something, but I couldn't put my finger on it. It was seven o'clock already, and I decided to pack up and go home. I had to get some money from the bank for Adriani. I also wanted to see the Christmas present she had bought for Katerina.

All the way home, I couldn't get my mind off the Hourdakis accounts. It was while waiting to turn left onto Spyrou Merkouri Street at the traffic lights on Vassileos Konstantinou Avenue that I suddenly realized what I'd been missing. I made a U-turn and went back down Vassilissis Sophias Avenue.

By the time I reached the office, all my people had gone. I spread out the accounts, one beside the other. First, Hourdakis's account at the National Bank, then his wife's in the Commercial Bank, his son's at Citibank, and, last, his mother-in-law's account at the Credit Bank. The largest amounts fell into two categories. Every month, Hourdakis deposited either 150,000 or 200,000 drachmas. Obviously, his fortnightly salary. But there was a second category of deposits with an odd regularity in all four accounts. Hourdakis had deposited 200,000 in his account on June 25, 1991. Two days later, his wife had deposited 300,000. Three days later, his son, too, had deposited 300,000. Last of all, his mother-in-law had deposited 200,000 six days after Hourdakis. The amounts differed each time. Sometimes it was Hourdakis who deposited the most, sometimes his wife, sometimes his son, and sometimes his mother-in-law. But the total amount was always the same: one million drachmas.

I unlocked my drawer and took out Karayoryi's file. I found the list with the Transpilar refrigerator trucks and compared the dates. The refrigerator truck run of June 20, 1991, recorded by Karayoryi, corresponded to the deposit made by Hourdakis on June 25, 1991, and subsequently by the rest of his family. Likewise on August 25, 1991. This time, Hourdakis's wife had deposited 200,000 on August 30, 1991, followed by the rest of the family, with the last deposit having been made by Hourdakis Jr. There was a series of deposits each time corresponding to the dates recorded by Karayoryi. There were also other deposits, along the same lines, that couldn't be linked to one of the recorded refrigerator trucks. Evidently, Karayoryi had discovered some of them but not all. The consignments were much more frequent, and I was certain that if we looked into it, we'd find that they continued with some other customs officer.

So that was the game, then. Hourdakis had got a one-million-drachma backhander for each refrigerator truck. He received it in cash, but channeled it into four different accounts. Anyone looking at each account separately wouldn't have been able to see any amount worthy of note. It was only the combination of the four accounts that provided the true picture.

I left a note for Sotiris telling him that I wanted Hourdakis brought in for questioning the next day, and I left to go home via the bank.

CHAPTER 37

The following morning I took Adriani to Larissa Railway Station, together with three suitcases that were hardly liftable. On the previous night, when I'd got home, I had found her in front of three open suitcases that she'd placed on the bed, struggling to get her entire wardrobe inside them. She took her clothes out of one and put them in another, reorganizing everything, pushing shoes wrapped in plastic bags into the corners. . . . In the end, I tired of watching, I took out my dictionary and made myself comfortable in the living room. By the time she'd finished, it was after midnight. I thought we'd make love, given that we wouldn't see each other for two weeks, but I had too much on my mind and Adriani was dead beat. She didn't have the energy to groan and fake an orgasm.

By the time I'd got the cases into the compartment, I was bent double. "Give my love to Katerina."

"So there's no possibility of your coming, then? Even for the weekend?" She knew the answer already, but she was having one last try, to not go down without a fight.

"Are you kidding? We're just beginning to get somewhere with the investigation, and there's no knowing yet where it's going to lead."

I kissed her on her right cheek, she gave me one on my left cheek, and I got off the train. She was leaning out of the window, but I had no intention of waving her off. I was in a hurry to get to the office.

"Call me tonight to let me know you've arrived safely."

The Mirafiori was waiting for me, squeezed into a little space on Philadelphia Street. It was already ten by the time I finally arrived at the station. Before going into my office, I called in on Sotiris.

"What did you do about Hourdakis?"

"We delayed and we lost him. He's gone away on a trip."

I was dumbfounded. "Trip? Where to?"

"To Macedonia and Thrace. So his wife said."

"By car?"

"No, by train or bus, she doesn't know exactly."

"Have his wife brought in." He looked at me in surprise. "Don't stand there gaping. Off with you. I want her in my office in an hour, together with her son. And find Hourdakis. Send a message to the Greek-Albanian border posts. He might be on his way to get rid of evidence that we don't know about."

A thought flashed through my mind, transfixing me. How come Hourdakis had vanished like that? Was it a coincidence? Like the murder of the Albanian before we'd been able to question him further? Hourdakis hadn't known we were on to him, so someone had tipped him off. Who? Someone from the bank? I'd have believed that if the business with the Albanian hadn't come before. The previous night, I'd left Sotiris a note to bring him in for questioning. Today he was gone.

I decided to tell Ghikas about it in order to be on the safe side. I was the one who'd asked him to delay the official investigation. I didn't want to pick up the pieces of some bombshell.

I was on my way out of my office when I found two men blocking the doorway. I recognized the first of them immediately. It was Demos Sovatzis. He was wearing a gray suit, made of English cashmere, a dark blue shirt, and a light-colored tie. His hair was swept back, like in the photograph. I wondered whether he combed it with brilliantine every morning or whether he had stuck it down to his head with fish-glue, once and for all. The other man was fat and balding, older, also impeccably dressed. Thanassis was standing behind them.

I tried to guess the purpose of Sovatzis's visit. Up until now, we hadn't been anywhere near either him or Pylarinos. So he couldn't have known that we were after him. Could someone have told him that we'd picked up Dourou? Who? The one who was distributing information all around? The same one who had tipped off Hourdakis? And then again, why would he come out in full view instead of lying low and pretending indifference? I would have been glad of an answer to all of those questions, the better to know how to handle him, but I didn't have one.

"Mr. Sovatzis would like a word with you," I heard Thanassis say.

I stood aside and allowed them into my office. They sat in the two chairs and I went straight to my desk without offering them my hand.

"This is Mr. Starakis, my lawyer," Sovatzis said. "Just this morning, Inspector, I heard that you had arrested my sister."

So this was the answer to my questions. Dourou was Sovatzis's sister. It was the only answer that would never have occurred to me. I swallowed it slowly, like children do ice cream, the more to savor its taste.

"We are holding Mrs. Dourou for questioning."

"On what charge?" said the lawyer.

"We haven't charged her. Yet." I didn't want to show my hand, so I added vaguely: "We had a tip-off that her nursery cares for Albanian children who have been brought into the country illegally and who are there to be sold."

"Who gave you the tip-off?" said Sovatzis.

"I can't possibly tell you that."

"And you arrest a qualified child carer who runs a perfectly legitimate nursery on the strength of a tip-off?" The lawyer intervened again. "There may be other motives behind the tip-off. It may have been for competitive reasons or professional envy or mischief on the part of one of the parents. Any number of explanations."

"We asked Mrs. Dourou to provide us with the names and addresses of the parents who had handed the children into her care. Up to now, she hasn't given us even one name. She says that the parents came to Greece, left their children, and returned to Albania."

"And do you find that strange in this day and age?" Sovatzis said.

"I find it strange to the point of highly unlikely. No parent hands over their child into care without leaving so much as a telephone number in case of emergency."

"Telephones in Albania, Inspector?" Sovatzis found the idea

amusing and smiled. "In Albania, not even the government ministries have telephones that work."

Now the lawyer started laughing. I opened my drawer and took out Karayoryi's photograph. The one with Sovatsis and his friend talking in the café. "Do you know this man?" I asked as I handed him the photograph.

The smile froze on Sovatzis's lips. "Where did you find this photograph?" he said, when he had recovered somewhat from his astonishment.

"It's not important where I found it. What about the man? Do you know him?"

"If I'm photographed with him, it means I know him." His composure was restored. "It's Gustav Krenek, a very good friend of mine from Prague. I grew up and studied in Czechoslovakia. I have many friends there."

"Did your sister know this Krenek?"

"Yes. She met him when Gustav came to Greece."

"We have good reason to believe that this man is behind the trade in children and that your sister was working with him."

"You can't be serious," he said, handing the photograph back to me. "Gustav Krenek is a most reputable businessman."

"A lot of reputable businesses are fronts for other activities. Both in Greece and abroad."

"You cannot accuse someone on the basis of generalities and vagaries, having no concrete evidence. I demand that you set my sister free."

"We'll let her go free once we are sure that we have no reason to hold her."

"When can I see my client?" interrupted the lawyer. He'd realized, it seems, from my tone, that I wasn't going to give way.

"Now." I called Thanassis on the internal line and told him to bring Dourou to the interrogation room.

"Can I see her, too?" Sovatzis said.

"I'm sorry, but while the preliminary investigations are still taking place . . . only her lawyer." I turned to Starakis. "If I were you, I would advise her to talk to us. It would certainly improve her situation."

As soon as they were gone, I got my breath back in Ghikas's outer office.

"He's on the phone," Koula said.

"He can just hang up," I told her succinctly and stormed in.

Ghikas had the receiver in his hand. He motioned to me to sit down. When he saw me pacing back and forth, he grasped that I was on hot bricks and hung up.

"What is it?" he said.

First I told him about Sovatzis and then about Hourdakis disappearing from under our noses.

"It's good news about Sovatzis. Now we know that Dourou is his sister and that he knew that—what was his name?"

"Krenek."

"Krenek, yes. It's not so good about Hourdakis. I would have preferred to have had his statement before talking to Pylarinos, but we can't put it off any longer. Leave it to me, I'll take care of it." He said it as if I'd put a huge burden on him.

"There's something else."

"What?"

"First the murder of the Albanian before Petridi had time to question him and now the disappearance of Hourdakis. Someone is getting hold of all this from inside the station and passing out information."

"Do you want me to order the official investigation right away? You were the one who asked me to wait."

I thought about it. "Let's wait another couple of days. Something tells me that everything will become clear. I'm just telling you so that you know."

He smiled. "You're finally learning," he said and picked up the phone again.

Waiting for me outside my office was the policewoman I'd sent the previous day to Dourou's nursery.

"I came to report to you something that happened yesterday."

Her expression made me curious. "What happened?"

"At around six there was a knock at the door and a foreign couple appeared. They spoke to me in English and asked for Dourou. I told them she wasn't there, and they asked me when she'd be back. I didn't know what to say so I told them tomorrow—to give me time to warn you about it. Then they went into the room with the playpen and the woman lifted one of the toddlers into her arms. She played with him and talked to him. From what I understood, with my basic English, she was telling the toddler how cute he was. I asked them if they had a phone number to leave me, but they said no and that they'd come again to the apartment."

"When they come, make sure you keep them there and inform me immediately."

"Yes, sir."

"Well done," I told her. "You'll get on." She went out with a smile from ear to ear.

When the policewoman had gone, I began thinking to myself, and gradually my mood improved. I took the list of arrivals from Karayoryi's file. Arrival of a refrigerator truck from Tiranë on June 20, 1991, arrival of a charter from London on June 22, 1991. Arrival of a refrigerator truck on August 25, 1991, another arrival of a charter on August 30, 1991. Another arrival of a refrigerator truck on October 30, 1991. This was followed by the arrival of a group from New York on November 5, 1991. The same pattern could be observed all the way through the list, with a difference of two to five days between the arrival of the refrigerator truck and the arrival of the charter or group.

I phoned the switchboard and asked them to connect me with the head of customs for the Greek-Albanian border. I asked him to give me a list of the most recent arrivals of Transpilar refrigerator trucks from Albania to Greece. The last one had crossed the border just four days previously; the one before that a week previously. One of them must have been carrying a load of children, which would ex- plain why the English couple had turned up at Dourou's nursery. The kids would arrive first, and a few days later the couples interested in adoption would arrive by charter or in package groups. They obviously had a child stamped on their passports and when they came here, someone from Prespes Travel would take care of the formalities. Because they were charters and package groups, the paperwork was taken care of all together and no one was interested in whether there was a child when they were leaving. They'd take the child from here and leave at their convenience. This is what Karayoryi had discovered and confirmed with her list. I couldn't but admire Sovatzis's organizational genius. He'd set up two illegal operations: exporting patients for transplants and importing kids for adoption, both of which were sheltered by Pylarinos's perfectly legal businesses. International operations on the part of Pylarinos; international on the part of Sovatzis, too. Perfect.

And Karayoryi, where had she got all this from? Perhaps I'd never know, but I could guess. During the trip she took with her sister and her niece, she'd found out about the transplants by chance and had begun looking into it. She'd found Dourou and had come across the nursery with the Albanian kids. She'd realized that she was on to something and had started delving.

Sotiris woke me from my thoughts. "Mrs. Hourdakis is here with her son."

"Show them in."

Mrs. Hourdakis must have been in her early fifties. She was fat and was wearing a pistachio-colored coat that made her seem even fatter. She was dressed to the nines. Gold necklace, gold bracelets, gold earrings, and a layer of gold rings on her fingers. Whatever she'd been deprived of in her youth, she was wearing now to get even. Her son dressed at the other end of the scale. Whereas you might have expected a smart employee with suit and tie, he had a beard and was wearing a thick anorak, jeans, and casual shoes.

"Where is your husband?" I asked Mrs. Hourdakis abruptly.

"He went on a journey yesterday. I've already told the lieutenant." She appeared frightened, worried. I couldn't read her son's expression behind his beard.

"Had he planned this journey for some time or did he leave suddenly?"

"No, he'd had it planned for days."

"And where has he gone?"

"Macedonia . . . Thrace . . . He didn't tell me exactly."

"How do you communicate with him?"

"He phones me because he's always on the move."

The son listened to the conversation without interrupting. Only his eyes moved back and forth from his mother to me.

"He's continually on the move, yet didn't take his car with him?"

"He never takes it when he goes away. He doesn't like driving."

Who was she trying to fool? He didn't take the car because we'd be able to find him immediately. Public transport made it more difficult for us.

The son decided to break into the conversation. "I don't understand, Inspector. It can't be against the law for my father to go on a trip?"

I picked up the photocopy of his bank statement and handed it to him. "Can you tell me where all these deposits of 200,000 and 300,000 came from?"

I don't know whether he heard me because he was poring over the statement. "Where did you get this?" he asked after a while, as if not believing that it was his.

"Don't worry about that. We looked into your account quite legally, with permission from the public prosecutor. I want you to tell me about the amounts."

He turned and looked at his mother, but she was busy admiring her rings. He saw that he wasn't going to get any help from there and so was forced to answer himself. "The 250,000 is my salary. The rest is—extra."

"Extra?"

"Jobs I do on the side."

I picked up Mrs. Hourdakis's statement and handed it to her. "And where are these amounts from? From a fashion house?"

"My mother gives them to me," she answered immediately. "She lives with us and pays her share of the housekeeping."

"Your mother also has deposits of 200,000 and 300,000 in her account, but I don't see any regular withdrawals or transfers to your account."

As soon as they saw that I also had the statement belonging to Hourdakis's mother-in-law, they didn't know what to say and clammed up. I started to get tougher with them. "Take a look at your husband's statement. Put it beside the others!" I said to Mrs. Hourdakis. "The amounts went into the four accounts with only a few days' difference. If you add them up, they come to a million drachmas each time. How did your husband, a customs officer on a reduced pension, earn all that money? I'm waiting!"

"We don't live on his pension alone. Lefteris does other jobs, too," she mumbled.

"And does he get so much from all those jobs that you're able to put millions in the bank and have a huge house in Milessi? Tell me the truth or I'll have the whole lot of you locked up!" I turned back to the son. "You'll be discredited and you'll lose your job. Your parents will lose their house and you will all, most certainly, end up in prison!"

At which, the son turned to his mother. "I told him so!" he screamed. "I told him I didn't want him putting money in my account, but he's stubborn, he never listens to anyone!"

"Quiet," his mother whispered, terrified.

But the son wasn't willing to sacrifice his life and his career for his father's sake. He preferred to talk and come clean. "I don't know where my father got the money from, Inspector. All he told me was that he wanted to put some amounts in my account and that I could give it back to him bit by bit. You can see that I withdrew small amounts of fifty thousand regularly. That's the money I paid back. He did the same with my mother and grandmother."

I took back the statements and examined them. That much was true. After two or three months, they all showed withdrawals of sums of fifty thousand or sixty thousand.

"And you never thought to ask your father where all this money was coming from?"

"No."

"Why not?"

"I was afraid to ask," he said.

I couldn't hold them with no more than the evidence I had. I told the woman to tell her husband that I wanted to see him in Athens immediately and I let them go.

"Take out an arrest warrant for Hourdakis," I said to Sotiris, when we were alone. He nodded and made for the door. "Didn't you catch on to the trick with the accounts?" I asked him just as he was going through the door.

"No, I didn't think to compare them."

I called down to the cells and told them to bring Dourou to me. She was in a state of some disarray. Her dress was wrinkled, her hair out of place, and she seemed to have had a bad night. Only her expression hadn't changed. It was calm and provocative.

"I asked to see you to inform you," I said, "that you had visitors at the nursery."

A ripple of concern clouded her expression, but she kept her eyes fixed steadily on me and asked skeptically, "What visitors?"

"A couple. We told them you weren't in, and they showed great interest in one of the children in the playpen. They picked him up, made a fuss of him, and played with him."

She tried to read some kind of guidance in my face, to see where I was leading, but I remained expressionless. In the end, she decided to smile. "They must have been his parents," she said. "Which is what I've been telling you. They must have come to see him."

"They must have been Albanians who'd studied in Oxford. From what I was told, you could have mistaken them for English."

"They were Albanians," she insisted. "Because your people only know pidgin English, they took them for English. Simple as that."

She didn't know that she'd insulted me personally with what she'd said. "My dear Eleni," I said, insulting her in my turn, "the puppet show is over. Why don't you tell us the truth, so we can start getting somewhere? As long as you tell us nothing, we'll keep looking, and in the end, we'll hang a lot more on you."

"They were Albanians and they were the child's parents. You probably scared them and they took off. Do you understand what you're doing to me? You're ruining my business!"

Obviously it had been arranged that the couple should talk only to her and she knew they wouldn't come back. That's why she was so cocksure.

"Did you speak to your lawyer?"

"Yes."

"Didn't he tell you that it was in your own best interests to tell us the truth?"

"The truth is what I keep telling you. I told the same thing to him."

"And what did you have to tell him about your friend Gustav Krenek?"

"He's not my friend. He's a friend of my brother's. I saw him once, that's all. When he was in Athens."

Her confidence was back. I stood up.

"Do you want me to send someone to bring you a change of clothes?"

"Why would I want that?" she asked, alarmed.

"Because I can see you being in here a long time," I said and walked out.

I could have rounded up all the foreign couples from the hotels and had them brought in for questioning, but I knew that Ghikas wouldn't give his approval. He'd only tell me that we were searching in the dark without any concrete evidence. We'd have all the foreign embassies on our backs and do damage to our tourism.

CHAPTER 38

We were both sitting facing Ghikas's desk. Pylarinos was poring over Karayoryi's two lists: the one with the patients wanting transplants and the other with the refrigerator trucks and the arrivals. He was holding them side by side even though there was no connection between them and was examining them. His hair was white and thinning; he was wearing a striped suit, light gray shirt, and a dark tie. I was sitting beside him with Karayoryi's file open on my lap and observing his reaction.

Ghikas had arranged the meeting the previous day. He'd phoned me at home at nine-thirty, while I was trying to kill time watching a comedy on TV, one of those that gets you laughing for a week. I usually give them a wide berth, but it was the first night that I'd been alone in the house. It was one thing to have quarreled with your wife and not be speaking, and another to be all alone. The former was a game, a counter-lull, "calm, tranquility, serenity," according to Dimitrakos. The latter was a killer, particularly when you've been married for twenty years and you have no life of your own. Not to mention that I'd been thinking how Adriani would be chatting away with Katerina, which had plunged me even deeper into despair. Such despair that I hadn't even felt like opening a dictionary. I'd sat there watching the box. Half of the female prosecutor, who was now all lovey-dovey with her husband, the businessman. Mercifully, I missed the second half because Adriani and Katerina had phoned. Then I watched the nine o'clock news with the rerun of the report concerning Dourou's arrest and, further down, the news that Hourdakis was wanted by the police. And finally, I'd watched the comedy. It was toward the end of this program that Ghikas had phoned to tell me that the meeting with Pylarinos was at eleven the next morning.

Pylarinos looked up slowly from the lists. "Do you have the evidence to back up your accusations, Superintendent?" he said. Ghikas glanced at me. Here, he couldn't sum it up in five lines as he did when making statements to the press. He left the explanation to me.

"Let me take things one by one. First of all, we have the Albanian who murdered the couple. Then he is himself murdered in prison. The girl who worked in the nursery recognized him from the photograph taken at the hospital. Among his possessions we found the address of Eleni Dourou, the sister of Demos Sovatzis. We know, too, that all the checks carried out on your refrigerator trucks returning to Greece from Albania were carried out by the same customs officer, by the name of Hourdakis. When we wanted to question him, he disappeared. We have Eleni Dourou's nursery, where we found only Albanian children. We have the English couple that visited the nursery and were evidently interested in one particular child. And finally, we have this."

I took the photograph of Sovatzis with the Czech out of the file and handed it to him. He examined it.

"One of them is Sovatzis, of course. Do you know the other man?"

He hesitated slightly. Then he answered categorically: "No, I've never met the man."

Bastard, I thought to myself. I'd like to see your ugly face after I show you the photograph of the four of you at the nightclub. "He's a Czech by the name of Gustav Krenek, who claims to be a businessman, though we have grounds to believe that he works with Sovatzis. Look at the date."

He noticed it for the first time. "November 17, 1990," he muttered.

You took them to a nightclub, and three days later they were plotting behind your back.

"Does that jog your memory?"

"No," he said again, but without the initial self-confidence.

Ghikas shot a glance at me and then turned to Pylarinos. "We have no doubt whatsoever, Mr. Pylarinos, that Demos Sovatzis uses his position in your business to carry out illegal activities."

"You understand, of course, that I know nothing about this."

"We know that you have no involvement. That's why we thought it proper to inform you before we speak to Sovatzis. We do not wish to put anything in motion without your knowing about it."

I'd known him for three years, yet every time I saw him perform, I couldn't help admiring him. With all that sucking up to Pylarinos, it was certain the minister would hear of how effectively and how discreetly he had handled the matter. That's how the points added up, Haritos!

"Is it possible that he's the murderer of the two reporters?" Pylarinos asked Ghikas.

"We're still not sure, but there is no doubt that he is somehow involved."

Pylarinos looked at the photograph again. He clutched it between his fingers and jumped up, furious. "The bastard!" he said. "I pay him a substantial salary, he gets a cut of the profits, and all that's still not enough for him! Ungrateful swine!"

"We need your help, Mr. Pylarinos," Ghikas said. "It's to your own advantage that we clear this matter up quickly and discreetly."

He stressed the word *discreetly* and Pylarinos liked that. "Tell me what you want me to do."

Ghikas turned again to me, as I was the one who'd gotten my hands dirty. "We want the names and addresses of the drivers of the refrigerator trucks that are on the list. Also, a list of the refrigerator trucks that made trips to Albania during the last six months, together with the drivers' names. We want the names of the passengers on the charters and package tours referred to in the second list."

"You'll have all that information before the day is out, Superintendent."

"I would also ask you not to say anything to Sovatzis about all this," Ghikas added. "Give us time to collect the rest of the evidence first. We can't exclude the possibility of him being party to the murders."

"That will be difficult, but you have my word on it."

He handed me the photograph. I put it back into the file and closed it. Pylarinos turned to Ghikas. He spoke to him, but he was addressing both of us.

"Gentlemen, I'm most grateful to you that you had the kindness to inform me of this melancholy business."

At least he was more polite than Petratos and Delopoulos, I thought to myself, as I watched him to the door.

Ghikas leaned back in his chair and let out a sigh of relief. "That's over with," he said.

He had every reason to be pleased. But I would have liked to bring Pylarinos in, too, even if I fell flat on my face.

CHAPTER 39

I was sitting in front of the TV with a plastic bag on my lap. The bag contained a souvlaki with all the trimmings, a bifteki with all the trimmings, a kebab with all the trimmings, and a portion of chips that had been hot when they went into the bag and had now become mush. I separated them mouthful by mouthful and ate them. I didn't use a plate, because I enjoyed eating the souvlaki like a gypsy. If Adriani had seen me then, she would have punished me with a weeklong suspension of contact between us.

The news featured a full report on Hourdakis. Where he was from, when he entered the army, where he served, everything. They had discovered his house, but his wife and mother-in-law had locked themselves inside and wouldn't come out. So they had to limit themselves to showing the tower from the Mani that had been transplanted in Milessi and to expressing the surprise that I felt when I'd first seen it: Where had a customs officer found the money for a house like that? The son, whom they tracked down in the street, was uncommunicative. Yes, he'd been called by the police to tell them where his father was. All he knew was that he was away. The reporters told him that a warrant had been issued for his arrest. "My father will answer any questions the police may have as soon as he gets back," he said with a conviction that he hadn't shown when I'd questioned him. Dourou had been relegated to the end, as there was nothing new in her case. They only stated that she was still being held. As for Kolakoglou, he had slipped out of the news altogether. No one was interested in him anymore, not even Sotiropoulos, the man who wanted to bring to light the miscarriage of justice and restore his name.

I finished the souvlaki along with the news. I was deciding be-

tween watching TV or taking refuge in my dictionaries, when the
phone rang. It was Thanassis.

"We've found them," he said triumphantly. "Evangelos Milionis
is here and is waiting for you. Christos Papadopoulos is arriving
tonight in Patras, on board the ferry from Ancona."

"All right, I'm on my way. Send a message to the police in Patras to
detain Papadopoulos without fail and to send him to us."

Pylarinos had turned out to be reliable. By five in the afternoon,
he had provided us with the information I'd asked for. Milionis and
Papadopoulos were the drivers of the refrigerator trucks that Karayoryi had noted. As for the lists of passengers, things were a little
more complicated. Those who were from EU countries got in simply
by showing their identity cards. I'd sent the lists of passengers from
America and Canada to the airport, but the chances of their being
able to locate which of them had come using a family passport or
had declared children as traveling with them were slim. Following
the appearance of the couple at Dourou's nursery, I was now sure of
the way the operation worked, but without the English couple it was
going to be extremely difficult to prove it. My only hope was that
Dourou or Hourdakis or one of the drivers would crack.

Waiting at the station was a spare man with a mustache and a three-
day-old beard—Evangelos Milionis. His criminal record was clean.
No convictions, no arrests, no accidents. He was thirty, unmarried,
and lived with his parents. He sat with his arms folded over his chest,
a tough truck driver, a man who wasn't going to be easily intimidated.

"Are you a driver for Transpilar?"

"Yes."

"And you drive a refrigerator truck?"

"Refrigerator truck, lorry, whatever they give me."

"And do you do runs to Albania?"

"Not only there. I go to Bulgaria and Italy and Germany too."

"When you go to Albania, what do you carry?"

"When I'm driving a refrigerator truck, frozen meat, frozen fish,
or cured meats. When I'm driving a lorry, anything from canned
foods to clothes, whatever you can imagine."

"And what do you bring when you come back?"

"Nothing. I come back empty."

"On August 8 last year, on April 22, July 18, and November 5 of this year, you crossed from Albania into Greece."

"Maybe. How should I remember with all the trips I make?"

"What cargo did you have when you came back?"

"I told you. I was empty."

"I know otherwise. I know that you were illegally carrying Albanians and young children."

He gave me an inquiring look, then laughed at me. "Since when have we been bringing frozen Albanians into Greece?"

I leapt to my feet and put my face up close to his. "Don't be a wise ass, Milionis, because you'll find yourself laughing on the other side of your face," I said. "I know that on all four trips you went to Albania loaded with frozen goods and came back loaded with Albanian kids! We're holding Eleni Dourou and she spilled everything!"

"Who's she?"

"Does The Foxes mean anything to you?"

"No."

"The Foxes is a nursery in Gizi, belonging to Mrs. Dourou. It was to her that you handed over your load of Albanian kids."

"I don't know any Mrs. Dourou and I've never seen a nursery. I grew up in the streets, getting beaten by my mother every day of my life."

"That may serve you in good stead, now that you're on your way to prison."

"Let's wait till I get there first," he said calmly.

"You're going, all right, because we've also picked up Hourdakis."

"And who's he?"

"The customs officer who turned a blind eye so you could pass untroubled with your illegal cargo."

He shrugged. "No one ever turned a blind eye to me. They kept me waiting there for hours."

"You're a blockhead, Milionis. Go on playing the tough guy and we'll hang everything on you, and those who feathered their nests will be rubbing their hands together because they'll have you to take the rap. Talk if you want to make things easier for yourself. Did you take your orders from Sovatzis?"

"I've never spoken to Sovatzis in my life. I saw him once, that's all, from a distance, when I went to the garage. He was speaking to the freight manager and didn't even turn his head to look at us."

"Where were you on November 27?" The day that Karayoryi was murdered.

"Let me think . . . On the twentieth I left for Italy, Germany. On the twenty-seventh, I took on a load in Munich."

He had to have been telling the truth, because he knew I could easily check. "And on the thirtieth?" The day that Kostarakou was murdered.

"Here, in Athens."

I could have checked him when it came to Kostarakou's death, but since he had an alibi for Karayoryi, it was pointless.

The interrogation went on till seven in the morning. We kept recycling the same questions and the same answers, sometimes with more aggression on my part, sometimes with more irritability on his. But it didn't get us anywhere. Milionis was a young truck driver, used to being at the wheel all night, and at seven he was as fresh as he'd been when we'd begun at ten the night before. He was relying on his endurance and was trying to exhaust me. I sussed him out and changed tactics. I went at him for thirty or forty-five minutes and then I sent him to Thanassis. I had a coffee, relaxed, and then took my shift again right from the beginning, as if nothing had gone before, for another thirty minutes or so. I thought that in this way I'd both break him down and keep myself awake through all the coffees, because after about three in the morning, my eyes had begun to get heavy with sleep.

I was on my fifth coffee, leaning back in my desk chair, and I closed my eyes to rest them, when the phone rang.

"Inspector, they've brought us someone by the name of Papadopoulos. He's for you," said the officer on cell duty.

"Get Milionis out of the interrogation room and take in Papadopoulos. I want you to isolate those two. There mustn't be any communication between them."

I picked up what information we had about Papadopoulos and tried to concentrate to read it. He had a wife and two kids. He was in his fifties. His daughter was married and had a one-year-old boy. His son was doing his military service.

I let another half hour go by and went back into the interrogation room. I found myself facing a bald-headed man with a potbelly that swooped over his belt. He obviously turned the steering wheel with his stomach, and, if he didn't wear moccasins, his wife must have to tie his shoelaces. As soon as he saw me, he propped himself up with his hands on the tabletop in order to support his weight.

"Why have you brought me here? What have I done? I haven't had any trouble on the roads or been involved in any accidents, nothing! I asked your people where they were taking me and no one has told me!"

He fell silent, thinking that I would tell him, but when he saw that he wasn't going to get any answer, he began shouting: "I've left my truck with a full load in Patras, at the mercy of all and sundry! If any thieves get wind of it and empty it, the company will be on my neck!"

He tried to pass this off as an outburst, but most probably he only wanted to quench his anxiety with his shouting.

"Sit down," I told him quietly. He obeyed immediately.

I began just as with Milionis. I received the same answers, but in a different tone of voice. He always came back empty and he knew nothing of any illegal children, what was all this that we were trying to pin on him, thirty years behind the wheel and he'd never had a single accident. Whereas Milionis was calm and above it all, Papadopoulos shouted and yelled, and deep down was scared. Things changed when we got on to Hourdakis.

"Do you know Hourdakis?"

"I don't know any Hourdakis."

"Hourdakis is the customs officer at the border, who stuck his head in the clouds while you crossed unchecked."

"I don't know customs officers by their names. Do you know how many customs officers I've seen in my time as a driver?"

"This one knows you at any rate. He was in on it. He was on the take in return for letting you through. He's the one who gave us your name."

He took a handkerchief from his pocket and wiped the sweat from his forehead. He looked at me, trying to guess whether I was telling him the truth or not. There was no way he could know that Hourdakis had slipped the net and that we were still looking for him.

"Listen to me, Papadopoulos," I said softly, in an almost friendly way. "I know that you're the last spoke in the wheel and that it was others who got the lion's share. They're the ones I'm after, not you. If you cooperate, I give you my word that you'll get off lightly. I'll talk to the public prosecutor and most likely you'll be able to buy off your sentence. But if you play tough with me, I'll send you down for five years minimum. Think of the effect that would have on your son, on his spell in the army. And on your daughter, who might lose her family. And you'll be stuck in prison, getting slapped around from morning to night."

I fell silent. He said nothing either. We just stared at each other. And then suddenly I saw this great lump of a man break into sobs. His stomach heaved and kept catching on the edge of the table, like a truck's tire scraping up against the curb. His tears found it difficult to roll down his fat cheeks, but then acquired momentum and ended up on the table. He let them fall unchecked. The spectacle was so sad that I wanted to turn my face away so as not to see.

"I did it all for my daughter," he said through his sobbing. "I'd promised her a flat for her dowry and I couldn't make ends meet with the payments. All the money I took went to my daughter's flat."

"Slow down, let's take it from the beginning. Who got you into the racket? Sovatzis?"

His sobbing was instantly arrested and he looked at me in astonishment. "Which Sovatzis? Ours? What did Sovatzis have to do with all this?"

It was my turn to be surprised. I stared at him without speaking and bit my tongue so as not to betray myself.

"Who then? Mrs. Dourou?"

"No. A foreigner."

"What kind of foreigner?"

"Around the middle of June in 1991, I'd gone with a cargo to Tiranë. A foreigner approached me. He was with a northern Epirot Greek. The foreigner spoke Italian to the northern Epirot, and he relayed it to me in Greek. They knew that I was going home empty, and they asked me if I wanted to transport a load for them on the quiet and make half a million for myself every month. I told them I didn't get involved in things like that, but the foreigner persisted. He told me that everything had been taken care of at the border and that I wasn't running any risk."

"And you believed him?"

"Not just like that. He offered to come with me on the first trip so that I could see for myself that everything had been arranged. And that's what happened. He came with me and we crossed the border at night without any check. From then on, on every trip, I took a cargo plus the 500,000 for myself."

"And the cargo was Albanians and Albanian kids."

"Only kids. Apart from an Albanian couple who took care of the kids. It was the same each time."

I'd begun to catch on, but I didn't want to interrupt him now that he'd gathered momentum. "And where did you deliver them to in Athens?"

"I didn't deliver them in Athens."

"So where to?"

"Ten kilometers outside Kastoria, I left the motorway and turned onto a side road. There, a closed van was waiting for me. The kids and the couple transferred to the van and I returned empty to Athens."

So that's why neither he nor Milionis had known Dourou. Krenek arranged everything from Albania. Sovatzis appeared nowhere. Krenek was in charge of the supply department, Sovatzis was in charge of the sales department, and Dourou of the warehouse. The only connecting link was the brother and sister: Sovatzis and Dourou. All the others vanished somewhere in between. I called

Thanassis and told him to bring me the photographs of the couple murdered by Ramiz Seki and the photographs of Seki himself taken by forensics.

"Where were you on November 27?"

The date didn't appear to ring any bells for him. He answered quite spontaneously. "Here, in Athens."

"What were you doing on that night between eleven and one? Do you remember?"

"Till twelve I was at my daughter's house. We were celebrating my grandson's birthday. Then I went home with the missus." Bringing his grandson to mind made him well up with tears again.

"Who else was there?"

"My daughter's in-laws and my son-in-law's sister with her husband. Why are you asking?"

"Because that was the night a journalist connected with this business was murdered."

"I'm no murderer!" he shouted in terror. "Okay, my daughter was going to lose her flat and I got involved, but I'm no murderer!"

"Calm down. No one's accusing you of murder."

Thanassis brought the photographs. First, I showed him the photograph of the couple. He glanced at it and turned his head so as not to see.

"Do you know them?"

"That's them," he mumbled. "The ones who accompanied the kids."

I moved the photograph away from him before he puked on the table. "And what about this man? Do you know him?"

"Yes. He's the driver of the van that waited for me outside Kastoria."

So that was it. The three of them had been stealing kids and selling them to feather their own nests. Seki had murdered the couple because they hadn't given him his cut. That's why we found the 500,000 hidden in the cistern in the hovel. Then others had put another Albanian to murder Seki because he was the only path that led to Dourou.

CHAPTER 40

"So, where does all this lead us?" Ghikas asked me. On his desk was the statement that Papadopoulos had just signed.

It was noon and my eyes were aching. "There are both good and bad points."

"Tell me the good ones."

"We know that the operation was organized by Krenek in Albania. We've got the two drivers. We know that Seki took charge of the kids just outside Kastoria and handed them over to Dourou. So far, it all fits, but then we come to the gaps. I can't find any link with Sovatzis. Krenek may have organized all this with Dourou without Sovatzis being in on it. Our only hope is Hourdakis. Unless, of course, we can prove that it was Sovatzis who murdered Karayoryi and Kostarakou."

"Do you rule out the possibility of Dourou having killed them?"

"At best, we can get her for being an accessory before the act. But too much points to the likelihood that the murderer was a man."

He looked at me pensively. I had ruined his good mood. "Let's not despair," he said, more to give himself encouragement. "We might get some light shed on it from elsewhere."

"From where?"

"From Dourou. With the case we can make against her, she's not going to get off. When her lawyer explains this to her, she may at last get scared and talk."

The telephone interrupted our conversation. Ghikas picked up the receiver. "Superintendent Ghikas." He always prefixed his name with his rank, whereas, being modest myself, I always said "Haritos" on its own and the other person might or might not take me for a police officer. "All right, I'll be right there." He hung up and smiled at me. "Things are looking up already. Hourdakis is downstairs waiting for you."

I ran down the stairs three at a time. The usual coven was outside my office, Sotiropoulos at their head.

"Have you got Hourdakis?" they all wanted to know.

"Later," I told them and tried to break gently through the ring. The questions rained down—had he talked, what had he said, did he really have any involvement in the case—but I paid no attention. I got into my office and shut the door.

Standing in the center of the room were two men. One was medium height, medium build, and medium hair. His coat was open and he was wearing a suit with a shirt buttoned to the neck, no tie. This had to be Hourdakis. The other was roughly the same age, fifties, thin, with a department-store suit and a tie so worn that it must have been dying of loneliness because there was certainly no other of its kind anywhere in his wardrobe.

"Where have you been, Mr. Hourdakis? We've been looking for you everywhere. We even had to put your wife and son to some inconvenience," I said.

"I've been on a trip."

"Christodoulou, Inspector, Mr. Hourdakis's lawyer," the thin one chipped in. "I would ask that it be taken into consideration that my client presented himself of his own free will as soon as he heard that you were anxious to speak with him."

"A warrant has been issued and we would have found him in any case."

"Nevertheless, it's not the same."

I didn't have time to waste on the lawyer and I turned to Hourdakis. "Do you know why we have been looking for you?" I said. "We want to know who was giving you the occasional million that you spread out over your family's accounts—payments for turning a blind eye to the Transpilar refrigerator trucks."

Hourdakis turned to look to his lawyer.

"I want you to know that my client came here to offer every help to the police, Inspector."

"Fine. We'll take that into consideration if his answers are satisfactory." Back to Hourdakis. "Well then, get on with it! Who was giving you the money?"

"I don't know," he said.

"Listen, Hourdakis. I've spent too much time on you already. Don't make me lose my temper. We've got the two drivers, Milionis and Papadopoulos. We've also got Eleni Dourou, who took charge of the children. We know everything. Tell us who was paying you so we can put an end to it."

"My client is telling you the truth," the solicitor interrupted again. "He doesn't know."

I stared at them and I felt something wasn't right. "How did you get the money?" I asked Hourdakis.

"Let me go back to the beginning. One evening, when I came home from work, I found a package waiting for me. It was an ordinary box, like those used for packing glasses. When I opened it, I found 500,000 drachmas inside. I thought there had been some mistake, but the package had my name and address on it. I was racking my brain trying to think who might have sent it when the phone rang and a man asked me if I'd received the 500,000. I asked his name, of course, but he wouldn't tell me. All he told me was that on the following night a Transpilar refrigerator truck would be crossing the border. If I let it through without inspecting it, he'd send me another 500,000."

"When did all this happen?"

"I don't remember the date exactly, but it must have been sometime in May of 1991."

"And so you let it through."

"Yes. Three days later, I received the other 500,000. After that, he'd phone me and give me the number of the refrigerator truck, I'd let it through without any inspection, and he'd send me the million."

It was that simple. The first refrigerator truck that had gone through in May '91 was almost certainly empty. If Hourdakis hadn't taken the bait and had inspected it, he wouldn't have found anything. What, after all, was Sovatzis risking in order to test him? A salary, perhaps not even. When he saw that Hourdakis had taken the bait, he began his operation.

"How was the money sent to you?"

"In a package, always. Brought by courier."

"And who was the sender?"

"It had a different name each time."

"And why did you stop, given that everything was going like clockwork?"

"The trucks always came at night. I had to change shifts in order to make sure I was there. At first it was easy, because no one wants to work at night. But eventually, they got suspicious because I kept asking to work nights. And then I got wind of the fact that someone had begun asking questions about the trucks."

"Who was asking questions?"

"Someone from Athens, I don't know who. I never found out."

I knew. It was Karayoryi.

"As I was eligible for early retirement, I applied and my application was accepted."

Now someone else was getting money in a package. We'd find him too, but I still had nothing on Sovatzis. Only if we got our hands on Krenek, but he'd be in South America by now.

I took out the famous photograph of the two of them, anyhow, and showed it to Hourdakis. "Do you recognize either of these men?"

He looked at it and shook his head. Then we went, together with his solicitor, to the photography records. I showed him the photographs of Milionis, Papadopoulos, Dourou, and Seki. He immediately recognized the first two, but Dourou and Seki he said he did not know, had never met. I sent him to make a written statement and then to the cells.

Sotiropoulos was waiting for me. "What happened with Hourdakis? Did he talk?"

"The chief will make an official statement."

"Oh, come off it."

I motioned him into the office. I told him briefly what I'd learned from Hourdakis. I wasn't doing him any special favor because Ghikas would tell the others the same.

"How involved is Sovatzis, Dourou's brother, in the business?" he asked me.

"Do you think he's involved?"

"He's involved, all right, but I'm afraid that you won't be able to prove anything," he said, puncturing my morale. "You've absolutely nothing on him. Your only hope is Pylarinos."

"Why Pylarinos?"

"Because Sovatzis is a pain in the ass for him. If he discovers anything whatsoever, he might just hand him over to you for the peace of mind."

I liked that idea. "What did you do about Kolakoglou?" I said as he was leaving.

"About Kolakoglou?" he turned and looked at me in surprise.

"Weren't you going to prove that he'd been sent down unjustly?"

It was no longer a priority; he'd virtually forgotten it. "I'd really like to, but it's not possible," he said and sighed. "Kolakoglou is no longer news. No one's interested in him. Even if I were to put together a report, the news editor would kill it."

Robespierre, employee of Media Inc., with a lump sum on retiring and a pension. It was already four. I'd been on my feet for forty hours. I decided to close shop and go to sleep.

Before leaving, I called Sotiris in and told him to leave no stone unturned until he had something on Sovatzis.

CHAPTER 41

They came one by one and handed me their reports. And with each report my hopes tumbled. In the end they were crushed completely. No one had been found who could recognize Sovatzis. Not at Hellas Channel, or on Karadimas Street, where the Albanians had been murdered, or in Kostarakou's neighborhood. No one knew him on Koumanoudi Street either. None of the building's residents or the neighbors knew him. The fox hadn't gone anywhere near The Foxes so as not to arouse suspicion.

I was in a state of despondency because the doors were closing, one after the other. In the end, I'd have to take the plunge. I'd bring Sovatzis in and lean on him. I tried to work out what the best tactic would be: to use the evidence I had on him and Krenek, or to try and scare him with the twenty years his sister would get. But before I had come to any conclusion, the telephone rang.

"Come up," Ghikas said in that curt manner he uses when he has someone with him and he wants to play the boss.

I wasn't wrong. "Big-shot visitor," Koula said to me as I went through.

"Who is it today?"

"Pylarinos."

My hopes were raised. For Pylarinos to have come back meant that he had something important to tell us. Could Sotiropoulos have been right after all, that he was going to sell out Sovatzis for his own peace of mind?

He was sitting in the same chair he'd sat in during our last meeting. As soon as he saw me, however, he got to his feet and shook my hand warmly.

"I've already congratulated Superintendent Ghikas, but I wanted to tell you personally, Inspector. You don't know how relieved I am that the case has been closed without any serious consequences for my businesses."

"The case has been partially cleared up, but it's still open," I said, correcting him. "Whoever murdered Karayoryi and Kostarakou is still walking free."

"I'm no police officer, of course, but in my mind the most likely murderer is one of the two drivers, or the customs official. The Albanians were killed to keep their mouths shut."

"The most likely culprit is Sovatzis. The others have alibis. And Dourou couldn't possibly have killed them. The murders were committed by a man."

He looked closely at me. "I have to admit that I thought of that too. That's why I phoned the superintendent and asked when the murders were committed. The first was on November 27 and the second on November 30. Mr. Sovatzis went abroad on November 25 and came back on December 2." He took a passport out of his pocket and handed it to me. "You can verify the dates from his passport."

I took it and thumbed through it. It was true. It had a stamp in Czech on November 25, another in Czech and in German on November 29, and an exit stamp in German from Vienna airport on December 2. The bastard had arranged Karayoryi's murder and made sure he was abroad on the day of the murder. Then he had given instructions to the murderer to kill Kostarakou too.

"The charge of accessory before the fact continues to weigh upon him," I said to Pylarinos. "Sovatzis is the only one who can lead us to the murderer."

"I am persuaded that Mr. Sovatzis has no involvement in the matter, Inspector," he said in a tone of voice that brooked no objection. "And I'm ashamed for having suspected him at first. You've done a wonderful job, you've arrested the guilty parties, and the case is closed. However, in order for me to put my mind totally at rest, I had Demos transferred to another position, with no administrative responsibility."

Ghikas couldn't restrain himself. "Where did you transfer him?" he said.

Pylarinos didn't answer immediately. "I made him vice president of the governing board," he said with some awkwardness, and immediately added, as if wanting to dispel an adverse impression: "It's a purely decorative position. The vice president has no executive involvement. He simply handles matters assigned to him by the chairman, and that's me. A bit like the vice president of America, who has the title, but effectively has no power." He laughed at his attempt at humor.

We were speechless. He took advantage of our surprise and got up to leave. "Gentlemen, once again, I offer you my warmest congratulations." He turned to me. "You can keep the passport to check the dates."

What was there for me to check? He'd made sure he was sitting pretty. "That won't be necessary," I said and handed it back to him.

As soon as Pylarinos was gone, I leapt to my feet. "If either you or I had done a hundredth of what Sovatzis has done," I said angrily, "we'd have been suspended right now and we'd be preparing our defense. He got promotion and a raise."

"Nothing would happen to us either if we had the minister in our hands," he said, smiling grimly.

"What does that mean?"

"Don't you see? Sovatzis knows about all the money that Pylarinos appropriated in order to become an independent businessman. He may even have concrete evidence. He threatened to reveal it and Pylarinos backed off."

True. I'd forgotten about that in my rage.

"The only thing," Ghikas went on, "is that, this way, they're pinning everything on Dourou."

I rushed to the door, as if Dourou were getting away from me. On my way out, I told Koula to call down to the cells and tell them to have her brought to me immediately.

I found her in the same seat at the end of the table. I went and sat next to her. "Eleni, I have bad news for you," I said in a friendly tone.

"Why, when did you ever have good news?" she said.

"Your little brother has sold you out, Elenitsa. He has proof that he was abroad when the murders took place. He says that you planned it all. He had no idea."

"Of course he had no idea. He didn't have any idea and I didn't plan anything. All that is your own fabrications."

"Wake up, dimwit! You've become as stupid as the Albanians you mix with! We've got the two drivers of the refrigerator trucks. We've got Hourdakis. We know that the drivers handed the kids over to Seki outside Kastoria and that he brought them in a van to your nursery. We know it all!"

"How do you know that he brought the children to me? Did you actually see him?"

"Your girl saw him and she has identified him."

"Ah, yes, the photograph," she said. "Just try proving from the photograph that this Albanian was somehow linked to me."

"We'll prove it, don't worry. Now that your little brother has made sure he's well out of it, it's you we'll settle for as an accessory to the fact for the murders of Karayoryi and Kostarakou. You'll go down for ten years at least. Your only hope is to cooperate with us. We know you didn't have anything to do with the murders. All you have to do is to tell me who your brother hired to kill the two reporters and I'll see to it that you only do half your time."

She looked at me, and it was the first time that she wasn't able to find anything to say. That was a good sign. Most likely, she'd begun to waver. I leaned toward her. "I can see that they're trying to pin everything on you and I feel sorry for you. These kinds of jobs only last as long as they do, and when they go wrong, everyone tries to save their own skin. That's what your brother is doing. Why sacrifice yourself on his account?"

She suddenly leapt up, like a wild animal. "Leave my brother out of it!" she screamed. "You don't know what he's been through! He was still in my mother's belly when she went to find my father up in the hills. She left me with my grandmother. I grew up scared stiff of policemen like you! They'd come to our house every so often and turn it upside down, terrorizing us! And when I wanted to enter the college for nursery carers, they made my grandmother sign a statement. Can you imagine? A seventy-year-old woman! Do you know when I first saw Demos? In 1978. One day there was a knock at my door and I found myself looking at a man. 'Are you Eleni?' he asked me. 'I'm Demos, your brother.' I knew that my parents had been killed in an accident, about a year before Zachariadis had been deposed as secretary of the party. But I knew nothing about my brother's fate. Demos had been brought up by the party. And though I was older than him, I couldn't help him or even send a letter to him. And now you're asking me to sign a statement just to save my skin? Leave my brother out of it! He doesn't have anything to do with any of this! He's innocent!"

I stared at her and my mind went to Zissis. I wondered what he'd have done if he'd heard all that. How he would have reacted. She had a triumphant smirk on her lips. She thought she'd cut the ground from under me.

I opened the door and strode out.

CHAPTER 42

Impasse = 1. a situation in which progress is blocked. 2. an insur-mountable difficulty. 3. stalemate. 4. deadlock.

The meaning given by Dimitrakos suited me to a T. Liddell & Scott, however, gave further meaning: *without outlet; unable to get out; the infinite (Aristotle* Physics *3.5.2).* So, according to Aristotle, *impasse* also meant "the infinite." In other words, I, who had reached an impasse, was spinning in infinity in my quest to nail Sovatzis. Put more plainly, I was looking for a needle in a haystack.

It was six in the evening, the day after Christmas, and I was lying on my bed with my dictionaries. The previous day had passed fairly painlessly. I'd been invited for Christmas lunch by Michos, Adriani's cousin who worked for the telephone company. I hadn't wanted to go, but Adriani and Katerina had telephoned to insist. It would not have been right for me to have said no, they would have been offended, and, in any case, it had at least passed the day. We had eaten our turkey, had a jolly time, and, at around seven, Rena, Michos's wife, had taken it upon herself to teach me gin rummy. What I know about cards begins and ends with snap, but out of courtesy I decided to comply. At some point, I thought I'd mastered it and they cleaned me out. I got home after midnight and went out like a light. I hadn't had so much as five minutes to think about Sovatzis.

This morning, however, he was on my mind from the first pee of the day. I racked my brain trying to find some opening, some way to trap him, but there was no ray of light anywhere. All right, we had put an end to a trade in children. I even knew who had taken Hourdakis's place at customs. Someone by the name of Anastassiou. We could send them all to the public prosecutor. The chances of the prosecutor charging Dourou as an accessory before the fact were fifty-fifty. The accessory before the fact wasn't Dourou, it was Sovatzis, and he was still at large, and so was whoever murdered the two reporters.

Adriani had been right. I should have left everything, gone to Thessaloniki, and been with my daughter. By noon, I couldn't take it anymore. I got into the Mirafiori and started driving aimlessly. Without a conscious objective, I suddenly found myself in Rafina. I got out of the car and took a stroll along the waterfront. The sea air cleared my mind and I saw the situation as blacker still. Never mind Sovatzis, we were even in danger of Dourou being released if the statement by her assistant didn't convince the court. Given the organization they had, it was nothing for them to come up with a handful of Albanians who would claim that the kids at The Foxes were theirs. They might even bring the real parents from Albania. The more I thought about it, the lower my spirits sank. I went into a café to unwind. The noise, the buzz of the card players, the dice rolling on the backgammon boards made me forget my cares. I got home at around four and settled down to a long browse among my dictionaries.

I was poised between sitting in front of the TV and going to see a film when the phone rang. It was Zissis.

"How's the bachelor life?" he said.

"Great. I'm having a ball."

He laughed. "That's always how it is at first. You try to convince yourself that you're better off alone. You have your peace and quiet; you don't have to answer to anyone. But before too long the loneliness gets to you and you slip into despondency. Ask me about it. I'm an expert after all these years."

I said nothing because I didn't want to admit that he was right.

"I made some roast goat in the oven yesterday, but I can't eat it all on my own. Do you feel like coming over and having a go at it with me?"

He took me unawares and I didn't know what to say. Okay, we knew each other and we helped each other out every so often, but it wasn't as if we were eating and drinking companions. I was about to say no, when suddenly I thought how difficult it must have been for him to invite me, how difficult it would be for him to have a police officer at his table, even one that he liked.

"I'll come," I said.

"When?"

"I can be there in an hour."

"I've got a surprise for you," he told me. "A kind of gift." And then he hung up.

The roads were empty and I arrived in Ekavis Street a quarter of an hour earlier than I had anticipated. I found him waiting for me at the door. He didn't let me get out of the car, but came and sat next to me.

"Where are we going?" I said. "To the baker's to get the roast goat?"

"We're going for the surprise, but first I want you to promise me something."

"What?"

"We're going to meet someone, but I want you to promise me that once you've talked to him you'll let him go. I gave him my word that as long as he was with me, he would not come to any harm."

"Who is it? Sovatzis?"

"Sovatzis? What on earth made you think that? No, it's not Sovatzis."

"And how do you know I'll keep my word?"

"I know," he said with certainty. "Take Dekelias Street and then turn onto Attalias Street. We're going to the AEK stadium."

It wasn't far and there didn't seem to be anything to say on the way. When we got to the stadium, he told me to wait.

"I won't be long." He got out and disappeared into the trees.

I tried to guess who he might be bringing to me, but my store of ideas had dried up. Presently he came back with a man, but I couldn't make him out in the darkness. As he got closer he began to look familiar. Then I recognized him: It was Kolakoglou.

They opened the doors and got into the car. Zissis in front, Kolakoglou in the back. He wasn't wearing any overcoat and was rubbing his sides to warm himself. He was wearing the same clothes he had been wearing when he was perched on the roof of the hotel with the gun to his head. He looked at me, suspicious and frightened.

"It's okay, Petros. There is no need to be frightened," Zissis said.

"Mr. Haritos gave me his word. You'll say what you have to say and then you are free to go."

"Why are you hiding?" I asked him.

"Because I'm afraid," he said. "I'm afraid that if I fall into your hands, you'll send me back to prison, and this time for murder."

"Why should you go to prison? Did you kill Karayoryi?"

He laughed despite his fear. "Do I look like a murderer to you?"

"That's beside the point. Most murderers don't look like murderers. The point is that after the trial you threatened her. You told her she'd pay for what she did to you."

"That's not what I meant."

"What did you mean?"

He fell silent. He wasn't sure he was doing the right thing by opening up to me, and he hesitated.

"Come on, say it and let's get it over with," Zissis encouraged him. "That's why you came."

"Karayoryi had a bastard child," he said.

I don't know what I'd been trying to imagine while Zissis was gone, but that was one thing I'd never have thought of. I quickly tried to work out what new paths this bit of information opened up. "Are you sure?" I asked him.

"I am."

"And how did you find out about it?"

"Before I opened my own tax consultancy firm, I worked as an accountant for the Seamen's Pension Fund. One day, it must have been April 'seventy-four, a woman came wanting to take care of some contributions. She was accompanied by Karayoryi, who had a huge belly. She must have been ready to give birth."

Without doubt, the woman must have been Antonakaki, her sister. She'd gone to take care of her contributions paid by her husband, who was a seaman, and Karayoryi had gone with her.

"Go on."

"When, years later, she approached me as a reporter, she didn't remember me of course, but I recognized her immediately. Apart from the pregnancy, she hadn't changed at all. 'How's the child?' I asked her at some moment. She was shocked and looked at me in astonishment. 'There's some mistake. I don't have any children,' she said. Then I told her I'd seen her at the office of the Seamen's Pension Fund and that she'd been pregnant at the time, but she insisted that she didn't have any children."

"Are you sure that it was her?"

"No doubt whatsoever."

"Maybe the child had died."

"If it had died, she would have told me so. She wouldn't have said that she didn't have any children. That's what I meant when I threatened her. That I knew her secret and I'd make it public knowledge. I got my lawyer to investigate. When I got out of prison, the first thing I did was to investigate it again myself. I wanted to expose her, to get my revenge on her, but I found no trace of the child. It was as if the earth had opened and swallowed it up. When she was murdered, I gave up on it." He remained silent for a moment and looked at me. Then he added angrily: "Do you understand how I felt? She had abandoned her child to some foster parents and she had me sent to prison because I loved children and caressed them."

Suddenly, the letters I'd found in Karayoryi's desk came to my mind. The unknown N was not Nena Delopoulou. It was the father of the child. He wanted to see his child and she was keeping it hidden from him.

"All I want is to get my life into some kind of order and to live peacefully from now on," I heard Kolakoglou telling me.

"There's no need for you not to go home, Mr. Kolakoglou. You're not wanted by the police and no one's going to bother you. If reporters start annoying you, shut the door in their faces. By now they will have found someone else to harass." He was no longer news. Robespierre had said so.

He looked at me uncertainly. He was afraid to believe it.

"I told you that if you told Mr. Haritos everything you knew, everything would work out. Go on home now," Zissis told him.

"Thanks," he said to Zissis, clutching his arm. He said nothing to me. He thought that if he said anything to me, I might change my mind and take him in. He opened the door and got out, but he didn't go back into the trees. He went in the direction of Dekelias Street, toward a bus stop.

"How did you ferret him out?" I said.

We were sitting at the table in his house, eating roast goat in a lemon sauce, and drinking retsina.

"I was surprised that you let him go, that time at the hotel."

"It was a big risk and it wasn't worth it."

"I don't imagine you did it only because of the risk involved. Deep down, you believed he was innocent."

It wasn't that I believed it. I knew it.

"Anyway, I know a lot of people in the area where you found him. They all know that for years the security police were after me too. That made it easy for me, because when I said that I wanted to help Kolakoglou, they believed me. Whoever knew anything told me. Eventually, I found out that he'd been taken in by a distant cousin of his, who lived between Petroupoli and Nea Liossia."

"I can understand those people. But how did you convince Kolakoglou?"

"I showed him these."

He put both hands inside his belt and lifted up his shirt and pullover. His back and chest were crisscrossed with scars from old wounds. I didn't need to ask him who had inflicted those wounds.

"I wanted to help him because I know what it means to be on the run," he said, tucking in his shirt. "After all, he'd paid for what he did. Why should he have to hide like a frightened hare?"

I watched him picking at the goat and eating it slowly the better to savor the taste. I remembered what he'd said to me a few days ago in the car: *You're the bottom. I touched bottom and we met each other.* Where? That first time in the security police headquarters on Bouboulinas Street, when we were chasing communists. Now with Kolakoglou, we were chasing pederasts. We were both sewer rats. That's why we'd met.

CHAPTER 43

It was after midnight when I reached home. Usually, I can't manage more than three glasses of wine, and Zissis had poured half a gallon down me. The moment I lay on the bed, I felt the room going around. I closed my eyes and tried to find a position in which I would feel less dizzy.

I woke up with a heavy head. I made a coffee and swallowed two aspirins. Then I phoned Thanassis. I asked him for Antonakaki's number. As I was dialing it, I prayed that she wouldn't have gone away for the holidays. Mercifully, she answered, and I told her that I needed to talk to her.

"Come around. I'll be here."

"I'd prefer that we be alone."

"We will be alone. Anna has gone away with some friends and will only be back tonight."

Athens was empty still. Those who had gone away had not yet returned. Most people went away right through to the New Year. Within ten minutes I was on Chryssippou Street in Zografou. She opened the door for me and showed me through to the living room.

"Would you like me to make you coffee?"

"No, thanks, I've already had one. Some new evidence has come up and I need some additional information concerning your sister."

"Ask me what you want." She sat down opposite me.

"In 1974 you went to the offices of the Seamen's Pension Fund to take care of some contributions for your husband. Your sister was with you. Do you remember that visit?"

"I've been there countless times. How am I supposed to remember after twenty years?"

"You might remember because your sister was pregnant at the time."

Her expression froze. She opened her mouth. To say something? To shout? I don't know, because she shut it again without a sound, without a word. And then at long last: "There's some mistake. My sister was never pregnant."

"Do you know who it was who dealt with your case at that time? Petros Kolakoglou. He was an employee at the SPF before he opened his own business. He told me that your sister looked ready to give birth in 'seventy-four.'" I remained silent and so did she. "What happened to the child, Mrs. Antonakaki?"

She came up with the easiest explanation. "The baby died."

"If that is so, there must be a death certificate. Do you know where it is? Is it at the Athens Registry Office?"

"It died during childbirth."

"All right. I shall need the name of the doctor and the maternity clinic so that I can verify the details."

She had exhausted her imagination and stared at me in grim silence.

"The fact of the child may have a connection with your sister's murder."

"No!" she screamed, terrified. "There's no connection! I swear it! None!"

I adopted my friendly tone. "Listen, Mrs. Antonakaki. The truth is always the least painful solution. If you don't tell me what happened to the child, we'll have to start investigating ourselves. We'll go through all the maternity clinics in Greece if necessary. And we will find what we're looking for, you can be sure of that. It will take time. Meanwhile, the gossip will start spreading. The reporters will hear of the investigation and say that Yanna Karayoryi had a child and abandoned it. Wouldn't it be easier for you to tell me the truth, instead of hearing your sister's name dragged through the mud?"

She still didn't reply, but this time she burst into tears.

"What happened to the child?" I repeated, still in a friendly tone. "Where is it now?"

"Here."

"Here? Where?"

"Here, in this house. It's my Anna."

Once I was over my initial shock and I thought about it, I saw that the dates matched. When Kolakoglou saw them at the SPF, it should have been Mina who was pregnant, but it was Yanna.

"Vassos and I couldn't have any children," she said through her tears. The doctors said that Vassos was to blame, but he wouldn't accept it. He said that I was the one who was incapable. In the end, he made up his mind to divorce me. He was about to leave on a long voyage, one lasting a year and a half. He'd signed up initially to get the money together to buy this flat. Afterward, he told me that he'd put the divorce in the hands of his lawyer and would leave, so that he wouldn't be around and we could separate without any fuss. I almost went crazy. Vassos was my whole life. I'd loved him from being a young girl. If we had separated, I would have committed suicide. Then one day, Yanna came around and told me she was pregnant. You've no idea what I felt when I heard that. I was getting divorced because we couldn't have children, and she was pregnant and going to get rid of it. I screamed like a shrew, I slapped her. She waited for me to calm down and then told me to tell Vassos that I was expecting a child. I didn't realize where she was leading. She had to explain it to me. Vassos wouldn't be here for the birth. She would have the child and give it to me."

She laughed and cried together. "It was all so simple," she said. "She went into the maternity clinic under my name. And when little Anna was born, we registered her as my child. Vassos was overjoyed. He worships his daughter. There's nothing he wouldn't do for her. He's coming home on New Year's Eve so we can be together."

"Who else knows that the child is Yanna's?"

"No one! Her plan was so perfect that no one ever found out anything. But you can't count on everything and to think we were seen by that pederast!"

"Who is the real father?"

"I don't know. Yanna would never tell me."

She suddenly jumped up from her seat. She came and sat next to me on the sofa and took hold of my hands and clutched them. "I beg you, don't say a word of this to anyone," she said, weeping again. "Anna and Vassos will find out. You have a home and a family. You understand what it will mean. It will be the ruin of us all."

I didn't know where this would lead and I felt a tightening in my heart. "Listen. If the baby has nothing to do with your sister's murder, you have my word that no one will ever learn anything about it from me. If there is some connection, then I promise to discuss it with you before proceeding any further."

Which is more important? To find a murderer or keep a family together? Both, and neither, and this was the problem. You're jinxed, Haritos, I said to myself. You're always getting into the deepest water.

"Tell me. Do you have any mementos of your sister?"

"What kind of mementos?"

"Photographs . . . letters . . ."

"I don't have any letters. Just a few photographs."

"I'd like to see them."

She got up and went out of the living room. Presently, she returned with a box of photographs. I looked through them one by one, but came across nothing of interest. Most of them were photographs of Yanna and Mina from their childhood; others were of Anna as a baby, with Yanna holding her in her arms. Some were from the trip that the three of them had taken together. And there was one photograph of Yanna wearing earphones and speaking—obviously taken during one of her radio programs.

"Are these all of them?"

"There's one more. One that Yanna had given to Anna, and she has it in her room."

"I'd like to see that one too."

She took me to Anna's room. It was a simple, pleasant room, with flowery curtains, a desk, a bookcase, and a single bed with a bedside table. On the bedside table was a photograph in a wooden frame, turned toward the bed.

"That's the one," Antonakaki said to me. "She told Anna to keep it close to her always, because it was one she was very fond of."

I looked at the photograph. It was of a group of young boys and girls in the country, in a clearing somewhere. I recognized Yanna in the center of the group. She was lying on the ground and had her head resting in the lap of one of the boys. Yanna was smiling at the camera. The boy's face was familiar to me. I leaned closer to get a better look and my gaze froze.

"Do you know when this photograph was taken?" I asked Antonakaki.

"No, but Yanna must have been about twenty."

That wily Karayoryi. She was still springing surprises on me even after her death. She'd given the picture to Anna so that every night before going to sleep, she would be able to look at her father.

CHAPTER 44

Before leaving Antonakaki's house, I phoned Hellas Channel and asked to speak to the backstreet marine, the one who had been on duty the night that Karayoryi was murdered. They told me he started work at four.

It was still only twelve-thirty, but I was in no mood to go to the office. The two aspirins had had no effect and my head was still heavy. I was angry with myself for having chosen the previous day of all days to get smashed, and now, when I needed a clear head, I didn't have one. I decided to go home and lie down. I had to put my thoughts into some order.

Sovatzis was off the hook for good. Now that it had been verified that he hadn't killed the two girls, nor had he hired anyone to do them in, we had nothing on him. Dourou would simply be charged with buying and selling children. There was no longer any question of her being an accessory to the murders. And given that we were dealing with Albanian and not Greek children, a good lawyer would get her off with a light sentence. The two drivers and Hourdakis would end up bearing the brunt.

If I hadn't come across the file with all the material on Pylarinos, I might have found the murderer more easily. It was the file that had led me astray. The file and the fact that I had let Kolakoglou walk away. Though I had won laurels for my competence by Ghikas and for my compassion by Zissis. What I really deserved was a slap across the face. Okay, getting led astray did have its advantages. I'd broken up the gang. At least, in part. The big boys had got away, but even so, I'd get a few points out of it. Yet I wasn't happy. I thought of what was in store for me, and my heart sank.

By the time I arrived at Hellas Channel, it was four-thirty. The backstreet marine was at his post. He recognized me at once and stood up. I told him we should go somewhere quiet to talk. He took me to the security guards' room, which was empty.

"I want to go over a few details," I said when we were sitting down. "You told me that on the night Karayoryi was murdered, she arrived at the studios at eleven-fifteen. Correct?"

"Yes."

"And was she alone?"

"All alone."

"Are you sure about that?"

"Sure I'm sure. I have a computer memory, I told you."

"Fine. And since you have a computer memory, you will have no difficulty in remembering how many times you left your post after Karayoryi had arrived."

"I told you. Only once for two minutes, when one of the other guards came and told me that she had been found murdered."

"I'm talking about before she was found murdered. How many times did you leave your post?"

"Not at all," he said quickly.

"Cut the crap, sonny. Don't try pulling the wool over my eyes, because I know you left your post. Are you going to tell me yourself or am I going to have to take you in and give you the business? If you make it difficult for me, that's also fine, because I'll go as far as having you fired."

His muscles relaxed and he sagged. "There was a basketball game on that night. Just before the end, I nipped along to find out the score."

"What time was that?"

"I don't remember exactly." His computer had gone down.

"And how long were you gone?"

"Five minutes at the most."

"Shall we say ten?"

He heaved a sigh. "Let's say ten," he agreed.

And during those ten minutes, the murderer entered the studios as easily as he pleased.

I let him go back to his post and took the elevator down to the parking lot. It was filled pretty tight at that time of day. Only one man was getting ready to leave. I stood there and waited for him. He opened the door with a magnetic card. I timed it. It took ten seconds to go up, remained open for another ten, and took another ten to close. Thirty seconds. It was not unlikely that the murderer had gone out by the main gate. He hadn't known whether the guard would be missing from his post and would have been afraid to risk it. He'd hidden in the parking lot, waited for the first car to leave and had walked out behind it, before the door had closed.

The elevator stopped on the ground floor and Petratos got in. He was surprised to see me. He shot me a hostile glance and adopted his tight-lipped expression.

"I was just coming to see you," I said.

"I thought we'd finished."

"I was coming to ask for your help. You owe me."

"Why do I owe you anything?"

"Because if you hadn't made Kolakoglou into a red rag for your own channel's bull, he wouldn't have gone into hiding and we'd have caught the murderer much sooner."

"So it was him, eh? I knew it!" he said triumphantly.

"You know damn all," I told him brusquely.

My reply made the atmosphere even more hostile and we didn't exchange another word all the way to his office. As we passed the newsroom, the reporters all looked at us curiously.

"Be brief," he said coldly, as he sat down. "This is the time we prepare the nine o'clock news and we're busy as hell."

"When did Karayoryi begin her career in journalism?" I asked him.

"In 'seventy-five, if I remember correctly."

"How did she begin?"

"Same as all of us. From newspapers, magazines. Afterward, when commercial radio began, she got into radio. And finally into TV."

"Could she have worked anywhere before 'seventy-five?"

He thought about it. "Now that you mention it, she once told me something about having once worked for National TV or the Armed Forces Channel. But I don't remember when that was."

"Fine. That's all I wanted," I said and got to my feet.

Late that evening, Adriani and Katerina called me. Adriani was over the moon about Panos. What a good kid he was, how he'd taken care of her, how he'd prepared the Christmas meal on his own, and how well he cooked. Her praises left me in tatters.

"Was it worth your while staying in Athens?" Katerina asked me, when she came to the phone. "Have you solved the mystery?"

"I've solved it, but I don't like it," I told her.

"Why?"

"Never mind. You'll find out soon enough."

My headache didn't seem as if it would go. I wanted to go to bed but it wasn't an option. I had to go out and deal with some heavy stuff.

CHAPTER 45

We were in his living room, which didn't look at all like Antonakaki's living room or mine. An old sofa, a leftover from the fifties, a Formica table with four plastic chairs, the kind sold by gypsies for a thousand drachmas. The table was covered with a hand-embroidered cloth. The table and chairs he'd bought himself. The sofa and tablecloth had been left by his parents.

He spoke slowly, with difficulty. Every so often, he passed his tongue over his lips.

"I met her when she was working at the Armed Forces Channel. That's when it all started." He stopped and tried to gather his thoughts. "You won't believe me, but I can't recall what year it was. I've forgotten."

"It was 'seventy-three. I had it confirmed by one of the technicians from the National Network, who remembered it."

"You're right. It was 'seventy-three. She was working on a police program and she'd been sent to do a report on the academy. She came in during one of our classes to ask us questions. When the lesson was over, she was waiting for me outside. She told me that she wanted to ask me a few more questions. I was afraid of getting into any trouble and I said no. But she reassured me. 'Don't worry. If there's anything objectionable, they'll cut it anyway,' she said. That's how we met." He let out a sigh.

"And so you saw each other again."

"We went out a couple of times. Then she introduced me to her friends, but without telling them that I was at the police academy. She introduced me as a law student. Yanna and her student friend. That's how they referred to us."

We sat at the table and stared at each other, just as we stared at each other every morning. Except that now, he was looking me straight in the eye, and not a fraction higher as he usually did.

"Tell me about the child. When did that happen?"

"It must have happened in August, when we went on vacation together. She told me in October."

The memory upset him and his voice grew hoarse. "I told her she must keep it. I'm from a village and when one of us gets a girl pregnant, we marry her. That's how I was brought up. But it wasn't just that. I was in love with her. I know how it is when you're only twenty-one. You fall in love at the drop of a hat. But we'd spent three weeks on our own in the islands and when we came back I couldn't bear to be apart from her for even one second. So I told her to keep it and that I'd marry her. She burst out laughing. 'Are you completely mad?' was what she said. 'I want a career as a journalist and you expect me to burden myself with a brat and a policeman in uniform for a husband? No way. I'm going to get rid of it.' I begged her. I kept telling her how much I loved her and how much I wanted the child. My passion scared her and she decided that we should split up. I went off my head. From begging her, I began threatening her. And after that she disappeared. She resigned from the Armed Forces Channel, moved, changed her phone number, and I couldn't find her anywhere. I became so depressed that I left the academy."

It was then that she'd decided to keep the child and give it to her sister. But Thanassis didn't know that.

"Then, suddenly, years later, I saw her one day at the station, right there in front of me. I was stunned. She was friendly and suggested that we go for a coffee. And while we were having a coffee, out of the blue she said: 'Your daughter is doing fine. She's nineteen now.' Can you imagine the shock? I'd begged her to keep it and she'd left me so that she could get rid of it. Because of her, I'd left the academy, and suddenly, all these years later, she told me she'd kept the child and that she was now nineteen years old. I told her I wanted to see the girl, but Yanna wouldn't hear of it."

He stopped, to catch his breath. He moistened his lips. Now he was talking without looking at me, as he'd covered his face with his hands. "I had an overwhelming urge to see my daughter. Don't ask me why. I don't know. Maybe it was because I had wanted the child so much. Or perhaps I simply dug in my heels because she'd deceived me. Probably both. When I saw that insisting wasn't getting me anywhere, I started to follow her. So, of course, I discovered that my daughter didn't live with her. And not only that, but no one around her seemed to be aware that she even had a daughter. The more I searched, the more my insistence turned into an obsession. I wanted to see my child."

How could she have shown her to him? She had turned her over to Antonakaki.

"One day, she came and said to me that I could meet the child if I did her a favor. She wanted me to give her all the reports that came into the department with connections to the buying and selling of children."

"And you gave them to her."

"I gave them to her because I didn't think I was doing anything criminal. All reporters get their information from somewhere. But when I asked her about the child, she kept stringing me along."

"And so you began writing letters to her and threatening her?"

"Yes."

"And why did you sign yourself N?"

"Nassos. That's what she called me. She didn't like Thanassis—she called me Nassos."

The solution is often under our noses and we can't see it.

"Until one day she asked me for another favor. She wanted to know when Pylarinos's refrigerator trucks crossed the borders and who was the customs official who checked them."

So he was the one who had been asking and had scared Hourdakis.

"I found it all out and gave her the information." He sighed again and lifted his head. "Things went downhill from there," he said.

"Why?"

"Because I was approached by Dourou."

"By Dourou?"

"Dourou, yes. She telephoned me at home. I don't know how she found my number, but she wanted us to meet. And she proposed working together."

"And did you agree?"

"I told Yanna that things had gone far enough, that I wasn't doing any more. But she had a demon inside her. She always had a way of getting around you. She told me to pretend that I was going along with them, to gather information and to give it to her. When she'd finished her investigation, she'd say that she'd uncovered the affair thanks to my help and she'd make me famous. And then she'd let me meet my daughter, because the girl had been brought up in a different environment and she couldn't suddenly tell her that her father was a common policeman."

Why hadn't Dourou admitted before now that she'd known Thanassis? Obviously because she was still not admitting her guilt to anything particular and was keeping him as the ace up her sleeve. She would let the bombshell drop when she realized that there was no way for her to get off.

"I agreed, but on one condition. That before she went on the air with it, she'd hand over all the information to you, so that you could go ahead with the arrests at the same time. She agreed and we went on with it. Whatever information I gathered, I gave it to Dourou. Whenever any kids were delivered, I made sure I was in the area so that if a patrol car suddenly appeared, I could send it away. At the same time, I also informed Yanna. When I saw Seki during the interrogation, I recognized him right away. I'd seen him coming in the van to bring the children. I told them that we were holding him. And when he signed the confession, I gave him 200,000. I told him it was a down payment and that he'd get ten times more if he kept his mouth shut. The stupid Albanian believed it and of course they silenced him for good. And it was me who told them about Hourdakis. I had heard that Sotiris was looking for him."

"Thanassis, it's me you're talking to, Haritos. Do you really think I believe that you did all this just to see your daughter?"

"You," he said to me sharply and with envy, "you've had your daughter with you to pamper for so many years. And even so, you're in a black mood every other day because you miss her. And when she phones you, you act like a little boy."

Put a sock in it, Haritos. There's nothing you can say to him. He was shaking his head back and forth to underline his despair. "I'm telling you. She had a demon inside her. And she knew how to keep your hopes alive. From the day I agreed to play along with Dourou, she started sleeping with me again. Not regularly, just now and again. Without actually saying so, she let me believe that what hadn't happened twenty years ago might happen now. That we might all live together. Her, me, and our daughter."

"When did you get wise to her?" I said.

"After the Albanian couple died, when she came to you and dropped the hint about the kids. You knew nothing, but I understood right away where she was going with it. She wanted to make you come out and announce to the media that you were looking for kids, and then she would go on the air and reveal everything, to show the public that whereas the police were only just beginning to be suspicious and were wandering about in the dark, she had everything already sewn up. She wanted to ridicule everyone, the police and the reporters, and to become a star. To show that she was miles ahead of her male colleagues. The only thing she didn't have, and which I couldn't find out for her, was how Pylarinos was involved in all this."

Because she didn't have Zissis. I had him.

"And that's why you killed her?"

The question was going to come eventually and he was expecting it. He looked at me for a moment. The thought passed through my mind that he might deny it, but he said slowly: "In part, it was your fault that I killed her."

"My fault?"

"You sent me off with her that night. I didn't want to go, but you insisted. When I told her that I knew what she was up to and reminded her of our agreement, she just laughed at me. She told me that she would honor our agreement but with one minor alteration. She'd hand over all the information, but only when the police called her, to show the public that without her we'd never have got anywhere. I threatened to tell you everything. She laughed again and told me not to even think about it, as I was involved up to the eyes and if I ruined her scoop, she'd turn me into a news item to make up for it. Before we left, she told me that she wanted to make a phone call. Then I took her as far as her car. In my madness, I hoped that she'd change her mind even at that last minute. But she rolled down the window and told me that she'd go on the air that same night with a small part of it, just enough to whet the appetite of the public, and that the next day she'd drop the bombshell on the nine o'clock news. And off she went so I didn't have time to say anything in answer to that."

Large drops of perspiration glistened on his forehead. He pulled out a tissue to wipe them away. And then, to break the intensity, he changed the subject to something completely unrelated.

"I'm sorry. I haven't offered you anything. Can I make you a coffee?" he said.

"No. I don't want anything. Go on."

He realized that he couldn't escape and submitted to his fate. "I didn't leave right away. I waited awhile so as to recover from the shock and to be able to think more calmly. It was then that I saw that the whole thing had been a lie. She never had any intention of allowing me to meet my daughter or of letting me share in her success. I got into my car and followed after her. Her car was parked outside the studios. I don't know whether I'd already decided to kill her, but perhaps I must have decided already, because I waited for the security guard to leave before sneaking inside. I knew my way around. She'd told me herself. I found her putting on her makeup in front of a mirror. She was angry when she saw me there. I told her that she hadn't kept her side of the bargain and either she tell me there and then where my daughter was or she would have to give me back all the information I'd handed her." He stopped and smiled. "Cometh the hour, cometh the words. I must have been completely out of my mind to talk about bargains. . . . She told me that she had given our daughter to some couple without children and that she certainly wouldn't take me to her or tell me where she was . . ."

He paused, then began to laugh. An insane laughter, paranoid. "I didn't have a gun with me. Which is why she wasn't afraid. How could she imagine that I'd run her through with the stand from the spotlight?" The laughter stopped. "I snatched her papers from her bag, together with her Filofax, just in case. I got into the elevator and went down to the basement. I hid among the cars and nipped out behind the first car that left."

She'd been afraid, but not of him. She was afraid of Sovatzis and Dourou and all their people. That's why she'd phoned Kostarakou.

He got up and went over to a cupboard on which his TV was sitting. As he opened it, it dawned on me that I wasn't carrying any weapon myself, and that if he were to take out a gun, I'd be in a fix. But he took out a brown envelope and a Filofax, and he handed them to me.

"Here, take these," he said.

I left them on the table in front of me, without opening them.

"You cannot know what a shock it was when you introduced me to her niece," I heard him say. "From the first glance I knew that she was my daughter, but it was far too late by then. What could I have said to her? That I was her father and that I had killed her mother?"

"And why did you murder Kostarakou?"

"It was you again who pushed me to do it. You told me that Yanna had telephoned Kostarakou to tell her to go on with the investigation. I was afraid that she might have given copies of the evidence to Kostarakou. And what if it contained my name somewhere? I couldn't risk it. I told her who I was and that I had something for her from Yanna. She opened the door to me immediately. I did in fact have the envelope with me. As she was going through it, I put the wire around her throat and strangled her."

He paused once more and again burst into that appalling laughter. "Then I came straight to you to report on Kolakoglou," he said. "You were my alibi. You were looking everywhere for the murderer and the murderer was sitting in your living room."

He stared at me and I reflected that this would be the last time. From the next day we would no longer be staring at each other, and so I wouldn't have the opportunity to reverse the rules of the game: to look him in the eye and tell him that I was a moron, and for him to answer: "I know you're a moron."

Then he became serious, "Now everything will come out, right?" he said, and heaved a sigh under the weight of his thoughts. "I'll be ruined and my daughter will find herself with a father who's a murderer."

"There's no other solution," I said.

"Are you going to arrest me?"

"That depends on you. I came alone to talk to you. If you prefer, I can have you arrested tomorrow."

"Tonight, tomorrow, what difference does it make? In any case, I'm done for. Let's go tonight and get it over with. Just wait a moment, if you don't mind, so I can get a few things to take with me."

"All right, I'm in no rush."

I opened Karayoryi's envelope. In it was another role of film, a pack of papers from a printer, and four photographs. One photograph was of Dourou. The other three were taken at night on Koumanoudi Street. Each one showed a different person taking a child out of the van. I recognized Seki. The other two must have been the Albanian couple, but it wasn't easy to make them out in the dark. I looked at them and felt like tearing up the prints. If we'd had this evidence from the beginning, we would have wrapped up the case within two days. And both Karayoryi and Kostarakou would still be alive. It's stupid, I know, but it's not at all pleasant to be told that you were the cause of two people dying, albeit unwittingly. Whatever, there was no way Dourou would get off now.

The sound of the shot came from the other room, shattering the silence. I rushed into the hall. The papers flew to the floor. The bedroom was at the back. Through the open door, I could see Thanassis's legs on the bed. When I went in, I found his head on the pillow. His left arm was hanging down, dangling loosely. His right hand, which was holding his service revolver, was on the mattress beside him. The bed was unmade and the blood slowly spread everywhere, dyeing the pillow.

CHAPTER 46

By the time the coroner and forensics boys were done, it was past three in the morning. I sent Thanassis to the mortuary in an ambulance and went home. I didn't want to go to the station because there would probably be reporters waiting and I didn't think I would know what to tell them.

I telephoned Ghikas as soon as I got home. He'd gone to spend Christmas at his wife's family home in Karavomylos. It rang for about ten minutes and then I heard a woman's frightened voice: "Hello?"

"Inspector Haritos. I'd like to speak to the superintendent, please. . . . Yes, it's very urgent."

I had to wait another five minutes before I heard Ghikas's worried voice: "What are you phoning me for at this time? What's going on?"

By the time I'd told him the whole story, he was wide awake, as if he'd drunk three coffees.

"And what are we going to do now?" he said. "What are we going to say to the press?"

I had a solution, but I didn't know if he would like it. "Crime of passion. Sergeant Vlastos had a love affair with Karayoryi. From the evidence we have, we suspect that Karayoryi started the affair with him in order to get information from him. Eventually, she decided to break it off. Vlastos took it badly. On the night of the murder, he had dinner with her and begged her to take him back, but she refused. He followed her to the studios. He made his way covertly into the offices, found her, and continued to plead with her. When he saw that she was adamant, he killed her in a moment of fury. Because everyone knows that Karayoryi had also dumped Petratos, they will fall for it."

"And Kostarakou?"

"He killed her because she knew of their affair, and he was afraid she would talk. When he realized that we were on to him, he put a gun to his head. And it goes without saying that with the evidence that Karayoryi had collected and that Vlastos was holding on to, Dourou will go down for ten years."

"Marvellous!" I heard Ghikas say at the other end of the line. "Not even the FBI could have come up with a plan like that to protect its good name."

I couldn't have given a shit about the good name of the FBI. What concerned me was that the case was wrapped up, Antonakaki and her daughter didn't come into it anywhere, and Thanassis escaped being denigrated after death as a crooked police officer. And the force with him.

Ghikas stirred me from my thoughts. "I don't think there's any need for me to cut short my leave. You can make the public statement." And he hung up.

Of course. He had his head screwed on. He made only the pleasant statements. The unpleasant ones he left to me. Good cop, bad cop.

I didn't have the energy to go to bed. I collapsed on the sofa. I mused that I had been persistently wrong about Karayoryi. I had thought she was a lesbian, but she simply hated men and exploited them. I had seen her exchanging looks with Thanassis and I had thought she desired him, whereas she already had him by the nose. Strange woman. On the one hand, she had had the child so that she could give it to her sister and save her marriage. And on the other, she'd driven Thanassis to murder and suicide out of a professional perversion. Why had the poor wretch got himself involved with a woman like that? I'd rather have Adriani a thousand times over, even if she does fake her orgasms.

Never mind, it was just as well that Ghikas would not be rushing back. I'd avoid having to write the schoolboy essay for him to relay to the reporters. It was even better that Adriani was away. She was fond of Thanassis. She would batter me with questions, moan about his fate, till she drove me around the bend and we would get into a flaming row. In the end, we'd stop talking to each other again. Till the next batch of stuffed tomatoes.